–

A Botanist's Guide to Society and Secrets

ALSO AVAILABLE BY KATE KHAVARI

The Saffron Everleigh Mysteries

A Botanist's Guide to Flowers and Fatality

A Botanist's Guide to Parties and Poisons

A BOTANIST'S GUIDE TO SOCIETY AND SECRETS

A SAFFRON EVERLEIGH MYSTERY

Kate Khavari

CROOKED
LANE

NEW YORK

Copyright © 2024 by Kate Khavari

Published in the United States by Crooked Lane Books, an imprint of The Quick Brown Fox & Company LLC.

Crooked Lane Books and its logo are trademarks of The Quick Brown Fox & Company LLC.

Library of Congress Catalog-in-Publication data available upon request.

ISBN (hardcover): 978-1-63910-662-2
ISBN (ebook): 978-1-63910-663-9

Cover design by Nicole Lecht

Printed in the United States.

www.crookedlanebooks.com

Crooked Lane Books
34 West 27th St., 10th Floor
New York, NY 10001

First Edition: June 2024

10 9 8 7 6 5 4 3 2 1

*For the seeds that grew, and the ones
that did not.*

CHAPTER 1

Cold rain soaking her boots, splashing her stockings, and leaking from the brim of her ruined hat and onto her face was the least of Saffron Everleigh's worries.

No, it was the lingering nausea of the crossing, clinging to her like a zealous strand of *Galium aparine*, combined with the exhaustion of traveling for over twenty hours, that made her miserable and desperate for the quiet comfort of her flat.

Thanks to the freezing downpour making the November night dreary, there were no cabs available as Saffron emerged on wobbly legs from the train station. She'd resorted to the bus, which had been a poor choice, given her uncertain stomach and London bus drivers' general propensity for driving like hellhounds were at their heels. Rather than risking vomiting all over the passengers of the cramped bus, she'd alighted three blocks before her stop and had to complete the walk with neither an umbrella nor an adequate raincoat.

Given the late hour, her quiet Chelsea street was dark, save for one flat. The warm lights emanating from the top floor of her building drew her like a bee to bee balm, promising a hot cuppa, a bath, and home.

She trudged up the stairs, her numb fingers fumbling with the pins of her hat. At the top, she eagerly pounded on the door. It swung open, and the anticipatory smile on Saffron's lips died.

Standing at the door to her flat was a stranger. He was youngish, tall, gangly, and wore wire-rimmed glasses and a look of haughty indifference. "Yes?"

Saffron blinked, checked the number on the plate next to the door, then looked back at the stranger. He had glossy blond hair in a washed-out shade of flax and very pale skin, which made the redness around his mouth and neck more apparent. His tie was loosened, she saw as she followed the color to his neck and then to his haphazardly buttoned waistcoat. At a loss, she asked, "Er—who are you?"

He lifted a brow. "Pardon me. Who are you?"

"Who's at the door, darling?" asked a voice from within the flat.

Saffron made to look around the man, but he moved with her to block her view. She glared at him and called down the hall, "Elizabeth?"

The man bristled, propping his hands on his hips and doing his best to loom over her. "Now, see here—"

Behind him, Elizabeth Hale popped around the corner at the end of the hall. "Why, hullo! You're back! Don't just stand there. Colin darling, move aside so she can come in!" She disappeared around the corner.

The haughty man—Colin, apparently—grudgingly retreated to the parlor without a word. Saffron stepped inside and negotiated removing her woefully soaked coat just inside the door. She could hear Colin saying something and Elizabeth's husky alto replying.

Just as Saffron discarded the floppy wet felt that used to be her hat, Elizabeth came down the hall in her stocking feet, arms open in welcome. Saffron took her in, sighing in exasperation to see that Elizabeth's clothing was as hastily donned as her date's.

"You look a right mess, Saff," Elizabeth said, embracing her in a warm cloud of Tabac Blond. "Did you swim the Channel?"

"Ha ha," Saffron replied flatly, allowing herself to sink into her friend's embrace. Elizabeth had returned from their trip to France two weeks ago, but it felt like a lifetime.

"You are freezing!" Elizabeth squealed. "Which would you like first, tea or a bath? Or tea in the bath?"

That brought a little laugh to Saffron's lips. "Tea first. You're entertaining, anyway."

Elizabeth winked at her. "Colin was just leaving."

As if summoned by his name, the man in question appeared from the parlor, his suit jacket on and his tie tightened to his throat. "Was I?"

"Yes, darling," Elizabeth said, not looking at him. "My flatmate has just returned from what must have been the world's worst crossing, and she needs tending." She shot him a coy look. "You've been tended to plenty. Scurry along, I'll see you tomorrow."

Colin's fair face heated, and he gave Elizabeth a hard look that only set her giggling. He squeezed by her and Saffron to reach for his hat and coat from the pegs on the wall. He gave Saffron an uncertain look. "My apologies for the confusion earlier. You are doubtless Miss Everleigh."

"I am. And you must be Colin Smith, from Elizabeth's office."

"I am one of Lord Tremaine's private secretaries, yes," he said, placing his hat atop his head.

"Of course," Saffron murmured as Elizabeth stepped forward and placed a gentle kiss on his lips.

"Ta, now," Elizabeth told him and shuffled him out the door. "Good night, Colin."

When the sounds of his footsteps had faded from the stairwell, Elizabeth flipped the lock on the door and wafted down the hall with an air of secretive satisfaction. Saffron made to follow her, but Elizabeth demanded she change from her wet clothing.

Five minutes later, Saffron was wrapped in her warmest and ugliest dressing gown of faded blue flannel, and the kettle was singing. Elizabeth busied herself with the ritual of tea.

"Well, Saff," Elizabeth said, settling the tray bearing teapot, sugar and cream, and cups and saucers on the little kitchen table, "I have all sorts of very interesting things to tell you, but you go first. How was the botanical conference? Did you go on to Belgium after all? Tell me everything."

The warmth of the kitchen, the familiar scent of steeping Earl Grey, and the kindness in her friend's eyes pried away the little that remained of Saffron's stiff upper lip. Her shoulders slumped.

"It was awful, Eliza," she rasped out. "All of it. I don't know what I'm going to do."

Alexander Ashton paced his office. Or attempted to.

Though the space was clear of the accumulation of flotsam that academia encouraged, his legs were long, and there were only so many strides his office could allow before he was forced to turn sharply on the heel of his polished oxfords. His office had become a kind of sanctuary this last week after his brother Adrian had stopped trying to be a pleasant houseguest and retreated back into old habits that left the sitting room and kitchen a mess and him sleeping past noon most days. But even the quiet order of his office couldn't lower Alexander's blood pressure when so much weighed on his mind.

On his fifth circuit of the room, he checked his wristwatch. It was ten past nine in the morning, well past the time he could expect to receive an answer to his question.

He left his office and strode down the hall of the North Wing. Thick clouds beyond the windows left the white-walled corridor gray. Below, the Quad was full of students and staff hustling to reach their lecture halls and offices. Few people lingered in the frosty morning air. The voices of those who'd already sought the warmth of the North Wing echoed through the tiled halls and scuffed wood-paneled staircase.

Alexander climbed the circular stair and saw his quarry at the door at the end of the hall.

"Mr. Ferrand," he called, lengthening his stride to catch him.

Considering the number of times the secretary had seen Alexander this week, the older man should not have looked so surprised as he paused in unlocking the door and turned to face him. But Mr. Ferrand was polite to a fault, even friendly, and so he greeted Alexander with silver eyebrows lifted and a bright smile. "Good morning, Mr. Ashton. How do you do this very English morning?"

His French accent was thick and his tone warm. Alexander managed a smile back, and Ferrand's grew into a knowing grin that might have chafed had it been on the face of a less affable man. "Ah, but I know what you are after. I believe if I just open these messages here"—he waved a hand bearing a handful of papers and envelopes— "I will have your answer."

Alexander followed Ferrand inside. The neat office matched the Frenchman's own appearance: tidy and polished. In all the years Ferrand had bounced from department to department at the University College London, Alexander had only ever known him to have his shining silver hair cut to suit a younger man and his stylish clothing tailored to perfection.

Ferrand did not move to sit behind his desk, which sat in the same place before the window that the last person to have occupied the position of secretary to the head of Botany had arranged it. He flipped through the messages and his face lit up. "Ah, but this must be it."

Alexander didn't reply. He knew he already seemed like an over-eager boy, asking daily for an updated itinerary, but he was getting desperate. Nothing he'd done to mitigate his brother's situation had borne fruit, and every day that passed wore on both their nerves.

Ferrand sliced the message open with a letter opener and scanned it, his brows dipping momentarily into a frown. "Wednesday," he said at last.

"As in the day before yesterday?"

"*Je le crois.*" Ferrand let the message fall onto the table and shrugged. "Miss Everleigh left France Wednesday. I suppose her plans changed. But that is good news, no?"

It was good news. Alexander had panicked when he'd learned Saffron had changed her plans to stay in France for an additional week following the conference she'd been attending. Learning that she was already back in London should have been a good thing. But it seemed nothing would alleviate the dread that had coalesced in his belly when Adrian showed up at his door.

"Indeed," Alexander said. "Thank you, Mr. Ferrand."

"This means our little daily chats are at an end, I think," Ferrand said, rounding his desk and sitting down with a sigh. "I did enjoy them. Anyone who manages to blink during a conversation is a welcome change from"—he tilted his head toward the double doors to his left—"the old *lézard.*"

That was an apt description of Dr. Aster, the head of Botany, for whom Ferrand had worked for several weeks. "I will make a point to say hello more often. Thank you again, Mr. Ferrand. And if you wouldn't mind—"

"I will say nothing to Miss Everleigh," Ferrand assured him with a wink.

Alexander nodded gratefully and took his leave. As glad as he was that Saffron had returned ahead of schedule, it meant that the time had come for him to ask her to do exactly what he'd warned her away from doing a dozen times.

He returned to his office for his coat before catching a bus to Chelsea. It was time to ask Saffron Everleigh to meddle in a police investigation.

CHAPTER 2

Saffron woke early Friday morning. She'd never made it into the bath the night before, having been too much of an exhausted mess after crying to Elizabeth, and so she took one first thing.

The bathroom, and indeed the whole flat, was not luxurious by any means. She and Elizabeth had secured it for an outrageous price, one that they could afford on Elizabeth's unimpressive receptionist salary. Little was new or in perfect working order, but they loved it all the same.

That thought recalled her current worries, and Saffron sank deeper into the hot water, allowing it to creep up the nape of her neck and wet her hair.

Money was a concern that had faded from her mind in the last year. She and Elizabeth had scrimped and saved to afford living in London on Elizabeth's salary while Saffron went to school, helped along by the money Saffron's mother had secretly passed along. Mr. Feyzi, the Everleigh family's solicitor, still mailed Saffron a modest check every month.

Growing up in her grandfather's household meant Saffron had never wanted for anything material, and though there had been a number of years without luxuries she'd once considered daily staples, Saffron had never truly known need. When she was hired by University College London as an assistant researcher, those cash-strapped years faded from her memory. Her recent promotion to full researcher had further bolstered their budget.

But after the conference last week, she was facing uncertainty from every angle, including the financial one.

The International Botanical Conference had been eye-opening. She'd expected the same sorts of discussions of scientific progress, methods, and adventures in discovering new species that she heard around the U. She'd prepared herself to face the same sorts of prejudices she experienced daily as the only female member of the biology department. She'd also anticipated coming away full of enthusiasm and ideas for her future research ventures.

What she had not expected was the proliferation of what was termed economic botany, the production of bigger, better, and more fruitful plants, nor that it would be the focus of the entire conference.

She hadn't thought herself so naïve, so idealistic, that she would not accept a more pragmatic shift in the focus of her field. It made her feel foolish to be so crestfallen that her personal interests in poisons and the plants they came from seemed to be relegated to two industries: medicine and government research. The former she had already dabbled in and would not care to venture further into. The latter she was determined to avoid.

Dr. Aster hadn't been subtle about his intentions in sending her to the conference; he hoped it would change her mind about participating in government research. It hadn't been successful. But what would she do if no one else would pay her to research the things she cared about?

She sank deeper into the water, which was quickly growing tepid in the chilly bathroom. Her class was showing, as Elizabeth occasionally teased her. She wanted to follow her passions without consideration for whether or not it would put food on the table and clothing on her back. Her father, when he began his journey into academia, had certainly never had to worry about that. He'd had the means to study and publish whatever he liked because he always had his father's money and the promise of inheriting the Easting viscounty to fall back on.

The words of Dr. Ingham, her father's former colleague, floated back to her. She'd run into him at the conference, and he had asked questions that she didn't want to contemplate the answers to. She pushed his voice aside, unwilling to let those concerns cloud her already muddled mind.

Saffron had no secondary plan if being a research botanist didn't suit her, unless she agreed to what her grandparents had been pushing her to do for years: leave the university and academic life and return to the stifling arms of the upper classes, where she would marry and reproduce. Marriage and children were not the repugnant part of that equation. It was the expectation that becoming a wife and mother meant she could be nothing else.

The distant trill of the doorbell jolted her from her thoughts. Her luggage was being delivered from the train station, she recalled. She hauled herself from the bathwater.

Teeth chattering, with clinging strands of hair soaking the neck of her dressing gown, she hurried down the hall on cold, bare feet, calling, "I paid the fee at the station. You can leave it on the landing, and I'll collect it later."

She came to a breathless standstill when she flicked open the little cover on the peephole. "Alexander?"

He stood a few feet from the door, peering at her through the decorative metal grate. "Hello, Saffron."

"H-hello," she replied, automatically drawing the lapels of her damp dressing gown tighter around herself, though he could see only a few inches of her face. "What are you doing here? It's ten in the morning. On a Friday."

"It is." He seemed to rock back on his heels, stoic features giving nothing away. "I was hoping to speak with you, if convenient."

"I, er—" She wet her lips. "I've just come from the bath, but—"

"Not convenient, then," he said. "Will you have dinner with me tonight?"

Her mouth fell open, and she quickly snapped it shut, forgetting again that he couldn't see her gaping like a fish. They'd had this conversation before, just a few weeks ago. He'd asked her to dinner but had relented when she'd made it clear that she did not envision a romantic future for the pair of them, not when he'd been adamant about her not continuing to help police investigations. He even went so far as to threaten to report her to Dr. Aster.

That didn't stop her heart from speeding up at the sight of him at her door.

"I just want to talk," Alexander added.

Saffron noted the softness of his voice, and between that and the darkness gathered beneath his eyes and the faint tension around his mouth, she found herself agreeing. "Of course."

He gave her the time and place and was down the stairs before she even had time to identify the feeling welling in her chest. After weeks of her vision for the future shifting and dissolving like a sand dune with no white-flowered *Oenothera deltoides* to anchor it, she felt hope once again.

The bell rang twice more that day, once just a few minutes after Alexander had left, announcing the actual arrival of her luggage, and once more midafternoon. The first made Saffron's heart leap with uneasy anticipation, imagining it was Alexander, impatient to reveal whatever was on his mind. When the bell rang at three, she'd squashed her anticipation and simply opened the door.

She was immediately confronted by a bouquet of flowers.

A confusing mixture of panic and appreciation flooded her at the sight of the blooms. A brief scan of the colorful arrangement assured her that none of them was poisonous, or at least not in the way the last bouquet she'd been presented with, and the casual manner of the delivery boy who offered them to her with a cheeky grin confirmed that this was the nice sort of flower delivery and not the deadly kind.

She locked the door firmly behind her regardless and took the flowers to the parlor.

With the radiator blasting and a fire laid in the fireplace for the evening, Saffron was enjoying a cozy afternoon. Her favorite plants grew in cheerful pots on the windowsill. Books and magazines sat in curated piles on the coffee table, and a blanket awaited her on the couch. She took a vase from the shelf and set it on the coffee table with the bouquet inside. Dark ivy twined through the bunches of purple verbena and lush, tall stocks of pink hollyhock. Nestled along the bottom were cuttings from a balsam tree, fragrant and sharp.

She puzzled over the flowers only until she recalled the card the delivery boy had sneaked into her hand. A familiar tight, neat script read:

Welcome back from your academic adventure! In case you've been missing the real fun, I've created a little puzzle for you. Drop by sometime, if you can bear to.

Yours,
Lee

Included was an elegant card providing Lee's full name and an address on Harley Street.

Saffron set the card and the note on the table with the flowers with a sigh. First Alexander, and now Lee. What was the world coming to?

Still, she was unable to resist the riddle Lee had created for her, so she went to the bookshelf for the well-worn floriography dictionary she'd refused to return to the university's library. It was a memento of her most recent adventure, one that was still useful, apparently. She quickly decoded the flowers.

Ivy: friendship
Verbena: regret
Hollyhock: ambition of a scholar

Her fingers smoothed over the pointed tips of balsam, puzzling over its inclusion, until she realized that Lee had likely meant balsam, *Impatiens balsamina*, rather than balsam fir, *Abies balsamea*. The mistake made her laugh despite herself. She understood his meaning, however—"impatience."

Saffron was not impatient at all to see Lee. With far too many problems nipping at her heels, she would be avoiding her former study partner for as long as her conscience would allow.

It wasn't long after the flowers arrived that the front door was unlocked, opened, then violently slammed shut. Saffron called out to Elizabeth, who didn't answer.

Warily, Saffron peered around the corner, only to be nearly bowled over by Elizabeth storming into her bedroom. She didn't close her door, so Saffron followed.

"Whatever is the matter?" Saffron asked her when she found her flatmate throwing her shoes into her wardrobe.

"I cannot *believe* him," Elizabeth snarled, starting on the buttons to her suit jacket. Her red varnished nails flashed with each button before she tore the jacket from her shoulders. "The sheer nerve!"

Saffron withheld a sigh. Colin Smith had no doubt done something romantically stupid. "Whatever it is—"

"And after so long!" Elizabeth's volume was steadily rising, along with the pinkness in her cheeks. "Years, he's waited!"

As Elizabeth and Colin couldn't have been stepping out for more than two weeks, Saffron asked, "Who, Eliza?"

Elizabeth's rambling became ranting as she shed her skirt and blouse. She only paused to detach her stockings from her garters and carefully roll them down, avoiding snagging them. When she was barefoot and in her camiknickers, she finally rounded on Saffron and exclaimed, "And he's coming here! He's just going to waltz in here like it hasn't been five *bloody* years since I've had more than a telegram from him wishing me happy birthday weeks late."

Saffron set her hands on her friend's shoulders, which were significantly higher than her own. "Who are you talking about?"

Elizabeth inhaled, and with the disgust she would display for a moldy potato at the back of the larder, she enunciated, "*Nick.*"

Saffron blinked. "Your brother?"

"Yes." Elizabeth brushed Saffron's hands away and bustled over to her dressing table, where she removed her earrings and rings.

"He's coming to London to see you?"

"That is what his note said," Elizabeth replied before half disappearing into her wardrobe. She came out with a man's union suit, which she pulled on. The long-sleeved undergarment could mean only one thing.

"And he's coming here, to the flat?" Saffron guessed.

Elizabeth did up the buttons and pulled a pair of denim overalls from the wardrobe, slipping them on over the cotton of the union suit. Saffron opened a dressing table drawer and extracted a plain scarf to hand to her friend. She knew better than to try to talk her out of what she would do next.

Elizabeth wrapped her perfectly set sandy waves with the faded pink fabric. "He said he'd be here in four hours. Four. Hours."

An unexpected visitor would likely put off any homemaker, but an unexpected visitor of this caliber meant that the cleanliness-obsessed Elizabeth was moments away from panic. All Saffron could do was stay out of her way and hope that she didn't wear through their floors with frantic scouring.

By seven in the evening, Saffron was more than happy to get out of the flat. It was spotless and redolent of bleach, dinner, and stress. She'd dressed alone for her dinner with Alexander, though she would have preferred preparing with Elizabeth to keep from thinking in circles about how things would go between them. She'd imagined everything from grand romantic gestures to a formal letter of termination, presented by Alexander on behalf of Dr. Aster. She'd known she was being ridiculous, but she couldn't help it. If the continued ranting floating down the hall was any indication, Elizabeth was equally on edge. She'd disappeared into her own bedroom to prepare to receive her brother.

The moment Saffron stepped into the street, where she was greeted by dreary dampness, she began rethinking her acceptance of Alexander's invitation altogether. She could have pressed Elizabeth harder about staying home, though her friend had seemed utterly resolute she'd greet her brother alone.

Though Saffron had grown up with the three Hale children, who'd lived on the property adjacent to the estate where she'd been raised, Nick was eight years older and had never had much time for Elizabeth and, by extension, Saffron. He'd tolerated the girls scampering after him during school holidays, but he'd joined the army right after school, and Saffron hadn't seen him since. She'd heard from Elizabeth and Mrs. Hale about his meteoric rise through the ranks but knew little about his service during the war, other than he'd received a medal of some kind. He hadn't returned to Bedford for the funeral services for the middle Hale child, Wesley, after he fell at Flanders.

Saffron guessed that was perhaps the crux of Elizabeth's problem with Nick—that he hadn't been present to grieve for their lost brother. Saffron, who'd been as much in love with Wesley as her fifteen-year-old heart had been capable of being, couldn't hold that against Nick. Even if he was as high ranking as she recalled, few men had been given leave to mourn their family members.

These thoughts took Saffron from her flat to Kings Road. When she reached the corner before the restaurant where Alexander had told her to meet him, she slowed her steps. Anxiety crept up her neck like the cold autumn chill.

At the very least, she and Alexander could talk about the Amazonian expedition as they dined. That was a safe topic of conversation, hopefully, one that would last them through the meal. She wanted them to be friends. That was the only hope she allowed to take root as she opened the fogged glass door of the restaurant.

CHAPTER 3

"I was half-convinced you wouldn't come."

Saffron stumbled over the threshold and reached a hand out to prevent herself from falling. Alexander caught it, steadying her.

She straightened up, gently withdrawing her hand from his grip. Even through her gloves, her freezing fingers could feel the heat of his touch. It felt far too intimate far too fast. Friends did not linger over simple touches like that. With a too-bright smile, she said, "Don't be silly. You promised me stories from the Amazon, if I recall correctly."

"That I did." By the intent way Alexander looked at her, she realized that he was taking in her appearance. She resisted the urge to fidget with her rain-dotted coat or check to see if her dark hair had slipped its pins. She removed her coat, using the movement to cover her own observations. He'd already given his coat to the maître d' and stood before her, tall and a little imposing in a navy suit that stretched a bit at his shoulders. His olive skin had lost some of the golden tan he'd brought back from the Amazon, but his sable hair and watchful eyes were as she remembered.

He offered his arm. "Shall we? Hard to reveal gripping adventures on an empty stomach."

That was precisely what occupied them for the meal. From the moment they were shown to their table, a cozy side booth, to the last bite of their excellent meal, Alexander regaled her with tales from the rainforest. His descriptions of encounters with creatures in the course of questing for the plants on her specimen list had her gasping, laughing, and groaning. For one who was usually economical with his words, he proved an engrossing storyteller.

"I refuse to believe that a monkey snatched the fruit from your hand," she declared after the waiter had swept away the remnants of their dessert.

Alexander chuckled. "But you believed the caiman story?"

Saffron narrowed her eyes. "You make it sound as though I should not."

"I would think that climbing a tree over the river to avoid a miniature crocodilian sounds more far-fetched than a monkey plucking a rumberry from my hand."

Smiling, she said, "Perhaps I like the image of you scrambling out of the water and into a tree too much."

The warmth that had danced in the depths of his dark eyes heated to something more than friendly. After replaying her words to herself, she realized she'd sounded more flirtatious than intended. It had been far too easy to slip into their rapport from the weeks they'd prepared for the expedition together. Thus far, he'd shown none of the surly, dictatorial attitude she'd been so upset by in their most recent encounters.

She cleared her throat, reaching for the now cold dregs of her coffee. "Now, tell me what's new at the U. I worry being gone for nearly a month will have put me quite out of it." Not that she'd ever been "in it" when it came to the inner circles of the biology and botany departments. Being the only woman in the North Wing of the University College had its challenges, including not being included in the gossip mill but still being one of its frequent targets.

"Let's see," Alexander said, humor fading as he smoothed the white tablecloth. His hand was mottled with shiny pink scars from his battlefield injury during the Great War. "Cunningham has me paired with St. John on something that bores even me to tears." Saffron laughed a little at that. Alexander's field of microbiology meant that his studies had titles that made even the most stalwart scholars yawn. "Miller and Aster have been arguing over funding, but that's not news. Ericson is making noise about another expedition soon, since he missed out on the Amazon. Something on the Mediterranean."

"That would be quite the thing," she said, straightening up. "Is there any real interest in the possibility?"

"There is, actually." Alexander shifted in his seat, his hands smoothing out the tablecloth once again. His eyes followed the movement, a restless combination that made Saffron's instincts perk up. When he swallowed hard, then cleared his throat, she was definitely paying attention. He was never one to beat around the bush.

"I had a visit from my brother," he said.

Her eyebrows winged up. He'd last mentioned his brother during a heated argument that had left Saffron feeling raw. "Is he well?" she asked cautiously.

"More or less," he replied. "He was on a train into town a week ago and a man in his compartment died."

"Oh, but that's awful," she said, checking her urge to put her hands on his if only to stop him from continuing to smooth the tablecloth. He was clearly perturbed by this turn of events. "Did he attempt to revive him?"

"Yes, he did," Alexander said slowly. "But a sudden death, when no one present knows the man or his circumstances, leads to a lot of questions."

"Naturally."

"Adrian was questioned," he continued, his words coming out with crisp intention, "at length."

Understanding rose through her, swift and painful. "Was he mistreated? What happened?"

His eyes met hers at last, full of wariness. "I do not believe he was mistreated. But he has been taken into the police station half a dozen times since, usually for hours at a time."

Silence fell between them, interrupted only by the gentle, distant clink of silverware on porcelain from the only other occupied table in the restaurant. Alexander was speaking so carefully, so roundabout, that Saffron wondered if he worried about offending her. But why . . . Suspicion gripped her. "Alexander, at which train station did Adrian's train arrive?"

"King's Cross."

"Which means the police officers on the scene—"

"Came from the King's Cross Road police station, yes."

Understanding sank like a lead weight in her stomach. "And the detective responsible for the case?"

There was no hint of apology in Alexander's gaze when he answered, "Detective Inspector Green."

Alexander resisted the urge to remove invisible wrinkles from the tablecloth yet again and withdrew his hands into his lap. He tried not to seem like he was avidly watching Saffron's every expression, but when they were displayed so plainly, it was hard not to. He'd never needed to make excuses to himself for why he looked at her so intently. She was every bit as fascinating as the specimens he spent hours gazing at through his microscope and just as unpredictable, never more so than in this moment. This time, however, it was a growing sense of having made a horrible mistake, rather than that deepening affection, that kept his eyes glued to her face.

Her fine brows came together as she pieced through the scant information he'd given her and drew conclusions he hoped were mostly wrong. At last, she spoke in a flat voice he didn't recognize. "So this was all a ruse to ask me to help your brother."

He felt like a caiman had snapped up his tongue. She'd skipped over the wrong conclusions and landed on the worst possible one. "No," he said firmly.

Her lips twisted in a humorless smile. "Asking me to dinner and plying me with entertaining stories was not a ploy to butter me up before you asked me to intercede with Inspector Green on Adrian's behalf?"

"I asked you to dinner because I wanted to see you." Beneath the table, his hands balled into fists. "But I can't deny that I wanted to ask for the benefit of your advice."

Saffron was obviously not convinced by his almost-truth. Resisting the feeling of defeat clawing its way over his shoulders, he added, "I do want to ask for your help. But that is not why I wanted to spend time with you."

He might have said more, explained about the way he'd stared at the chair in his office, imagining her there over the past few weeks. And passed by her empty office unnecessarily. And now had a strange collection of office mates. But she abruptly slid from the booth, color high in her cheeks and her lips tightening into a line.

He followed her. "Saffron, give me a moment to explain."

"I don't think I require any further explanation." She snatched up her handbag from the table before rounding on him. "Whenever I become involved in a police investigation, you encourage me to cry off. The last time, when I was helping to catch a murderer who'd killed three women, you threatened to go to Dr. Aster, whom you know would have sacked me for misusing my work hours and resources. And now, when it's convenient for you, you *want* me to interfere. I'd never taken you for a hypocrite, Alexander."

Her words stung all the more for their truth, one he'd accepted the moment he realized things were going south for his brother faster than he could work out how to fix them. She seemed to be missing a key point: the lack of danger in her becoming involved in Adrian's situation compared to those other investigations. But he certainly wasn't going to point that out now. "You're right."

Saffron nodded firmly. "I am."

"I am being hypocritical in the extreme."

"You are," she confirmed, though with less confidence.

"And I apologize."

"You should."

The barest twinkle of amusement in her eyes encouraged him. He stepped closer, gently taking her handbag and setting it on the table. "I am sorry. For threatening to tell Aster and thereby threatening your career. And I am also sorry for the way I acted toward Lee." The words burned, but they needed to be said. "You were right. I did not make the extent of my feelings for you known when I left for the expedition, and you were right to tell me off for having expectations I had not communicated. I'm sorry for all of it."

Her eyes narrowed. "But?"

He shook his head. "There is none. I did not react well when I returned, about us, or the case, or Lee. And I'm sorry for apologizing in combination with asking for help regarding Adrian's situation. But"—he rushed on, seeing her ire rekindling—"I want you to know that I would have apologized at the first chance regardless."

After an interminable moment, Saffron nodded. She slipped her hand from his and made her way to the door, where the maître d' assisted with her coat. Alexander followed, donning his own coat and hat before they stepped outside.

"May I walk you to your flat?" he asked.

From beneath her umbrella, she gave him another narrowed-eye look. "I suppose."

Though he'd rather they shared an umbrella, he opened his own. The rain had turned to a fine mist, haloing every light they passed with gold.

It brought to mind the night they'd walked together in search of a taxi following their adventure in Berking's garden. He bit his tongue on bringing it up. He had no idea how to walk the line between wanting to rekindle something of their past affections and not putting Saffron off after asking for her help. Even as he needed to give her time to accept his apology and move past his mistakes, he felt the urgency of every passing moment that Inspector Green and the others cemented their opinions about his brother's guilt.

He waited until they'd reached her street to bring it up again.

"I know the timing is poor," he said, pausing outside her building. She stopped and angled her umbrella so they could look at one another. Her neutral expression only made him warier. "And if there was another option, I would have taken it."

"What do you want me to do, Alexander?" she asked impatiently. "I don't expect the inspector would appreciate me walking into the station and demanding he dismiss one of his suspects."

"Of course, that isn't what I'm asking."

"Then what?"

"Adrian said that the man appeared unwell. The police have asked him again and again if the man consumed anything on the train, if Adrian gave him anything, even a cigarette. He didn't, but they don't seem to believe him."

Saffron frowned, ignoring the water dripping from the umbrella's point onto her shoulder. "They think he was poisoned."

A mixture of relief at her understanding and worry for Adrian made his stomach turn uneasily. "Yes."

To his surprise, Saffron let out a laugh. "Just because I know things about poisonous plants doesn't mean I'll be of any use in proving your brother didn't slip the man something! How can you expect me—"

"The man who died was a scientist. A horticulturalist. He worked in a lab," he said quickly, "so you might be familiar with some plant or chemical he worked with."

"And now I'm supposed to snoop around his lab?" She lifted an arm in exasperation. "Should I run up to change my shoes so I might creep around his garden too? Alexander, you're asking me to do exactly what you told me off for doing before. That isn't fair."

He hung his head, wondering how the conversation had gotten so off track. "I'm not asking you to do anything of the kind. You have knowledge that might help the inspector *solve* the case. I'm not asking you to do anything more than offer your help to Inspector Green. Showing that the man died from ingesting some chemical from his lab will help Adrian."

"Simple. Easy," she said sourly. "I'll just tell Inspector Green to hand all the information over to me. He knows you and I have—had—a relationship of some kind, and he won't suspect I'm up to something. No, not the detective inspector. He'll never suspect a thing. Excellent plan."

She turned and stomped up the steps to the flat. He took the steps two at a time to beat her to the top, where he held open the door. She shot him a dark look as she closed her umbrella and stepped inside.

That didn't put him off. Even though he could feel his chances of fixing things between them dwindling with every sarcastic word from her mouth, he needed to do something to help his brother. At present, that looked like chasing Saffron up the stairs to her flat.

CHAPTER 4

Saffron barely noticed Alexander next to her as she pounded up the steps. Her mind was too loud with all the things she wished she could throw at him, accusations and more sarcasm and outright shouting about him being a selfish, manipulative man.

None of it would come out, however, because underneath all that frustration at his hypocrisy was an appreciation for the absoluteness of his apology and his loyalty to his family. Even if she couldn't trust that his apology was entirely genuine, it was very hard to be completely angry with a man who'd humble himself to help his brother. Not to mention he said he thought she could actually help the inspector solve the case.

But that too could easily be a manipulation. He knew that saying such things would work in his favor.

At the top of the stairs, Saffron shoved her key into the lock and pushed the door open. A wave of warm air scented with a savory dinner and traces of lingering bleach poured into the cold hall.

Saffron turned to tell Alexander good night, but before she could get a word out, Elizabeth was clattering down the hall.

"Saffron! And Alexander, what a pleasant surprise!"

Saffron opened her mouth to explain that it was not a pleasant surprise at all, but her words died as Elizabeth came to a stop before them. She wore one of her best dresses, burnt orange with yellow floral lace appliqué, and flawless makeup that left no hint of her cleaning frenzy on her person. But the smile stretching Elizabeth's scarlet lips was more of a desperate baring of teeth.

"Is your brother still here?" Saffron asked.

"Yes, and I've just brought out coffee," she replied. "Won't you join us? Alexander, come and meet my brother, Nick."

Alexander's sudden stillness behind Saffron drew her attention away from the obvious subtext of Elizabeth's invitation, that she didn't want to spend another moment alone with her brother. Saffron turned to see that his face, which had been open and earnest during his plea, had shuttered. After a brief glance at Saffron, he said, "Of course."

They removed their coats and were chivied down the hall by Elizabeth. She briefly squeezed Saffron's cold hand in her own warm one, though Saffron didn't know if it was in warning or gratitude.

The parlor was bright and inviting. The table that Saffron used as a desk had been dragged from the window to stand before the fire, lingering debris from supper layered atop.

A man rose from the couch as they entered. He was tall and solidly built, as all the Hale family were, and had the light, sandy coloring all three siblings shared. But that was all that Saffron found familiar in the man smiling broadly at her.

His eyes were crinkled into a warm smile, his teeth even and white. He wore some of his weight in his jaw and neck, both giving the impression of a sturdy character to go with his frame. His thick hair was short and neatly brushed back on his high forehead.

He stepped forward to meet her. "But this is never little Miss Everleigh, terror of all Bedfordshire," he said with a chuckle.

Saffron offered him her hand. "How do you do, Nick? It's been a long time."

"An awfully long time," he agreed, not releasing her hand right away. Instead, he held her away slightly, taking her in with friendly appreciation. "Long enough for you to be unrecognizable, apart from those Everleigh blues."

A slight flush rose in her cheeks, and she slipped her hand from his. "I'm afraid even ten years won't change my eyes."

Nick chuckled again. Saffron wasn't sure what she'd expected, but he was nothing like the stuffy sort a decorated military man was likely to be. He was all ease and smiles, perhaps even a hint of flirtation.

Scowling, Elizabeth said, "Well, don't let the two of us interrupt your jolly little reunion."

Saffron cast her an exasperated look as she took Alexander by the elbow to draw him further into the room. He'd stopped just inside the door.

When the two men were face to face, she said, "Nicholas Hale, this is my colleague, Alexander Ashton."

"Pleased to meet you," Alexander said somewhat stiffly, offering his hand.

"Mr. Ashton." Nick took it with a still broader grin. "Call me Nick. I'm Elizabeth's older brother."

They broke their handshake, and an awkward silence fell, with only the soft ticking of the clock and the occasional snap of the fire in the hearth to ease it. Alexander looked at Nick, Nick looked steadily at Alexander, and Elizabeth seemed to be trying hard to look anywhere but at her brother.

"Coffee," Saffron said, recalling it just as the scent found her over the smell of eau de cologne and rain-dampened wool. "Shall we?"

They settled onto the couch and armchairs, with Saffron pouring and doctoring each cup to the liking of her companions.

"So," Saffron began as she handed Nick his black coffee, "I'm afraid I haven't any idea what you're doing these days, Nick, so much so I cannot even introduce you with your proper rank. What does the army do to keep you occupied these days?"

"Not enough," Nick replied cheerfully. "Not enough entertaining things, anyway. I'm now former Major Hale. Though king and country still pull my puppet strings, as it were."

"Nick works for the Agricultural Ministry," Elizabeth said rather acerbically, accepting a cup from Saffron. "It appears our home county has gotten its claws deep in him after all. Agriculture, after the thrills of war. I can hardly credit it."

Nick shot her a grin. "Thrills and a lot of unpleasantness, I assure you. I find the quiet life of paperwork and farms suits me." He turned back to Saffron. "Eliza says you're a scientist, Saffron. Botany, like your father. I'd wager Lord Easting is not pleased by that."

Saffron couldn't help but sigh at Nick's guess. No, her grandfather was not at all pleased with her following her father into the sciences. "I believe my grandmother has the greater objection, but no, neither are pleased."

"Now that a terrifying prospect," Nick said, playing up a little shiver. "Viscountess Easting always knew how to express that infamous displeasure with such bone-chilling hauteur. I don't envy you in the coming weeks." He caught the confusion on her face, for he added, "Returning home for the holidays. A very frosty Christmas welcome is in your future, I'm sure."

Like a trowel cutting into damp earth, a hollow opened inside of Saffron. She hadn't been home for Christmas in three years, since the last time she'd subjected herself to her grandparents' scolding in person.

Elizabeth snapped, "Neither Saffron nor I have been back to Bedford in a very long time." Saffron could practically hear her continuing on, *something you'd have known if you'd bothered to write more than once a year.* Did he know that Elizabeth was all but estranged from their parents, as Saffron was from her grandparents? What had Nick said when he learned his parents had planned to marry Elizabeth off to an old man in a foolish attempt to repair the fortunes that the war had cut in half? Had he known that his sister had all but fled for London, following Saffron when she began studying at the university?

Nick's eyes bounced between Elizabeth and Saffron. "I see I have misstepped. I apologize."

Saffron was aware of Alexander's gaze on her, but when she met his eyes, she saw he was not idly watching her reaction to Nick's apology but looking at her with such intensity she felt she might be scalded if she didn't break eye contact.

"It's no matter," Saffron said, turning back to Nick.

Saffron didn't think Nick missed the glare Elizabeth shot in his direction, for a few minutes of idle chat later, he rose to his feet.

"The hour grows late," he said dramatically, almost like he was quoting a play. "Thank you, Eliza, for the matchless hospitality. The dinner was exquisite, only trumped by the company." He smiled at Saffron and Alexander. "I'll be in London for a few weeks. I hope to repeat this treat soon."

Saffron agreed, privately thinking she'd rather take a stroll in a patch of giant hogweed. She could hardly believe Nick was oblivious to the tension laying like a thick fog in the parlor.

After a round of polite goodbyes, Nick departed. Before the door had even closed, Saffron was pointedly looking at Alexander to make his own exit, and he complied, murmuring a promise to talk more the following Monday, when Saffron would return to campus.

When they were finally alone, Saffron and Elizabeth exchanged weary glances. By mutual unspoken agreement, they tidied up the flat and retired to their rooms in anticipation of the morning, when they would inevitably dissect each word their unexpected guests had said.

CHAPTER 5

B risk wind greeted Saffron on Monday morning. The considerable walk and bus journey to reach the University College London campus seemed especially interminable, what with the promise of another tense conversation with Alexander. What worried her more, however, was the meeting she anticipated between her and Dr. Aster.

The head of Botany, though he was still new to the position, was as intimidating as he was old. That was to say: very. Aster had been the friend of her mentor, Dr. Maxwell, but Aster had never shown her any of the warmth Maxwell had for Saffron.

Stepping onto campus after a break had felt for many years like a welcome home, a return to the place she believed she'd one day belong, contributing to the world and its knowledge. Now she felt none of that thrill, or even that comfort, that she'd once taken from walking into the Quad. The stone buildings bracketing the circular drive seemed to watch her with their darkened windows like somber eyes as she crossed the pavement on her way into the North Wing.

She climbed the steps to the second floor, where she unlocked her office, set her things down, and surveyed the room. Her desk had a tall stack of files atop it, and her collection of plant cuttings in the window sill were in dangerous need of water. Their pale roots tangled at the dry bottoms of the test tubes she'd arranged them in. She took the wooden rack in hand and headed back out into the hall.

She planned to go down into the bowels of the building to the breakroom, but going into the basement and facing dim halls lined with furniture covered in white fabric was deeply unappealing. She didn't care for being underground, for one thing, but her general dislike had bloomed into full-blown reluctance in recent months. Surprisingly little had bothered her about the conclusion of her last case, but two things continued to emerge in her dreams or catch her off guard in her waking hours: flashes of fleeing through moonlit rooms full of covered furniture, and the dead, empty face of Mrs. Keller. She'd known Mrs. Keller's corpse would haunt her for a long time, but the former surprised her. It wasn't the villain's chilling confession nor having her head mercilessly bashed that lingered . . . but white-swathed furniture. It made her feel rather like an idiot to have her heart pound at the prospect of the basement and its rows of discarded desks and shelves, but she'd avoid the reminder all the same.

Dr. Miller and Mr. Feinstein, two members of her department, had paused to talk just before the staircase. Usually, she would have turned tail rather than interrupt a conversation between the pair, but if she was going to work out how to be a contributing member of the department, and to the study of botany in general, she needed to be able to have conversations with them that did not end with her wanting to hide from their sneering comments.

She exhaled, straightened up, and walked toward the stairs. "Good morning."

Feinstein nodded politely, pausing his complaint about fertilizers to reply. "Good morning."

Dr. Miller eyed her, his enormous mustache twitching. "Your galivanting on the continent lasted quite a while. How are your samples from Brazil faring?"

Ice trickled down her spine at his tone. What had happened to her samples to make him smile so smugly? Aster had approved her tropical pigmentation study on the condition it wouldn't take her a year to complete, and if something happened to her samples, it could put her back months.

She didn't bother forcing a pleasant expression in return. "I'm sure Mr. Winters has done an excellent job managing them."

That was an utter lie. Taciturn Mr. Winters despised foreign plants, especially the dangerous sort. She'd thought that his relative kindness in the past meant he could be trusted to keep all her samples alive, but had that been a mistake?

She nodded to the two men, murmuring "Excuse me," before quickly retreating down the stairs. She had to ensure nobody had sabotaged the only step in her career she'd been sure of.

The chilly morning meant the glass walls of the five greenhouses belonging to University College London were entirely opaque with milky condensation. Saffron bustled inside, set down her still-dry test tubes, and snapped off her hat, gloves, and hat. She stowed them on the hooks just inside with practiced inattention. Her eyes were already sweeping over the greenery within.

She didn't see any of her samples, but she hadn't expected them in the first greenhouse. That space was reserved for the full-grown species that belonged to tropical regions. She'd likely find them in the second or third greenhouse, where it was still warm but less crowded with massive fronds of every shape and shade of green.

She tied on her apron and pulled on her heavy leather gloves as she slipped into the second greenhouse, where lines of tables were spread like miniature roads. Each surface was covered in tiny pots. Some looked like nothing but dirt lay within, while others showed the first promising signs of life in minute green sprouts attempting to push through the black soil.

A quick sweep of the room showed that her specimens were not among the little pots.

Growing worry increased her pace as she strode from the greenhouse. Greenhouse Four was the dry one, and she was relieved to see her tropical plants had not been mistakenly put in there. But that meant that her samples—the ones that were retrieved for her from Brazil by Alexander and could not be replaced unless she begged cuttings or seeds from institutions notorious for their lack of cooperative spirit—were in Greenhouse Five. Where plants went to die.

Or, in the case of the xolotl vine, went to thrive. The toxic yellow vine had taken over the entire back wall of the greenhouse, not caring that the building was a little too drafty, a little too dry to suit its origins in the warm jungle of the Yucatan peninsula in which Dr. Maxwell had discovered it.

She ignored the vine, though, for she immediately saw that her plants were not in the greenhouse.

The now all too familiar sense of dread returned to squeeze her lungs. Her samples were nowhere to be seen, and she was meant to promptly visit Aster for a report on the conference and finalize her decision to keep her name off the paper she'd written with Lee. She'd have to tell him that her plants were missing.

She hurried back to the germination greenhouse. She read each and every label, stooping low over the tiny sprouts as she scrutinized each one. Sweat prickled her forehead, the heat and humidity of the greenhouse working in tandem with stress to overheat her.

"Blast," she whispered, straightening up and surveying the room once more. No hint of her tiny, poisonous plants. It was nearly nine in the morning, and Dr. Aster would be expecting her. She needed to get back to the North Wing, but how could she face him, knowing she was bringing only bad news? A hundred excuses and prevarications circled in her mind, but she knew Aster would accept none of them. What was she going to do?

Chapter 6

She'd made it only two steps into the North Wing before Saffron was accosted by someone calling her name.

Despite her worry, a smile tugged at her lips to see the man hurrying forward. Mr. Ferrand was a sweet man, quite the opposite of Dr. Aster, to whom he was secretary. "Monsieur Ferrand, *bonjour.*"

She accepted his hand, and he squeezed it briefly. "*Bonjour, ma charmante amie. Pardonne-moi*, but Dr. Aster wished me to find you as soon as you set foot on campus."

Saffron swallowed her misgivings and attempted to reply adequately. Since learning she would be going to his homeland a few weeks ago, Ferrand had insisted on speaking to her in French. She'd responded in kind though her command of the language was middling at best, her accent worse, even after three weeks of speaking French nonstop. He was gracious enough not to cringe as she said, "*Montrez le chemin.*"

She followed him up the stairs, dodging clumps of students. As they reached the third floor, an idea struck her. "Monsieur Ferrand," Saffron said, "have you heard anything about my samples from the Amazonian expedition? Perhaps Mr. Winters—"

"Ah!" Ferrand opened the door to his office and swept an arm for her to enter. "I believe you must speak to Mr. Ashton."

Saffron blinked. "Alexander Ashton? From Biology?"

Ferrand merely winked in reply. Nonplussed, Saffron allowed him to shuffle her across the office and to the double doors that led to Dr. Aster's inner sanctum.

After the busy halls, Aster's office resembled a tomb, silent and gloomy. The only light came from the green banker's lamp, which illuminated only the top of Aster's highly polished desk, on which a pair of pale, age-spotted hands were folded.

"Miss Everleigh," came Aster's sharp voice from the darkness above those hands.

Saffron couldn't help it—she shivered. It was downright spooky in there. It didn't help that the windows were covered by thick draperies.

Ferrand tutted softly as he pulled them open. Saffron winced at the cool light. Ferrand gently took her test-tube rack with her cuttings out of her hand. She'd rather forgotten she'd been carrying it.

Aster sat at his desk on the opposite side of the room, a sour expression pinching his wrinkled face. He was an old man, but not the jolly old sort like Dr. Maxwell. There was no softness to him, from his precisely parted white hair to his gray eyes glimmering like melting snow over metal.

He nodded, and she sat in the chair before him.

"I trust the rest of your travels were sufficient," he said without preamble.

Her fingers linked together in her lap. The reason she'd extended her stay on the Continent had been among the worst experiences of her life—and she'd recently been held at gunpoint, poisoned, and abducted. Traveling to Ypres and Flanders had been a mistake but one she would never admit to Aster. "Yes, sir. I appreciate greatly your flexibility."

"Have you changed your mind about the case study paper?"

"No, sir."

He didn't miss a beat. "I see." Curiously, Saffron was sure that this was what Aster had been expecting. "What are your plans for ensuring your position within the department and your spot in the master's program?"

This was the question for which she'd rehearsed her answer, and so she said what she'd been planning, even if it stuck a bit in her throat considering what she'd just discovered in the greenhouses. "My initial analysis for the pigmentation study is on track to meet your first deadline. I will be more than capable of carrying out the study when classes for second term begin in January."

She held her breath as Aster watched her. Determination warred with fear. She *was* more than capable of carrying out a study while earning her master's degree. But should Aster not be willing to keep her on as a researcher, should she be sacked, finding another position after being dismissed from a university . . .

"Very well," he said.

Saffron didn't allow her shoulders to droop in relief. "Thank you, Dr. Aster."

Ferrand was not at his desk when she retrieved her cuttings, but she didn't slow to feel relieved that Aster gave her a reprieve. She had plants to find.

She directed brief, polite nods to the other staff members in the hall, who either nodded back or ignored her. News of her choice to keep her name off the paper would be known by the end of the day, and she had no doubt any acknowledgment would further dwindle. No one in the department, or likely the entire scientific community, would understand her reluctance to participate in government research. Even if their fathers, brothers, sons, and friends had been killed in the same manner her father had, at the hands of new and violent technology, she doubted any of them would be willing to put aside a potentially enriching opportunity out of principle. None of them was likely that idealistic—or that stupid.

She'd just started down the stairs to the ground level, lost in thought about where exactly one might stash her specimens, when a hand landed on her elbow. "Saffron."

Her hands fumbled, sending her test-tube rack flying. "No!"

She dove for it, but it was unnecessary. Alexander caught the rack easily, handing it back to her. She swallowed, hugging her cuttings close. "Thank you."

"Sorry," he said, shoving his hands in his pockets. "I've been calling your name."

Heat rose in her cheeks. "I was lost in thought. My Brazilian samples have gone missing—"

"I have them."

Her mouth fell open. "You took my samples?"

"They're in my office."

She didn't bother asking why, she wanted to see her plants.

She followed Alexander to the second floor and around the corner to his office. It was so clean and sparsely furnished as to be sterile, but near his window stood an unfamiliar cart.

A trio of massive glass jars sat overturned on the cart. Next to them stood a lamp, shining directly on them. Condensation obscured what she hoped was beneath. She held her breath as Alexander moved aside the lamp and lifted the first jar.

Twelve tiny pots stood in two concentric circles. Bending, her face inches away from the dark soil, Saffron's heart swelled. Tiny green specks were just visible through the dirt. The *Strychnos toxifera* seeds she'd planted just before departing—the only plant that hadn't survived the journey from Brazil, and the only sample she was growing from seed—were alive and well.

She reached for the next jar. Alexander obliged her, lifting the other jars in turn so she could examine each plant. She counted her samples, mentally ticking off each specimen. *Brugmansia sanguinea*, now a thick stalk with a fringe of leaves, would someday grow into a tree with massive, trumpet-shaped flowers. The vines of her *Chondrodendron tomentosum* cutting were already budding with new leaves.

They were all there, all accounted for and apparently thriving in this rather unorthodox setup.

Unexpectedly, a lump formed in her throat. It was silly, perhaps, to care so much about a collection of plants that could kill someone so easily, but she did. She was so very glad to find them alive and well and not sitting at the back of some classroom rotting away. They couldn't help being dangerous, after all. The tropical pigmentation study was the only forthcoming project she had, and thus far the only thing keeping her from losing her position at the U.

"All's well?" asked Alexander from behind her.

She turned to the man who had apparently saved her plants and her study. "Not that I mind you brought them in here—you've done a wonderful job tending them—but why?"

He crossed his arms over his chest, a hip leaning against his desk. "I thought they had a better chance of survival if they were not in the greenhouses."

"You doubt Mr. Winters's ability to tend to them? Or you were concerned for your reputation if the samples you retrieved did not bear fruit?" Her questions were meant to come out teasing, but she couldn't conceal the growing certainty that she really didn't want to know why Alexander had taken her plants from the greenhouse.

"I overheard some people talking about how it would be rather amusing should some of your specimens be found to be ineligible for your study."

Any buoyancy she'd felt at finding her plants faded at this confirmation, her mood returning to the same low levels as when she'd left Aster's office. "I appreciate you rescuing them, then."

"I was happy to," he said, his gaze not leaving hers.

No doubt Alexander knew that saving her specimens was the surest way to her heart. She'd nearly melted in a puddle on the greenhouse floor when he'd shown her the collection when he returned in October, and he would remember that. She'd not be so easily swayed to forgiveness, even if the instinct to throw herself into his arms in gratitude was strong.

She turned back to the makeshift terrariums. "I'm going to help your brother, you know. That was never in question, even if every last one of my specimens died. I just wish this entire thing didn't feel like an act to secure my cooperation." She risked a look behind her to see his reaction.

Alexander's dark eyes flashed. He stepped into her space, making her lift her chin. "*Nothing*," he said with quiet intensity, "about this is an act, Saffron."

His palm met her cheek, his fingers brushing her neck. Then he was leaning down, bringing his face to hers . . .

She leaped away from him half a second before the office door swung open. "Mr. Ashton—" Mr. Ferrand paused with his head just inside the door, his open mouth snapping shut as he took in Saffron and Alexander standing close together. "*Ouf!* My apologies, my apologies." He made to duck out.

Face burning, Saffron called to him. "Wait, Monsieur Ferrand."

He opened the door just wide enough for his shoulders and smiled broadly. "I see you have already found each other. *Quelle chance*, eh?"

"Very good luck," Saffron said, giving him an exasperated look. "You might have mentioned Mr. Ashton had my specimens. I was quite concerned."

"I can see that now, *mon amie*, and I apologize once more." He winked at her. "Good day, *adieu*."

Saffron huffed when he closed the door. The sooner she left this office the better. She had loads to do, the first of which would be figuring out the finer points of the miniature terrariums. She nudged the cart experimentally and found it was heavy but not impossible.

"I can move them to your office for you," Alexander offered. "I would suggest keeping them in your office until you can have a word with Mr. Winters."

That was advice she would certainly be taking. "I can manage it myself. Thank you for all you've done." She looked up and saw he wore a strange expression. "I'll go to Inspector Green at lunch and see what I can do for your brother."

"It isn't that." He shot her a sheepish smile. "I'll miss those plants. We've become rather good friends."

It was infuriating that he'd decided to be so utterly charming. Why couldn't he have been like this when he came back from Brazil, rather than behaving like a disgruntled badger?

She gave him a tight smile. "I suppose you are welcome to visit them at your leisure."

"I'll do that."

It was inelegant work, navigating the cart with the jars and lamp to her office, and she had no doubt it made for an interesting spectacle for the students. But once she and her samples were safely ensconced in her office, among her books and cuttings and files, she felt as if all was right in the world, though she knew quite well it was not.

Catching up on her work was slow but not as intimidating as she'd feared. Budgets for second term were due soon, and the following week would bring the college faculty meeting where she would be expected to present a brief report on her current project. She'd have to prepare a statement that promised progress while striking the perfect balance of confidence and humility, knowledgeability and openness to learning. All while making sure her appearance did not detract from her presentation by being too eye-catching or too dowdy.

She turned to her *Strychnos toxifera* seedlings, which she'd placed directly on her desk beneath the articulating lamp. "It is wildly unfair, isn't it?"

When her stomach began to growl, she pulled out the sandwich Elizabeth had left for her and ate it while she reviewed what she knew of Adrian Ashton's situation.

Alexander hadn't told her much. Adrian had shared a train compartment with a man who was a horticulturalist who'd appeared unwell before he died, supposedly of some sort of poisoning. She knew less about Adrian himself, just that he was older than Alexander and was also a veteran of the Great War. Alexander had suggested that his brother had also required treatment from doctors, but she didn't have a clue as to what for. Alexander had received a serious injury from a grenade, leaving him with scarring on his right arm and possibly elsewhere. He also struggled with shell shock, though Saffron knew he'd worked hard to overcome it with meditation.

When her ham and cheese sandwich was finished, Saffron donned her coat and hat and left the university. If Adrian was similarly blighted by shell shock, and the police knew about it, that could be troublesome. The prejudice against those with the mysterious affliction could be strong, and if Adrian had given them any reason to believe he was unstable, they could have leaped on him as a suspect simply because many believed those afflicted with shell shock were prone to violence.

But her task was not to prove Adrian innocent but to offer to help find who was responsible, if anyone. She hoped Alexander was right and it was simply a matter of some accident in the victim's lab, rather than secrets she had to dig up before they could sprout like seeds.

CHAPTER 7

"I suppose one might consider this visit providential," Detective Inspector Green said, eyeing Saffron, "but I think I know what brings you here."

Saffron shifted in the hard seat across from the inspector's desk. "I hope you believe me when I say I mean only to offer my help, Inspector."

It was difficult to know exactly what the inspector was thinking. When she'd arrived five minutes ago at the King's Cross police station, he'd been standing at the desk sergeant's desk, conversing tersely with a handful of black-clad bobbies. Compared to the gangly young men, Inspector Green's plain, middle-aged face seemed ancient. His brown eyes, which usually regarded the world without emotion, looked at her with what she suspected was something between amusement and exasperation.

"This offer of help was not prompted by a certain friend of yours?" Inspector Green asked.

Amusement, she decided. "I assure you, I mean only to—"

"Help, yes," he said. "As it happens, I was planning to go to the university this afternoon."

Saffron straightened up. "You were?"

He caught on to her excitement, shaking his head. "My needs are less botanical and more chemical, Miss Everleigh."

"But they're agricultural chemicals," she said quickly. "Things one might use in a laboratory."

The inspector's mouth flattened. "I take it Mr. Ashton informed you of the circumstances."

"Of course he did." She softened her voice. "Inspector, his brother is in trouble. He wants to do all he can to help him, and he knows I have some expertise in the very clues you're seeking."

"And I'm to trust that any information you provide is not going to be influenced by your relationship with the younger Mr. Ashton?"

Saffron's fingers twisted together in her lap, but she spoke calmly. "My *friendship* with him and our professional relationship have raised your concerns, quite rightly. But was I not able to provide you useful information when you investigated Dr. Maxwell? I was honest with you about my own little investigation, however misguided it was."

"Be that as it may," Inspector Green said, leaning back in his chair, "I cannot accept your offer of assistance. You have a significant conflict of interest."

Saffron deflated. "I understand."

"Not to mention there are . . . ramifications beyond what you've assisted with in the past," he added, seemingly as an afterthought though his finger tapping on the file on his desk suggested he was still thinking hard. He glanced down at the file, opened it, perused its contents briefly, then sighed.

A knock came at the door. Saffron turned, half expecting Inspector Green's usual companion, Sergeant Simpson, rushing in haphazardly as he'd so often done, but it was one of the bobbies who peeked in and asked for the inspector. After a moment's pause, the Inspector patted the file before rising from his desk. He left the room, murmuring, "Excuse me a moment."

Saffron idly took in the plain features of Inspector Green's office. Like the man himself, it was rather nondescript. Graying white walls, a network of rootlike cracks in the ceiling, and furniture that was once average and now had devolved into shabby. Since the last time she'd visited, several more maps had been added to the walls, though she doubted they were decoration. A Bacon's Gem Map of London had a series of red pins that formed a line, resembling a curiously stretched-out caterpillar.

One little leg was in Kingston, to the southeast of London. The line plodded along the train line, marked with minute tracks, up through Twickenham, Richmond, Kew, S. Acton, and Willesden Junction, where another pin went off the train track and up to Harlesden.

Two paths diverged at Willesden Junction, where Saffron knew there to be a confluence of several railways. One went to the northwest, up to Watford, where the map ended. Another map was pinned beneath it, continuing the line, though to a different scale. The pins finished in Harpenden.

Something tickled at the back of her mind at the name, but before it crystalized, she scanned the path of the other line of pins, the one leading into London. She knew what these paths meant; the culminating pin at St. Pancras in King's Cross Station made that apparent. These train journeys were obviously related to the man Adrian Ashton supposedly poisoned.

Her eyes drifted from the maps to Inspector Green's desk, where his file lay open.

Another time, she might have lingered on the edges of guilt and indecision. She did feel bad for looking at something she wasn't meant to, but it was a vague and distant concern that didn't stop her from delving into the information on the top paper.

Inspector Green's handwriting, if the neat black writing on the report was his, was very easy to read. The victim's name was Demian Petrov. He'd journeyed from Harpenden to London on November seventh on an afternoon train. She dared to lift the paper and turn it over to continue reading the report. Petrov had been seen to be ill by not only Adrian Ashton but by two other witnesses.

According to the report, Adrian Ashton, age thirty-four, lived and worked in Kingston upon Thames as an engineer at Hawker Engineering. Saffron dashed away her surprise at learning Alexander's brother was also a scientist, albeit a different sort, and kept reading.

Adrian had been to visit a colleague in Harlesden, then got on the train to come to London. It was noted in the same neat script that he'd not planned to go to London but had decided last minute to visit his family in town. Her lips pursed. That was no doubt suspicious, as was the detail that Adrian did not appear sober during his interview.

A scrape of noise in the hall beyond the office door made her jerk away from the desk, but no one entered. She bit her lip. Eyes locked on the door, she eased back over to the file and nudged aside the top papers. Another page caught her eye: the coroner's report.

Her experience with Lee had taught her much about the human body and the language used to describe the ways it could be injured, but it proved insufficient in deciphering the majority of text on the page. The only thing she was confident of as she finished scanning two pages of the coroner's scrawl was that the victim, Petrov, had died of nephritis, which she knew to mean something to do with the kidneys.

Glancing at the door, she scrambled for her notebook to dash down the collection of words included in the rest of the report. She'd head to the library at the first opportunity to see what she could make of them. Just as her pencil marked the last letter of "xanthochromia," the sound of footsteps had her swiftly closing the file and returning to her seat.

Inspector Green entered, muttering under his breath. He did not resume his seat, going instead to his desk and picking up the file. Saffron's fingers spasmed as he briefly paused over the papers. He'd left the file open, and she'd closed it.

She cleared her throat to claim his attention. "If you are unable to accept my help, Inspector, I hope I can make a recommendation to you about another botanist who might assist you."

"I would appreciate that. University College is close enough to the station to make it extremely convenient should I find an expert there I could consult."

As much as she didn't want to give disagreeable Dr. Miller any more credit than he was due, he would be the one within her department to ask about agriculture. "We don't have a separate agriculture department at the U, but Dr. Eugene Miller's research comes the closest to it. He'd likely be able to give you some insight into whatever you might need. But I have to ask, Inspector, haven't you inquired with the lab itself what sort of things the victim was working on? They ought to be able to tell you what work he was doing and what he was exposed to."

Inspector Green nodded, looking somber. "They ought to, indeed. The difficulty is that this is a government laboratory. They tend to be touchy about such things. They've given me a list of chemicals the victim was regularly exposed to but not the amounts or configurations." His nostrils flared slightly. "The director seemed concerned about spreading word of anything more definite than that was a matter of security."

From his dry tone, she could tell the inspector's opinion about that. She was inclined to agree; providing the police with information for a possible poisoning seemed vastly more important than maintaining the secrecy of a new breed of potatoes or something.

She rose and thanked the inspector for seeing her and repeated her suggestion of Dr. Miller. Should he take her up on it, she'd be poised to learn far more about Petrov and his demise than she'd been able to glean in this office.

Medical jargon truly was a language all its own, Saffron decided with a glare at the medical dictionary. Upon her return to campus, she'd nabbed a tome Lee had regularly used from the library and hauled it up to her office, where she'd been squinting at the minuscule text for an hour.

Perhaps it was the burden of the tasks she was leaving undone, sitting on the corner of her desk, that made it more difficult to connect the Latin and Greek words to their meanings. More likely, Saffron conceded, it was that this was most certainly not her strong suit. She'd figured out that Petrov's kidneys had failed and that he was jaundiced, but apart from that, her progress was slow. She'd hoped that her visit would at least inform her as to the reason the police believed Petrov had been poisoned or why Adrian, in particular, was under suspicion. She'd seen nothing to answer either question, nor had she written down anything that would effectively assist her with diagnosing a poison, botanical or inorganic, and that sent rivulets of panic creeping down her spine. Alexander and his brother were counting on her to help, and she'd done nothing more than get some words on paper and send Dr. Miller a visitor.

She sighed, cupping her chin in her hand. She knew the quick solution to this problem.

Harley Street was a brisk fifteen-minute walk through Fitzrovia and into the neighborhood of Marylebone. The buildings became grander, the brick and pale gray stone cleaner. Black iron pickets separated many homes from the pavement, and a good many shining automobiles rested before residences.

Saffron reached Number 67 and paused on the pavement to take it in. She knew Dr. Lee, senior, must have had a successful practice from how Lee, junior, had spoken about it. The tall white stone building with four levels of gleaming windows suggested it was not just success that kept the place looking so prestigious but the support of the wealthy Lee family as well.

Saffron went up the shallow steps and into the portico before the front door. A gold plaque next to the door announced whose bell she was about to ring.

It took moments for a young maid in black and white to open the door and invite Saffron inside. The entry was formal and elegant, with marble tile and a large staircase with an ornate wrought-iron balustrade. The maid led her into a sitting room that one might have found in any well-to-do townhouse rather than a medical office. After giving her name and her request to speak to the younger doctor, to which the maid gave her a beady-eyed look, she disappeared with the promise to summon him at his leisure.

Saffron had scarcely turned around to take in the elegant furnishings before Lee was bounding into the room.

Dr. Michael Lee was a shockingly handsome man, with hair like gold, eyes shining green, and a sharp jaw. With his stylish, colorful shirts and ties and his inclination to flirt, to many, he was a veritable sheik. To her, he'd been an unwelcome colleague, an enemy turned ally turned friend, and almost something more. Despite her hesitance to see him after their uncomfortable last meeting, her heart was glad to see her friend.

"Good Lord, old thing," he said, coming forward with hands outstretched, "but it did take you an age to come by."

Somewhat ruefully, she placed her hands in his, which he used to draw her to him to place a kiss on her cheek. She removed herself from his grasp and gave him a severe look. "I do hope you don't greet all your patients that way."

His humor evaporated, leaving him looking serious in his white doctor's coat. "You're ill?"

She waved a hand. "No, of course not."

He tutted. "You are tiresome. I wish I had a medication for that to give you. Tea will have to do, however."

He led her to an office off the entry. It was painted fresh, antiseptic white, and the single window offered a view of the street.

"Sit down, won't you?" Lee leaned his head out of the door and called, "Betsy, tea and biscuits, if you please!"

Lee had been perennially messy when they'd shared her office at the U, but this room was as tidy as could be. Papers and files were stacked neatly on his desk, and every surface shone like it'd been polished that morning. The benefits of a maid, she supposed.

When they were settled, Lee's gaze danced over her face. "How was France?"

The strong urge to tell Lee the truth of how exactly her trip had gone caught her off guard, but she had more pressing matters to attend to. She shrugged, plucking off her gloves. "It was very French."

"Didn't care for the food? You're looking a bit peaky."

Saffron glared at him.

He laughed. "You are! You're looking pale, Everleigh. Though that could simply be because you're no longer traipsing about the countryside with naught but a flimsy hat to keep you from burning."

The maid knocked softly before entering with the tea service. Lee waited until she'd departed to say, "Pater doesn't approve of coffee, and barely approves of the stimulating effects of tea, so we'll have to make do with this weak stuff."

"How has it been?" Saffron asked, accepting a cup from Lee. He was right; even taking the tea as she did without milk, it was the palest of amber in the porcelain cup. "Working for your father?"

"All well and good, I suppose. Bit boring after chasing down criminals and being shot." As if sensing she was about to ask, he patted his left leg. "All healed up, by the way." He took a sip of tea and grimaced. "I can't say working here isn't full of its own problems, but it's quite hard to take seriously someone complaining of a stomachache after a lifetime of too much rich food and wine when you've seen people fighting for their lives."

Saffron hesitated, but her curiosity outweighed her other concerns. "You didn't follow up with the Defense Committee's offer."

"No, I didn't."

His green eyes did not leave hers, something of a challenge in them. She'd been furious at the notion of the vague offer of employment from the Imperial Defense Committee at the conclusion of their study. She'd been even angrier that Lee had considered accepting their offer. She hadn't known the government was funding their research, and Lee somehow hadn't seen the problem with the government gathering information about poisonous plants, their effects, and where they grew.

But perhaps he did now. Maybe that was why he hadn't followed through and landed himself a job at one of the science parks the government ran across the country.

Lee tapped a fingernail against the porcelain of his teacup. "I take it your own return to work is not to your satisfaction. Otherwise, you'd not be here at half past three in the afternoon on a Monday."

From the look he gave her, something more tender than usual, she imagined he was asking more than his words suggested.

Saffron set her cup down on the saucer. There was no point pretending she'd come merely to socialize. "I came because I need your advice."

He let out a dramatic sigh. "And here I thought it was because you liked the flowers I sent you. What's the matter?"

She blew out a breath, knowing how it would sound. In a rush, she said, "Alexander Ashton's brother, Adrian, is suspected in the death of a Russian horticulturalist with whom he shared a train compartment. They believe poison of some kind is involved, and naturally, Alexander asked me to help, but Inspector Green has rejected my offer of assistance due to my conflict of interest, being friendly with Adrian's brother. I saw the coroner's report when I was alone in his office, however, and I have some questions that I'd like to ask you."

Lee tilted his head in a rather feline motion, his eyes narrowing. "You know," he said slowly, "I used to think you were a dull person. Obsessed with plants, of all things. Perpetually glaring at me for making jokes. Closeted in your office poring over the most tedious books. But now I realize you're actually a rather chaotic bit of goods, Everleigh." He let out a laugh, shaking his head. "How I did miss you."

Saffron couldn't even bring herself to be annoyed. "Things do have the tendency to get a bit complicated, don't they?" He hadn't said no or seemed offended, so she retrieved her notebook from her handbag. "Will you take a look?"

"Hand it over, hand it over," he said, waving her forward. She gave the notebook to him, open to the right pages, and he removed a pair of gold spectacles from his white coat's breast pocket and slipped them on. "You were in a rush, I take it."

"I wasn't supposed to be looking at the report." She stood and wandered to the window. "The inspector could have caught me at any moment."

"He left you alone with it in his office. Knowing you as he does, he ought to have known you'd be unable to resist."

She hummed, considering that. Inspector Green did know she had a tendency to snoop. "He seemed preoccupied. I suppose he didn't think about it."

Lee settled into reading, nibbling the end of a pencil and occasionally humming. After a few minutes, he said, "Toss me that big blue book, will you?"

From the nearest shelf, Saffron hefted a blue book as thick as her wrist was wide. She allowed it to thunk on the desk rather than attempt to do anything resembling tossing.

"This word here is a mystery," Lee said, tapping "xanthochromia" in her notebook with his pencil. "'Chrom' obviously means color, but 'xantho'?"

"It means yellow. I thought that referred to the jaundice." She pointed to the note she'd copied about the victim's yellowed eyes.

"I've never seen it referred to as xanthochromia." Lee flipped to the end of the book, then flipped a few dozen pages until he found it with a soft "Ah!"

Saffron leaned over his shoulder. She didn't know how to feel when she caught a whiff of his cologne mixed with the subtle scent of cigarettes. It was so familiar as to be comforting, and that was disconcerting. She read aloud, "'Xanthochromia, referring to yellow discoloration, such as may be seen in the skin, as in jaundice, or the cerebrospinal fluid if it contains the residue of haemoglobin from red blood cells.'"

Lee frowned. "Hmm. Why this word, though? They already referred to his jaundice. Xanthochromia must have another meaning."

"Shall we check another book?"

They did, and within half an hour, Lee had found not a definition but a case with xanthochromia reported in a patient's feet and hands.

"So we might guess the coroner referred to yellow discoloration on the feet and hands," Lee said.

He didn't sound convinced, and neither was Saffron. She strained to recall if the report had mentioned hands or feet.

She sighed, and Lee turned in his chair to say, "Come now, old thing. That's still something. I don't recall any nasties we worked on that made someone's skin turn yellow."

"Perhaps not in our study," Saffron replied, "but numerous poisons affect the kidneys."

"The liver too," he said, tapping her notebook where she'd jotted down "hepatotoxicity." "I don't suppose you noticed the weights of these organs."

"The weights?"

"An autopsy includes the weighing of individual organs," Lee said, as casually as one might discuss the weather. "Gives a great deal of information, same as looking at samples under a microscope. A liver plagued with certain illnesses may swell or shrink, depending. Same as the kidneys. If the coroner said the fellow died of kidney failure, though, that likely means the liver bit was just wear and tear from heavy drinking or something."

"But there isn't a way to know without you seeing the report?"

"Or the organs themselves." Now his nose wrinkled. "I haven't done something like that since school. Can't say I'm in a rush to do it again."

Saffron nodded absently. Breaking into a morgue would be a thousand times worse than any of the snooping she'd already done. She'd find another way to solve this. Then she'd find a way to tell Inspector Green without him being angry she'd meddled again.

CHAPTER 8

Saffron parted with Lee with a surprising degree of comfort. He'd been his normal self, complete with smiles and near-flirtations. The only awkwardness had come when he'd asked her to give Alexander his regards as she'd departed. It was on the tip of her tongue to mention she was assisting Alexander and his brother only out of friendship and a sense of justice, but she held her tongue. She was loath to give up any sense of equilibrium after the discomforts and disappointments of the last month.

She spent the rest of the day on her actual work, staying in her office well into the evening, which was beginning to creep up on her faster and faster with the changing of the season.

Tuesday morning brought the news she'd been hoping for. Word quickly spread through the North Wing that Dr. Miller had received a visit from a police inspector asking his advice.

Saffron had to fight off a scowl hearing it; when she'd been visited by the police, the rumors were always something nasty, like she'd been accused of harming someone. But it was good news, because it meant that she'd soon have the list of chemicals from Inspector Green.

At lunch, she made her way into the breakroom. Gregory Spalding, the research assistant Dr. Miller shared with another professor, was eating with two other members of Biology. Spalding was a ruddy-faced blond man, rotund but tall, and his demeanor was so loud and jolly that one often missed he was without his left arm. He kept his jackets and shirts neatly pinned back and his body usually turned slightly to the side to hide his wartime loss.

Saffron liked Spalding, for he was generally more pleasant to her than the others. His loss made it difficult for him to assist in the greenhouses, but he always made an effort, and she'd seen him gain more skill in manipulating specimens one-handed. He was, however, not very enthusiastic about journals and books, ironic as that was for a professional researcher. Saffron had often heard him proclaim that he joined the biology department to look at living things, not *read*.

Saffron sidled into the room, keen to not disturb the men as they finished their meal. She quietly lit the spirit lamp to heat water for a cup of tea. After a few minutes of their chatter, the men stood. Saffron tensed at the silence that fell as they noticed she was in the room.

"Ah!" Spalding said. "Good afternoon, Miss Everleigh. Didn't see you there."

She returned the greeting with a smile. "I hear Dr. Miller has had rather an interesting visit."

He grinned. "Indeed. Your old friend, I reckon. Detective inspector something or other. Same fellow who came 'round asking about old Maxwell."

"I suppose he wasn't asking about Dr. Maxwell this time."

His companions left the room as Spalding guffawed. "No, nothing so interesting as that!"

"Not an attempted murder?"

With a rueful grin, Spalding said, "No, indeed! Of course, I'm the one to handle it, Miller hasn't got the time." He shook his head with a chuckle. "Lord knows why he keeps fussing over his beets when he might be helping the police! I admit though, it's tedious stuff."

"What is it?" Saffron asked, stirring her tea. She couldn't appear too eager, but Spalding liked an audience.

"Wants to identify some fertilizers, of all things. Damned if I know why."

"Fertilizers? Strange thing for a policeman to ask about. I wonder if there was some sort of crime involving them."

He shrugged. "Don't know, wasn't there when the inspector dropped off the list. Now I'm stuck in the library this afternoon."

"Me too," Saffron said with a commiserating sigh. She blew on her cup of tea.

Spalding smirked. "Loads to do after your little vacation?"

She bit her tongue from replying that her vacation had been a trip to a professional conference, which no one else from Botany had been sent to, but that would have been counterproductive. "It's a pity, too, since I heard Winters was going to be preparing the greenhouses for the cold. I've always liked that sort of thing. A nice break from sitting looking at books." She wrinkled her nose slightly. "We'll be sharing books, then, as I'm going to be investigating fertilizers myself. I want to see if I can give my specimens a little boost now we've less sunlight."

His pale brows soared. "Are you, now?" He leaned a hip against the table, and it squeaked loudly as it lurched under his weight. He hastily returned to his feet. "Don't suppose I could give you that list to research? You know, a favor?"

Saffron tamped down the sense of victory threatening to show on her face. "A favor?" She frowned somewhat melodramatically. "I don't know . . ."

He held up his hand, saying, "If it wouldn't be too much trouble. You'll be in those journals and books anyway, won't you? I'll owe you one."

She pursed her lips as if considering, while inside she was beaming. Nearly everyone liked Spalding, and his word in her favor could be useful. "Very well."

Ten minutes later, she was on her way to the library with Inspector Green's list in her hands.

Light seemed to slip through the windows of the library like water through fingers. The afternoon had barely begun, in Saffron's mind, and already the warm sunlight had dimmed to a blue-tinted glow.

It *had* been hours since she'd begun picking through texts. Inspector Green's list of chemicals was lengthy, not to mention they were given as a combination of brands and unnamed mixtures. Haber-Bosch was featured alongside monocalcium phosphate. Deciphering those wasn't difficult, as she was already familiar with some, but determining what any of them might to do the human body was quite another thing.

Asking Lee was a possibility, but she'd just been to see him. After his parting comment about Alexander, she was wary of asking too much of him. He undoubtedly thought she and Alexander were together, and she didn't want to make Lee resentful when she believed there was a possibility of resuming their friendship.

There was an entire chemistry department at the university, but she knew no one who worked in it. With her reputation lingering near the bottom of the list of desirability, she didn't know if she could get any of them to assist her.

But Lee had a friend in Chemistry, she recalled. Hope lit in her chest. Romesh, his name was, and he'd analyzed some cocaine Lee had once been given. Lee had mentioned that Romesh hadn't been happy about it, but Saffron wasn't going to bring him illicit substances.

She got to her feet, checking the clock on the far end of the quiet library hall. Over the heads of two dozen students and staff bent over the rows of long tables topped with glowing green lamps, she saw it was a quarter to five. Some would already be gone from their labs and offices, but perhaps Romesh—was that his surname?—might not be.

The Chemistry Hall, just across an alley from the North Wing to the east, had a strange smell. It wasn't pleasant, but Saffron couldn't quite put a finger on what was bad about it. It was like the gentle stink of pear tree blooms mixed with the strange fruit a researcher had once brought to the North Wing to share after an expedition to Southeast Asia. Saffron, a student at the time, had wondered if the long journey back to England had made the durian fruit overripe and thus unpalatable, but Maxwell, who'd given her a piece to try, had insisted that the sweet onion flavor was as expected.

The building itself was not so different from her own haunts, white-walled and tiled. Many of the windows were open, likely in an effort to air out the place. They let in the late afternoon chill and the sounds of busy Gower Street beyond. The halls were mostly empty. It was easy enough to find the lab of the man she was searching for or at least make an educated guess. Romesh was not a typical English name, so she searched for a name that was equally non-English sounding.

Datta, she thought, might match. The light was on within, she noted with some excitement. Perhaps she could make further progress in her investigation this evening after all.

She knocked and then knocked again when no one answered. A sound like a chair scraping across the floor preceded footsteps approaching the door.

It swung open, and a petite woman blinked up at Saffron. She had deep brown skin with large brown eyes framed by a messy Eton haircut that, at first glance, made the young woman look almost like a young man. She wore a man's shirt, complete with a starched collar, tucked into a narrow skirt. Neither her clothing nor her short hair could conceal she was a woman, however.

She looked expectantly at Saffron.

"I'm looking for Romesh . . .?" Saffron offered, preparing to ask if the woman belonged to that name.

Just then, a man in a white lab coat came striding down the hallway. He was reading a file and came up short when he saw her.

He matched the woman in coloring, his skin a rich bronze and his hair thick and black. His eyes were huge behind his spectacles, not from surprise, but because the lenses magnified them significantly.

"Are you Romesh?" Saffron asked him.

"Yes." He sounded and looked baffled. He glanced toward his office, saw the woman with the Eton crop, and scowled. "What do you want with my cousin?" He turned to the woman. "Savita, what have you done now?"

Not appreciating the harsh tone, Saffron said, "I came in search of you, Dr. Datta."

His cousin snorted. "Romesh hasn't a doctorate. He's too busy trying to appease his fiancée."

"Vita!" Romesh scowled at her. "Get back into the office and stop being troublesome."

The girl's protests were cut off by Romesh chivying her back from the doorway.

Saffron cleared her throat. "Mr. Datta?"

Romesh turned around, looking exasperated. "I apologize for my cousin, Miss—?"

"Everleigh. Saffron Everleigh, in Botany."

"Everleigh—Everleigh?" Romesh looked agog at her. "You're Lee's associate?"

"Yes," she replied. "Dr. Lee and I worked on a study together earlier this year."

Romesh's eyelids fluttered for a moment behind his spectacles. "And you're . . . speaking to Savita? What about?"

"I came to speak to you about a list of chemicals. I need to know some things about them quite urgently, and since Lee spoke so highly of your abilities . . ." She trailed off hopefully.

"I . . . well." He darted a glance up and down the hall. "This is all above board, isn't it? I told Lee I wouldn't be testing anything untoward for him again."

"This is nothing of the sort, I assure you," Saffron said quickly.

"If you won't do it, Romesh, move aside and let me tackle it," his cousin said, appearing over his shoulder. A grin lit up her face. "I'm a chemist too."

Romesh attempted to block her. "Ignore her, Miss Everleigh. Savita is untrained. She likes to mix things together and see the reactions, that's all."

"But that's wonderful," Saffron said, angling herself to see Savita again. "Do you study here, Miss Datta?"

"Yes," Savita answered, attempting to knock her cousin aside with her hip.

"No," Romesh grumbled. "Not until second term."

"But that's very exciting, isn't it?" Saffron took Savita's lead and ignored Romesh. "Have you any experience tracking down chemicals and breaking them into their components?"

"I do," she said brightly.

"I have a list," Saffron said, drawing her notebook from her handbag and passing Savita the list. "I need to know what exactly these chemicals are, and what they might do to the human body if consumed."

"You need someone with more experience, Miss Everleigh." Romesh attempted to pluck the list out of Savita's hand, but she dodged away. "If you need it before the new year, I will look up the chemicals for you. Savita barely knows boron from barium."

Behind him, Savita gasped. "You are—how dare you! I spend nearly as much time here as you do. I should tell her about all the times you've complained about missing points on your exams!"

Romesh opened his mouth to argue back, but Saffron said quickly, "If you could both take a look, I would be much obliged. But I do need the information as soon as possible."

"Police business again?" Romesh asked, dropping his voice low.

Saffron nodded. Savita had crept closer, nearly pressing her face between Romesh's arm and the door frame. "Police business? I'll have it done by tomorrow."

"Tomorrow morning," Romesh said.

Saffron bit her lip. "It is an extensive list."

"It will be done, I assure you."

"I assure you too," Savita added.

"Thank you both very much," Saffron said, not bothering to hide her smile now. "I'll come back tomorrow, then."

CHAPTER 9

Saffron was ready to fall into bed when she returned home that evening, but Elizabeth had other ideas. "Where have you been?" she demanded, tugging Saffron's coat from her shoulders the moment she walked through the door at seven-thirty.

Nonplussed, Saffron replied, "At work, of course."

"Nick telephoned," she said, now tugging Saffron's gloves off. "He's taking us to dinner."

"Tonight?"

"Yes," Elizabeth said, giving Saffron a dark look before pushing her toward her bedroom. "He'll be here at eight o'clock to collect us, destination unknown. He said dinner, drinks, and dancing, and you are woefully unprepared for any of those things."

"What's the occasion?" She ought to have noticed when Elizabeth first attacked her that she was dressed to the nines in her best evening dress. The pink silk shimmered with embroidery as she crossed to Saffron's wardrobe.

Elizabeth barked out a laugh, pushing around Saffron's anemic collection of evening gowns. "My birthday."

"He does know that isn't until Sunday, correct?"

"I didn't deign to inform him of his mistake."

Saffron submitted herself to Elizabeth's expert ministrations. By eight o'clock, her long brown hair was perfectly waved and bundled at the back of her head, pinned by a glittering faux sapphire barrette; her matching blue dress dripped its handkerchief points to her calves.

Saffron eyed her reflection in the mirror in the parlor, where she and Elizabeth waited. She was dressed as she might have to portray Sally Eversby but without the heavy coating of makeup. Only her lashes were curled and her lips were red with lipstick. She looked really quite nice.

Nick seemed to agree. He was generous in his praise of both his sister and Saffron when he arrived at eight sharp. He cut an impressive figure himself in his evening kit. They packed tightly into the waiting cab, with Saffron in the middle. The night was cold and had a tang of woodfire mixed with automobile exhaust, but within the cab, Saffron was assaulted by Nick's and Elizabeth's opposing scents, muddled by the slightly musty smell of the cab.

"Where are we going?" Elizabeth asked.

"A surprise" was Nick's only reply.

A surprise it was, for when the cab rolled to a stop and the door opened to reveal their location, Elizabeth could not hide her wonder.

"The Savoy," she breathed, her face illuminated by the lights of the grand hotel. The building soared overhead with a hundred windows reflecting colorful pinpoint lights of the Strand.

Saffron bit her lip, glancing between Elizabeth and Nick. Elizabeth looked like she might cry; Nick looked as if his desired outcome had been achieved.

Elizabeth gasped as she put out her hands to grip Nick's arm. Eyes huge, she demanded, "Is Ada Coleman here?"

The famous lady bartender of the Savoy's American Bar would be at the top of Elizabeth's list of things to see at the Savoy. Nick only grinned and tucked her hand in the crook of his elbow. "Let's find out."

Either Nick had observed that Elizabeth had a great love of gastronomy or he was banking on any young woman being dazzled by the Savoy. Dining at a world-famous restaurant might have been enough to thaw the ice between Elizabeth and her brother, but treating her to a Hanky-Panky at the American Bar first left Elizabeth close to putty in his hands before the meal had even begun.

Elizabeth laughed at Nick's quips, of which there were many during their excellent meal, and didn't roll her eyes when he smiled broadly at Saffron, which was even more frequent.

"And the entire time I failed to notice that the cow was, in fact, a bull," Nick said, concluding yet another amusing tale of his seemingly bumbling service in the Agricultural Ministry.

"Little wonder they moved me to crops," he said, turning to Saffron once again.

She had enjoyed the meal—certainly not as much as Elizabeth, but it had put her into a very good mood. The cocktail at the bar and the expertly paired wines with each course had helped her forget the trials of the day. "What sort of trouble do you get into in fields, rather than pastures?"

Elizabeth paused with her fork just before her mouth. "There will be no talk of *manure* at the Savoy."

"Of course not," Nick said mildly before stretching an arm out and over to the back of Saffron's chair. "It's a recent change, I'm to set out for my first assignment soon. Some sort of fungi is plaguing a couple of farms to the north, so I'll be heading that way to investigate." He stretched his other arm to touch Elizabeth's chair, adding, "That's why we had to celebrate your birthday early, my dear. I'll be ducking out for a few days and might not be back until Sunday night."

Elizabeth blinked slowly at him. "I see. Your consideration is exceptional."

Saffron narrowed her eyes at her friend across the table. Elizabeth was a handful when sober, and she was downright troublesome drunk. Saffron's hopes that the Savoy's glamor would maintain her friend's pleasant mood may have been a bit high.

Saffron glanced around the stunning dining room for a waiter. To the table at large, she said, "I do hope dessert is on its way."

Either Nick did not notice the slow shift in his sister's mood or he thought that dancing would help it, for when the meal ended, he whisked them into another cab.

The band could be heard before the cab stopped.

Saffron shot Nick a questioning look as he hopped up onto the pavement next to her. The club, while evidently very popular, was a far cry from the elegant extravagance of the Savoy. She'd never heard of Lou's Place in the West End, its name illuminated by pink neon and tucked in among a dozen other shops, hotels, and venues. This part of town was exactly up Elizabeth's alley, however.

"Ah," she said with a lazy grin, "good ol' Lou's."

Inside, Saffron was forcibly reminded of the Blue Room, the staging place of her last adventure. Though the room did not glow with eerie blue light, it was smoky and loud enough to rattle her bones.

She tightened her arm around Elizabeth's as they were shown to a tiny table on the edge of the dance floor. The place was done up in silver and pink, with a glittering stage to one side and a large bar covered in mirrors on the other.

Nick summoned a waiter and ordered a trio of cocktails. The band incited cheers from the dancers as they rattled out song after song of popular dance tunes. Saffron wasn't sure how their party was to manage dancing with only one man. Though from the sort of dancing happening on the floor, it was unlikely Elizabeth would want to be paired with her brother.

She'd just opened her mouth to murmur the question to Elizabeth when she caught sight of a familiar face through the haze of cigarette smoke.

"Alexander?" Saffron breathed.

Elizabeth cast her a sidelong glance. "Sorry, love, but I am in no mood to hear about the most recent chapter in the Ashton saga."

Saffron watched Alexander's figure as he wove from the bar through the crowd. He reached a table and slipped into the booth to sit.

She was on her feet before she could determine what exactly she'd say to him when she reached him. She was angry he was there, but why was that? Had she imagined the protestations of his interest in her meant he would never go out dancing? Was he there with someone else?

Her last question was answered when she reached the table. A pretty red-haired girl was leaning close, tracing her finger along the rim of the martini glass on the table before him. Her stomach clenched. Not only was he with another woman, but he was drinking alcohol, which he'd told her he never did anymore.

"Excuse me," she said, her voice cold and clear over the noise of the club.

The couple turned to look at her. The girl's eyes dipped to take in Saffron's appearance with an unimpressed smirk. The man, however, was not Alexander.

His coloring was the same, with black hair pushed back from his olive-toned face and eyes the same shape and color. But his face was longer, thinner, and his eyes far more deeply shadowed. Not to mention that Alexander had never smiled at her so openly as this man did.

Her mouth snapped closed the moment she realized it was hanging open. "I beg your pardon," she mumbled, "I thought you were someone else." She turned away and attempted to disappear into the crowd.

She'd taken not three steps before a warm hand on her shoulder stopped her.

A strong sense of déjà vu claimed her as she turned. It was the man from the booth, and the action of turning her just as Alexander had done the day before sent her head swimming. She was *never* having a cocktail and wine in such rapid succession again.

"Excuse me," he said, shouting a bit to be heard over the band. "But you are . . . ?"

"Er—I'm mistaken, that's all. I thought you were a friend of mine. Sorry."

The man's smile only grew, threatening to overstretch his thin face. "What friend?"

Nonplussed, she replied, "A colleague."

"Ah, you are from the university?"

Between the man's slight accent barely audible over the music and his surprising supposition, it took Saffron a moment to understand him. "I—sorry?"

"You thought me to be my brother, I think," he said. "He works at a university not far from here, so you must as well."

Saffron's mouth fell open again. "You're Alexander's brother?"

A laugh broke out from the man, and he threw his head back with the force of it. "I am. I am Adrian Ashton. But who are you?"

CHAPTER 10

"Adrian," cut in a hard voice from Saffron's left. Alexander, the actual Alexander, had materialized at Adrian's side. Seeing the brothers next to each other made her question how she'd ever confused the two. Alexander was slightly taller, broader, and infinitely more serious looking. "Would you excuse us for a moment?"

Adrian's grin didn't disappear, but he seemed to deflate. Saffron couldn't make out his reply, but he leaned closer to Saffron and said, "A pleasure to meet you. I hope to see you again, miss." He disappeared into the crowd.

Saffron rounded on Alexander. "How dreadfully rude you are."

"May I speak to you?" His eyes only met hers on the last word, following Adrian out of sight.

"No." A distant, entirely sober part of her knew she was being silly to refuse him after being angry with someone who'd turned out not to be him, but he had been abominably rude, sending his brother away without an introduction.

"Please," he said through gritted teeth.

She glared at him but waved for him to lead the way. He took her hand to guide her, but rather than using the front door as she'd expected, he led her to a nearly invisible door off the side of the dance floor. It led to a dim corridor devoid of any of the interior's glamor with its scuffed floor and the paint stained and peeling. With the sound of the band slightly muted, she could make out the sounds of a busy kitchen at the other end of the hall.

"What are you doing here?" Alexander asked the moment they came to a stop.

"Dancing," she shot back.

The long look he gave her suggested he imagined otherwise. "I'm here with Elizabeth and her brother," she added, exasperated.

"Nick and Elizabeth are here," he said, not as a question.

"We're celebrating Elizabeth's birthday." He examined her in a way that brought heat to her already flushed cheeks. "What?"

"You've been drinking."

She bridled. "I am enjoying a night out with friends. Or I *was* enjoying it. What is the matter with you, Alexander?"

He didn't reply, merely swiped a hand over his jaw. It was not clean-shaven, suggesting he'd not made the effort to prepare for an evening out, or he hadn't had the time. She took in the rest of him. His dinner jacket did not fit him as well as it had before. It strained at his shoulders, as the rest of his suit jackets did. Hadn't he said something about rowing after he'd returned from the Amazonian expedition?

Perhaps her scrutiny made him uncomfortable, for he took half a step closer to her, dropping his voice. "I'm sorry for being abrupt earlier. It's just . . . I did not intend to introduce you to Adrian this way."

Saffron grimaced. She obviously hadn't made a very good first impression, interrupting his date so aggressively, only to babble like an idiot when he confronted her.

His expression matched hers. "Adrian does not present the best image of himself in . . . such circumstances."

"Adrian was perfectly nice," Saffron said, confused. There was something about him that tickled her mind, however, something she couldn't quite put her finger on. Possibly she just found it odd that a man accused of murder was enjoying a night out.

She sighed, recognizing that some of the glow of the evening that had been lost was not going to be regained. "I'll have to speak to him eventually, for the case. I'm afraid my involvement is not off to a good start. Inspector Green did not accept my offer of assistance."

"Why not?"

"You know why," Saffron said impatiently. "Conflict of interest. But it doesn't matter, I managed to get some information to start with. Between the chemists helping with the inquiries and Lee look-ing at the autopsy notes, I—"

A gabble of male voices startled them as two waiters carrying trays of food and drink emerged at the end of the hall. Saffron and Alexander had to press themselves to the grimy wall, and the pair gave them amused glances as they passed.

Alexander frowned down at her. "Lee is helping?"

She returned his frown, silently daring him to make an issue of it. "Yes."

"That is . . . decent of him," he said, his tone leading to an unspoken question.

"It is. But friends do favors for friends, don't they?"

He didn't reply but gave her a thoughtful look that lasted only a moment before he was offering her his arm. "Enough of my interruption. You were here to have a good time. Let's return you to it."

⚘

Saffron thought Alexander had changed his mind about her spending time with his brother when they emerged back into the smoke and music of the club, since he did not immediately usher her toward her companions. Pleasantly surprised by his change of heart, for reasons she didn't care to identify, she searched for the tall, gangly form of Adrian on the dance floor.

But Alexander twirled her, sending her tipsy head spinning, and she landed hard against his chest a moment later. When her eyes could see straight, she realized they were moving in time to the beat. He was dancing with her.

It was perhaps unfair to have assumed that because Alexander was rather a reticent man, and a scientist at that, dancing would not be something he'd be good at. But he moved as if he'd taken to the dance floor as often as he scrutinized bacteria in a microscope.

A giggle bubbled up in her chest at the thought. Alexander looked down at her with a small smile.

"You can dance," she said through a laugh.

"I can."

"I'd never have guessed." His smile faded somewhat, and the loss made her feel unexpectedly sad. "Odd, we've never had the opportunity until now."

"Hopefully we will again."

Saffron had taken dance classes growing up, the waltz and several other steps that she found she rarely even thought about, let alone used in the ballrooms she'd been expected to swan around in. Even if she hadn't relocated to London, she doubted she'd have found herself often using them. The world had changed so much since she was a girl, standing up with the younger of Elizabeth's two brothers, Wesley, to learn dances in the stuffy ballroom at Ellington. Grand estates with their monthlong house parties, grandiose balls, and tightly rehearsed teas were increasingly a thing of the past. Fortunes had been lost and made in the war, not to mention the shifts in society meant the world to which her grandparents belonged was dwindling. Saffron found, as she twirled the floor of a somewhat disreputable dance club in the arms of a man her family would likely not approve of, that she was rather glad not to belong to it any longer.

"Where did you learn to dance?" she asked Alexander when the song ended and a slower one began. "I was given lessons. They were dreadfully boring, even with the amusement of watching Elizabeth attempt to flirt with our instructor constantly."

"That must have been quite the sight."

"It was. She'd bat her eyelashes and find excuses for him to correct her form. It made her brother very cross." She laughed to remember how Wesley would grumble under his breath about it as they toddled through the steps of the polka.

"Nick attended dance lessons with you?"

"No, Wesley. He was the middle child in the Hale family. You saw his photograph at our flat."

His expression, which had grown remote, softened. "Your sweetheart who died at Flanders."

Saffron swallowed, looking away. She didn't want to think about Wesley at Flanders, not now. "And you? Where did you gain your mastery?"

"In clubs not unlike this one," he said. "My brother and cousins are all several years older than me. I was always pulled along with them on their misadventures. They had a friend who used to own a place similar to this, and I spent many evenings as an undergrad with them."

The answer was so unexpected that she laughed again. "I can't imagine you making plans to dance all night!"

"I assure you, I did not. Adrian and my cousins, on the other hand . . ."

"I think it's nice they wanted to bring you along. I'm not very close with any of my family save for my cousin, John." But speaking about John would require her to think about France again. "Are you still close with them?"

"They were not thrilled I chose to pursue academia rather than join their business. But bacteria called to me." He chuckled, and she could feel the vibration of it in her own body.

The sensation lasted only a moment. The band erupted to life, and their conversation died as the foxtrot demanded their attention.

When her legs felt as if they would give out and her cheeks hurt from smiling, she dragged Alexander from the dance floor. He was not even winded, though sweat dotted his brow. As she looked for Elizabeth or Nick, her eye caught on Adrian Ashton once again. He stood at the bar, laughing with a trio of men who shared his dark features. Saffron squinted at them through the smoke. "Are those the famous cousins of yours?"

Alexander turned to follow her gaze, and she thought she saw unease cross his face. He cleared his throat and drew her arm tighter through his. "We ought to find Elizabeth. It's getting late."

Saffron allowed him to pull her away. It was likely very late, and she would already be regretting the hours dancing, not to mention drinking, come the morning.

Elizabeth's dancing partner seemed disappointed when she abandoned him to drape her arm around Saffron's shoulder and babble about how grand Lou's was and how they had to come back soon.

Nick materialized soon after, looking as fresh as when he'd arrived on their doorstep. "Ashton! Good to see you, old man. How do you do?" He offered Alexander his hand. "Like jazz, do you?"

Alexander nodded. "I trust you'll see the ladies home safely."

If Nick was bothered by Alexander's rather rude lack of greeting, he didn't show it. He bobbed his head with a pleasant smile. "I will. Girls, let's heave-ho and find a cab."

Alexander escorted her outside alongside Elizabeth, who seemed to be leaning heavily on her brother. On the curb, Nick summoned a cab and helped Elizabeth inside. He made as if to offer Saffron a hand inside as well, but Alexander subtly moved ahead of him to hand her in himself.

"I'll see you tomorrow," he said firmly.

Then Elizabeth was saying something, and he backed away. At the sound of the cab door closing, Saffron turned back to see Alexander had shut it. She peered out, wondering if Nick had decided to stay at Lou's, but he was speaking to Alexander.

She could only imagine what was making Alexander look so serious as they spoke. Nick, on the other hand, clapped Alexander's shoulder and grinned before swinging the door open and clambering into the cab himself. He gave the driver their destination, and the cab rolled away. Through the window, she could see anger lingering on Alexander's face, cool and controlled but present nonetheless.

What in the world had that been about?

CHAPTER 11

A rmed with a headache powder and a thermos of very strong tea, Saffron made it to her office without regretting the previous evening too ardently. The sight of her cuttings and seedlings happily ensconced within the makeshift terrarium helped her nearly forget that her head pounded and her feet ached.

She resisted the urge to stroke a tiny cotyledon that was just poking its head from the dirt. The seed leaf was the promise of something thrilling, and she couldn't risk damaging it. So she merely gazed down at it, pleasure permeating her like warm sunshine.

She allowed it to fuel her work for a few hours until she deemed she'd waited long enough to return to the Chemistry Hall. Would Savita Datta or her cousin have found anything useful, or would Saffron find she'd wasted a day when she could have been making progress in helping Adrian Ashton?

The Chemistry Hall was humming with activity, but Romesh's office was quiet and dark. She ought to have been more specific in asking the time Romesh would be available.

She sighed and left the pungent hall for the Quad. Students cluttered the pavement and grass. She imagined Savita Datta joining their ranks in a few weeks as a student. She'd been so bright-eyed, it reminded Saffron so much of herself as she anticipated life at university.

Unfortunately, Saffron could see into Savita's future. Despite the prominence of women like Martha Annie Whiteley and Marie Curie, a fellow woman in the sciences would experience the same arbitrary, misogynistic opinions of others that had made Saffron's own academic life so unpleasant. It could only be made more difficult by Miss Datta's race.

That frustrating thought was eased as Saffron passed by a cluster of students who were speaking a language she thought was Arabic. Savita might be a woman, but perhaps at an institution like the University College London, her ancestry would matter less. People from all over the world came to the U to study, something Saffron had always enjoyed. In fact, it wasn't uncommon to overhear conversations in half a dozen languages over the course of the day, and—

Saffron froze, a puzzle piece clicking into place in her mind. The peculiar thing she'd struggled to identify about Adrian Ashton was suddenly crystal clear.

"How absolutely *ridiculous*," she breathed.

The light glowing under Alexander's office door and the slow tap-tap on a typewriter within assured her that she would get to confront Alexander the moment she'd climbed to the second floor of the North Wing.

She did not bother to knock.

Alexander sat at his desk, shirtsleeves rolled to his elbows as he pecked away at the Noiseless sitting on his desk. He looked up from the typewriter, somewhat startled, but then broke into a smile that soon faded when he took in her angry expression. "What is it?"

"You," she said with a huff, tossing her handbag onto the chair before his desk, "are the most obnoxious man I've ever met."

He blinked. "Why is that?"

"What is the real reason you kept me from your brother last night?"

"Because he was drunk and I didn't wish you to believe anything he said or did while in that condition was a true reflection of his character."

He said it so readily that she was taken aback. Still, she felt it was important to confront the issue. "Adrian speaks with an accent." Alexander's nostrils flared. That was evidence of . . . something. "Why?"

"Because he spent a good deal of his childhood with our mother's side of the family."

"And they are?"

"Greek."

"And so you are Greek."

He nodded.

When confronted with a mystery, Saffron generally felt some sort of satisfaction when it was solved, especially if she'd been the one to do it. It was part of the reason science so appealed to her; it was all about finding answers to questions. But now, having pulled apart this minor mystery, she felt not victorious but hurt. She and Alexander had grown rather close before he'd left. They'd spent hours in this very room, talking about their work and their ideas and a dozen other things that were quite personal. She'd told him a good many things about herself and her family. She could count on the fingers of one hand the things she knew about Alexander's family, including this most recent revelation.

"I do not tell many people," he said, apparently sensing her disquiet.

She refused to voice the hurt threatening on her lips, *why didn't you tell me?* They were merely friends and stilted ones at that. The fun of dancing together the previous evening had made her forget.

She exhaled, feeling the last vestiges of burning curiosity drain out of her. Why did she find it so hard to remember that she was simply helping his brother avoid an accusation of murder? "I will need to speak to Adrian about the case—regardless of what secrets you fear he might reveal to me—if you want me to help him."

When he merely looked at her with that shuttered expression, she retreated from the room.

Saffron sought the sanctuary of her office but stopped short when she saw a familiar tall figure pacing before it.

"Hullo, Nick," she said, forcing a pleasant tone.

"Saffron," he said jovially. "I was worried I'd missed you. I was in the neighborhood and thought I'd stop by and see your digs." He tapped a finger on the plaque on her door stating her name. "Impressive. Show me around, won't you?"

Saffron opened her mouth to beg off as politely as possible but realized she didn't have her handbag, which contained the keys to her office. She'd left it on Alexander's chair, and she didn't care to see him until she'd stopped steaming. "How thoughtful. Allow me to show you our greenhouses. They'd probably appeal to an agent of the Agricultural Ministry."

Nick was pleasant company as they exited the North Wing and joined the flow of students from the Quad and onto the street. Saffron took them on the long way 'round, despite the fact she didn't have her jacket and the sun had long since fallen behind the tall buildings, leaving the streets in cold shadows. The Church of Christ the King, a grand building with buttresses and parapets and a lovely rose window, was tucked up next to the university buildings on Gordon Street. Through the opened doors hummed the varied sounds of the choir warming up their voices.

The greenhouses, across the street in a square fringed with young trees, were still illuminated by fading afternoon light.

"Have you visited any of the botanical research stations?" Saffron asked at the conclusion of yet another of Nick's diverting tales. Sometimes it felt as if he had a catalogue of them, ready to pull out to amuse at a moment's notice. "Have you seen any of their greenhouses?"

"I've seen a few," Nick said, dodging around her to open the door to the greenhouses for her. "None to rival this, however!"

It was rather impressive, especially in the dying light, to see the mass of leaves upon entering Greenhouse One. With deepening shadows sharpening the diverse shapes, the exotic plants seemed multiplied and alien.

He reached up to brush a fanning leaf out of his way as they ventured inside. "I'm used to rows upon rows of seedlings, numbered and carefully measured. And fertilizer. And manure! I suppose Elizabeth is not here to complain. So much manure, Saffron, I cannot even begin to say."

Saffron laughed. "We've our fair share of manure, though I rarely have to cope with it these days. They have the students assist with things like that."

"And you're a researcher," he said. "Recently promoted. Very impressive indeed."

"You are very kind."

"I am not, I assure you." He shot her a devious look. "Don't think I haven't lured you here under false pretenses. My boss is always saying I lack initiative. I'm plotting to convince you to reveal all your secrets so I might claim them for my own."

"Ah, yes," she said dryly, "the great secrets of seedlings and fertilizers."

"You say it as if that is not our bread and butter," he said with mocking severity. "Though truthfully, these days I suppose fungi is mine. Don't suppose you have any molds hanging around?"

"There are fungi everywhere," Saffron said, considering. "They're in the soil, their spores are floating in the air."

"And, unfortunately, they can cause quite a bit of trouble."

She led them toward the door to the second greenhouse. "Indeed. That's why you're heading up the northern line later this week."

"Indeed," he said. "I'll be visiting a research station while I do, come to think of it. I'll be able to compare your greenhouses to theirs and see who reigns supreme."

Saffron rolled her eyes at his dramatics. "I will wait with bated breath." She turned back to him, hand paused on the door's latch. "Nick, where exactly are you going?"

His cheeks were flushed, likely from the heat of the greenhouse. "Little place called Harpenden. Can't imagine you've heard of it."

"Actually," she said slowly, "I have."

"Ah, now this is more like it," Nick proclaimed, rubbing his hands together as they passed into the next greenhouse. "Rows and rows of little nothings ready to become somethings."

Saffron glanced at the lengths of workbenches covered with pots. "I didn't realize the research station in Harpenden studied fungi," she said casually. He hadn't replied to her earlier bait, being too overawed upon entering the room. She hadn't been lying earlier; fungi could, indeed, be very troublesome, to plants and people alike. If Petrov had been working with fungi, some strain could have done him in, and that should be easy enough to determine if the coroner knew what to look for.

"Fungi is just the start of it," Nick said. "Anything to do with growing plants is their domain up in Harpenden. Rather like you lot." He leaned over Dr. Miller's beet seedlings.

Saffron bit her lip. So much for that. "What sort of people do they have there? I imagine it's all old fogies in places like that."

He chuckled, moving on to another series of pots. "Bit like here, they have all sorts. Young, old, locals, foreigners. Harpenden has a number of women working there too."

"Foreigners," Saffron repeated, though she was curious about his last comment. "Where from?"

Nick meandered over to where she stood. "Forgive me, I should say they had one. One was an old fellow, recently snuffed it."

"Oh," Saffron said, feigning surprised sadness. That was no doubt Demian Petrov. How could she guide the conversation where she needed it to go?

Nick crossed his arms over his broad chest and leaned toward her, his voice low but clear. "There's a bit of a mystery clouding the old man's death. Intrigue, you know. I daresay that must appeal to you, eh?"

Saffron laughed nervously, excitement coursing through her. "You've my attention, Nick."

"Well," he intoned dramatically, "the fellow died rather suddenly. On a train, here, in town."

"Oh, my," she breathed, keeping her eyes wide and bright with curiosity. "Whatever happened?"

"They don't know. But the old man was a White. Fled the Bolsheviks and sought shelter here right as the revolution was heating up. His work in exchange for safe haven, or at least, that's what I'm guessing from his employment records. The whole thing sounds fishy, doesn't it?"

Saffron opened her mouth to agree that it did seem fishy, but if Nick was going to visit Harpenden, perhaps speak to the other scientists there, she didn't want to encourage his belief that something was going on in the laboratory. Stoking the fire of suspicion likely wouldn't do Inspector Green any favors in discovering the truth of what had happened to Demian Petrov.

Instead, she blurted out the first thing that came to mind. "What do you know about Greece?"

Nick cocked his head. "Is that some sort of odd London turn of phrase I haven't learned the meaning of?"

"No," Saffron said with a laugh. "I just wondered, with all the changes the war caused . . ." She strained to recall anything she'd read about Greece in the newspapers from that time or after, something that would make Alexander keep his origins to himself. "They had a sort of power struggle, didn't they? They ended up on our side, I think."

Still looking at her curiously, Nick nodded. "They had a king, and that king wasn't too certain he wanted to fight against his closest neighbors. Their prime minister disagreed, and eventually they joined up with us. The people, naturally, had strong opinions either way, and it all came to a head after the war ended. Bit of a mess over there now, Greece and the former Ottomans and all of them. I was stationed in that part of the world for a good many years. It all seems so far away now." He smiled down at her. "I find myself rather glad to be home."

The longer he stared down at her, the more aware she became of their nearness, the way Nick leaned over her, not quite crowding her, but not quite giving her enough space either.

A throat cleared. Saffron looked around Nick to see Alexander in the doorway of the greenhouse. He held up her handbag. "You left this in my office."

"Oh, thank you." She rushed forward to retrieve it. "Nick just stopped by the U."

Alexander nodded, barely flicking him a glance.

"Since he works in agriculture, I thought to show him the greenhouses," she said.

"Ever the educator," Nick quipped.

The conversation stalled, and Saffron found herself looking determinedly at a beet sprout. Why were they so awkward with each other?

Alexander excused himself a moment later, and Saffron would have preferred retreating to her office to contemplate what she'd learned and what it meant, but Nick insisted on touring the rest of the greenhouses. When they reached the xolotl vine, she explained its involvement in the poisoning of one of the university staff's wives.

Nick let out a low whistle. "If I recall correctly, your father was also a botanist. He had that massive conservatory."

"He did. A separate one he constructed on the property—"

"Near the stables, I remember now. A mysterious old place, wasn't it? Locked up all the time, if my memories of my bored adolescence are correct."

"Yes, my father kept all his specimens well away from the smaller conservatory connected to the house. He studied plant diseases." And more, if reports from others were to be believed. Her mind turned to Dr. Ingham and his suggestions. A few days ago, she'd been determined to ignore his questions, too distraught over everything that had occurred in France. A tiny spark of curiosity was lit at the mention of the greenhouse at Ellington. Had her father housed only sick plants he was experimentally treating or had other plants grown within? Something to do with the lab Dr. Ingham said her father had been invited to join?

"I can understand their concern, having seen the disastrous results of illness among plants," Nick said. He let out a sigh. "I still cannot believe that my career has come to center around *plants*, of all things. You, at least, have the excuse of your father as your entry into botany."

"That is something Elizabeth and I have puzzled over," Saffron replied, starting toward the door. "Why are you working in the Agricultural Ministry? Aren't you meant to be some sort of war hero?"

A smile played on his lips. "Deliver one message while under fire, and the world wants to vaunt you as a hero."

Nick walked her back to the Quad, where lamps now glowed gold at the twin gatehouses on Gower Street. He bade her good night with a promise of another dinner with Elizabeth when he returned from Harpenden, and Saffron returned to her office.

She tidied up her things, contemplating Alexander and his so-called secret. Most of Europe had been involved in the war; she didn't know why he should feel the need to hide his Greek heritage, especially when they'd ended up on the same side as England.

She checked once more that her samples were well insulated and was just reaching for the blinds on her window when she saw two tall figures just beyond the gatehouses.

They stood in the pools of light cast by the lanterns, allowing her to see perfectly the angry expression Alexander wore as he spoke to Nick.

CHAPTER 12

He'd been waiting for Nick in the shadows of the oak trees just inside the Quad. He had lingered there until Saffron had crossed the drive, huddled slightly without a coat on, and slipped inside the North Wing. Then he hurried to the street.

Nick was there, lighting a cigarette. The match flared in the gathering gloom, momentarily lighting up his face. With a deep breath to steady his nerves, Alexander began, "Nick." Nick looked up, shaking out his match before flicking it to the ground. "Look, I'm not sure what job you're here on—"

"Job?" Nick released a train of smoke as he spoke. "I'm here visiting my sister. And popping by to visit an old family friend. As I said."

Alexander took a step forward. "I don't know why you're onto Saffron, and I don't care. Leave her alone."

Nick raised an eyebrow, puffing on his cigarette. "I don't know what you're talking about."

His smile was gone. The amiable older brother act that had grated on Alexander had finally given way to the man with whom he'd been acquainted.

The change in demeanor only strengthened Alexander's resolve. "I don't know why you're here, but I know that Saffron shouldn't be a part of it."

"And *I* don't know what you're talking about," Nick repeated. "I'm just here spending time with my sister. If Saffron happens to be around, and she finds my company appealing, what can I do? She's a pleasant, attractive woman."

Alexander glared at him, unwilling to rise to the bait Nick offered. "Fine. But I've warned you."

"A warning is hardly friendly." Nick's eyes bore into Alexander's. "That sort of talk will get you into trouble."

Alexander refused to look away first; it meant the same thing to humans as it did in the animal kingdom.

Nick cocked his head slightly to the side, blowing out more smoke. "Have a good night, Alexander."

He turned and walked away, disappearing into the shadowy bustle of the street.

Alexander waited only a moment before retreating to his office. His hand shook as he paced the room.

He'd known right away who Nicholas Hale was; he'd recognized him nearly a year ago when he first saw the photograph of Elizabeth's family in Saffron's flat. An odd coincidence, he'd thought at the time.

He hadn't been concerned about Nick's presence in London until tonight. Nick had shown a marked interest in Saffron and her work, which made perfect sense if one believed he was working for the Agricultural Ministry. But Alexander knew better.

There was nothing he could do. Nick was right; trouble would come for him if he said the wrong thing. He'd have to find another way to keep Saffron out of whatever Nick was doing.

"The answer is obvious," Elizabeth told Saffron that evening at the kitchen table. "They know each other from the military."

Saffron paused in picking at the food Elizabeth had had waiting when she'd arrived home. She'd barely eaten any of the roasted chicken and vegetables, a rare treat for them, as she poured out the strange interaction she'd seen between Alexander and Nick. "But why wouldn't they have mentioned it?"

"I'd wager they didn't recognize each other at first," Elizabeth said. "If the reports are to be believed, those poor men were covered head to toe in mud for the entirety of their service. I barely recognize you after you work in the garden on a spring day. Imagine how disconcerting it must have been for them to realize who the other was."

"Be serious," Saffron said, glaring at her.

"I am, darling. What I find far stranger is that Nick showed up at the U. Do you think he's developed fond feelings for you?"

"After a reacquaintance of a few days?" Saffron shook her head. "No. He is remarkably friendly, though. I don't recall him being so . . ."

"Goofy?"

Saffron smiled at the strange word. "Yes, exactly. I always thought he was very serious."

"War changes people," Elizabeth said. "Colin served under some major who worked in government, and his idol-worship of the man led him to become a private secretary. And you mentioned, during your long-ago fawning over Alexander, that he decided to study biology after the war. It isn't unreasonable to assume that Nick changed because of his service."

"I suppose . . ." Saffron attempted a few more bites of food in the ensuing silence. "You seemed to have changed your tune about Nick."

Elizabeth sighed. "It is very easy to forgive a man who takes you out to the Savoy and then dancing." She frowned at Saffron as if realizing something unpleasant. "How the devil did Nick know about Lou's? He'd only been in town a few days. Lou's certainly isn't in any London guidebooks."

"I don't know. I'd never heard of the place myself," Saffron admitted.

When they retired to the parlor, Saffron wandered to the mantle to examine the photograph of the Hale family.

Their black-and-white faces looked back at her steadily. Her eye went first to Wesley, as it always did. Face bright with anticipation, his lips were almost tipped into a smile. Five years on, it still made her heart ache. He'd been so full of life and energy, and it had been snuffed out so easily.

Tears blurred his image, and she blinked them forcefully away. Her tears had wet the very ground where he'd fallen, and she'd resolved to put it all behind her. Not her love for Wesley—she'd never wish that away—but the guilt she carried that she was alive and he was not. The feeling of unworthiness because she had allowed her heart to be touched again, when she'd promised to love him forever in their last words to each other. She knew that was a childish promise—she'd been only fifteen at the time, after all—but it had been sincere, and knowing it was a young girl's promise didn't make her feel less guilty for feeling how she had about other men.

She turned her eyes from Wesley to the rest of the family. Nick and Wesley both wore army uniforms as they stood behind young Elizabeth and their mother, an older, less cheerful-looking copy of Elizabeth. Mr. Hale, a crag of a man, stood in the center, a hand on his wife's shoulder. She examined Nick's cool and collected expression. He'd have been something like twenty-three years old when this photograph was taken, still with some of the softness of youth in his face. His angles were sharper now, as if life at war had chiseled away every last trace of boyhood.

Saffron wrinkled her nose as the thought emerged. That sounded like something out of Elizabeth's lurid poems.

Nevertheless, he looked older now, more mature despite his silly gentility. She wondered if Alexander's childhood photographs showed the same. Had he once looked as hopeful as Wesley, or had he always had the same sort of cool confidence as Nick?

The army did seem to be their only connection, but Alexander had served briefly in France, his deployment cut short by his injury, and Nick said he'd been in the east.

"Where exactly did Nick serve?" Saffron asked Elizabeth.

She was curled on the couch, paging through a magazine. "Don't know."

"He received a medal, something about delivering a message under fire?"

"Don't know," Elizabeth repeated, turning another page.

"Do you think your mother knows?"

"Don't know, don't care."

Saffron sighed. Her friend's family matters were just as touchy as her own. She couldn't ask Elizabeth to telephone her mother to find out.

"You should ask him," Elizabeth added, not looking up from her magazine. "I'm sure he'd love the chance to impress you with his exploits."

Saffron sighed at the sourness in Elizabeth's tone. "I don't think he would. He seemed more interested in talking about plants."

She snorted. "Darling, if I were a man trying to win your affections, that is precisely where I would begin."

Hadn't Saffron just been thinking that about Alexander? "He knows about the Petrov case, Eliza."

That got her attention. She straightened up, tossing the magazine aside. "*Does* he? Well, well . . ." She exhaled, shaking her head. "I suppose he does have to be interesting somehow." She tapped a finger to her chin, a wide smile stretching across her face, the sort that promised mischief. "Petrov was an émigré, you said. Lord Tremaine might have been the one to look over his case. He's in charge of immigration matters, you know. I could find his file—"

"And be found poking around in a possible murder victim's file? Absolutely not, Eliza."

Elizabeth rolled her eyes. "So, it's all good and well for you to do the same a dozen times over, but not me? It's fine for you to quite literally *risk your life* to solve your mysteries, but I can't pick up one little file?"

Saffron blinked. Elizabeth's temper could be volatile, but it usually took a few minutes to be riled. "Elizabeth—"

"No," Elizabeth snapped, getting to her feet. "Why can you investigate murders and I can't even look at a piece of paper?"

She marched out of the room, punctuating her anger with her bedroom door slamming.

Nick coming into town had bothered her much more than Saffron had imagined. Even if her friend said she was feeling warmly toward her brother now, she knew that this explosion of frustration was linked to his presence. Having Nick around brought back to the surface unresolved family problems: Wesley's death, Elizabeth's attempted betrothal to restore the Hale's fortunes, her subsequent estrangement from her parents. She wondered if either Elizabeth or Nick was aware of all the things left unsaid between them.

Elizabeth's position as the receptionist for Lord Tremaine was a very good one, despite her constant complaints. Saffron could never ask her to risk that, even though she now burned with curiosity as to what Petrov's file would say. Perhaps it would reveal that he'd been a high-level government scientist for the late tsar, and there was a possibility that there was some sort of political motivation for Petrov's death. That would put Adrian in the clear for sure.

Alexander arrived at the Coleridge Gardens Hotel, a nondescript hotel a ten-minute walk from Saffron and Elizabeth's flat, just after three in the afternoon. He strode into the lobby and up to the spotty man at the counter.

"How may I help you, sir?"

"I needed to pick up a package from Mr. Nicholas Hale. He should have left something for a Mr. Johnson."

The clerk went to through a door behind the counter, presumably to check for a package. Alexander nudged the guestbook further into view and scanned the page for the right name until the clerk returned and replied nothing had been left for him. Alexander frowned and spoke forcefully. "He must have forgotten it in his room. Is it possible to check? I'm afraid I must have it as soon as possible."

The clerk regarded him nervously. "No, sir, I'm afraid that's against our policies."

Alexander affected a frustrated sigh. "Check again, then, the safe, perhaps. It's valuable, he might have had it locked away until I arrived."

"Yes, sir," the clerk said, already scurrying away.

Alexander had just slipped the right key off the wall behind the desk and into his pocket when the clerk returned, shaking his head apologetically.

"What time is Mr. Hale returning?" Alexander asked. When the clerk had no answer, he said, "I'll have to telephone his office then. Where is the telephone?"

After receiving directions to a room down the hall, Alexander instead found the staircase. Ignoring the creaking floors and garish wallpaper, he found the correct number. It was midafternoon and the hall was empty. He softly knocked, and when no answer came, he slipped the key into the lock. He opened the door and stepped inside. There was nothing unusual about the room. It had a bed, neatly made, the usual arrangement of toiletries, and a range of normal clothing in the wardrobe. Alexander checked the usual places, not expecting to find anything. A man in Nick's line of business wouldn't hide anything meaningful under the bed.

Ten minutes later, he was glaring down at the dust smudging his fingertips. The gravity of what he was doing hit him. What *was* he doing? Breaking into a hotel room and searching it?

Nick was dangerous, plain and simple. But even if Alexander had found something to reveal what Nick was up to, he didn't know what he could do about it.

CHAPTER 13

The next morning was miserably cold, suitable to the chilly mood within Saffron's flat. Elizabeth had all but ignored her this morning; she'd left a cold boiled egg and toast for her on the kitchen table, which for Elizabeth was tantamount to active torture.

Romesh Datta seemed pleased to see her, however, when she knocked on the door to his laboratory. He proved himself a much more pleasant fellow when his cousin was not around, apologizing for the delay in having the information prepared and even proclaiming he'd be quite happy to assist her further should she need it.

She accepted the dense packet he offered her and thanked him, adding her hope he'd pass on her thanks to Savita, which he promised to do with a strained smile.

The folder contained a report on each chemical on Inspector Green's list from Petrov's laboratory. She was pleased to see two different sets of handwriting; Savita had gotten to contribute.

Unfortunately, she had to turn the packet over to Spalding, who'd give it to Miller, who'd pass it on to Inspector Green, which meant she didn't have long with the information.

Back in her office, she scanned each document, making hurried notes in her notebook as she did. Most fertilizers were made of some variation of nitrogen, phosphoric acid, and potash, and she recognized those easily as she passed through the documents. She'd need to see what an overabundance of each might do to the human body, especially the kidneys or liver.

Other pages listed sulfur and sodium, then the contents changed more toward detergents and cleaning products, no doubt used to keep the lab clean. Petrov would have contact with those also. Bleach was certainly dangerous, she mused, examining the chemical components of the brand used by the lab, which the Dattas had provided, but Petrov would have known if he'd been poisoned by bleach. It wasn't exactly subtle.

At the end of her frantic note-taking, she'd learned nothing useful. It was either time to retire to the library to research the effects of the chemical components, or it was time to return to Harley Street.

The latter was far more appealing.

Lee was pleased as punch to see her, especially as it was the lunch hour.

"We're eating, Everleigh," he declared, and she didn't argue. She was hungry, and Lee's buoyant demeanor was pleasant after the dramatics of the previous day.

Rather than walk down the street to find something, or eat a meal at the Harley Street office, Lee drew her into a cab to Berkely Square.

"Are you sure you want to risk another meal here?" Saffron asked him as they climbed out of the cab before a familiar gleaming window with gold lettering. "Last time we ate at the Grove, I ran out on you."

"You did," he said, opening the door for her, "and missed a delicious lunch. Don't make that same mistake again."

The Grove might have been styled the Orangery, for the cafe was filled with miniature trees that now bore miniature oranges. They stood in earthenware pots strewn across the black-and-white tiled floor, giving diners the sense of dining al fresco. The greenery inside made up for the lack of it outside. Beyond the large glass windows was a view of the square, where few people strolled among the bare trees.

Saffron, for her part, was pleased to be seated inside next to a particularly large tree. It smelled divine and gave their table a sense of privacy, which she appreciated when discussing gruesome matters.

They parried quips as they ate, Lee offering a few amusing anecdotes of his patients, and Saffron explaining about her temporarily missing samples.

Lee patted his mouth with his napkin and eased back into his seat, knitting his fingers over his abdomen. He looked rather more severe than usual in a navy suit and tie, but his pale pink shirt and loudly patterned tie expressed his usual personality. "Now, to the real reason you've torn me away from my work. Let's have it, then."

She passed him her notebook, having given the file to a grateful Spalding on the way out of the North Wing.

"This is absolutely useless," Lee sighed, flipping between pages. "Singular components aren't going to give you answers, Everleigh. Especially when we don't know which he ingested or inhaled. It might be a combination of things, anyway."

"But you can tell me something," Saffron said, taken aback. "These chemicals were things he might have worked with every day. If someone slipped some into his tea, or—"

Lee shook his head. "Even if that was the case, they'd have tested his blood and such to see what chemicals lingered there. If he'd been doused with ammonia or something, his blood and tissues would show it."

"But that would only be if it was an acute poisoning," she reasoned. "Many chemicals don't leave that sort of evidence behind with a chronic poisoning."

He lifted a brow. "Someone has been keeping up with their medical terminology. Yes, an high dose of something would likely be evident in a different way than a poisoning taking place over time."

"But if it was chronic poisoning that killed him, why would they believe it was Adrian Ashton?"

Lee shrugged. "He might have been acting suspiciously, or someone wanted to pass blame on to him. What did the inspector say?"

"Nothing," Saffron said dully.

"And Ashton? The elder one, that is?" He frowned. "Good Lord, that is annoying. Adrian, then."

"I haven't asked him."

Lee blinked. "You haven't asked Adrian, the one accused of murder, about the case?"

Heat rose in her cheeks. "Alexander doesn't want me to speak to him."

"Why the devil not?"

"He's afraid I'll get the wrong impression of Adrian. Or their family. Honestly, I'm not entirely sure."

"Wasn't Alexander the one to ask for your help?" Lee asked with genuine confusion. "And he won't let you speak with his brother?" He scoffed. "Forgive me for saying so, but your beau is an idiot."

"He isn't my beau." Despite herself, she felt the need to defend Alexander. "And he isn't an idiot. He's protective of his family. He'd kept it from me this entire time that his mother and her family are Greek. As if that's something that ought to be some great secret."

Lee's finger traced his lower lip, eyelids lowered as he considered her. "Alexander Ashton is Greek, keeping secrets, and decidedly not your beau. Fascinating."

She scowled at him. "Lee. Be serious."

"I might be, if you'd allow it," he said, winking. He hurried on before she could scoff at him. "What other secrets have you dug up about Ashton?"

"You are a wretched gossip."

"I have only the maid to chat with these days." He wiggled his fingers at her. "Out with it, Everleigh. What gruesome skeletons are in Ashton's closet?"

"He knows Elizabeth's brother somehow," Saffron admitted. It felt good to tell someone other than Elizabeth, who'd not thought anything of it. "They were . . . having what seemed to be a rather unpleasant conversation just last night. Nick came to the U to see our botany facilities since he works in agriculture, and—"

Lee scoffed again. "Sounds more like he was trying to make nice with you."

"A man might actually have an interest in plants, you know," Saffron replied hotly. "He might actually care about what I have to say about my work."

"Of course. Forgive me, do go on."

"Alexander looked very angry when I saw them from the window speaking on the street."

"And I don't suppose he told you why?"

"I have no reason to think he'd tell me anything," she said. "He's been remarkably opaque. I think they must know each other from the war."

"Well, I can do one thing for you, since I was useless with your chemicals. My Uncle Matt has his finger in every governmental pot, and I daresay he could dig up some information about Ashton. See if he and Nick might have bumped into each other on the march. What's Nick's full name?"

Mattias Lee was a rather important figure in British politics, though Saffron didn't imagine he'd know anything about the average soldier. "Nicholas Andrew Hale. A major, I believe."

Lee rubbed his hands together excitedly. "Very good. I'll see what I can find out for you. I'm guessing they didn't get on in the army and now find themselves butting heads once again. As for everything else, let's just hope whatever secrets Ashton is keeping don't tie a noose around his brother's neck."

CHAPTER 14

Employment records, Saffron found, were quite useful. Lee's suggestion of finding Alexander and Nick's military history inspired her own foray into the university recordkeeper's office, and she soon emerged with an address.

Alexander lived in a second-story flat in the exact kind of place she'd guessed he would live. Respectable and practical, just a six- or seven-minute walk from campus. She climbed the stairs, bracing herself. She was tired of arguing with him at the university, where she guessed he didn't feel comfortable speaking about personal matters. He'd clammed right up the previous day, and she didn't want to give him any excuses this time.

Invading his privacy was possibly not the best way to do it, but he might also see it for the olive branch it was. She was coming to him, ready to apologize for being so upset about not being told something he obviously felt was private, and ready to needle him until he gave her what she needed to help Adrian. Everything she'd learned about Petrov's death—admittedly not much—suggested that Adrian wasn't responsible. She needed to figure out what about Adrian had made the police suspect him if she was to counter it.

But when she knocked, it was Adrian, not Alexander, who opened the door.

She immediately lifted her eyes up and toward the corner of the doorway. He'd answered the door in trousers with braces dangling and an undershirt, his curly hair wild and his jaw stubbled. Voice too high, she said, "I'm terribly sorry, Mr. Ashton, but I was hoping to speak to Alexander."

Adrian chuckled. "*I* am terribly sorry, Miss Everleigh. You must think me brash for opening the door like this, but I thought you were my brother. He'll be back any minute. Come, come inside and let me put on a shirt, hmm?"

He was gone before she could tell him she'd wait outside.

She ventured into the hall, unable to stop her curiosity. The walls were bare but for coat hooks, and the floor was spotless but worn hardwood.

"Come in, come in," Adrian called. "The kitchen is warm."

Hesitantly, she stepped down the hall. The flat was set up similarly to her own, with doors likely for bedrooms lining the hall and a parlor off to one side. The state of that room, from what she saw passing by, shocked her. Alexander was tidy to the point of obsession, and it looked as if the room had been caught in a whirlwind. The furniture was covered in books, newspapers, magazines, and to her surprise, bottles of wine and spirits.

That was Adrian's doing, then. Alexander must have hated his brother's mess and likely his liquor too.

Adrian found her in the hall, a collarless shirt now buttoned beneath his braces. He grinned and flung a hand out. "Please, this way." He shepherded her into the tiny kitchen, which was indeed very warm. "If you please." He pulled out a chair for her at the shabby kitchen table.

She sat, looking around. This room was equally bare of personality, though from the pots and pans on the stove Saffron guessed that cooking did happen there. She had never heard of bachelors cooking much.

"Forgive me for not entertaining you elsewhere," Adrian said, settling across from her. "But the kitchen calls to me. The warmth, the smells of food. When I go home, I spend more time in the kitchen with my mother than anywhere else in the house."

"My flatmate is much the same. She finds the kitchen to be the most agreeable place in the flat."

"A smart girl," he said. "You came for Alex, but it cannot be for business, otherwise you would have spoken to him at the university." His thick brows lifted, and his smile turned suggestive.

"I came to ask him to speak with you, actually," Saffron said, adding quickly, "Alexander asked me to assist with your situation with Mr. Petrov's death. I'm sorry you've come under suspicion."

Adrian's smile slipped momentarily, but then his eyes went wide and he let out a laugh. "You are the poison girl!"

She blinked. "I'm sorry?"

"The one he met before his expedition! You are the one he told me about!"

Heat flooded her cheeks. "I . . . yes, we did meet before the expedition. And I do study poisonous plants."

"Excellent!" Adrian's curls shook with each shake of his head. "I am glad to know he is still, ah, speaking with you. Alex is so quiet, you know, I had no idea—"

"We are friends," she said. "He asked if I could look into the case, since I know poisons and I'm familiar with Inspector Green."

At the mention of the inspector, his expression darkened. "Ah, yes. The inspector is very . . ." He let out a humorless laugh. "He is not unlike my brother, in fact. Prefer to present a blank face, don't they?"

"They do," Saffron agreed. "Can you tell me what happened?"

Adrian knitted his fingers together atop the table and spoke with a tone that suggested he'd told this story too many times for his liking. "I work for Hawker as an engineer—"

"You build aeroplanes?" Saffron interrupted.

"Yes," he said absently. "I went to school for it, then flew during the war. When I came out, I wanted to make something better than the flimsy things they sent us up in. Hawker is in Kingston upon Thames. My boss, he tells me I'm to go see Sir Gavin Montfried. He lives near Roundwood Park in Harlesden."

Saffron nodded, picturing Inspector Green's map in her mind.

"I took the train from Kingston to Willesden Junction, then I took a tram. I saw Sir Gavin, got the plans he was working on—he was wing commander to my boss and still likes to play with designs—and then I returned to Willesden Junction." His words were quick, his accent making them emphatic and earnest. He shot her a furtive look, however, as he said, "Once there, I went to a pub. Drank some, and got to thinking I should go into town, see my brother, my mother." He flashed a grin. "She misses me. Worries for me. For us both, you know. Alex is her baby." He chuckled, shaking his head.

Warmth for the affection Adrian suggested between Alexander and their mother eased Saffron's impatience. She really had never thought much about Alexander's family, since he so rarely brought them up.

Adrian tapped his long fingers on the table. "After a few drinks, I got on the train to St. Pancras. I chose a seat in a compartment with only one other person. He was an old man, with gray hair and a face like cracked pavement." Saffron quirked a brow, and Adrian waved a hand toward his own face. "Heavy, wrinkled. Looked like he'd never smiled. He was asleep, anyway. But when the train lurched, he woke. He said something polite to me, maybe 'Good evening,' then closed his eyes again. He stayed that way for ten minutes or so, then he let out a moan, like he was ill. I asked if he was all right, he mumbled something." His lips flattened briefly as if irritated. "He said it in Russian, I know now. I didn't know at the time he was a Russian."

Curious, Saffron asked, "Why do you say that?"

He huffed a laugh. "The police asked me many times if I knew who he was, where he came from, what work he did, even where he lived. I suppose I am used to denying knowing anything about him. All I saw was an old man who looked ill. He went pale and began to shake, moaning nonstop. This was around"—he squinted—"Kilburn, maybe. I called for help. An older woman with a young boy poked her head in but went away. There was a fellow who said he'd call for an attendant, but I did not see him again. Another two people came and stayed there until we reached St. Pancras. Mrs. Sheffield and Mr. Crawford."

"Who were they?"

"Mrs. Sheffield was an older lady, said she was the wife of a physician, but she only patted the old man's brow with her kerchief. Mr. Crawford, he wore a bad suit and a bowler hat. He and I spoke about what was to be done, and he said he would go for the stationmaster or a doctor or something when we arrived at St. Pancras. But the police said they hadn't heard about him."

"But Mrs. Sheffield confirmed he was there?" Saffron asked.

"I don't know," Adrian said. His voice had grown taut. He reached behind himself to the kitchen counter for a pack of cigarettes and a lighter. He lit one with unsteady hands, and the pungent scent of burning tobacco filled the small room.

"What happened when you reached the station?" Saffron asked.

"There was a great commotion as soon as people discovered there was a dead man aboard the train. Mrs. Sheffield and I stayed in the compartment until the police and doctor arrived. I felt for the man, Petrov. He was dying and alone, with only our sorry company. I wanted to make sure he was taken care of." His lips twisted. "But that was suspicious, I was told later. It was also suspicious that I had aeroplane plans on my person. And suspicious I sound and look like this." His cigarette left behind a hazy ring as he waved around his face.

"Because you are Greek," Saffron said cautiously.

"Because I look and sound foreign," Adrian said. "They don't care that I was born and raised here. They see only the darkness of my features and hear my mother's people in my voice." He tapped ash into a dish on the counter. "Because being foreign is itself a crime, eh?"

"I've never thought so."

Adrian shrugged, but this time the motion did not look to be casual punctuation to his thoughts, but like he was trying to shed the suspicions others held toward him.

"It would have been better," he said somewhat sullenly, not looking at her, "if I'd done as Alex did. Forced myself to speak like our father."

Saffron said nothing, at once deeply uncomfortable to hear something so private about the Ashton brothers and breathless to learn more.

Adrian obliged her silent wish. "He watched our mother be treated poorly and listened to our cousins complain about prejudices. Even as a very young boy, he never let our mother's voice take root like I did. It didn't matter though, he was kicked out of dance halls and pubs same as the rest of us, when we went out all together and spoke our mother tongue."

He leaned slightly forward on the table. "We came back broken, you know. People, they don't understand how it is, to be stuck." He tapped the side of his head. It occurred to her then that Adrian was perhaps not entirely sober, for his dark eyes were hazy. "Makes it hard to tell what's in your head and what's real. The street becomes a sky full of bullets. A fellow sweeping the street looks like he's holding a bayonet. God knows it can be frightening, dangerous."

Usually, soldiers did themselves harm rather than others. Saffron's uncle, her cousin John's father, had killed himself not long after returning from his deployment. She'd never considered that he might have done the other members of the household harm too, but that had been a bone-chilling possibility.

"Alex, he knows this. He knows what people see when they look at him, what they think about those with the shock. He wants to be seen as strong, smart, in control." Adrian chuckled. "Oh, the control! It is something he never cared for before, and now he needs it badly. So, he stepped away from it, from the family. Removed one strike against him by hiding in our father's name, his manner." He seemed to recollect his cigarette, now heavy with ash, and took a long drag. "But we all hide, do we not, eh?"

Saffron cleared her throat, wishing she could open a window and clear out the air too. Adrian was delving into very private matters.

"Alexander mentioned you'd been to the police station a number of times," she said, hoping to get him back on track. She still had things she wanted to know about the case. "What did they ask you?"

"What did they not want to know?" he mused. "I have been to the police station three times, and they have come here twice. They asked me what I did that day, who I saw, when I'd last been to London, if I'd ever visited a place called Harpenden. What I saw the man eat, drink, or smoke. What I gave him, what he said when he woke, and where he came from. If I noticed anything strange about the circum-stances, our train compartment. They asked me why I chose to sit there with him." He shook his head with a faint smile on his lips. "They didn't believe I wanted a quiet place to take a nap."

"And it was Detective Inspector Green interviewing you?"

"Yes, and another fellow. A big, tall man, blond hair."

"What was his name?"

"He didn't give one," came a voice from behind her. "But I'm sure you can guess who it was."

Saffron winced slightly at the hard edge of displeasure in Alexander's voice. He stood with arms crossed, shoulder leaning against the door frame. A parcel dangled from one hand.

Adrian frowned at his brother. "Do not be rude, Alex. Your friend Miss Everleigh is here."

"I came to speak with you," she told Alexander. "But I found your brother instead. He's been giving me his account of the situation."

"I see" was his only reply. He skirted her to place the parcel on the table before his brother.

Adrian opened the parcel and exclaimed something in what Saffron presumed was Greek. "It's as if you went straight to Kyllini!"

Saffron darted a glance at Alexander, and she found he was looking at her already.

"Kyllini is the town where my mother grew up," he said evenly.

"I see," Saffron said. She watched Adrian unpackage a series of small crocks, all emitting smells that made her mouth water. "I will leave you to your supper," she said to Adrian, and he looked crestfallen.

"But you must stay!" he exclaimed, getting to his feet as Saffron rose.

"Thank you, but I ought to go," she said as warmly as she could manage when she felt so suddenly out of place. Adrian glanced between her and Alexander, and whatever he saw made him resettle into his seat.

Alexander stepped back so she could enter the hall and followed her to the door. "I'll walk with you to the bus station."

Saffron hadn't noticed how late it had become until they reached the street, and it was all but silent. Distant rumbles of automobiles and the gentle tap of their heels on the pavement were the only sounds as they went toward the Euston Square bus stop.

It might have been quiet on the street, but in Saffron's head, there was a riot of thought. Adrian's story mixed with his revelations about himself and Alexander, but one question kept surfacing in her mind, and she spoke it aloud to Alexander.

"Why does Inspector Green believe Adrian has something to do with Petrov's death?" she asked. "There has to be something. Some connection. It can't be only because they were in the same train compartment."

They paused on the street corner as a messenger slipped past on a bicycle.

"I don't know," Alexander said, not looking at her. They crossed the street. Alexander's long legs ate up the distance, and Saffron had to scurry to keep up with him.

"There has to be a reason, Alexander," she insisted. "Inspector Green doesn't just make decisions based on no evidence!"

He glanced at her. "Dr. Maxwell—"

"The inspector arrested Dr. Maxwell because he had a motive to poison Dr. Henry and access and knowledge of a unique toxin." She stopped him with a hand on his arm. "*You* were the one to convince me of his possible guilt, if you'll recall. And now, Adrian is still under suspicion despite nothing in Inspector Green's notes connecting him to the actual murder. It has to be something else."

He didn't reply, and they began walking again.

"He mentioned he doesn't come to London much," Saffron said. "Why not?"

"He doesn't get on with our father," he muttered, then shook his head. "You've done far more than I could have hoped, thank you."

Frustration had her gnashing her teeth together. He was shutting her out again, and it was going to prevent her from doing anything useful. She'd already wanted to help, but speaking to Adrian and seeing the lurking helplessness behind his smiles, she had to do something.

They reached the bus stop and came to a rather abrupt halt. After a beat of silence, in which Saffron realized Alexander wouldn't be leaving until she'd boarded the bus, she asked, "Have you found a lawyer?"

Alexander ran a hand through his hair. "Adrian refuses to hire someone who might get word back to our father that he's in trouble. He's a solicitor."

Saffron bit her lip. The only solicitor she knew was Mr. Feyzi, who worked for her family. "I know someone who may be able to help," Saffron said slowly. "I don't believe he handles these sorts of cases, but he might be able to offer advice. I will search up his card and give it to you tomorrow."

He nodded. "Thank you."

The bus ambled around the corner. She told Alexander goodbye, then hopped aboard. He was out of sight before the bus pulled away from the pavement.

CHAPTER 15

When Saffron knocked on Alexander's office door the next day, he was ready.

Ready to accept this unexpected offer of her assistance with a lawyer, ready to do something productive to help Adrian, and ready to put aside some of his misgivings about being more open with Saffron.

He did not like being wrong, but when he was, he admitted it freely. He'd been wrong in his behavior toward her before, for which he'd apologized sincerely, and he was beginning to realize that the way he'd handled Adrian's situation and personal history had not been the right one. He'd nearly destroyed Saffron's regard for him with his impulsivity and jealousy; he'd not make the same mistake again.

Not to mention that the rebuke Adrian had given him upon his return to the flat the previous evening had been thorough and, Alexander suspected, had been partially motivated by Adrian's hurt. He'd seen how Alexander had spirited Saffron away from him twice now, how irate he'd been to find her at the kitchen table listening to Adrian spill God only knew what about his own life or Alexander's. Adrian could be trusted to be candid but not prudent. Alexander could only be trusted to be the opposite. And Saffron thought his unwillingness to speak had to do with her.

He rose at the first sound of her knock and was opening the door before the next knock landed.

She wore her lavender coat and matching hat. She'd not put off giving him the information about the solicitor, and he felt that was a positive sign.

"Good morning," he said, stepping back to admit her.

She didn't move forward. She dipped her hand into her handbag and brought out a worn card instead. "Good morning." She offered it to him.

He took it, looking down at the name on the worn cream paper. It was good quality paper, with an engraved name upon it with an address in Marylebone.

"Feyzi?" he read, peering up at her.

"He is my family's solicitor," she said. "He's exceedingly pleasant, don't worry."

It was not the notion of meeting with a solicitor that made Alexander wary, though it should have, but rather that this man was in business with Saffron's family. Viscount Easting was her grandfather, something he'd been embarrassed to learn after Nick had mentioned it in their first meeting at the flat. Ellington was the estate where Saffron had grown up and had she been a man would have inherited. He'd not known of the Everleigh family's status when he'd been taught by Professor Thomas Everleigh, for he'd never been called a lord or an honorable or anything other than "Professor."

But that was a problem for another day. Saffron stood before him, offering assistance when she didn't have to. He'd make do with what he had, then see what the next step was in making her see he felt something more than the friendship she kept bringing up.

Alexander cleared his throat. "Have you met him?"

"I have, several times," she said. "He was a friend to my father in addition to managing the family's legal affairs." Her eyes clouded momentarily before flicking up to meet his again. "I should accompany you to see him. He's a very busy man, but he always makes time for me."

"I would appreciate that."

"Noon?"

He agreed, and she gave him a small smile before bustling off to her own office.

The lunch hour came upon him sooner than expected, leaving him rushing to tidy his space before struggling through doing up his cufflinks and donning his jacket. He was just tugging on his overcoat when Saffron's knock came upon his door again.

They caught a bus to Marylebone. Unfortunately, traffic left them at a standstill. Just outside the bus's window stood a sign marking the Warren Street Underground station.

"We ought to just get off and take the Underground," he said.

She shuddered next to him. "Absolutely not."

He quirked a brow, and to his surprise, her cheeks flushed pink. "Why not?"

"I do not care for the Underground."

"Because it's crowded? Smelly? Did you have a bad experience with a train getting stuck?"

"I don't like that it goes underground," she said almost plaintively. "And don't bother to poke fun at me, I've heard every jest about a botanist fearing being underground that could ever be told. Elizabeth has even invented new ones to make fun of me."

Alexander chuckled. "And said them far better than I could, I'd wager. Why do you dislike that it goes underground?"

"I don't know." She sighed. "I used to think it was claustrophobia, actually."

"Ah." Alexander had done research into phobias, thinking it might help him overcome his own neurosis after his injury. His research had led him to Freud and his examinations of anxiety hysteria. He wondered if Saffron was aware that Freud believed claustrophobia had to do with an excess of libido, and decided not to mention it.

"But this," she went on with a wave of her hand, "doesn't bother me in the slightest."

The bus wasn't packed as it might have been later in the afternoon, but they were standing with a handful of others near the rear, with every seat filled.

"And the greenhouses are packed with plants," Alexander added.

"Exactly. So it's not to do with crowding or being in a place with a closed door. I believe it's actually being underground that bothers me. Subterraphobia, if you will."

Alexander laughed. "You're mixing your roots. Phobia comes from *phobos*, which is—"

"Greek. I am well aware," she said wryly.

"It could be *bathophobia*," he mused, emphasizing the Greek pronunciation of the words. "Fear of deep things. Or . . . *ypógeios* means underground, so *ypógeiosphobia* is the most accurate if you truly don't like anything subterranean. Rather a mouthful, though."

He couldn't resist smiling at the way Saffron watched his mouth form the words.

The traffic eventually cleared, delivering them to New Cavendish Street. Saffron led him to a red brick building with white window trim and black wrought-iron lattice work around the door and transom window.

They were admitted to a parlor to wait but had barely sat on the comfortable couch before a man in his late forties or early fifties entered the room. He was dressed in a smart, dark suit with a ruby-red tie. His black hair was generously threaded with gray, and his skin was tanned and creased in a way that suggested he smiled widely and often. He reminded Alexander of Mr. Ferrand.

"Miss Saffron," he said warmly, kissing the air next to Saffron's cheek as she took his hand. "And you have brought a friend, I see."

"This is Alexander Ashton, Mr. Feyzi," she said, smiling back. "Might we steal a moment of your time?"

Feyzi smirked. "It will not be stolen, I promise you. But your grandfather never too carefully analyzes his bill, so I would not concern yourself."

They were shown into an impressive study so heavily scented with pipe smoke that Alexander imagined it saturated the wine-colored walls. Volumes of law texts lined the walls, the dull titles vaguely familiar to Alexander from hours spent in his father's study being scolded.

"I love coming here," Saffron whispered to him. "He has the best tea."

Mr. Feyzi requested tea and it was excellent.

"Well, my dear," Mr. Feyzi said, settling at his desk, "what brings you?" He glanced between them as he took a sip of tea.

"Mr. Ashton is in need of a solicitor on behalf of his brother, but I will let him explain the particulars to you so you may determine if you could help him, or if you have a recommendation for another solicitor who could."

Feyzi took it in stride, nodding and looking at Alexander with interest. Saffron excused herself to wait in the parlor, ignoring Alexander's protest that she was welcome to stay.

The solicitor was polite as he gently prodded him for details on Adrian's case, and after a quarter of an hour, Feyzi had given him three names of barristers who might be helpful and discreet. He'd smiled knowingly when Alexander mentioned his desire to avoid his father's notice.

"I understand perfectly," he said. "Family is the trickiest of assets, but an asset it is. Jeremy Ashton is well spoken of. I would not avoid his involvement unless absolutely necessary."

Alexander privately agreed, but this was his brother's affair. Even acknowledging that, though, he knew that should his brother actually be arrested, Alexander's first telephone call would be to his father. Adrian and their father might not agree about much of anything, but they cared for each other. Not to mention Adrian would need their father's support.

"Please send the bill to me," Alexander said, rising to his feet along with the solicitor.

Feyzi stood but did not move to the door. Crossing his arms over his chest, he scrutinized Alexander with a slight squint. "Thomas Everleigh was a friend of mine, you know. School chums. Then when Lord Easting needed a solicitor after his old retainer died, Thomas insisted he take me on despite the fact I'd only recently finished school. He was a loyal friend, a good man."

"He was one of my professors," Alexander said. The brief but warm interactions between Feyzi and Saffron made it clear that Feyzi cared for her well-being. Alexander wanted him to understand that he also cared for her. "I was very fortunate to meet Saffron earlier this year. We worked together and became friends. She is also a loyal friend."

"That she is."

Alexander almost smiled at the hint of something in Feyzi's voice. It was meant to be threatening, he'd wager, but it only made him glad that Saffron had someone in the city she could turn to. But she *hadn't* turned to Feyzi when she was facing suspicion in the Berking and Blake poisoning. Now he thought of it, she had mentioned a solicitor in one of her letters to him when he was in Brazil, something about a visit from a lawyer had changed her plans for testifying in the case against Berking and Blake. He'd assumed it was from the prosecution, but now he wondered if it had been her family's lawyer.

He didn't want to get her in trouble with her family by asking. So he merely said, "I appreciate your assistance, Mr. Feyzi."

He rejoined Saffron in the parlor, but Feyzi was not done with them yet.

"Miss Saffron," he said, beckoning to her, "a word, if you please."

Saffron flashed Alexander a quick smile, and followed the solicitor back out of the parlor, leaving Alexander to wonder exactly what Feyzi would be saying to her.

"An interesting fellow," Mr. Feyzi said as they settled in his office.

"He is," Saffron agreed.

"This is the same man you were involved with during that incident in the spring," he said, stating it not as a question.

"Yes, he is."

Mr. Feyzi was quiet for a moment, watching her in that uncanny way of his that was both kindly and assessing. At last, he said, "I will not mention this visit to your grandfather, of course, but I must caution you, Miss Saffron, that you risk further angering both Lord and Lady Easting—"

"I don't care, Mr. Feyzi," Saffron burst out. "You know that I do not."

"But you care about your mother," he said, a sharpness to his words that she rarely heard. "And she cannot refuse to open their letters as you do or simply run off to London."

Saffron bit her tongue. She would not correct him about running off to London; it would only sound childish. "You're right. But my mother has told me numerous times that I am to stay the course if this is what I want. You are the one to pass on her . . ." She released an embarrassed breath. "Monetary support. You know that staying here is what she wishes me to do."

"That does not mean your actions do not have consequences," he said. "Consequences your mother faces as a result of your disagreements with Lord and Lady Easting."

Again, she bit her tongue. Being friends with her father and watching Saffron grow up, albeit from afar, had given Mr. Feyzi a fatherly attitude toward her. She could not deny there were many times she appreciated it. Now was not one of those times.

"I appreciate the advice," she replied. "Mr. Ashton needs assistance, and it was within my power to help him find someone who could help his brother. That is all."

"I know how your mind works, Miss Saffron," Mr. Feyzi said wryly. "If there is a mystery afoot, you will poke into it. From what I gathered, this is a serious situation. I cannot in good conscience, allow you to—"

"I am helping a friend," she interrupted. "That is all."

Color touched his cheeks, and Saffron felt sorry for it. She did not want to offend him, but neither would she be "allowed" by Mr. Feyzi to do anything. She'd not left Ellington and her grandparents only to find another keeper—one that answered to them.

She cleared her throat. "I beg your pardon, Mr. Feyzi. I simply wish to do what I believe to be right." She got to her feet to take her leave, but Mr. Feyzi made a sudden sound of enlightenment and rose, crossing the room in quick strides.

"The tenants at your father's flat in Bloomsbury sent something over a few weeks ago," he said, extracting a file from a cabinet. "They said they were worried there was a pest of some kind inside the walls. They found a few things and sent this over by messenger. I had thought to send it to your mother, but . . ." He turned and brandished the file at her.

Not missing the way Mr. Feyzi's large eyes clouded over, she took the file, letting her fingers rest against his for a moment. "I understand," she said softly.

Mr. Feyzi had stayed at Ellington for a few days immediately following her father's death, helping her grandfather put affairs in order since he had lost his heir. Along with the rest of the household, Mr. Feyzi had been aware that her mother had slumped into something like a catatonic state of shock, unable to leave her bed for days. He knew now, from his visits to Ellington as well as his communications with Violet Everleigh to assist Saffron, that she still did not leave the manor. It touched Saffron that Mr. Feyzi was so saddened by it. He had known her mother for years and knew how brightly Violet Everleigh had shone before her light was doused by grief and fear.

Saffron peeked inside the file, her heart clenching at the sight of her father's handwriting darting across the papers within.

"I will give you a moment," Mr. Feyzi murmured somewhere behind her. The door snicked shut.

There were receipts, train tickets, letters between Thomas and Violet Everleigh and a handful of others in no particular order. She wouldn't read her parents' letters; what had been said between them during the months her father had spent at the university was private.

As she paged through the other notes and letters, however, familiar names caught her eye. She grinned at a note from Dr. Maxwell, reminding her father about a meeting. He'd been something of a mentor for her father too, she knew. There was a lengthy letter from a well-known French plant pathologist whose name she saw frequently in *Annals of Botany*. And a name that made her fingers falter, nearly dropping the file.

Dr. Jonathon Calderbrook's name was like a lightning strike straight to her heart. The name Dr. Ingham had mentioned during their brief meeting at the conference, the name Saffron had wondered over for weeks now. Paired with the words "Kew Botanical Gardens," it was enough to make Saffron break out in a cold sweat.

Dr. Ingham had asked Saffron if she'd known whether or not her father had accepted the position in Dr. Calderbrook's lab at Kew. The lab had been government-run, Ingham had mentioned. And Saffron hadn't wanted to know what, exactly, the government had wanted her father to do. Plant pathology, her father's specialty, was innocuous enough. But her former department head of Botany at the university, Berking, had mentioned he'd used her father's research to strengthen the toxins of a poisonous plant, which he'd then used to create a poison that had nearly killed someone. He'd planted a seed of doubt in her mind, and she'd allowed it to flourish. What if her father had been working on something dreadful? What if he had created something that could hurt people, just like the scientists who'd labored over the gas that had flooded the battlefield where her father met his death?

Indecision kept her frozen, but an acute wave of fury overtook it. She'd allowed Berking's words to worm their way into her mind, corrupting her memories. For months, she'd avoided mention of her own father, because she was afraid she'd find Berking was right. She did not want her worst fears about her father to be confirmed.

But no more.

She read the letter.

When she was finished, she needed the telephone, which she promptly was given access to by Mr. Feyzi.

After directing the operator, she only had to wait a moment to be connected.

"Immigration Ministry, the offices of Lord Tremaine," came the coolly professional tones from the telephone's handset.

Saffron straightened up. "Eliza—"

"How may I assist you?" Elizabeth's voice took on the strident tone of an impatient clerk.

"I hope you are of a mind to have fowl for dinner," Saffron announced.

There was the sound of shuffling, followed by an irritated "What the devil are you on about?"

Saffron grinned. "I hope you're in the mood for fowl tonight, Eliza, because I just realized I must eat a heaping serving of crow."

"If you don't start making sense immediately, I am ringing off."

She laughed. "Eliza—I am *eating crow.* I'm eating my words. I need you to look into Demian Petrov's file after all."

As Alexander did not fail to see the energizing effect of her newly formed plan, he asked what was on her mind the moment their feet touched the pavement outside Mr. Feyzi's office.

"I'm going to look around Demian Petrov's flat," Saffron declared.

Alexander stopped in his tracks. "Why?"

She waved an impatient hand. "Isn't it obvious? I've failed to come up with another way to prove your brother's innocence, and so I'm changing my tactic. My hypothesis about the chemicals he may have ingested has proven insufficient, so I must make a new one."

Alexander's brows lowered into a frown. "You plan to break into Petrov's flat and you're looking for what?"

"From what Lee said about the notes I took from the autopsy, it sounded as though it was not an acute poisoning, meaning it was something he'd been exposed to over time. Breaking into the Harpenden laboratory is an unlikely possibility, so I plan to look for anything that might have made him sick in his own home."

Though he shook his head in the slow, unbelieving way she was accustomed to, Saffron didn't miss the hint of a smile on his lips.

"Elizabeth can find his address in his immigration papers, I am hoping," she continued, "and as soon as I learn where he lived, I'll be able to find what may have been damaging his kidneys and liver. After I do that, I can tell Inspector Green that he may not have considered a chronic poisoning that couldn't be linked to Adrian." Alexander opened his mouth, no doubt to question her, and she raised a staying hand. "I plan on insisting very firmly that he take a look at other possibilities without revealing that I've been doing any sort of poking around."

"This is assuming we find anything in Petrov's home."

"We?"

His eyebrow quirked. "This is for Adrian's benefit. How could I let you go alone?"

She buried her pleasure at his words, giving him a severely doubtful look instead. "Considering the last time you helped me break in somewhere I was nearly caught and ruined a pair of stockings by hiding under a desk, I'm not sure I want your help."

To her surprise, he took a step closer, forcing her chin to tilt up to keep meeting his eyes. "Have no fear. I've been practicing my technique."

Her throat suddenly quite dry, she merely nodded.

They continued down the street, and when they'd boarded the bus to return to campus, Alexander asked, "What was your inspiration for this new plan of attack?"

Saffron's grip flexed on her handbag, in which sat the file of her father's papers. With a tight smile, she said, "I was merely reminded of how much can be hidden within someone's home. Important clues could be easily missed, if someone doesn't know what to look for."

Chapter 16

Elizabeth, her anger toward Saffron forgotten, found Demien Petrov's file after two days of searching the records room with Colin's help, she explained enthusiastically upon presenting Saffron with a piece of paper in her perfectly executed typewriting. She had gotten his last known address as well as quite a bit of other information, including a photograph of the man.

"Eliza!" Saffron gasped, taking the black-and-white photograph in her hand. "You can't just take this!"

"I'll return it on Monday," she said, rolling her eyes. "It's not like anyone will miss it. I thought you might like to know what he looked like." She sighed, inching forward on the couch they shared in the parlor to look at Petrov. "I can see the pain of his losses so clearly in his eyes."

Saffron had to agree. Adrian had described him as having a face like concrete, and he was rather lined and aged-looking in this photo, taken in 1919 when he'd immigrated, but there was softness in his shadowed gaze. Saffron felt for him having run from his homeland to start anew. He'd been sixty-one when he'd arrived in England, and nearly sixty-five when he'd died. He'd been married, but his wife had died young and he'd never remarried. He'd had no known children and no family in England. He'd lived a long life, but Saffron wasn't certain it had been a good one. It certainly hadn't ended well.

It put a pall on her mood the next morning when she met Alexander at the bus stop nearest her flat. Any sense of adventure from their planning had dissipated, leaving her unsure of their course of action. The prospect of looking through Petrov's things felt like an invasion of privacy after the reminder that he was no longer a living, breathing person. Looking at her father's papers had had a similar effect; she'd learned her father had been in communication with Dr. Calderbrook just before his deployment to France, rejecting the offer to join Kew. The letter had alluded to a private research project her father believed would soon bear fruit. Seeing her father's handwriting spike with telltale excitement had given her a strange, out-of-body feeling, as if she watched him write it. She could so clearly imagine him pushing his eyeglasses up on his forehead as he reread his words.

"Harpenden is rather far from Tottenham," Alexander said, recalling her to her task for the day. "I looked at the train timetables; it would have taken Petrov at least an hour to travel from there each day."

She'd looked at the map herself; Petrov had lived in Tottenham, north of London proper. Harpenden was also north of London, but the train and bus lines would have taken him through the city to get there. "I wonder why he would live so far away from the lab."

Eventually, the neighborhoods became less crowded, the buildings alternating between new and old the further from the Thames they went. They switched from bus to tram, and, at long last, they emerged onto a rather plain-looking street.

Saffron didn't know what to expect when they set out on the journey, but what she found was a busy neighborhood street opposite the train tracks. The day was overcast and promised rain, but that didn't stop women from hanging their laundry in the tiny yards, or a handful of young men standing around smoking as they chatted at the end of the street.

They passed one street, then another. Saffron resisted the urge to get out her map and examine it to assure herself they were headed in the right direction. Seeing her craning her neck a bit to see what street came next, Alexander caught up her arm and threaded it through his own. "You will draw the wrong sort of attention doing that," he muttered.

"I know," she said plaintively. "I just want to know we're not wandering around, missing it."

"It'll be just up here."

"Did you memorize the map?" That would be a very Alexander thing to do. He was so exasperatingly competent and assured, it was both extremely annoying and extremely attractive, neither of which was useful when she was anxious about their housebreaking.

"Yes," he said, "but I can also see what we're looking for."

Saffron followed his nod toward carts stationed at the end of the next street. As they grew near, she could make out the hum of conversation, laughter, arguing, and calls for customers.

The street sign affixed to the building announced Durban Street, the one Saffron had been searching for. The market seemed to spill out of the street, a colorful display of produce, clothing, books, and an assortment of housewares.

Women with their hair draped in colorful patterned scarves went from cart to cart. In the small gardens of the houses before which the market was set up, older men sat across chessboards with steaming cups of tea. Children shrieked as they ran, hopping over the short fences and rubbish bins and anything else in their way.

"I feel as if they've just picked up their Russian neighborhood and set it down in England," she said to Alexander after watching a boy no older than six insist on carrying an enormous bag of produce for his mother, or that was Saffron's guess, since their conversation had not been in English.

Alexander surveyed the street thoughtfully. "There's a lot of talk in the papers about the émigré population and their plans for the future. Some think this is temporary, that when things settle down and order is restored to Russia, they'll just go home. I've known a few people in similar situations who feel there's no point in learning to be English. Or they just don't want to."

"Your family?" Saffron asked.

"Some of them. A few have gone back to Greece, but most have stayed and plan not to leave again. Greece has had troubles of its own."

One thing that struck her, as Alexander was beckoned from her side by an old fruit vendor, was that the whitewash of the buildings was gray, the linens hanging from the line were gray. Alexander's shirt collar was brilliant by comparison. Yet the place was not drab; it was vivid with color and movement and *life*. It might not look particularly familiar—particularly English—but it was life all the same. It was full of pockets of jolly conversation and good-natured arguments between neighbors, the scents of cooking food, cigarette and pipe smoke, and spices.

Alexander returned to her side with a pair of oranges. He began peeling one and offered her a piece. She took it, rather surprised to be eating on the street, but it was delicious.

They took their time, matching the pace of other shoppers, taking in the shapes and colors of the produce, sacks of dried herbs and ground spices, the stacks of secondhand books in Russian and other eastern European languages.

The line of carts stopped abruptly in the middle of the street, and it became quieter, though life still puttered on. Children played and neighbors chatted over stout garden walls. Saffron and Alexander garnered some curious looks, but no one approached them.

They reached the house marked with Petrov's address. Saffron walked right up and knocked, hoping that her prepared story would work.

An old woman opened the door. She looked between Saffron and Alexander, wispy white eyebrows raising as she said, "*Da?*"

It hadn't occurred to her that they might need to be able to communicate with a person who didn't speak English. That was a foolish oversight. Saffron put on a sad smile and offered the woman the photograph of Petrov from Elizabeth's file. She said, "I come from Mr. Petrov's work. I wish to see his rooms to collect some of his equipment."

Alexander gave her a sidelong look as if uncertain about the bluntness of her plan.

The woman took the photograph and frowned down at it. She sighed heavily and returned the photograph to Saffron. She turned and began hobbling deeper into the house.

She had not shut the door in their faces, and that was a victory in Saffron's book. They followed her inside.

Demian Petrov's rooms consisted of a parlor and a bedroom. The kitchen and bathroom were shared by a handful of others, not uncommon for a boardinghouse. Streaks of dust marked the paths of hands over mismatched bookshelves stacked high with academic texts in English, Russian, Polish, and French. A teacup stained with brackish liquid sat on the single small table. Saffron leaned over it and caught a sickly sweet scent.

"I'll check the bedroom," Saffron said, and Alexander volunteered to look around the parlor.

The first thing she noticed in the bedroom was the only movement in the place: a rubbish bin with flies buzzing around it.

Dreading what she would find inside, Saffron peered into the bin, but it turned out to be only fruit peels and cores. That explained the vaguely fruity scent which accompanied the nameless scent a place took on after a person had lived there for a long time.

The rest of the simple bedroom consisted of an iron bed frame, the bed made rather messily with worn quilts, a bedside table, and a wardrobe.

The table at the bedside was a rickety thing with a drawer, in which sat a Bible, recognizable though the characters were Cyrillic. She thumbed through the pages until she came across a trio of photographs. One was an old-fashioned portrait of a somber woman, dated May 5th, 1884. Saffron guessed that if Elizabeth checked Petrov's file more carefully, she'd find Petrov was married on or near that date, for the woman held flowers.

The other two photographs were not photographs, she saw on closer inspection. One was a postcard from Russia depicting a city on the water. The other was a postcard of Brighton, the word typed neatly in the corner of a photograph of the famous pier. Neither had been posted or written on.

Saffron puzzled at the postcards, wondering what was so important about these two specific places.

"Saffron," Alexander called, "you'll want to see this."

She replaced the photographs and the Bible in the drawer and returned to the parlor.

Alexander had turned on the single lamp standing between two shelves. He stood next to the largest bookshelf, a solid piece with a cabinet at the bottom. It was open, and Alexander crouched to point out what was within.

She crouched next to him and peered inside. "A spirit lamp!"

Carefully, she reached inside the cabinet to lift out the small glass bottle. The tip of the wick was blackened, and it still carried a burnt smell. She loosened the cork surrounding the wick to get a whiff of what was inside and caught the heady scent of strong alcohol. She coughed lightly.

"Was he doing experiments here?" Alexander asked, looking deeper into the cabinet.

"Let's find out," Saffron replied. The interior of the cabinet was too dark to make much out. She offered him the spirit lamp. "Light this?"

He stood, going to another of the shelves with drawers and withdrew a pack of matches. She'd forgotten he didn't smoke, unlike Lee who was ever ready with a light.

With the spirit lamp lit, the contents of the cabinet were revealed. More laboratory equipment lay within.

Heart pounding, Saffron began carefully bringing each piece out. A weighted stand with an adjustable arm, somewhat rusty. A glass beaker, the neck of which would fit into the stand, tinted brown around the bottom, came out next. Finally, two glass jars containing dried leaves.

She carefully pried the lid of the first container off and took a hesitant sniff.

"He used it to make tea!" Saffron exclaimed, unexpectedly delighted.

"Bit elaborate," Alexander said, accepting the container to smell its contents. "It's not tea."

"No, but it is definitely herbal. And we know well the dangers of making tea from things we ought not to. What if these were what made him ill?" She held up the two jars.

"It is possible," he said cautiously. "But how could you prove it?"

"We figure out what's in the jars, of course. And I know just where to start."

CHAPTER 17

They returned to the market, where Saffron marched up to the first spice vendor she saw. Jar held up, she asked, "I would like to buy more of this herb."

The vendor squinted at her, making her already narrow eyes almost disappear into her layers of wrinkles.

Saffron repeated herself, and the woman waved her hand for the jar. She opened it, sniffed it, then shook her head. "Grigory." She pointed to another cart.

They thanked her and went to Grigory's cart. He was a thin, middle-aged man, his gaunt cheeks ruddy and his gray eyes sharp under a swath of black hair sticking out from beneath a worn cap. He'd seen the other vendor point to him and watched them approach.

"Good morning," Saffron said. She held up the jar. "I would like to buy more of that."

He beckoned for it and stared at its contents. He then looked her up and down in a rather offensive way. In heavily accented English, he said, "What you want it for?"

"For my own reasons," she replied. "Have you any?"

"Is for milk," he said, looking between her and Alexander now with the same sort of rude speculation. When Saffron merely looked at him blankly, he held his hands out in front of his chest with cupped hands. "Milk for baby."

"*Oh*," Saffron gasped, face flaming. Next to her, she thought she heard Alexander choke on a laugh. She shook her head vigorously. "Not for me. For my, er, grandfather."

"Oh," repeated the man, nodding. "Grandfather. He has pain?"

Saffron nodded, relieved. "Yes."

Grigory knelt behind his cart, sorting through crates. "Hands? Feet?"

"Er, both," Saffron said.

Grigory returned with a burlap sack. He waved for the jar, and Saffron shook her head. She had to return this jar to the flat for Inspector Green to find later. "I need a new jar."

Grigory grunted and stooped down again, returning with another jar. He scooped it into the sack, coming out with it brimming with dried flowers and leaves.

He sealed it, then handed it to her. She compared the two containers.

It was clear they held the same dried plant. The bits of faded magenta petals mixed with olive-green leaves and stems matched. "Thank you. What is it called?"

Grigory replied with a word in what she guessed was Russian, but she would have had no hope of repeating it, let alone writing it down. "Do you know the name in English?"

He screwed up his face in thought. "No."

"What about this one?" Alexander handed Grigory the next jar, and he frowned at it.

He shook it like the first vendor had, then opened the jar to sniff it. "Ah," he said, nodding, "*Oreshnik*. I have this."

"What does it do?" Saffron asked as he scooped dried leaves into a new jar.

"Help with pain," he said, patting his belly. "Mix with *medovyy*." He waved a hand to another vendor who had a number of amber-colored jars sitting on his cart.

The vendor's sign was written in Cyrillic, but from the bee drawn on the sign, Saffron could guess his ware. "Honey?"

"Yes, yes, honey," Grigory said with a grim sort of smile. "It for pain." He waved his hands.

That was the second time he'd mentioned pain in the hands. Perhaps Petrov had suffered from rheumatism, in addition to ailments of the kidney and liver. "Rheumatism?"

Grigory shrugged, but then brightened. He barked something at a young man with a minuscule cigarette between his thin lips loping down the center of the lane. He rolled his eyes and swaggered over. He answered Grigory in an insolent tone, and when Grigory nodded to Saffron and Alexander, he said flatly, "How I can help you?"

"We want to know what this herb is used for," Alexander explained.

"And what it's called in English," Saffron added.

The young man consulted Grigory for a moment before saying, "It is leaves from *Oreshnik* tree. We do not know the English name. You mix with honey and drink like tea. It helps with pain of the stomach, and pain in the hands or joints. It is for old people." He surveyed Saffron doubtfully.

Grigory added something in Russian, and the young man nodded, saying, "He says it is also good for thin blood."

"Thin blood?" Saffron repeated, perplexed.

"For anemia," Alexander said, accepting the jar from Grigory. "I see. Thank you."

Before the young man departed, Saffron pulled out the photograph of Petrov. "Did you sell herbs to this man?"

Grigory nodded slowly, looking from the photograph to Saffron with suspicion, but said nothing. The young man flicked away the butt of his cigarette.

Saffron paid Grigory for the herbs and the jars, and offered a further coin to the young man, who took it without compunction, and she and Alexander set off back to Petrov's flat. Saffron took samples from the jars before replacing them.

When they returned to the main road across from the train tracks, Alexander asked, "Off to the library?"

The library would possibly supply answers, but it might take weeks to find the correct plants to match the dried flower's characteristics or Grigory's descriptions. There was an alternative that would likely get her the answers they needed faster, and she really didn't like it.

"No," she sighed. "Off to see Dr. Aster."

A note was stuck in Saffron's office door when they returned. Color rose in her cheeks as her eyes flicked over the words.

"Good news?" Alexander asked mildly.

She shook her head, tucking the note into her coat pocket. "Just need to return a telephone call."

That enigmatic statement did nothing to abate his curiosity. She darted into her office to drop off her things, then returned with her notebook and a file. "Will you give me the second jar, the one with the *Oreshnik* leaves?"

He passed it to her. She held it up, squinting at the broken shapes of the leaves as she'd done several times during the journey back to the university. "If you'll wait in your office, I'll just nip up to Dr. Aster's and see if he can tell me anything."

"What are you going to tell him it's for?"

She shrugged. "I'll come up with something."

Uncertainty swirled in his mind as she vanished up the stairs. She was putting her position at risk again, taking Aster clues. Aster would be curious why she was looking into something so unrelated to her own work.

His thoughts stopped at the sight of a paper jammed into his own door. His right hand shook as he tugged it loose and opened it.

Adrian had been summoned to the police station again. Considering the last time he'd been summoned there his brother had nearly been arrested for attacking one of the bobbies for antagonizing him, Alexander needed to get there as soon as possible. Saffron's clues would have to wait.

Ferrand had never asked him for Saffron's office key back after Alexander had used it to raid her files for information about how to manage her cuttings and seedlings, so he used it to deposit the other jar on her desk before taking himself off to the police station.

Alexander's memories of the police station hadn't been fond before his brother had been brought there, and now the crowded, dim space was one of his least favorite places in the city. The disorganization alone would have been enough to make his skin crawl, but entering the station now, he wanted to burn the place down. Bobbies and officers eyed him when he walked in, doubtless both because he resembled his brother and because the last time he'd visited the station, he too had been on the belligerent side of irritated. He was not proud of it, but nor would he back down when he was Adrian's only defense. He hadn't even had time to contact the solicitors Mr. Feyzi had recommended.

Just as Alexander started toward the desk sergeant, a cool voice said, "Mr. Ashton."

Alexander turned to the man at his side with dread pooling in his stomach. "Inspector Green."

The older man raised a hand in the direction Alexander knew his office was in. "I'd like a moment of your time."

But rather than guiding Alexander to his office, Inspector Green took him to a small room with a pair of chairs on either side of a scuffed table. Alexander forced himself through the door and into the seat.

"Why am I being questioned?" Alexander asked the moment the door closed.

Inspector Green sat opposite him at the table. "We've had some new information regarding the Petrov case." He paused, giving Alexander the chance to ask what it was, but Alexander merely stared at him. He pulled his notebook from his pocket and flipped a few pages. "For the record, please state your name and address."

Alexander did so.

"Your brother is staying with you at your flat."

"Until you tell him he is free to leave London," Alexander said, wanting to emphasize that his brother was following Inspector Green's directive to stay in the city.

"I see."

The inspector's eyes rose to his, locking him in a stare that was neither eager nor bored. It was the look of a man with an extremely good hand of cards and the means to mask his anticipation of victory. It raised Alexander's hackles.

And with the coolness of a man setting an ace on the table, Inspector Green said, "Tell me about your brother's involvement in the royalist political movement during the war."

CHAPTER 18

Alexander was nowhere to be found when Saffron emerged from Dr. Aster's office, but she was too eager to delve into the volumes at the library to wait for him to turn up. She went to the library, pulled several of the more ancient-looking texts from the shelves of the botany and medical sections, and got to work.

Without mentioning the police case or any Russian street markets, she'd gotten one of the identifications from Dr. Aster in a startlingly short time. Saffron had utilized one of the oldest tricks in the academic textbook: competition.

In the years she'd been mentored by Dr. Maxwell, who was a friend as well as colleague to Dr. Aster, she'd watched their interactions with fascination. Dr. Maxwell was as warm and fuzzy as a blooming *Acalypha hispida* while Aster had all the charm of a rocklike *Argyroderma*. Their research was very different, but they both had a passion for taxonomy, and their enthusiasm always reached a fever pitch when there was a bet to be had. Before, Aster could be found in the company of her mentor nearly every day, but Saffron hadn't seen Aster speak to anyone but Mr. Ferrand for a long time. She knew how isolating it could be to be the odd man out in a close-knit department. She felt somewhat guilty for using that loneliness for her own purposes, but she needed help. Saffron had never risked asking Aster before, not even when she'd needed to know the name of a plant to help solve the poison bouquet murders, but she'd managed to find the right plant in the end. She didn't feel she had weeks to spare this time, however.

After fibbing that she'd received a letter from Maxwell containing the dried leaves, she'd admitted to Aster that she'd been unable to identify them. She wasn't asking for his help, she'd assured him, as she'd known the department head would abhor the notion of helping Saffron cheat. She *did* plan on sending a sample of the dried leaves for Maxwell to attempt to identify so that they might play their game through the post.

She didn't even ask Aster to take a look at the leaves. He'd demanded to see them and had even deigned to observe them through his own microscope. She'd hoped that Aster's expertise in leaf morphology would enable him to identify the leaves quickly, and she'd been right.

"*Corylus avellana*?" he'd muttered with disgust. "Not even a challenge, Maxwell."

Saffron had pretended not to hear.

And now, all that was left to do was learn what toxins might lurk in the leaves of the *Corylus avellana*, the common hazel tree, and determine if any of them caused liver or kidney problems. She also had to identify the other plant, for which she did not even have the Russian name, and determine if that plant could have killed Petrov.

In truth, she had a long way to go before her search of Petrov's flat would garner results, but that was the way of science. One planted many seeds in the hope that one would germinate, then one tended it carefully to see what fruit it might bear. Hopefully it wouldn't take as long as the life cycle of a plant.

Minutes turned to hours, and Saffron remained in the library until the librarians told her it was time to leave. She trudged up to her office, wondering why Alexander had not come to find her. He might not have expertise in botany, but he could read and examine botanical illustrations as well as anyone. But he had not come, and she couldn't help but be a little hurt.

Two of the century-old folk remedy tomes had indicated that common hazel reduced inflammation. Honey, it was known, also reduced inflammation as well as prevented wounds from going foul, which Saffron took to mean it was antimicrobial. Combining the two would likely work to calm pain in the joints, as Grigory had said. She could not confirm the suggestion that the mixture would help reduce anemia, its other use according to the vendor, nor had she determined what were the actual chemicals in the plant. She'd asked another favor of Romesh Datta, for Savita was not in his lab, and asked him to analyze all of the plants for their chemical composition. It was a start, and she could only hope they quickly revealed useful information. It was likely too much to ask that someone had poisoned one or both of Petrov's herb jars. Perhaps Grigory the vendor had some grievance with Petrov and had added something nasty to his purchase, or his landlady or another tenant had broken in . . .

She planned to go home, to allow Elizabeth's nattering about her daily complaints and victories to lull away the trials of the day, but as she patted her pockets for the key to her office, she found the folded note from earlier that day. Lee's message indicated he'd heard from his uncle about Alexander and Nick's military records. She'd forgotten in the rush to find something useful about the herbs.

Given the hour and Lee's propensity for going out with whatever attractive female was at hand, she doubted he would answer her telephone call, but she asked the operator to ring him up anyway. She perched on the stool in the telephone nook on the ground floor of the North Wing, listening to the dwindling echoes of footsteps drifting down from floors above.

"Yes?" came Lee's voice.

Saffron dropped the wire she'd been coiling around her finger. "Lee, it's Saffron."

"So I surmised. Who else would be calling from the U at this hour? What are you still doing there, anyway?"

She told him about Petrov's flat and the herbs, and to her surprise, he said, "Bring 'round a bit of the one you don't know. It'll be like old times, trying to figure out the identity of some nasty plant, won't it?"

She agreed, unsure if she wanted to revisit those old times. "Did you learn something from your uncle?"

"I did, indeed. Let me see . . . Yes, Corporal Alexander Theodoros Ashton. *Theodoros*, Everleigh." He chuckled. "Enlisted in 182nd Brigade out of Warwickshire—"

"Warwickshire?" Saffron repeated in disbelief.

"—belonging to the 61ˢᵗ Midlands. Saw action in Fromelles, injured 16 July 1916 and sent home to coalesce 3 August." Lee hummed, and she imagined him stroking his jaw. "Warwickshire. That's Birmingham, isn't it?"

"Near it, I think," she replied absently. "But . . . Alexander lives in London. He was born and raised in London, I thought. What was he doing enlisting close to Birmingham? That's hours away."

"Not sure. Shall I tell you about Major Nicholas Andrew Hale now?"

"Go on."

Lee rattled off details of Nick's service. Nick had joined a staff college well before the war to be trained as an officer, then had served in various places over the course of the war. He'd received a Distinguished Conduct Medal in 1915 for service in a place called Chunuk Bair, which Lee said he'd discovered was in the former Ottoman Empire.

Alexander had served briefly in France, and Nick in what was now Turkey. There was no overlap there.

"There was also," Lee said slowly, "something about Salonika."

Surprise had her staring blankly at the scuffed wall of the telephone vestibule. "That's in Greece, isn't it? Wasn't there a campaign fought there?"

"Yes, quite a long one, too. Not really in the city, of course, but that was the sort of headquarters for our side. Ashton went there in 1916. Might be a reference to his family, but my uncle mentioned it, so—"

"It might be in reference to his military service," Saffron finished, mind racing. "Could Nick also have been in Greece?"

"Not a clue, old thing. 'Fraid you'll have to ask Ashton about it," Lee said. "The younger one. How go things with the elder Ashton?"

"I don't know. Thank you, Lee."

Saffron rang off and stared at the receiver, still swinging from its handle with the force of her hanging up.

Alexander had lied to her. She'd asked him about his service in the military. She'd thought he'd been honest—open, even—about his injury and his service. She'd cherished that conversation, carried out in the early hours of the morning after a shared adventure when the mysterious man she'd dragged along had offered her the story of his scars. She'd been touched that he'd shared something so personal with her.

Had it all been a lie?

She stood and slipped from the telephone nook. She was going to find out.

The knocking on the door was polite for the first two or three times, but soon became an impatient pounding that would no doubt disturb his neighbors if Alexander didn't answer it soon.

He swung the door open, half hoping it was Adrian. It wasn't.

Usually, the sight of Saffron at his door inspired enthusiasm, even excitement. But after the afternoon he'd had, and the evening he'd made for himself, he'd rather it be Adrian, sloshing over with drink.

Her color was high and her mouth held tightly. "I would like to speak with you."

He stepped back. "Come in."

He led her to the parlor. She stepped inside and blinked, looking from wall to wall, then she turned and gave him a swift, scrutinizing look. "What happened?"

He wasn't sure what about the parlor he'd spent the last hour cleaning indicated anything had happened, but he told her the truth anyway. "Inspector Green is questioning Adrian again."

Her irritation fell away. "But why?"

"Inspector Green learned some new information," he said heavily.

"About Petrov?"

"About Adrian." He turned away, running a hand through his hair. He'd relived every detail of his brother's life with Inspector Green that afternoon, every stupid choice his brother had made. He'd laid everything out. Nothing else had anything to do with Petrov, or Russia, or Greece, but he didn't want to be taken off guard by a "discovery" again.

Behind him, Saffron asked, "What was it?"

"Adrian . . ." He let out an impatient breath, resigning himself to an explanation he'd prefer never to give. "Our cousins were born and raised in Kyllini, as I said, and many of our aunts and uncles and distant family members lived there until the Great War. My family supported King Constantine, regardless of his perceived allegiance to Germany, and my cousins did so very vocally. Many of them left Greece when Constantine was removed from the throne during the war. They were not happy that the prime minister, Venizelos, circumvented him to join Greece with the Allies.

"A few of my cousins came here and riled up the Greek community in London. They protested, called on members of Parliament to try to get their support for the king." He shook his head, his frustration just as acute as it had been when he'd learned what had happened. His father had written to him at the convalescent home he'd been living in at the time, explaining what Adrian had done. "It was stupid. Some of the younger ones went too far and were arrested, including Adrian. He was on leave and they swept him up in their nonsense."

"He was arrested for protesting?"

"He was arrested for participating in a protest that turned violent," he said grimly.

"Inspector Green knows he has been arrested before," Saffron said. "It would have been in his record."

"For protesting."

Her brows lifted. "And something else?"

His shoulders slumped. "A number of small, harmless offenses."

"Such as?"

Through gritted teeth, he said, "Things related to his drinking."

She dropped her chin to her chest, sighing. "I don't understand why you bothered to ask me to help at all, if I have to pry every bit of information out of you! What's the point?"

"I asked you to help Inspector Green solve the case," he said, "not investigate my brother."

"Your brother's past matters here, Alexander. You're implying Inspector Green suspects Adrian because of his prior involvement in the"—she waved a hand— "whatever that was with your cousins. Supporting the king of Greece. What does that have to do with anything?"

It was nearly too convoluted for Alexander to explain. "King Constantine and the tsar were first cousins."

"The tsar, who was ousted during the Russian Revolution, was friendly with King Constantine," Saffron said slowly, clearly trying to make sense of how that related to Adrian and Petrov. "And your family supported the king. Inspector Green thinks that because Adrian supported the king, he might in turn support what remains of the tsarist Russians? Or he believes that Adrian aligns himself with the Germans since they were on opposing sides?"

"It's ridiculous," Alexander ground out, repeating what he'd spent the afternoon explaining to the inspector. The powers and politics of the world had shifted so often in the last five years, it seemed impossible that the police could believe that Adrian, of all people, would risk murder for an allegiance that might change any day.

"I suppose it is ridiculous."

Silence fell between them, taut and grating. Nothing came to mind to say.

"I'll be going."

Alexander swallowed, realizing how rude he'd been to not even offer her a seat. "I'm sorry—"

"Don't be." Her voice had a practiced evenness to it that he didn't like. "I'll leave you to your thoughts."

"I don't want you to leave," he said, surprised that a large part of him meant it.

"I don't much see the point in staying here." Her voice inched higher as she looked to the hallway. "I don't know why you bothered to ask me to help Adrian. It's clear you'd rather not tell me a thing other than what I can find out myself, about him or you."

"I'd rather not lay all my brother's failings at your feet," Alexander said before he could think better of it. "I'd rather you not see the worst of him, the worst of my family."

She swung around to glare at him. "I don't care if you have a hundred cousins who've been arrested, Alexander! That doesn't have any bearing on you." Her blue eyes searched his face. "What I care about is that you are so reluctant to tell me anything about yourself. You've told me nothing about your family, your life before the war, and even the things you told me about the war aren't true!"

Dumbstruck by the accusation, he scrambled for words. "*Everything* I've told you is true."

"You told me you were hurt at Fromelles, but not how, or when, or where you convalesced, or for how long!" Alexander opened his mouth, prepared to tell her anything she wanted to hear despite his annoyance at her sudden need to know irrelevant details just then, but then she said, "You didn't tell me anything about going to Salonika during the war."

A strange blankness suffused his brain, like the aftereffects of an illuminating grenade's detonation. The first coherent thought he had was to wonder how she could have possibly known about his visit to Greece. Nick wouldn't have told her, so she'd found that information somewhere else.

That only stunned him more. How had she found out? And why had she gone digging into his past?

Anger and fear swirled together into a heady mixture that had words rushing from his mouth. "I don't talk about my war because it was bloody and miserable and ended in a goddamn explosion that ought to have killed me just before my entire company was slaughtered. I don't tell people about my family's origins because they've no right to judge who my mother is or where she came from. I'm not the one under investigation. I am not a mystery to solve." His breath was sharp in his lungs, and it strained his tight throat to breathe. He'd thought they were on the right path, but now he realized that she'd simply been looking for information, more pieces of the puzzle of his and Adrian's involvement in Petrov's murder.

At his side, his fingers were tingling. It was cold. He'd been whipped into such a fury he hadn't remembered to turn the radiator on when he'd returned to the flat. He glared down at his hand before burying it in his pocket.

"I know you're not a mystery to solve," Saffron said quietly. "I just thought . . . I just want to understand. Why your brother is under suspicion. How you know Nick. Why you're keeping so much from me."

Alexander's whole body flushed with heat before a wave of cold overtook him. "I don't know Nick."

"You do," Saffron said flatly. "I saw you two arguing the other day at the U."

"So you are spying on me."

Saffron's head snapped back, eyes wide and angry. "I am not *spying* on you! I am simply trying to—"

"I am trying to keep my word," Alexander interrupted. "There are things you cannot know, Saffron. You must accept that."

He hadn't meant to sound so desperate. But he hoped that her wide-eyed look of surprise meant he'd gotten his point across.

"Very well," Saffron whispered and turned away.

He didn't follow her out of the flat, but he did wait until she was well away before ruining the order he'd been so careful to create.

CHAPTER 19

There were voices within her flat when she arrived, Elizabeth's alto responding to two male voices. Saffron could have hidden in her room after greeting her and Colin, ignoring whatever good time her flatmate had planned for her beau, but it would be rude to abandon two guests.

Saffron sighed and pushed the door to the flat open.

The irresistible scents of tea and fresh ginger biscuits drifted down the hall to her. If she was required to be social after arguing with the inscrutable Alexander, at least she would enjoy the refreshments.

She hung up her coat and hat, and paused when she recognized the coat and hat just next to hers. Lee.

As she approached the parlor, his voice could be heard, and immediately cut off when she stepped into the room.

"Everleigh!" he called jovially from an armchair. He rose, as did Colin and Elizabeth, and greetings were exchanged.

"I was worried I'd miss you," Lee said, resettling into his seat.

Saffron accepted tea and biscuits from Elizabeth. "Just staying late at work. Lots to make up for after the conference."

Elizabeth launched into her own complaints about all the filing that had awaited her after her own brief absence from the lord's office. Lee shot her a sly smile when Colin began his own account of the last time he took leave from his work.

"Ah, but the pot's gone cold," he said with exaggerated sadness when he reached for more tea.

Elizabeth glared at him. "It has not."

"I'll tend to it," Saffron volunteered. The two men rose as she did, and Lee followed her out, saying over his shoulder, "I'll help."

"You're about as adept in the kitchen as I am," Saffron grumbled. "It'll be a shock if we don't burn the whole place down."

Lee chortled and planted himself at the kitchen table. He looked around the kitchen with curiosity. He'd visited the flat a number of times during their work on the study, but Saffron couldn't recall him ever being in their kitchen before. She glanced around the room herself, wondering what he observed.

The stove was old but spotless, as was everything else in the room. Elizabeth refused to let dirt, crumbs, or a hint of mold within their home. The kitchen was her sanctuary, and so it was scrubbed daily. Bits of Elizabeth were visible in every corner, from the particular brand of wine she kept on the counter to the new painting she'd bought in Paris from a street vendor. It was a market scene with warm colors that matched the autumn season during which they'd visited.

"Not that I'm not pleased to see you," Saffron told Lee as she lit the stove, "but why are you here?"

"I'd say it was merely because I wanted to drop in on Elizabeth and irritate her, though I did that expertly anyway. She was clearly planning on a quiet night in with her beau." He wiggled his eyebrows. "Though the choice of this fellow is quite . . . unexpected. He's as dull as toast. Why is she stepping out with him?"

"'There are only so many penniless poets one can stomach before one realizes they are more often after a hearty meal rather than one's heart,'" Saffron recited, leaving off the dramatic phrasing Elizabeth had used when Saffron had asked her the very same thing. "And Colin is nice." That was the highest praise she could give him, unfortunately.

"He doesn't seem the sort to take a shine to naughty poetry, eh?" He took on a serious air and straightened his cuffs unnecessarily. "I had a thought about Ashton and his little Greek adventure."

Saffron paused in her preparation of the teapot. With a heavy sigh, she said, "I think it's best if we leave that in the past."

Lee leaned forward to peer out the small window at the black night beyond. "I believe that was a piece of the sky that just fell."

"Do shut up, Lee."

"Leave it in the past? Do you know the favors I promised Uncle Matt to get that information?"

"Oh, woe is you. You likely have to attend one of his hunting weekends at his manor. How very dreadful."

Lee grimaced at her sarcastic platitudes. "I am required to go up for the entirety of the Christmas holiday. I'll miss the bloody Chelsea Ball!"

Of course, Lee had planned to attend the notorious New Year's party. "However will you survive?" she said dryly.

"I'll not be wasting my favor," he said with a stubborn moue. "I believe I know what Ashton was doing in that ridiculously hard-to-pronounce place in Greece with Nick."

"Any Greek city would be nothing to the mouthfuls of syllables that you regularly pronounce in your work," a tart voice said.

Saffron and Lee turned as one to the kitchen door, where Elizabeth stood with hands on hips. "What on earth are you talking about? And where is the tea?"

"I've dug up information about your brother and Ashton that might explain how they know one another," Lee said.

"They know each other from the army," Elizabeth said dismissively, nudging Saffron away from the stove.

"Yes, but they served on opposite fronts. Your brother was an officer fighting the Ottomans, and Ashton was in France. My uncle said Ashton went to Greece during the war, and it was in his military service record, so I doubt it was for a friendly family visit." He pointed to Saffron. "Did you ask him why he enlisted in Warwickshire?"

"No." Saffron suppressed a groan at Elizabeth's arched-brow look. "Drop it, Lee. I don't want to know anything more."

"Why the devil not?"

"Because he does not wish me to know," Saffron said. "And he . . . he is not some puzzle I must assemble."

Lee and Elizabeth turned on her with appallingly similar narrowed eyes. They glanced at each other, and Elizabeth said, "An argument."

"Tonight, I'd wager," Lee said. Elizabeth hummed in agreement and crunched into a ginger biscuit.

"Pardon me!" Saffron waved a hand. "I am not suddenly gone from the room, you know."

"Well, sounds like Ashton doesn't want you poking around in his secrets after all," Lee said. "I do wonder why. Perhaps it is because he doesn't want you to know he was on a *diplomatic* mission to Greece."

Saffron's mouth fell open, but she quickly caught herself. "I do not want to hear about it."

Lee tutted. "Whatever Ashton said is all smoke, Everleigh. He's trying to cover it up."

Elizabeth nodded avidly, the teapot abandoned. "Of course he is! And it makes so much sense, too, that Nick knows Alexander if they were both in Greece together during the war. Nick is not just a drone for the Agricultural Ministry. He's very obviously a spy of some sort."

Saffron rounded on her. "*What?*"

Elizabeth wiped ginger biscuit crumbs from her fingers into the sink. "Of course, darling. Why else would my brother just happen to be in town the moment one of his supposed employees—a Russian, no less—drops dead suddenly and suspiciously? Colin quite agrees with me."

"A spy, eh?" Lee stroked his jaw. "His records were rather sparse, according to my uncle. That'd explain it."

"Have you all been eating nightshade berries?" Saffron looked between her friends, incredulity raising her voice. "You cannot actually believe that Nick is a spy and Alexander knows him from some—some mission during the war! What would that make Alexander?"

"My guess is that his role was dreadfully boring," Elizabeth said. "For all his mystery, he's chosen to study bacteria, which is the dullest thing I've ever heard of."

Saffron propped her hands on her hips. "And yet you believe your brother, who is tasked with manure analysis and tracking down grain fungi, is a spy."

"So you *do* think Alexander is also wrapped up in government conspiracy," Elizabeth said sweetly.

Perhaps Saffron was the one who'd consumed hallucinogenic berries, for she was clearly the only person in the room with a sliver of rationality. "No, I do not. I think you are both in desperate need of excitement in your own lives and should stop inventing trouble where there is none. I'm up to my ears in dramatics already. I do not need any more!"

Rather than allow herself to dwell on whether or not Alexander wanted her to continue helping with Adrian's case, the next morning Saffron spent a bit of time in front of a microscope with the mystery plant from Petrov's stock of dried herbs. While she was able to identify several salient features, she hadn't been able to place it on the taxonomical lines with certainty. She could guess that it belonged to the group known as *Sympetaly*, but past that, she could not be sure. The rest would be a mystery until she returned to the library or gained the courage to approach Dr. Aster again.

She decided this was worth calling in that favor from Spalding and gave him a sample. He raised a brow at the request but agreed. Saffron didn't trust that her mystery plant would be a priority for him, however, so to the library she went.

She forced her steps to click but not clatter across the polished wood floor of the Flaxman Gallery and had just reached the steps to the library's double glass doors when she caught sight of Nick walking down the hall adjoining the North Wing to the Wilkins Building. He wore a dark brown suit beneath his overcoat and still had his hat on.

"Saffron," he called brightly. He strode to where she stood on the steps. "How do you do?"

"Quite well, but I'm afraid I'm rather in a hurry."

"I must speak with you," he said, his smile fading.

Cold sliced through her. "Is it Elizabeth? What's the matter?"

He shook his head. "Nothing to do with her, I assure you. Could we pop over to your office?"

"I can't at the moment, Nick, I've got something urgent—"

He took her by the arm in a movement too quick for her to process, and suddenly her back was pressed against the wall in one of the small alcoves next to the library's entrance.

His face was inches away and his voice little more than a rough whisper. "I've got something far more urgent, I assure you."

Saffron blinked at him. Was this . . . a seduction? An attempt at intimidation? She wanted to roll her eyes. "Nick, I do not have time—"

"There's been another murder."

Saffron stared at him. From this distance, she could count the faint freckles on his nose. She fought off chills at the intensity of his gaze. It was not friendly or pleasant but direct and utterly serious.

"The laboratory in Harpenden," he said. "You remember I mentioned the old man who died abruptly." Saffron nodded. "One of his colleagues has gone missing. I'm sure he's dead too."

She swallowed. "W-why is that?"

"Because he's been missing for three days, and the boy who delivers the milk just reported a smell coming from his house."

"Dear God."

Nick nodded grimly. "I want your help."

"But why?"

Something of his humor returned to his face, softening the lines a bit. "You've been involved in several murders, Saffron."

Elizabeth probably told her brother everything about her murder investigations while they were at Lou's.

"And," he continued, raising a questioning brow, "our mutual friend Alexander Ashton has an unfortunate connection to the death of Demien Petrov, doesn't he? I imagine you were asked to intercede on Adrian Ashton's behalf."

Saffron swallowed, shaking her head. "I don't know where you got that impression, but—"

"Otherwise, I very much wonder why you and Alexander were seen on the dead man's street earlier this week. Coming out of his flat, even."

"No one prevented us from seeing his flat—"

"I'm not suggesting you did anything wrong," Nick said in an unhurried fashion. "But I am suggesting you know far more about Demian Petrov than anyone suspects. I imagine you've already gotten halfway to solving his death. Work with me to finish it, and learn what happened to the missing man."

Saffron found she had no idea what to say. Nick was asking for her help in investigating the death, possibly deaths, of government laboratory workers. Surely these were matters for the police, not the Agricultural Ministry. "Was . . . is the other man, the missing one, also Russian?"

"No, English as the Union flag," Nick replied.

If the other man was dead and the two cases were related, Adrian would likely be exonerated. The other man had been missing three days, and Adrian hadn't left London in over two weeks, according to Alexander. If she helped prove that the other man's disappearance had nothing to do with Adrian, it would likely go a long way in proving his innocence in Petrov's death. And if Nick endorsed her involvement as an agent of a government ministry, then Inspector Green could not fault her for her involvement. Nor could Alexander.

"What exactly is the lab researching?" she asked. "You've mentioned fungi."

"They do study fungi, as well as a number of agricultural topics," he said.

"Anything worth killing over?"

Nick gave her a long, evaluative look. Without breaking eye contact, he leaned so close his breath brushed her cheek. "Are food supplies of the entire country worth killing for? Learning how to combat disease? Or possibly . . . spread it?"

Saffron couldn't see the movement of the students filing up and down the stairs to the library just before them. All she saw were fields, fallow fields just like the ones she'd seen in France. Decimated. Unable to produce anything but grief and panic. She swallowed hard.

"Is it worth killing for, to keep enemies from learning what the greatest minds in our nation—and others—are developing?"

She didn't need to put herself in the place of the sort of people who gave those orders or carried them out to imagine the answer. The Harpenden lab might not be mixing chemicals to attack men in trenches, but they were creating things that could prevent starvation—or cause it. Not to mention Saffron already had a connection to Petrov's lab that, now she'd been presented an opportunity to examine it, was far too tempting.

"Yes," she said aloud, confirming it to herself just as much as Nick. "I will help you. What do I need to do?"

CHAPTER 20

Nick was a good sport about her endless questions on the half-hour train ride to Harpenden. By the time they reached the correct stop, she'd learned that the lab was a compact operation with a chief and assistant of mycology, entomology, horticulture, and botany, as well as a small staff for administrative and maintenance purposes. Petrov had been the chief of Horticulture. The man who was missing, Jeffery Wells, had been his assistant. Nick also told her that there was a sister lab, housed on an estate not five miles away, which also specialized in studies related to agriculture.

He continued to look at her with delighted surprise with every question she asked. Now he'd shown her the other side of himself, the intense, serious side, Saffron imagined this overly friendly demeanor was nothing more than a mask. "You needn't pretend everything out of my mouth is brilliant, you know," she told him. "I understand what's going on."

"What's going on?" he repeated with an innocent blink.

"I've agreed to help you. You needn't feign interest in me," she said. "Elizabeth thinks you're some sort of spy, you know."

"Does she?" he asked mildly.

"You are clearly not just an employee of the Agricultural Ministry. I'm not convinced you're dealing in international sabotage, but I'm also not convinced your usual duties give you much chance to investigate the deaths of employees."

"You'd be surprised," he said, and she couldn't tell if the humor in his voice was false.

They left the train and emerged onto the platform, a simple concrete slab before a tiny station house that reminded Saffron of the out-of-the-way places she'd visited with Lee. The weather was a far cry from the sticky warmth of summer, however. The day was cool and the sun kept hiding behind clouds, leaving her shivering.

On the map, Harpenden seemed inconsequential, merely an agrarian town some thirty miles from London. But a hotel and three different public houses greeted her upon exiting the station. The lively main road was lined with businesses, and down the road to either side she could see houses.

"This way," Nick said, offering her his elbow.

They began to the east, passing pedestrians, red brick houses and shops, tall trees and hedges whose autumnal colors had begun to bleed away to brown. They came to a long stretch of road that was bordered by thick trees. Saffron tried to peer through them.

"Does this belong to Rothamsted?" she asked, referring to the other laboratory in the area.

"No, Rothamsted is the other direction," Nick replied. "Quite a lot of land, they have. Far more than the Plant Pathology Lab."

"Jodrell Lab at Kew Gardens became the Plant Pathology Lab when it was moved from Kew to Harpenden," Saffron said. Nick had told her as much on the train, and she hadn't mentioned she was already familiar with the Jodrell Lab. "Where did Rothamsted come from?"

"Some wealthy man decided to make his scientific hobby into something more. He already owned the house, and rather than let the old place molder, he invited other scientists to work there. Did well enough for a few decades, but by the turn of the century, it was on its way out. They brought in a new director and he turned things around. Made it over, expanded their program of study, gave some new people a chance." He slanted Saffron a look. "Their head of Botany is a woman, you know, Dr. Winifred Brenchley."

Saffron swallowed an excited gasp. "She graduated from University College. She studied alongside my father. I've read so many of her papers—"

"And now she runs the Rothamsted botany lab," Nick said. "Ever thought about leaving the university to do something like that?"

"I . . . No, I've never considered it." Her plans had always been to stay at the university, the place her father had loved so much, and perhaps eventually teach as her father had.

"You may want to," he said lightly. "From what I hear, the university hasn't exactly been welcoming. Not all places are like that."

It had been hard, without a doubt, to find her place at the U. Even now, years after arriving and months into being a proper researcher, she felt out of place more often than not. What would it be like to work in a place like Rothamsted, being led by a woman?

Next to her, Nick gave her a conspiratorial grin. "You're what, twenty-three? I hope you don't believe that just because you started at UCL means you must stay there."

"You were already entrenched in the military at twenty-three," Saffron said, not wishing to think too hard about her current circumstances, then wrinkled her nose at her poor choice of words. "And you've stayed within the government all this time."

He shrugged. "Alexander was twenty-three when he was injured at Fromelles. I'm sure he's told you a little about how that changed his plans for his life." His lips tilted into a smile as if he knew how frustrating it was for him to casually indicate he had such deep knowledge of Alexander's life. "And you can't tell me you believe Elizabeth will be a receptionist forever. Twenty-three is too young to decide who one will be for the rest of one's life."

They subsided into silence, eased only by their footsteps on the brick path along the road and the occasional whisk and whirl of a passing bicyclist.

When another street came into view, Nick directed them south. The curving brick wall lining the road was partially obscured by vines both brown and green. Nick's demeanor seemed to focus; his spine straightened and his pace increased fractionally. Saffron recalled their purpose, and her growing sense of dread made the crisp air sharper in her lungs.

They passed two neighborhoods on opposing sides of the street, then, at last, reached Poets Court.

A collection of homes dotted a clearing in the trees with little poetic about them. The plain red brick and whitewashed houses, the gardens already slumbering for the winter, were rather bleak beneath a watery white sky.

Nick approached the house directly ahead, skirting the circular drive and stepping up to the door. Saffron darted a look around, but the court was empty. She wasn't sure why, but she'd expected something of an uproar. But perhaps the neighbors in Harpenden were not so nosy as in London.

They slipped inside the house and Saffron immediately stepped back out. Her unconscious retreat was irresistible in the face of such an unholy reek.

"This was what I was afraid of," Nick muttered. He delved into his jacket pocket and retrieved a small bottle of something. "Give me your handkerchief."

Saffron did, one hand clamped over her nose. Nick tipped the bottle onto her handkerchief and handed it back. "Keep that to your nose."

It was scent, spicy and blissfully strong enough to prevent the worst of the stink from invading her nostrils. Nick waved her inside.

The open front door cut a swath in the gloom. After a moment to allow her eyes to adjust, Saffron followed Nick down the hall to the back of the house. The kitchen was silent, cold, and messy. Discarded dishes and cups cluttered the counter and sink.

Nick surveyed the room, then checked the back door. It was locked. He turned and nodded back the way they'd come. "Up the stairs."

Saffron reflected that she really did not want to go up the stairs. But she'd agreed to help both Nick and Adrian. This was a part of that promise.

At the top of the stairs, there was just one room, and the door was ajar.

Saffron attempted to take a deep breath to steady herself, but the smell was worse up there and she gagged, barely catching herself from vomiting on the landing. Nick turned to her in question.

"It's just the smell," she forced out.

"I'll open a window," he muttered and went into the room.

When she heard the slide of a window opening, she followed.

The bedroom was plain, with a battered wardrobe in one corner and an old-fashioned writing desk next to it below the open window. The curtains were parted and the window open, letting in a brisk breeze and just enough light to see the rest of the room. Saffron slowly turned toward the bed, next to which Nick stood.

His somber face said it all, looking down at the man in the bed. "It's as I feared. Jeffery Wells is dead."

Jeffery Wells lay in his bed, pale eyes open and bloodshot. His ginger hair was a mess around his head, and his middle-aged face was gray and contorted as if he was, even in death, experiencing pain.

The scent of death and illness overpowered her. A rush of dizziness overtook her and she swayed, catching herself against the bed frame.

"Don't touch anything," Nick said sharply. "Even with gloves."

Saffron stepped back, clutching her hand to her chest like it'd been burned. Her thoughts caught up to the situation. "Where are the police?"

"They haven't been informed yet," Nick said. "Are you able to come closer?"

Saffron swallowed down her revulsion and took a small step forward, then another. She'd been in a room with a dead body before. The brief glimpse of that woman haunted her dreams. She had no doubt Jeffery Wells would show up, as well.

She kept her eyes firmly off the stains in the bedclothes that were no doubt causing the wretched smell. An old-fashioned wash basin on the bedside table answered for the rest of it. It was full of old sick.

Saffron moved as far from it as possible, coming to stand next to Nick.

"Look here," Nick said, carefully pointing to Wells's hand.

Wells had cupped his hand to his chest just as Saffron had moments before. A horrific gash, crusted and black, seemed to peel away from his flesh in layers

"Dear God," she whispered, daring to inch closer to lean over Wells. "What on earth happened to him?"

"I'm guessing it's the same thing that got Petrov," Nick replied. "Petrov was also sick on the train."

Adrian hadn't mentioned that, but most people wouldn't discuss the unsavory things the human body did while in distress.

"Petrov didn't have any injuries like this," Saffron said.

Nick turned to look at her in surprise. "How do you know that?"

She had little emotional capacity left for embarrassment or guilt, and she doubted Nick would object to her snooping, considering he'd invited her along for this. "I looked at the coroner's report in Detective Inspector Green's office. It said he died from kidney failure, and possibly liver failure as well. I don't suppose we'll know what killed Mr. Wells until his own autopsy, but Petrov did not have a black gash on him anywhere. It would have been noted." She turned away from Wells. "I don't believe Petrov was poisoned all at once, if at all. I think it would have been a chronic poisoning, like spouses do to each other. They add a bit of arsenic to the sugar basin, and let their spouses drop poison into their tea each day until it finally kills them."

"You are unexpectedly macabre, Saffron Everleigh," Nick said with a hint of teasing.

"I am a scientist who looks at the evidence, Nicholas Hale. It's not my fault the evidence is so ghastly."

Saffron left Nick to examine the body more thoroughly, promising to inform her of any further grisly details. She went to search Wells's things.

She hadn't expected, necessarily, to find the same herbs as Petrov had in his flat, but it would have been convenient. As it was, Wells had only the usual headache powders and digestive tonics in his medicine cabinet.

Nick found her in the kitchen, looking through piles of receipts Wells had shoved into a drawer. She'd learned nothing from them other than Wells had bought a pack of cigarettes every few days and frequented the Dancing Sparrow, one of the pubs in Harpenden's main square.

"I saw nothing else worth noting on his body," Nick said. "He's been dead longer than a day, but less than three."

"How do you know that?"

"His body is cold but no longer stiff." At Saffron's baffled look, he added, "Rigor mortis lasts about twelve hours. He's no longer stiff but has not begun to bloat yet. The grate in his hearth was also cold, meaning the house has been cold for some time. Cold slows decomposition, if you'll recall. Not to mention there are no longer signs of blood pooling in the low points of his body. I am estimating he's been dead much longer than twelve hours but no more than seventy-two."

"How will you ensure the police won't notice he's been moved?" she asked. She'd kept her gloves on, as had Nick. But that didn't mean the police wouldn't notice if Wells had been rolled over for Nick to examine his back or legs.

"I have arrangements in place, don't worry," Nick said.

"That is not very assuring."

"Be assured," he said with a small smile, "that I have leave to be here."

"Wonderful," she muttered, setting the receipts back in the drawer. "What now?"

"Now, you return to London. I have some business here in Harpenden."

The truth was that she didn't want to be in this house any longer. She'd managed to soldier through seeing the body, but her own didn't feel right.

Nick walked her back to the train station and saw her to her train. Saffron sank into her seat, ignoring the squabbling children in the next row over. She ought to feel some relief. Nick had confirmed it had been in the last seventy-two hours that Jeffery Wells had died.

Adrian couldn't be responsible unless he'd snuck away. That was possible, but she did not believe him a murderer. She held on to that belief on the journey back to London. It didn't prevent her from reliving all she'd seen of Jeffery Wells's terrible end, however.

Saffron emerged from St. Pancras Station in a daze. The train had felt like some sort of purgatory, where she was neither a part of the world nor separate from it. She'd been unable to think of anything but Wells and Petrov, Adrian and Alexander. The idea of sitting in her quiet office or returning to her flat with nothing but silence to accompany her was unthinkable. She couldn't go to the police station, though her conscience screamed for her to do so and tell Inspector Green everything. Nick hadn't required her to promise not to reveal matters to anyone, but as he helped her onto the train he said something about appreciating her discretion and that her cooperation had made a difference. She had no desire to betray his trust, even if she wished he hadn't given it to her in the first place.

She passed through the gate into the Quad, hardly realizing she'd made it back to campus. Her eyes lifted to the columns of the Wilkins Building. The library. It was safe there.

It was quiet in the gallery and the stacks of the library. It was as if the sun's disappearance behind the city's buildings had reduced the volume of the city itself. The rows of shelves stood like silent soldiers, steady and assuring.

Saffron sank into one of the worn wooden chairs without thinking. As she sat, she realized her legs were shaking. Distantly, she found her whole body was shaking. She was cold.

Cold like Wells.

She was glad she was nearly alone in the library. There would be fewer people to see her lose her tenuous hold on her self-control.

She closed her eyes and breathed deeply. The scent of books and dust was nothing like the stink of death and decay. It did not stop the erratic pounding of her heart, but pressing her hands to her forehead helped the world from spinning quite so fast.

But the longer she sat there, the faster the images of the dead man flashed in her mind. The more detailed they became, from the yellowed whites of his eyes to the blackened flesh peeling away from his wound.

Saliva pooled in her mouth, the sure warning of impending vomit. She swallowed convulsively, her eyes flying open in panic. She couldn't vomit in the library.

A man stood over her.

She let out a shriek, shoving her chair back with a matching screech. She didn't realize it was Alexander until he knelt before her, shushing her gently.

She stared at him for a moment, the concern written into the lines of his face. Heedless of the place and the potential for an audience, she dove into his arms and pressed her face into his collar.

Warm skin scented with shaving lotion and starch. Warm arms, wrapped around her without question. Warm breath at the nape of her neck as he bent to embrace her fully. She closed her eyes and allowed Alexander to overpower her senses with no other thought than gratitude for his presence.

After a long moment, he pulled away. Arms still around her waist, his dark gaze searched hers. "What's the matter?"

"I saw a dead man," she whispered.

His hands twitched on her waist. "What happened?"

She told him. When she got to the part about Nick mentioning he had leave to examine the body, he stood and took a few paces away. She hadn't realized he'd been kneeling in front of her the entire explanation and looked about sheepishly. She saw no one, to her relief.

"He took you into a house where a man had died?" Alexander asked. His voice was quiet, but his tone was sharp.

"I agreed to go," Saffron said. "I wasn't expecting . . . what I saw, but Nick made it clear he suspected the worst."

His nostrils flared on a heavy exhale. He shook his head, then his eyes caught on something on the opposite side of the library. "The faculty meeting. I came to look for you. It started ten minutes ago."

Saffron turned to the clock on the other end of the room and bolted to her feet. "Blast!" It *was* Friday, and that was why the library was deserted. The students were off enjoying their weekends, and the staff belonging to the sciences were at the meeting. She followed him out of the library, out of the gallery, and down a hall. Why had she fallen apart just when she needed most to be put together?

CHAPTER 21

Their steps were quick as they made their way to the hall where faculty meetings were held. The long room was filled with several massive tables, along which department heads and professors were seated. Researchers who didn't teach and assistants sat in chairs lining the walls. Saffron followed Alexander inside. His overcoat was slung over two chairs next to the door.

Alexander had saved her a seat. She glanced at him, but he'd given his attention to the person currently speaking at the table. It took her only a moment to see that he was angry. His jaw was clenched, his nostrils still flared. In his lap, his right hand rested, fisted so tightly his scars were white.

"I'm sorry for making you late," she whispered to him as they sat down.

He shook his head slightly.

"I appreciate you coming to collect me," she added.

"Don't mention it," he said from the corner of his mouth.

She fell silent for a minute, listening to someone from finances drone on about budgets. "You saved me a seat." He glanced at her and nodded. "Why?"

She could barely hear him sigh. "I wanted to speak to you about what I said the other night."

"You did?"

To Alexander's left, someone cleared their throat. Alexander was quiet until the talk of budgets ended and the main table moved on to the class schedule for the next semester. "I wanted to apologize. I spoke without thinking, and I wasn't being fair."

"*I* wasn't being fair," she said, putting her hand on his hand for the briefest of moments. "I had no right to demand to know anything. I'm sorry."

Alexander turned just enough to look at her. He was frowning. "I would like for you to have the right to . . . ask me things. I would like for us to be able to speak to each other openly. About personal matters."

Her mouth fell open for a moment. "You—you want me to ask you things. Personal things."

He nodded slightly.

Naturally, the first question that came to mind was "How do you know Nick?"

Next to her, Alexander stiffened. She poked his arm. "Well?"

"That isn't something I can tell you."

"But you just said—"

"I find it difficult to discuss Nick with you when you smell like him."

Saffron gasped with embarrassment and surprise. "What?"

Half the room turned to her with a mix of curiosity and annoyance. She hastily coughed.

She forced herself to be quiet for five minutes. When she was sure the newest topic of discussion, the question of wage increases, had riveted the entire room's attention, she leaned over to Alexander and whispered, "The house with Wells's body stank to high heaven and Nick doused my handkerchief with scent. I smell like him so I didn't have to endure the stink Wells left behind."

Alexander slanted her a glance, but she couldn't discern his expression. "I see."

He was infuriating! "Forget it. Forget all of it. I see your notion of personal questions means questions like a favorite book or food. Nothing real."

His fist tightened further in his lap. "Nick and I met in Greece."

Her heart leaped. "During the war?" He nodded, and she asked, "In Salonika?"

With another shallow nod, he said, "I can't say more."

"But why were you there? Why was Nick there?"

He shook his head slightly.

She thought furiously about the theories that had crowded her mind over the last day. Despite her protestations, she'd been unable to prevent herself speculating. Lee had mentioned it was a diplomatic trip. Alexander might have had family in political positions, but he likely would have mentioned that when describing Adrian's unintentional pro-Constantine activities. That would have had greater implications if their family was in a place of political power.

Alexander would have been coming out of healing from his injury then, and if he'd been well enough to travel, he might have been shipped out to fight again. That left only a few options.

Her first guess was the one she'd thought was the most likely. "You were a translator?"

She could feel him going still next to her. She tried to peer into his face. He gave her the smallest of nods.

Relief and something else overtook her in a warm wave. A translator. That was so simple, so reasonable. He wasn't some sort of spy, like Elizabeth imagined Nick to be. He could speak Greek; he was already in the military. It made sense that he could have been chosen to come along to assist with communication.

And the idea that he'd served England in that way, after he'd already been injured, was admirable. Very admirable.

Saffron did not ask more questions after that. A mystery had been solved, the answer something simple and logical. Alexander had allowed her to figure it out, helped her to understand him. It made sense, too, why he hadn't simply told her. He'd been keeping his word, he'd said. Of course, he couldn't just go talking about it; the things he must have heard were confidential.

She was lighthearted when she was called upon to speak. She found the usual self-consciousness that a hundred staff members all watching her brought on was absent from her brief speech about the progress of her pigmentation study.

She was still in the clouds when the meeting adjourned what felt like hours later.

"Will you come to visit the strychnos seeds now?" she asked Alexander as they stood. The words were polite, but the look she gave him suggested it was not the seeds that a visit to her office promised.

His face gave nothing away when he agreed.

The sound of the office door closing was loud in contrast to the utterly quiet building. With the sun disappeared beneath the city horizon, the university had settled into a relaxed state of slumber.

Saffron didn't feel relaxed in the least. She'd convinced Alexander to follow her up here, but now she wasn't sure what she wanted next.

"They've sprouted," Alexander commented. He'd moved to the window, where he bent over the third makeshift terrarium. "I was worried I wouldn't be able to do any better than Winters. But your notes were very thorough"—he slanted her a smile—"if a little disorganized."

She couldn't help but smile back. "Not everyone wants their world to be as strictly organized as you."

He straightened up to his impressive height. "That is true. I do like my world to be orderly. I like to know precisely where things are, how they fit together." He reached a hand to her cheek. His touch was feather-light along her cheekbone. "You drive me mad, you know."

"Oh?"

"When Lee told me you were missing, it hit me very hard. I'd been through a war, I'd been threatened with a pistol and forced to drink poison—but that was a distant, numb sort of fear that could be put aside in order to survive." His hand cupped her cheek, his fingers threading through her hair. "But when you were taken, it was different. It was immediate. Hot. I felt like I would tear apart the city." He exhaled, a rueful smile on his lips. "I hated it."

Saffron held still, worried that if she moved or interrupted him, he would stop speaking. She didn't necessarily enjoy his words, but she was desperate to understand what he was saying.

"The meditation I do helped me ease the fear and anxiety I felt— feel, still. It helped me let go of my feelings. I stopped dropping dishes, smashing beakers, losing myself when a loud sound jolted me." He swallowed. "I have sat, cross-legged and barefoot on the floor, for hours since I met you. No amount of meditation helps. You are too bright, too captivating for my mind to let go of."

Saffron had no words to match his quietly spoken confession. She kissed him.

He returned her kiss but only for a moment. "The window," he murmured.

With her office illuminated, anyone below in the Quad would see a pair of shadows doing things better left in privacy. She dragged him from the window and toward the couch.

She started their kiss anew, fierce with a determination that stemmed from his words and her own need to stave off the despair at the sights of death and pain she'd seen that day. This was warmth and life and something somehow better than logic and evidence and method, a rightness that did not need words to define.

That feeling of rightness was peerless in her experience. Perhaps that egged her on, encouraged her hands to tangle deeper into his hair, her body to press closer against his. Saffron believed in reason and answers to the questions of why and how, and she wanted to know why Alexander cared for her if she drove him mad, and why she wanted to understand him when he was so insufferably inscrutable, and how they could make things work between them.

Things were working very well, in her lust-hazed opinion. She'd managed to situate herself very nearly in Alexander's lap, and she could see his face perfectly. The way his brows furrowed as if in concentration as he returned her kiss, the hints of wrinkles across his forehead that would grow deeper with time, the three gray hairs hiding in the black at his right temple.

Likely sensing her distraction, his lips slowed, then stopped. He gazed up at her. His eyes, which were so often as impenetrable as his mind, were deepest brown. She could see the striations like layers in the soil. She could count each thick eyelash.

He leaned so his lips touched her throat. She shivered. His lips inched upward.

"I want you to do something for me," he murmured, breath tickling her ear.

She sighed with pleasure. "Yes?"

"Please leave off this business with Nick."

It was like she'd been drenched in cold water.

"Oh, no," she said, scooting off him, batting his hands away. "I will not put up with that again, Alexander." She got to her feet. "You were the one to ask me to investigate on Adrian's behalf!"

"This is different."

She glared at him. "I'm helping solve what might be a murder. And helping your brother in the process! I am not doing this with you again!"

"Nick is dangerous."

She opened her mouth, then closed it. She could no longer dismiss the idea of Nick being more than what he seemed. He'd shown her he was. He had permission to examine a body before the police had even visited the scene, and he knew about measurements of a dead body's decay. Alexander had known him while on a diplomatic mission during the war, during which Nick had no doubt killed men from the other side. More than anything else, however, Saffron had seen how Nick had changed his entire personality like he was switching hats. She'd seen his intensity, his coolness in the face of death. She could believe Nick was dangerous.

Deflated, she said, "There will always be danger of some kind. I might be hit by a bus on the street or catch 'flu. I work with poisonous plants for a living! Why is working with Nick any different?"

Alexander ran a hand through his hair, mussing the curls she'd already disordered. "I just want you to know that he isn't as he appears."

"One doesn't watch a man go from making quips about cows to examining a dead body with the clinical air of a professional without something being not quite right," she said flatly.

Alexander shot her a look of consternation. "Yet you agreed to help him."

"In part to help Adrian."

"And in part because . . .? Did you find it hard to say no to Nick?"

The tone of his question rankled her. She crossed her arms over her chest. "I found it hard to say no to a member of the government asking for my help in solving mysterious deaths because figuring out if it was accidental or intentional is important to the security of the laboratory."

Alexander watched her with a grim look. "He told you that the investigation was a matter of securing the lab?"

"Well, it's true, isn't it? If someone is killing off members of the lab, it might be because of something they're researching. Perhaps the Russians are after it."

He sighed and got to his feet. "It's late, Saffron."

"Come to my flat." She didn't want to lose the ground they'd gained. He was not arguing with her, or threatening to prevent her involvement, but giving information in his subtle way. She wrapped her arms about his waist, and he eyed her with a sort of wary curiosity that she found delightful. "For *supper*. Elizabeth no doubt is cursing my name for being so late, and she does love to show off her culinary efforts."

He agreed, and Saffron found herself unable to stop smiling the whole way home.

CHAPTER 22

Elizabeth declared that a special dinner party was in order. To Alexander, she said it was because her birthday was Sunday, and she wanted to celebrate him and Saffron making up.

"I am truly so glad, darling," she told him during their shared late supper, "that you and Saffron have made up. She was in tatters over it, you know." She'd shot Saffron a wink well within his view, somewhat ruining the impression of sincerity.

To Saffron later that evening, however, Elizabeth revealed that she wanted to needle Nick about his true occupation. Saffron reflected that she really ought not to have told Elizabeth about Alexander's diplomatic mission or Jeffery Wells's body if she didn't want her friend to obsess over her belief in Nick being a spy. Elizabeth was now certain, and Saffron couldn't entirely dismiss the idea.

With characteristic determination, Elizabeth pulled together a plan that ought to have taken a week of preparation within two days. She'd invited her brother, Colin, and Alexander for dinner, and Saffron had undertaken a long list of tasks to prepare for their arrival that evening. She'd cleaned, under Elizabeth's careful supervision, and then she'd been sent to the market with an extremely detailed list of ingredients. Then she was shooed from the kitchen and left to her own devices for two hours before their guests arrived.

Saffron used the time to scrub up and dress, then found herself alone in the parlor with nothing to do but fiddle with the perfectly set table they'd moved into the center of the room. It glistened with their nicest secondhand glassware and the excellent set of elegant dishes Elizabeth had gotten on offer. Saffron prodded a stalk of vibrant blue beardtongue she'd spotted at the market, aligning it more perfectly next to the equally bright asters. She hadn't been able to resist including the flower in the arrangement, perhaps in tribute to Dr. Aster for not sacking her, or to thumb her nose at him for being so vexatious.

The bell rang. Elizabeth howled her dismay at the very early arrival of their guests.

Saffron poked her head into the kitchen. Elizabeth's face was flushed and her apron was marked with a colorful collection of stains. She looked ready to boil over. "I'll shoo them away for half an hour," Saffron soothed her. "Not a worry."

She went to the end of the hall and pulled the door open.

And froze.

It was none of the gentlemen they'd expected, and the last person Saffron expected to see.

Lord Easting stood in the hall of her building.

"Grandpapa," Saffron said, coming up short.

Her eyes traced the familiar lines of his face, noting the appearance of new wrinkles and the dry, papery quality of his skin. Lord Easting had always been the robust, active lord-of-the-manor type. More comfortable in tweeds than a suit, more likely to be found examining a newborn calf than the stock reports in the newspaper. He'd taken the loss of both his sons hard, noticeably slowing. But the past few years had brought about even greater change; he looked like a man of eighty rather than sixty-some years. White hair had overtaken the gray, and his usually ruddy complexion was sallow. Her mother had obviously understated the poor quality of his health in recent letters.

"I—do come in," she said, scuttling back to give her grandfather admittance. "Would you like me to take your coat and hat?"

"No," he said stiffly, eying the narrow hall.

"Please, this way."

She felt his eyes on her back as she led him to the parlor. She watched for his reaction to her home but was distracted by the man himself. He walked so painfully, and he was so pale—

"Do sit down," she said, pulling out a chair for him at the table. "May I offer you tea, or water, or—"

"Sit," he said, voice thin.

Saffron swallowed and obeyed. She perched on the edge of the chair across from his.

His pale eyes, Everleigh blue but with the slight haze of old age, swept over the table, then her.

"Feyzi tells me you've been to see him," he said.

Her heart stuttered. Mr. Feyzi had told her grandfather about her visit with Alexander?

"You've been poking about in your father's things."

Saffron's lips parted in surprise. *That* was what he'd told her grandfather? "I . . . saw some of his papers," she said slowly.

Her grandfather's scowl deepened. "Not enough for you to go digging around in the garden, no. You had to make it a profession. Now you're digging about in my son's things." He shifted in his seat, looking restless and disgruntled. Saffron realized it wasn't just because of the scolding he was giving her, but because he would have usually gotten up to pace at this point, and he perhaps couldn't. Guilt stirred up anew in her chest.

"And not just Thomas's things! You've meddled in police business. *Twice.*" He shifted again, his eyes going to the mantle, where the photograph of Saffron and her parents sat. "You were never able to sit still when something interested you." Saffron thought there was a hint of warmth in that comment, but it disappeared with his next words. "But I never expected that incessant curiosity would assert itself so irresponsibly."

"It is one thing to embarrass the family by taking up a profession," he went on, "but another to drag our name through the muck. I kept it quiet the first time, never expecting to have to do it again. I barely had the influence to suppress reports of your involvement with police matters a second time." His gaze had wandered, but he focused on her again, lips twisting bitterly. "I never saw much point in dallying about in town, making nice with the sots who hang about in clubs rather than manage their land. But that means that when I need favors from those same sots, I'm at a disadvantage." His derisive snort turned into a cough. Saffron made to stand to fetch water, but her red-faced grandfather waved her back into her seat. His cough subsided, and his color faded. "I've had enough of this, my girl. I'm too old and tired to indulge you any longer, and I'm ready to give your grandmother what she's wanted from the beginning, which is you, back at Ellington where you belong."

Saffron's mouth fell open, a rushing in her ears. "I'm not going back to Ellington."

"You are," her grandfather said firmly. "Your grandmother wants you there, and your mother . . ." He shook his head. "Your mother would benefit from your presence too. I allowed you to stay in London, thinking that you would tire of the challenges of city life without my support. I admit, I had moments when I wanted you to succeed. One has to challenge their spouse on occasion, and your grandmother looked like she'd bitten into a lemon each time I said I'd let you stay."

That hint of the rascally man she'd known her grandfather to be made Saffron sit forward and say, "Sir, I have succeeded. I'm a researcher now, just like Papa. I—"

Her grandfather gripped the edges of the table and with, a grunt of effort, hoisted himself up. Saffron leaped to her feet, just stopping herself from offering a hand for support. When he was steady, Lord Easting gave her a beady look. "I don't care, my girl. You could be running that university yourself and I would still bring you back home. Thomas did not work so hard—"

He broke off, coughing again. Saffron took his arm to help him back into his seat.

He rasped out, "You are coming home. Now."

"I am not," Saffron said automatically, forgetting to be cowed. "I'm staying here, Grandpapa. This is my home. London is. The university is. There's nothing for me at Ellington."

"Your family is at Ellington."

That stymied her for a moment. When she spoke, her voice was soft. "I can't go back. I would be expected to live as Grandmama dictates until she finds me a husband who will then expect me to live as he says." She covered his gnarled hand with hers. It was cold, and she squeezed it gently. "You have always said that we are the sort of people who do things, Grandpapa. You would consign me to a life of sitting in a parlor pouring tea?" He seemed unmoved, so she added, with some measure of guilt, "Is that what Papa would have wanted for me?"

He looked away, lips thinning. "It is not a matter of what I want for you, but what I want for my family. I will not tolerate this tarnish on our family because you would rather avoid a few boring callers."

"That's not it at all—" Saffron's hand tightened on his, but he shook her off.

"Pack whatever you need for the journey. I expect a few of your things are still in your room at Ellington. We can send for the rest."

He pushed to his feet, steadier this time. He walked to the door, stopping at the threshold expectantly.

"I'm not leaving," Saffron insisted.

His eyes went cold. "You will."

The challenge in his words shifted the air between them. Saffron could see her future if she capitulated now. Her life would be nothing but compromises until she had nothing left of the life she'd built for herself here: living independently, exploring the world through plants, earning money of her own with a position that challenged her and gave her opportunities. No more Elizabeth, no more Lee, and no more Alexander.

That was unbearable.

"Don't make me do this," she said, suddenly desperate. "Don't make me choose."

Her grandfather stiffened. "There is nothing to choose."

The doorbell rang.

Neither of them moved. Behind her grandfather, Elizabeth tip-toed by, flashing Saffron a wide-eyed look over his shoulder before slipping down the hall to the door.

A low murmur sounded. Alexander.

Her already knotted stomach twisted. She'd barely begun to imagine introducing Alexander to her grandfather, but this was quite possibly the worst moment to do that.

Her grandfather must have read the panic on her face, for he turned and slowly made his way around the corner. Saffron hurried after him.

Elizabeth, now in her evening dress, stood at the open door with Alexander. Elizabeth's rapid whispering fell silent at the sight of Lord Easting coming toward them.

Elizabeth nudged Alexander out of the way, and they both stepped into the hall to give Saffron's grandfather space to leave the flat.

It was an uncomfortable tableau. Alexander was frozen but for his eyes, which flashed to Saffron and back to the older man. Beside him, Elizabeth smiled broadly. "Good evening, Lord Easting."

Lord Easting paused at the end of the hall. "Eliza," he said curtly. "I see you've not come to your senses, either."

"Quite so, my lord," Elizabeth replied cheerfully.

Lord Easting grunted and finally exited the flat. Cold air from the stairwell had crept inside, leaving Saffron with gooseflesh. She made to follow him, unsure if she ought to help her grandfather down the steps.

"Grandpapa—" she began, stopping when he cut her a scowl.

He was right next to Alexander, plainly ignoring him. She could feel Alexander's focus on her, and a sense of helplessness swamped her. It would be terribly rude not to introduce them, but it would likely be disastrous to do so.

"Have a safe journey home," she said, internally wincing at the squeak in her voice.

He grunted again and began toward the stairs. With his back turned, she turned to Alexander and mouthed, "I'm sorry," before inching down the hall after her grandfather.

Saffron did not breathe easily until Lord Easting had made it out of the building. She rushed back inside and into the parlor, where she knelt on the armchair in front of the window to peer out to the street. Her grandfather was being helped into an old motorcar by the driver.

She slumped into the armchair and closed her eyes.

"That was your grandfather?"

She flinched. She hadn't noticed Alexander in the room. "Yes," she said with a sigh.

"I take it his visit was unexpected."

She opened her eyes to look at the ceiling. "Whatever gave you that impression?"

He chuckled at her sarcasm, and she looked at him. He was sitting on the couch on the opposite wall. The table was between them, the flower arrangement partially blocking her view of him.

"Lucky guess," he said. "Come here."

She rose, skirted the table, and dropped onto the cushion next to him. He was no longer wearing his coat, and he was wonderfully handsome in his dinner jacket. A little severe, with his darker coloring, but softened by a small smile.

Her throat grew tight at the kindness in his expression. "I'm sorry I didn't introduce you."

"He didn't look to be in the mood to make a new acquaintance."

"He came to take me to Ellington."

"I gather you disappointed him."

She nodded. He placed his arm around her shoulders, gently drawing her to his side. "Good."

CHAPTER 23

Dinner was off to an awkward start. Saffron was still shaken from her argument with her grandfather and hadn't much spirit for conversation. Elizabeth had the opposite reaction, raving about the absurdity of the patriarchal society in which it was acceptable for a woman to be yanked from her life like a puppet from the stage.

Colin and Nick arrived nearly at the same time, cutting off Elizabeth's rant. Saffron saw the moment when it occurred to Elizabeth what she'd put into motion: Nick, her estranged brother whom she couldn't help but want to impress, was going to meet her beau. Nervous energy drenched her the minute Colin strolled into the parlor.

And it was an uncomfortable introduction. Colin, looking cool and collected in his own expensive dinner jacket and perfectly starched white shirt, offered his hand to Nick. Nick straightened to his full, impressive height and took just a moment too long to accept his hand to shake.

"Smith, is it?" Nick drawled. "I feel I must have met you before somewhere."

Colin quirked a pale brow. "I don't recollect—"

"Ah!" Nick dropped his hand with a grin that was not entirely pleasant. "I've got it! I saw you at the racetrack, didn't I? Ascot, for the jumps a few weeks ago?" Nick squinted at Colin as if trying to remember. "No! It was cards at—" He broke off with a glance at Saffron and Elizabeth, then winked at Colin. "I'm sure we've met before."

Colin had slowly flushed to brick red. Through a tightly held jaw, he said, "Indeed. I might have seen you around town, but I should be surprised. Eliza tells me it's been years since you've been to London."

Nick's eyes gleamed. "Just so, I'm afraid. My work keeps me busy, usually with travel. I don't mind though—work is the god we must all kneel to, eh? A better master than Lady Fortune, though."

No doubt sensing the strange hostility between the two men, Elizabeth announced it was time for drinks. She supplied everyone but Alexander with sherry, provided Alexander with a glass of tonic mixed with some concoction of juices, then slipped out of the room to check on the roast.

That left Saffron with Alexander, Nick, and Colin. Alexander, who was angry at Nick for taking her to see a dead body. Colin, who was not pleased by Nick's obvious references to gambling. And Nick, who was cheerfully pretending to be unaware.

Nick leaned on the arm of the couch, putting him nearly on eye level with Saffron, and said, "How is your work faring, Saffron? Plucked anything interesting out of the ground lately?"

"No," she said, unsure if he was referencing dead Jeffery Wells or something else. "How was your trip up the northern line?"

Saffron wondered if Nick was aware that everyone in the room knew that he was no mere agent of the Agricultural Ministry. He shrugged, sipping his drink, and said, "It was highly productive, though examining decay is never pleasant."

Saffron darted a glance at Colin. Nick must have known Alexander knew it, but she doubted he was aware that Elizabeth had told Colin all her mad ideas about Nick's real job, including that Nick had found another dead member of a government lab. Colin showed no signs of anything more than vague interest.

It was then that Alexander decided that he would fill the conversational void with a tangentially related tale from one of his expeditions. Saffron was relieved he'd made the effort. It lasted until Elizabeth returned with hors d'oeuvres.

Elizabeth took up the mantle of conversation after that, playing perfect hostess, so that even Colin seemed relaxed by the time the main course was served.

In true Elizabeth fashion, the entire meal was flawless, though conversation continued to be somewhat lacking. Saffron had never thought that Colin's long, droning stories from his days at Eton might be considered pompous, since many of her and Elizabeth's friends from their youth had had a similar education. But when Colin asked Alexander about his own school days, and his reply made clear that his days had been spent in average London primary and secondary schools, Saffron realized that the conversation might embarrass either man. Colin did not seem daunted, though he was plainly taken aback.

"I see," he said leaning back in his chair and idly swirling his glass of wine. "I thought I'd understood from Eliza that you had some connections at that university."

"No, darling," Elizabeth said easily, "that's Saffron. Her father was a professor there."

"But I thought your father was your grandfather's heir," he said, frowning at Saffron. "Or did I misunderstand that too?"

Saffron shifted uncomfortably. "He was, but he had a passion for science, and so he taught at the university for a few years," she said, hoping that would put an end to the conversation. She didn't care to have all this family drama laid out on the dinner table.

"I see," Colin repeated. His tone suggested he didn't quite see.

"Tell us about your people, Smith," Nick said. He'd been quiet for most of the meal, responding with his jaunty amiability when addressed, but Saffron had caught him eyeing Colin on more than one occasion.

Colin shrugged. "Not much to tell, really. Pater works in investments."

"They live in town?" Nick asked.

"Gads, no," Colin said with a laugh. "No, they live over in Bath, of all places. My mother is convinced her health requires it, though everyone knows that nonsense about Bath water is drivel."

"The minerals found in spring waters can be very effective in treating a number of ailments," Alexander said. "Magnesium, for example, has been well documented in improving muscle and nerve function in mammals."

This sent Colin into another long tale involving his mother and his aunt and their quest for the most efficacious curatives that ended up being a costly waste of time. Saffron couldn't help but suspect that Alexander was rather enjoying Colin's blathering on, she guessed because it so clearly bothered Nick. He'd lost some of his blandly pleasant manner through the evening, as if even his brotherly mask couldn't stand up to his active dislike of Colin.

Saffron didn't know whether to be amused, impressed, or concerned. But at least she was no longer thinking of her grandfather and his demands.

Dessert arrived at last. When Elizabeth disappeared into the kitchen to bring the butterscotch cake, Saffron nipped out to the landing to retrieve the bottle of champagne she'd hidden out there to keep cool. Alexander had obliged her by taking the champagne glasses out of the cabinet in the corner of the parlor and had them ready for her.

"Oh!" Elizabeth said softly when she returned to the room, cake-laden tray in her hands, and saw her guests were all raising a glass to her.

Saffron beamed and took the tray from her to set on the table. "To the dearest friend anyone could ever ask for, happy birthday. I wish you health, happiness, and the very best of what life has to offer."

In a few weeks' time, when it was Elizabeth's turn to toast her on her own birthday, she'd no doubt come up with something more elaborate and polished to say, but Saffron received a watery kiss on the cheek from Elizabeth all the same.

Nick added his own well wishes. Everyone drank. Alexander's barely passed his lips, Saffron noted, and Colin was eying them all in a strange way as he finished off his glass. Saffron ignored his obvious lack of celebratory spirit. Elizabeth seemed happy, especially once Saffron had passed her a generous glass of champagne for herself, and that was enough for now.

"You were no help with Colin at all," Saffron hissed at Alexander, adding a playful elbow jab to his stomach for good measure. They'd been left alone in the parlor when Elizabeth walked Colin to the door and Nick excused himself for a moment.

He caught her elbow and pulled her down so they sat hip to hip on the couch. "If you were in the jungle and saw a hapless deer about to be eaten by a jaguar, would you try to help the deer, or let nature run its course?"

Shocked by the macabre joke, and perhaps a bit giddy at his closeness, she burst into a nervous laugh. "I suppose not, but goodness, why on earth would you call Nick a jaguar?"

"Alexander obviously finds me a mysterious, dangerous creature," Nick drawled, entering the room with a cigarette between his lips.

"Do not light that," Saffron warned. "Elizabeth will flay you alive. She doesn't permit smoking in the house, it causes an awful mess."

Nick's brows lifted, but he replaced the cigarette in a slender gold case he returned to his jacket pocket. He sat on the armchair opposite them and grinned. "I think that went perfectly, don't you?"

"I think Elizabeth might flay you even if you don't smoke," Saffron said crossly. "You were perfectly awful to Colin."

Nick settled more comfortably in the chair. "*He* is perfectly awful. Did you see his face when you toasted Eliza? He had no idea we were celebrating her birthday."

She agreed, but she'd never betray Elizabeth by saying so. She'd act as if she liked Colin well enough until Elizabeth saw what a dreadfully dull, pompous fellow he was. "They've only been stepping out a few weeks."

Nick tapped his fingers on the arm of the chair. "Well, on with the show, eh? I've had word about Wells."

The warm ease she'd felt from sitting so close to Alexander evaporated. "What did they say?"

"And from whom?" Alexander asked.

Nick flicked him a glance, a smile curling one side of his mouth. "I see this is now a team effort instead of a partnership. Very well. Wells died of respiratory and heart failure. His liver was enlarged, to boot. Perhaps most significantly, that nasty cut on his hand was infected with fungus."

Saffron stared at him. "But what killed him?"

"The report didn't say. They need more time to do the full workup."

"But?"

Nick tilted his head thoughtfully. "But I suspect the fungus will have something to do with his death. It looked god-awful. Something funny is going on at the Harpenden lab."

"So you'll return there to investigate?" Saffron asked.

"I will," he said. "But I'm not trained for lab work. Couldn't muddle my way through pretending, even if I hadn't already been in the lab in my current capacity."

"As an agent of the Agricultural Ministry?" Alexander asked dryly.

"Just so." He rubbed a hand over his jaw, frowning. "It'll take ages to find someone to be a mole in the lab. They're a tight-knit group, with only a handful of scientists working there. They'd spot a true outsider in a moment."

"I'll do it."

Saffron spun in her seat to face Alexander. He was looking at Nick without expression.

"I appreciate the offer," Nick said, "but you're not subtle, Alexander. A great tall brute like you would only put them on their guard."

Saffron scoffed. "You're practically the same size, you know."

Nick gave her a wicked smile. "He's certainly not the type to strike up friendly conversations that lead to free-flowing information, is he?"

Saffron had known it would come to this the moment Alexander had spoken, knew why he'd offered. But she'd do it anyway. She wanted to know what was going on. "I'll go to the lab."

Nick studied her. "No, I don't think so."

"But why not?" she asked, surprised. She'd thought he'd been angling for her to volunteer.

"First of all, it *is* dangerous," Nick said. "Two men are dead. I know you know your way around a lab, especially one that deals with plants, but should something happen, I'd be responsible. You're a civilian."

"*You* are meant to be a civilian," Saffron muttered, a bit put out.

"Second, the value in sending you would be, in part, your name. Everleigh is a name known in botanical circles, and your father worked in plant pathology, which is what this lab deals with. I doubt you'd be willing to go as yourself."

"Why not?"

"Aster," Alexander said. "He'd hear about it before long."

Saffron finished his thought. "And sack me for working in another lab."

The room fell silent. She didn't want to dance along to Nick's tune and jump at the chance to go to the lab, but it did make sense for her to go. She knew lab work, and her name would give her clout that an assumed identity wouldn't have. And, truth be told, she wanted to see what she could learn about her father and what he might have done there.

She blew out a heavy breath. "Would your . . . office be willing to explain to Aster what I was doing in the lab when it is all over?"

Nick considered it. "If and when Petrov's and Wells's deaths are adequately dealt with, and if you provided assistance, I think that would be possible."

"Aster would have done the government a favor," Saffron said, "by allowing me to work in the lab temporarily."

"We could phrase it that way."

A slight shiver went through her at the way he said it, with the cool authority of the mysterious "we."

"And it would only be for a few weeks, at the most, wouldn't it?" Nick nodded. "Then I think it's a good idea."

A glance at Alexander told her that he did *not* think it was a good idea, but he said nothing.

"I'll just make a telephone call, then." Nick rose from his seat and left the room.

Saffron stood and began to collect the champagne glasses. Alexander silently assisted.

Elizabeth was in the kitchen, elbows-deep in soapy water. From the aggressive way she washed the dishes, Saffron guessed that she did not agree with Nick's positive assessment of the evening. She left her to her scrubbing.

Nick hung up the telephone when she emerged from the kitchen. "Looks like we're all set. I'll let you know the plan tomorrow, Saffron."

He left. Alexander departed soon after with a kiss and an enigmatic smile, and Saffron was left to wonder if she'd made a mistake in offering to go to the lab, while at once confident that she'd had no other choice.

CHAPTER 24

Though the day was as bright and cheerful as a November morning in central England could be, Saffron was uneasy exiting the railway station in Harpenden. There was a fair amount of traffic on the street and the pavement, but it eddied away as she walked from the town's center. Nick had given her directions to the laboratory, and Milton Road was just across the train tracks, in the same direction as Jeffery Wells's house.

The train ride had given her plenty of time to second-guess herself and to ruminate on the part of the evening she'd willfully forgotten about in the excitement over news of Wells's cause of death and the plan to infiltrate the lab. The way the unexpected visit from her grandfather had ended was awful. He'd told her to choose, and she'd chosen her life in London. She didn't know where that left her with him or the rest of her family.

Her cousin, John, and his little family would always accept her. The brief time she'd spent with them in France, where they lived, had affirmed that. John was a barrister, stubbornly refusing to return to England after the war despite the fact that Lord Easting thought he ought to be at Ellington, learning all he needed to know about being the heir to the viscounty. John disagreed, uninterested in forcing his French wife to abandon life in their charming town. Saffron couldn't relate more, though she doubted their grandfather would go all the way to France to harass John about returning home.

Her mother, too, would never abandon her, though Saffron didn't know what it meant for the future of their relationship if Saffron wasn't permitted to go to Ellington. Her mother did not leave the house, and she wasn't sure the inducement of seeing her daughter would be enough to enable her to overcome her fear of the outside world.

As much as her grandparents frustrated her, she loved them. They were terse and distant but loving in their own overbearing way. They had provided for her and permitted her to go to university, even if they'd preferred she hadn't. She didn't want them to disown her, though she was afraid that might have already happened.

It took Saffron only a few minutes to walk from the train station to Milton Road, but another five to ascertain she was in the right place, lost in thought as she was. The street was residential, and the homes were more or less the same, two- and three-story red brick buildings with white trim and trees and gardens. They were spread out enough to have privacy but not so far apart that the homes might have been considered estates. Everything one might expect in a nice suburban neighborhood—but nothing like one might expect of a government laboratory.

It wasn't until she noticed the small brass plaque on one of the houses that she realized she'd already walked past the building twice. She passed through the gate into the low-walled garden and approached the door, next to which the plaque read, "Harpenden Phytopathological Service, No. 28 Milton Street."

She let out a nervous breath and rang the bell.

A young man with an eyepatch over his left eye opened the door. Scars peppered the left side of his face and over where an ear used to be. "Yes?"

Saffron gave him a perfunctory smile that he did not return. "I'm Saffron Everleigh, and I have an appointment with Dr. Calderbrook."

He stepped back so she could enter.

The entryway was shabbily gentile, with an unpolished wood floor covered in rugs of decent quality and questionable cleanliness. The pattern of the wallpaper was barely decipherable beneath row after row of scientific art: illustrations, paintings, and photographs of plants, birds, insects, and fungi. An empty sitting room with mismatched furniture and an empty hearth despite the chill outside was to her right, and a library packed with books and journals stood to the left.

They went up squeaking stairs lined with more framed prints and paintings. A window provided a view of the bare front garden, contrasting with the flourishing ferns on the sill and ivy dripping from a pedestal in the corner.

At the top of the stairs was a row of closed doors, and the young man tapped on the first.

"Yes," called a male voice.

Saffron straightened and followed the young man as he opened the door and stepped inside.

The room had clearly been made over from a bedroom. The rosy walls and delicate moldings along the ceiling and along the mantle of the fireplace made it clear it had been a feminine space.

The man sitting at a desk in the center of the room matched it, strangely enough. His face was as round as his spectacles, his skin smooth and unwrinkled. His light brown hair was shining with pomade, and his full lips were topped with a mustache a bit more gingery than the rest of his hair. Dr. Jonathon F. Calderbrook was a phytopathologist, just like Thomas Everleigh had been. He was forty-two, unmarried, and lived at Number 28 in a set of private rooms, Nick had explained to her once he'd secured her this interview. This was not his personal bedroom, of course; the large desk and masses of filing cabinets along the walls made that clear, in spite of the pink floral wallpaper and fussy lace curtains.

"Miss Everleigh, sir," said the young man.

"Thank you, Joseph." Dr. Calderbrook got to his feet and smoothed a hand over his green tie. "How do you do, Miss Everleigh?"

Saffron came forward and offered her hand. "How do you do?"

"Have a seat, if you please." They both sat, and Joseph left, closing the door behind him. Dr. Calderbrook looked at her for a long moment before saying in quick, precise tones, "I was . . . surprised to see your application for the assistant position. You studied botany at UCL, and you work there now. You are aware that the position for which you've applied is in horticulture?"

"I am," Saffron said. "But I'm of a mind to switch fields." It displeased her to say it, and she worried for the moment her words would no doubt trickle down the grapevine to Dr. Aster's ears. She'd written a proposal for Dr. Aster detailing all the reasons why she needed to stay off-campus in order to explore resources for her study for the next several weeks. He had accepted it but without any enthusiasm. It was a weak excuse for her absence, but she had to hope it gave her enough time to find the information Nick needed.

To her surprise, Dr. Calderbrook's lips twitched. She realized she'd made a pun and allowed herself to smile. "I love botany, of course, but I recently attended the International Botanical Conference in Paris—"

Dr. Calderbrook looked taken aback. "Did you?"

"Yes. I attended the conference and saw just how urgent the need for horticulturalists and agriculturalists is, especially following the war, and decided it was time to make a change. I've worked as a research assistant before. I can learn the specifics of horticulture as I go."

The director shifted in his seat, easing forward and then back, his eyes flicking to her, then to the paper on his desk. "I am aware . . ." He cleared his throat. "Your father was Thomas Everleigh. He was a friend of mine, a colleague, though we never worked together officially."

"I didn't know that, sir," she lied.

"Yes, well, he was a good sort of fellow and I liked him very much. Tried to get him to come to my lab up at Kew, you know." His smile was brief and nervous. "I didn't know he had a daughter in the same field. I see Dr. Aster once a month, you see. We get together with a few colleagues for supper. One would think he'd mention Thomas Everleigh's daughter working for him."

Saffron didn't reply, merely kept her pleasant expression frozen on her face. She was all but certain to be found out by Aster now. But hopefully, this would be cleared up before they next met.

"I do need a horticulture assistant, and if I'm honest, rather desperately. We have several experiments going that will put us ages behind if we do not have the bodies to run them. I feel as if Fate has placed you in my lap!" He let out a laugh, then seemed to choke on it. "Oh, goodness, do excuse me. I simply mean it is a relief to have an Everleigh show up just now."

Saffron mashed down her annoyance. She didn't mind that Dr. Calderbrook had misspoken; she minded that he, like so many others, would reduce her to her surname, rather than the fact she had a degree and was already working as a researcher at a prestigious university. But she smiled brightly regardless. She wasn't there for an actual position, just the appearance of one. "It does rather seem that way."

"Very good." He got to his feet, extending his hand, and Saffron shook it. "Welcome to the Harpenden Phytopathological Service."

CHAPTER 25

Joseph reappeared and, at Dr. Calderbrook's instruction, gave her a tour of the place. He was quiet, borderline rude, in the gruff way he pointed out rooms and features and tersely responded to her questions. He also did not provide her another name by which to call him, so she simply called him Joseph when necessary, and he didn't correct her.

The rest of the first floor contained the offices dedicated to the seed catalog and the mail, which Joseph described as "a hefty pile on the daily." The ground floor was made up of the laboratory, a sitting room, a library, a lavatory, and a kitchen and scullery from which a kitchen maid provided a simple lunch each day.

The second floor, he mentioned as he led her into another wing, was off-limits to the regular staff.

"Why?" Saffron asked him.

"Director's rooms," Joseph replied.

It was good to know Nick hadn't been wrong. "Where do the other staff members live? Here in town?"

"Some are in Harpenden," he said, opening a door for her and standing dutifully to the side as she passed into a long corridor of more worn hardwood floors. There was no carpet here, and their steps echoed as he led her down the hall. "Some are up from London every day."

"I'll be coming up from London," she said. "And you?"

He shrugged and pointed to an open door. "Mycology."

"Joseph!" barked a man from within. "Get in here."

Joseph sighed and went to the door. Saffron followed, peering over his shoulder.

A man in a white coat had turned from the microscope sitting on a high counter before a window. He looked to be fifty years old, with thinning brown hair and a hefty, slightly bowed frame that suggested too much time bent over his work. "Tell Mary to get back in here!"

His accent was flat and clipped, indicating origins somewhere to the north.

"Aye, Dr. Sutcliffe," Joseph said without feeling. Dr. Sutcliffe began to turn away, but Joseph added, "New staff, by the way. Miss Everleigh."

Saffron edged around him into the lab for an introduction. Sutcliffe whipped around and roared, "Don't you set one foot into my lab!"

Stunned, Saffron jerked back and ran into Joseph. He steadied her for the merest instant before stepping well away from her.

"For heaven's sake!" cried a muffled female voice. A moment later, a tall woman also in a white coat threw open the door of the room at the end of the hall and strode toward them. "If you didn't want anyone coming into your lab, why'd you leave the door open, you daft old bear!"

The woman stomped up to Saffron and Joseph and stuck her head into the lab. "No terrorizing the new staff, you hear me?"

Sutcliffe jabbed a finger at the woman's foot, which was just inside the door. "Get your feet out of my lab! You're not wearing your gear!"

"*You* aren't wearing your gear!" she shrieked back before reaching inside the room.

Sutcliffe got to his feet, apparently enraged, but the woman had taken hold of the doorknob. She slammed the door.

The ringing silence of the hall was broken by low grumbling from within Sutcliffe's room.

The woman turned to Saffron and Joseph. She had an angular, middle-aged face. She topped Saffron by a head or more, even in the flat walking boots she wore with her dress beneath her white coat. "Ignore Sutcliffe. He's spent too much time with his growths to understand the ways of *Homo sapiens* any longer." She stuck out a broad hand and shook Saffron's enthusiastically. "Edna Quinn—call me Quinn, everyone does. How do you do? You're here for Horticulture, I hope."

"Yes, I'm the new assistant," Saffron said, then gave her name.

"Welcome to the Path Lab. I assure you, we're not as cracked as we seem. Joseph!" She turned to him, and Saffron saw he was already halfway down the hall. He flushed, displeased he'd been caught in his retreat. "You must come to introduce Miss Everleigh to the rest of us!"

Joseph wordlessly acquiesced, and Quinn didn't bother to keep her voice low as she leaned over to Saffron and said, "The boy needs interactions with people! He's always hiding away in the greenhouses when Calderbrook doesn't have need for him."

Joseph's shoulders tensed before them. They passed a door marked Records, and another marked Samples, before they reached the large, bright room at the end of the hall.

Agriculture and horticulture had always been considered far more pragmatic sciences, and to some, not even sciences but practices. The Paris conference had reminded Saffron that this was not the case, and the laboratory she now stood in confirmed it. This was no rustic outpost stocked with a few tins of soil or seeds but a bustling center of science. She ought not to have expected anything less, it being the child of the Jodrell Lab at Kew.

The room might have once been a modest sort of ballroom, for it was a single large, open space. A maze of workbenches topped with shelves laden with chemical containers of amber, blue, and clear glass had been erected within. The windows let in streams of light, ensuring that all the benches were adequately lit, though each one had several articulating lamps at the ready. Dark wood beams crisscrossed a high ceiling that had been stained in several places.

A smile tugged at Saffron's lips. The lab might be in a strange place, full of odd people, but this was very familiar ground.

"A fresh face to greet, everyone," called Quinn. She sounded very much like a schoolmarm, a bit overbright and forceful. It matched her appearance: perhaps in her forties and tidy, with streaks of gray in her brown hair. Her nose was rather red, including red marks on the bridge which suggested she'd recently removed a pair of spectacles.

Two people emerged from the maze of shelving. From the far left side stepped a willowy man with hair that was either very pale blond or had gone white. He had large features: a wedge of a nose between light blue eyes that reminded her of a basset hound's. The other was a polished woman Saffron's age with a stylishly cropped head of brunette hair. She wore a white coat, like everyone else, and looked at Saffron with friendly curiosity.

"Where is everyone else?" Quinn demanded.

"Crawford and Burnwell will be gone for another two weeks yet, remember?" said the younger woman. Her voice was soft, but she spoke with the same flat vowels as the shouting scientist. She stepped forward and offered a hand. "Mary Fitzsimmons, Mycology. I believe you've met my colleague, Dr. Sutcliffe."

Saffron could feel heat rising in her cheeks. "I did, yes."

Mary gave her a sympathetic look. "Don't mind him. We must take our safety protocols more seriously than the rest, else we risk contaminating the whole lab. I'll explain the rules after you've met everyone and gotten settled a bit."

"This is Dr. Narramore," announced Quinn, beckoning the blond man. "He runs Entomology, and I am his assistant."

Saffron was surprised to hear this; with her masterful manner, she'd have guessed she was in charge of her own department or even several. She shook Dr. Narramore's hand.

"And you know Joseph Rowe, of course," said Quinn, waving at Joseph.

He was standing unobtrusively behind them. He nodded solemnly as Quinn added, "He is our man of all work. Nothing he can't do or fix, apart from his determination to be quiet." Quinn barked out a laugh. "Speaking of which, I would like you to run to the post office, Joseph. We've been promised new specimens from Devon and I'm getting a bit impatient for them!"

"They'll arrive when they will," Dr. Narramore said, his voice low and resonant.

Quinn gave him a fond look and sighed. "You're quite right. We've enough to be getting on with already. Never you mind, then, Joseph."

Taking that as his dismissal, Joseph retreated from the room.

Narramore disappeared into the shelving, Quinn following him and speaking enthusiastically about something to do with phosphates.

Saffron looked to Mary hopefully. "I don't suppose you could tell me what I'm meant to be doing?"

Mary sighed, giving her another commiserating look. "I really ought to return before Sutcliffe starts shouting again. I was only in here for another set of these." She held up a few white pieces of fabric Saffron recognized as lab masks. The white cotton filtered out some of the potentially harmful things one might breathe in working in a lab. "Come with me. Horticulture is set up over here."

Saffron followed Mary to a series of waist-high benches against the wall in the far right corner of the room.

Mary glanced around the workspace. "Usually there's a set or two of keys wandering around the lab, but you'll need to ask Dr. Calderbrook for your own if you're to get into the files to see what you're meant to be doing. You'll learn more at our meeting later this afternoon. Most of your duties will be tending the pyrethrum daisies. You'll find your spot in the greenhouses easily enough. Joseph can always help if you have trouble."

Mary left the room, and from her seat, Saffron could see her pausing outside Mycology's door to don one of the cotton masks.

Saffron let out a breath. She'd made it past two hurdles—getting Calderbrook to hire her and meeting the staff, but now the real work was to begin. She began with searching for keys among the instruments and files before resolving to do as Mary suggested and ask Dr. Calderbrook for a set of keys of her own.

Saffron took the rest of the day to familiarize herself with the work that Demian Petrov and Jeffery Wells had been doing before they died. She was there to investigate the lab, but she was also there as herself, and she refused to do a shoddy job.

Her tasks seemed simple enough: manage and observe the growth of pyrethrum daisies. Each batch of *Chrysanthemum cinerariifolium*— not a daisy at all, though the cheerful blooms closely resembled them—was planted in a different kind of soil, with a different variation of fertilizer and companion plant. Her duties included measuring their growth, watering and fertilizing them in careful amounts, and recording it all on the provided charts and graphs. It was easy work, tasks she'd done as a student.

She read over the horticulturalists' notes, hoping for a hint of might have led to their deaths, but found only fretting about the growth of the plants in plot thirteen. The masses of daisies in that plot *were* a bit shorter, growing a little unevenly, she supposed, but even her desire to do good work during this temporary job couldn't bring her to worry much about it. The plants in these plots were intended for the harvest of the toxins in the daisies—pyrethrins—which the other scientists would test on pests. There were other plots being grown for strength and productivity.

Joseph acquainted her with the greenhouse procedures and where things were located, and by teatime, apparently a firm ritual at Number 28, she felt she'd found her footing.

She said as much to the staff as they stood around in the ground floor library, sipping tea around a table laden with a large tray the kitchen girl brought in. She was perhaps fifteen or so, with a rosy complexion and her hair hidden beneath her white cap. She must have been shy, for she set the tray down and darted from the room without a word.

Quinn poured the tea for everyone, and Saffron watched her ministrations carefully, wondering if this was the way whatever killed Petrov and Wells had been disseminated. It was unlikely, from the random way the cups were distributed and the fact that everyone drank from the same pot. Sugar and milk were also too randomly consumed to target a specific person.

"Glad you're getting into the swing of things," Quinn said in a motherly tone as she handed Saffron her tea.

"Just with the daisies," Saffron admitted. "There's far more to catch up on with the other projects, I'm afraid."

"We do like to keep busy," Quinn said. "Each department has at least two other studies in addition to the pyrethrum daisies. We've all got a hand in that study."

Saffron glanced at Sutcliffe and Mary, who were speaking near the window, the curling steam from their teacups catching the light.

"Yes, Mycology too," Quinn said, following her look. "You are growing the stuff as robustly as possible, and Entomology and Mycology are finding ways to kill it." She chuckled when Dr. Narramore, who'd been silent at her side, sipping his tea, gave her a sour look. "Come now, Neville, that is what we are doing."

"We're not killing the plants," he protested. "We're researching what insects might kill it."

"It's easy work, I don't mind saying," Quinn said to Saffron. "The entire reason we're researching the stuff is that insects don't care for it. *Chrysanthemum cinerariifolium* has been used for hundreds of years as a deterrent, a companion plant like marigolds, you know. We're just experimenting to see just how effective it can be in other forms as well."

"I see," Saffron said. It was not particularly interesting work, she thought, but she was glad someone was excited to do it. "What part does Botany play, if Horticulture is the one to grow the specimens?"

"Botany covers physiology, mainly, in addition to the pathology aspect. They diagnose what mechanisms are affected by what disease. They pass that information on to us if it's related to insects, or to Sutcliffe if it's a fungal problem. Viruses and bacteria were dealt with in cooperation with Petrov."

"Petrov was the chief of Horticulture," Saffron said, more a statement than a question.

"Yes," Quinn replied. She sighed, glancing at Narramore, who'd retreated back into his abstracted gaze. "Poor Demian. He was an émigré, you know, but never did he give me a moment of doubt about his ability."

Rather than frown at Quinn's assumption, Saffron thought of the books in Petrov's rooms, the range of subjects in so many different

languages. He certainly seemed very intelligent. "He died unexpectedly, I understand."

"He did, yes," Quinn said. "His assistant too, if you can believe it."

"Were they in an accident of some sort?"

Saffron's question drew the attention of Mary and Sutcliffe.
Mary's face pinched with what might have been sadness or concern.
"It was so tragic, to lose two members of our lab so close together. I
worry—"

"Petrov was an old man," Sutcliffe said flatly, cutting her off.
"Looked like a stiff wind could blow him over most days. It was
nature at work, nothing tragic about it."

Mary gave him an admonishing look. "But Mr. Wells wasn't so
old."

"What happened to him?" Saffron asked.

Next to her, Quinn went still. Saffron glanced at her, then followed her attention to the hall, where Joseph's back disappeared into
the kitchen.

"Excuse me," Quinn murmured. She slipped from the library as
Mary answered Saffron's question.

"We were told he died of a sudden illness," Mary said, her frown
tightening further.

The horrible sights and smells of Wells's house crashed into
Saffron, almost as if she'd stepped inside the house once again. She
swallowed convulsively.

"Are you all right?" Mary asked, looking concerned.

"I'm fine," Saffron said quickly. "Just got a bit dizzy, is all."

"You've been wearing your protective equipment, haven't you?"
Mary asked anxiously. "Without it, you can breathe in all sorts of
nasty things."

After assuring Mary she had been taking precautions, she excused
herself to the ladies'.

The lavatory was at the back of the house, once elegant with marble and wallpaper that now showed decades of wear. Saffron pressed
her back against the door. She wished she hadn't closeted herself in so
close and stuffy a space, but there was a tiny window over the toilet,
so she climbed atop it and pushed the window open.

A blast of cool air hit her face, and she sighed in relief. She needed fresh air to forget the awful things she'd seen—and smelled—in Wells's home.

Saffron inhaled the scent of winter air, touched with the smell of manure and fresh earth that emanated from the nearby greenhouse. She supposed dead bodies were a reality that she should inure herself to, considering this was the third time she'd assisted in some sort of criminal investigation. It was perhaps the worst part—or the second to worst, considering the danger she'd found—but she rather thought she ought not to get used to dead bodies. She wanted to help those who'd lost their lives, not necessarily look at them.

Those squeamish thoughts were interrupted by a low voice coming in the window on the wind.

"I haven't seen them, I told you," a sullen male voice said. She was sure it was Joseph.

"You're in and out of the lab all day," Quinn's clipped voice replied. "You could have taken them by accident—"

Joseph grew louder. "I haven't seen your papers."

"A mere mistake can be forgiven, my boy," she said patronizingly.

"Then admit you lost the papers. Don't go blaming me."

Quinn's tone turned sharp. "What about the vivarium? You expect me to believe that one of our costly vivariums just happened to fall off the counter and shatter? We didn't even get to collect the specimens inside before it was swept away. It was almost as if someone was trying to cover up they'd broken it."

"I've already told you, and Dr. Narramore, and Dr. Calderbrook that I had nothing to do with that." He spoke over Quinn as he added, "I'm going back to work."

The sound of a door slamming came a moment later. Quinn grumbled something under her breath, then the door sounded again, more quietly.

Saffron latched the window and stepped to the floor, mind racing. Missing papers and a vivarium, in addition to two dead scientists? Perhaps there really was something going on at the Path Lab.

Chapter 26

Saffron dedicated the next few days to unraveling the mystery of the missing papers. Nick had shown great interest when she'd telephoned him about it and had encouraged her to quietly look into discovering what papers were missing.

She had no idea if anyone else was missing documents, apart from Quinn. Saffron wandered to the entomology section of the lab to chat with her and attempt to speak with Dr. Narramore, though that was only moderately successful. She did discover something interesting, however.

Edna Quinn was in love with Dr. Neville Narramore. And he had no idea.

Quinn moved around him like a planet around the sun. Narramore would wander from microscope to specimen container, and Quinn would nudge vials and beakers out of his way just before he would have knocked them over. Saffron had believed herself a very good assistant to Dr. Maxwell, but she'd never been able to predict his movements so well. A china cabinet's worth of broken teacups could attest to that. Saffron imagined it was because Quinn and Narramore had worked together for a long time, but she heard from Mary that they had been paired when the lab moved to Harpenden just three years ago.

It made Saffron rather sad. Narramore never sought out Quinn except to ask her to make a note, bring a specimen, or discuss their work. Saffron had listened to her discourses with others and was quite certain she was brilliant. She wondered why Quinn settled for being an assistant at a minor government lab, rather than teaching or running her own lab.

She'd found the answer: love. It was a strong binder, Saffron considered. And a strong motive.

Everyone knew that people committed crimes for just a few reasons, and love was certainly one of them. Did the missing papers and dead scientists have anything to do with Quinn's pining for Narramore?

Her gentle prodding at lunch about the papers brought little result. Saffron mentioned that the horticulture files were missing pages here and there—true, though Saffron did not know enough about the notes she'd been left to be certain what they related to—and Quinn's response was a lengthy lecture about the various relationships between the Path Lab and the research stations and farms that had agreed to send data and samples to them.

"Have you noticed any of your samples or notes missing?" Saffron asked Quinn rather bluntly. "I heard Dr. Sutcliffe, er, sound rather upset that he'd misplaced something, and that wasn't the first I'd heard of missing items around here." That was not a lie, either, since she and the rest of the lab—even the whole of the street—had heard Sutcliffe's bombastic displeasure at being unable to find a report the previous afternoon.

"That ogre," Quinn muttered. After a moment of thought, her bespectacled eyes darted to Narramore, and when she saw he was gazing at the ceiling with a thoughtful frown, she must have deemed it safe to answer more fully. "You've come just when our lab is at far less than normal staffing numbers, what with the untimely deaths of Petrov and Wells, and the Botany lot being off in the field. Usually, there are many more bodies coming in and out of the lab, sharing workspaces and such. It's really not that surprising to have papers or notebooks—or even samples—go astray. Much easier to search out a package of crickets, though, isn't it?" She laughed, but it was a high-pitched, nervous sound.

"Indeed," Saffron said, laughing herself. "Besides, it's not as if there were anything worth stealing around here."

Narramore blinked as if their laughter had woken him from a waking sleep. "No, nothing to steal here. Come along, then, Quinn."

He rose and left the dining room, and Quinn hurried after him with a fawning look.

Quinn had accused Joseph of having something to do with missing papers, and so it was to Joseph that Saffron went next.

It was easy to find him, since they both were regularly in and out of the greenhouse. She waited until they'd been working in silence for some time. He knelt on the ground to fiddle with one of the pipes that cycled hot water through the floors to maintain the warmth of the building. Meanwhile, Saffron carefully measured each sprout of green that emerged from the earth in a nearby plot.

"Your duties seem vast and varied, Joseph," she said, not looking at him. She'd seen early on that he was shy in addition to reserved.

He paused briefly and glanced her way. "They are."

"Do you like working here?"

"I do."

A loud hiss accompanied a cloud of steam. Joseph swore soundly and jerked out of the way. He moved to the other side of the hole in the path and stuck a hand clutching a wrench into the hole. The steam ended a moment later.

"Told Calderbrook this fixture needs replacing," he grumbled.

"How did you come to work at the Path Lab? Have you any interest in plants or insects?"

To her surprise, Joseph sent her a look that might have indicated humor. With his good eye turned mostly away from her, it was hard to tell. "It's good work. Puts food on the table."

"And the people here are kind," she said, leaving him an opening for contradiction.

He grunted as he stood and replaced the bricks he'd removed to access the pipe. She'd nearly tripped over the stack when she'd come into the greenhouse, since it was just inside the door. Then he took up a broom and began sweeping the floor.

"You've been here long?" she asked.

He was quiet for so long, face to the floor as he swept, that she thought he would not answer. "Worked as a gardener at Kew. Came back from war, couldn't hack walking the grounds like before. Dr. Calderbrook needed someone to manage the post."

"And he brought you with him when he became director of this lab."

He nodded. "Like Mary."

"Mary was at Jodrell too?"

Joseph jerked his head in disagreement. "Sutcliffe brought her, when he moved down from Yorkshire. They were neighbors. She worked for him when she was a girl, then went back to work for him when she was finished at university. Sutcliffe told the director he'd only come down here if he could bring her. Best assistant he'd ever had. Never put off by his yelling." He broke off. Saffron noticed his remaining ear had gone red.

Was there more than one set of affections at play in the Path Lab?

"The two staff members who are out in the field," she said, hoping to keep him talking. "I'm sorry not to be able to meet them. I'm trained as a botanist, actually. But Dr. Calderbrook seems to think that Dr. Crawford and Mr. Burnwell have it well in hand."

Joseph snorted, then swung the broom around, perhaps to hide that he'd made such an undignified sound.

Smiling, she asked, "What is it?"

He glanced over his shoulder, and for a moment, she caught a glimpse of how he might have been before the war: a young man full of mischief. It was gone in an instant.

"Dr. Crawford isn't bad," he said. "But that Burnwell doesn't know what he's doing."

"He doesn't?" Saffron asked, curious.

"He's rude," he said. "And always smoking, even in the lab."

Saffron swallowed a groan. "Is Burnwell—he's not Victor Burnwell, is he?"

Joseph straightened up and regarded her with wary surprise. "You know him?"

Victor Burnwell had been her classmate for years, and a foul man he was. Competitive, acerbic, and with disgusting habits he'd leveraged against her and the others in their classes. He'd lick his finger before turning each page in a report and spit into the eyepieces of microscopes to polish them, then scoff when others didn't want to use them. She'd caught him flicking the butts of cigarettes into the greenhouse beds on more than one occasion.

"I do know him," she said, barely refraining from wrinkling her nose. She hoped she was gone from the Path Lab before she had to cope with his odious presence again. "Forgive me for saying so, but I almost wish it had been Botany to lose its members rather than Horticulture."

It was a crude, thoughtless thing to say, but it made Joseph's mouth hitch up into half a smile and that snort of a laugh break free again. "Think you might be right, miss. Burnwell'd yell at Mary—or anyone else—when they told him to keep to the safety protocols. Refuses to wear a mask or gloves. Coughs and spits and smokes all the time. I told the director he'd burn down the building with those damned cigarettes of his. Burnwell is a right git."

"No disagreements here." She sighed. "I ought not to have said that, though. I can't believe the horrible luck, to have both the chief and assistant of Horticulture die so unexpectedly. I almost worry for myself."

Joseph merely shrugged as he returned to sweeping the bricks. "Nothing to worry about. Keep up with the safety protocols, and it'll be fine."

CHAPTER 27

That evening, Saffron compiled all the information she'd found for Nick. He'd mentioned his intention to drop by the flat to catch up with her, but she had plans that night. She'd just give him the notes and be on her way to the university to meet up with Alexander. He'd telephoned the previous evening saying he wanted to see her. She was rather excited.

She forsook reading one of Elizabeth's old copies of *The Sketch* magazine, where she'd been catching up on installments of Agatha Christie's latest mystery on each train ride to and from London, and jotted down all her thoughts about Harpenden's Path Lab. She sketched out the characters of each of the staff members, including what she knew of Victor Burnwell. She half wished the wretched man was involved in this plot, but he and the chief of Botany had been away at another research station for almost a month. While she was confident Petrov had been suffering longer than that, according to the Path Lab staff and his autopsy, Wells had appeared not to have such a long illness prior to his death. It would be hard to prove the botanists had anything to do with their deaths from their post in Northumberland. Burnwell was a perfect villain, crude and disgusting. Mary Fitzsimmons's cheeks had flushed an angry red when Saffron mentioned the man during lunch earlier that day. It appeared Saffron and Joseph were not alone in their dislike of him.

Elizabeth was not home when Saffron arrived, nor half an hour later when she was preparing to leave, so she wrote her a quick note

saying she was off to meet up with Alexander. She left behind her
notes for Nick and asked her to pass them along if he showed up.

Anticipation made it hard to draw a full breath as the bus
approached the stop. She and Alexander had stepped out a few times
before his departure for Brazil in the spring, but now that they seemed
to be a couple, it felt different, important. This date marked a change
in their relationship, she was sure. A chance to start anew.

It did not bode well, then, that he was nowhere to be seen at the
bus stop where they'd agreed to meet. She looked all around the circular drive surrounding the memorial statue and considered going
into the train station to see if he'd sheltered from the misty rain. It
was cold enough to make her fingers hurt within her gloves as they
clutched her umbrella.

She didn't believe he would have stood her up. She did believe he
could have lost track of the time while working, however, so she
made for the U.

The Quad's pavement glistened gold in the glow of the lamp-
lights. She hopped up the step and into the North Wing, peering
around the entry to see if anyone was lingering. The place was
empty.

She darted up the stairs, slipping slightly on the damp tile, and
saw Alexander's office light was on. She opened the door.

Just as she had in the nightclub, Saffron thought it was Alexander
standing with his back to the door, looking out over the Quad. But
she recognized Adrian after only a moment, for his bearing had not
the strength or the quiet confidence of Alexander's. He grinned
widely as he turned toward the door, which made his identity more
obvious.

Alexander was sitting on the couch just inside the door. He, too,
smiled at her, but it was a smaller, more secretive smile. She loved it.

"Hello," the brothers said with such synchronicity that she burst
into laughter.

"Hello, Ashtons."

"I was just leaving," Adrian said. He was in front of her in a
moment, lifting her hand to his mouth and kissing the air above it
with a cheeky wink. "It has been a true pleasure, Miss Everleigh."

"Saffron, please," she said. "And don't hurry away on my account."

"But I must, alas, or I will miss my train."

"Your train?" Saffron repeated, glancing between the brothers in question.

"Adrian was told today that he could return home," Alexander said evenly.

Saffron beamed at Adrian. "But then you must no longer be under suspicion!"

He grinned back. "So it seems."

Adrian thanked her and wished her well, then embraced Alexander before departing.

When the door clicked shut behind him, she turned to Alexander. "How has he been cleared? I haven't told Nick or Inspector Green any of what I've found out."

Alexander gave her a wry smile. "Is it wrong of me not to care? I'm far too relieved he'll be heading back to Kingston."

She noted the exhaustion lurking in the darkened depressions beneath his eyes, the deepened tension lines on his face. She felt as if she hadn't seen him in weeks rather than days.

She wrapped her arms around his middle, resting her head on his chest. "I'm relieved too. Whatever the evidence, I'm glad the inspector found it."

They stood like that for a long moment, his arms resting gently around her back. When he spoke, it was a rumble against her ear. "How is Harpenden?"

She was pleased to snuggle close to him on the couch for a few minutes as she explained all about the laboratory, the staff, and the missing papers.

"I wonder how much of this Inspector Green knows," Alexander said. "Especially about the pyrethrins."

"They weren't on the list of chemicals, strangely," she said.

Alexander, who'd been absently toying with her fingers, paused and gave her a significant look. "If this is proprietary research, I'm not surprised they're reluctant to reveal it. Look what happened to the list of chemicals they did give the Inspector. You managed to get it into the hands of six different scientists who have no connection to the

Path Lab, several of whom would have an interest in replicating their research before they could publish."

"I'd thought of that," Saffron said, "but that doesn't explain why it wasn't included. This is a murder investigation. I can't imagine anyone picking and choosing the information they give the police."

"Unless they have something to hide."

"But everyone in the lab knows about the pyrethrins' effects!" Saffron scowled. "Oh, this is maddening."

"It is," Alexander murmured, bringing her hand to his lips. His words tickled her skin. "Here we are, discussing murder once again when I'd planned to wine and dine you." His soft laugh at her doubtful look skated over her palm before he pressed another kiss there. "Not the wine, but certainly supper."

"I could put off supper for a while," she whispered.

And so they did, filling the time with an embrace that left Saffron's head spinning.

A rap on the door had her jerking dizzily away from Alexander. He looked as dumbfounded as she felt, his lips full and red and his hair tousled. Saffron couldn't help but smile sheepishly at him as he stood and attempted to fix it.

"Yes?" he called. He was doing a poor job, so she rose to her feet and reached up to smooth her hands through the dark curls.

"Alexander."

Alexander dropped his head onto Saffron's shoulder with a sigh. "Nick."

"Saffron with you?"

Saffron patted Alexander's shoulder in commiseration. "Yes, I'm here."

"Might I come in, or . . .?"

Alexander straightened up with a questioning look. She gave him a rueful smile and straightened his collar and tie, which she'd also mussed.

She opened the door. "What do you want, Nick?"

His understanding smile made her cheeks heat. "Is that any way to treat the man who ensured your beau's brother is no longer on the hook for murder? Petrov's case has been taken out of the police's hands. I understand Adrian is already on his way out of London." He smirked at Alexander over her head. "You're welcome." He withdrew a note from his coat pocket and Saffron recognized her own handwriting. "Now, while I appreciate the note, I feel we needed to debrief about the Path Lab properly. Not to mention . . ."

Nick slipped around her to enter the office. He set down a briefcase on Alexander's desk, unlatched it, and took a small round object from within. He straightened up and held it out in the palm of his hand.

"What is that?" Saffron asked, peering down at the lidded petri dish. It was stained with a yellow growth that made her stomach turn just looking at it.

"I have no idea," Nick said, "but it's what killed Jeffery Wells."

The laboratory lights were turned down low and a breathless silence filled the room. Saffron sat with her thigh pressed against Alexander's as they took turns peering into the eyepiece at the fungus culture contained in Nick's glass dish.

It was hard to give the culture her complete attention when Alexander sat so near her, radiating focus and calm confidence. His body was bent low over the microscope, his brow furrowed when he took a turn at the eyepiece. Every once and a while, he bit his lower lip as he made a minute adjustment to the magnification. It was terribly distracting, but it was hard to ignore the lingering presence in the laboratory that prevented her from making meaningful designs on Alexander.

Saffron couldn't tell which ruined the mood more: the deadly fungus they were examining or Nick.

As if to win another point in his favor, Nick heaved a sigh from behind them. "When you suggested examining it yourselves, I imagined it would save time."

"If you are feeling impatient," Alexander murmured, "you are welcome to leave."

Saffron imagined she could hear Nick's eyes rolling. "I very much doubt anything will get done if I leave you two to it."

Alexander glanced up from the eyepiece and winked at Saffron. She enjoyed the tingle of a blush on her cheeks.

"You might as well leave," Alexander said, returning to the specimen. "We'll identify it before long."

"'Before long' has to be before that specimen dies," Nick said, but it sounded more to himself. He'd said the sample had been sealed so he could transport it, meaning the culture was cut off from oxygen and nutrition.

"Mycology may not be either of our specialties," Saffron said, "but we are well acquainted with the process of specimen identification. Alexander is developing a rapid identification system for bacteria found in water and soil, you know." She patted his shoulder. "He's gotten to know dozens of fungi in the process. Once we've done the measurements and observed the salient features, it's merely a matter of finding the right entry in the right book."

Nick cast a doubtful look at the stack of books on fungi she'd retrieved from the library before it closed.

"It helps that it's yellow," Alexander said. "Narrows it down."

Alexander continued calling out features that Saffron examined herself before recording in her notebook. They took turns thumbing through pages of the textbooks until Alexander let out a soft hum.

He tapped on a page. "I think this is it."

Nick came to loom over them.

Saffron read the heading of the entry. "*Mucor indicus.*"

"The challenge in identifying it is that it is dimorphic," Alexander said. "It forms both filamentous and yeastlike growths, or a mixture of the two."

He didn't bother to explain the terms to Nick, but Saffron tapped on the drawing she'd done in her notebook of the stringlike growth pattern and the circular one in turn.

Alexander continued, "I don't know what it looked like in the tissue samples from the autopsy"—Saffron shuddered at the thought—"but it is very possible only one form showed up, making it harder to identify. The cell wall in the filamentous growth—"

"Thank you, I think I've heard enough," Nick said. He quickly swooped between them, planting a hand on Saffron's shoulder to steady himself as he put his own eye to the microscope's eyepiece. He hummed, then stepped back.

Saffron glared at him and rubbed her shoulder. He was far too heavy to use her as a support. "What now?"

"Where does one find this fungus?" Nick asked.

"Soil, among other places," Alexander replied, looking at the textbook again. "And considering where Wells worked and the way it was likely introduced into his body, from the wound in his hand, it's possible it was an accidental infection."

"An accidental infection he didn't see a doctor about, even when he was deathly ill?" Nick asked, his disbelief plain.

"It is possible both Wells and Petrov died accidentally," Saffron said slowly. "Will Petrov's body be checked for a *Mucor indicus* infection?"

"Of course it's possible," Nick said impatiently. "And his body will be checked, now we know to look for it. But considering what we know about Wells . . ."

"What do we know about Wells?" asked Alexander nonchalantly.

Nick ignored him, looking instead to Saffron. "I need you to find out if the lab works with *Mucor indicus* specifically. That'll give us a clue as to this being an incidental infection or something else. See you tomorrow."

CHAPTER 28

The train's whistle jerked Saffron from a dream. The last visions of it faded in a swirl of steam beyond the window as the train came to a slow stop, something about growths of yellow smothering her Amazonian samples, though Saffron couldn't be sure if she'd dreamed it was the xolotl vine, or if it was *Mucor indicus*. Regardless, the lingering image bothered her as she made the trek from the train station to the Path Lab that morning.

She'd stayed out far too late with Alexander—thus the impromptu nap on the train—and now felt a bit like a flower on its last legs in autumn. Such flowers had been killed off just a few days ago with the first frost. Perhaps not the best analogy for herself, then.

The Path Lab was quiet with Dr. Calderbrook shut up in his office, as he usually was, and Joseph nowhere to be seen. The door was closed to Sutcliffe's lab. She could hear Sutcliffe's rumbling voice and Mary's bell-like tones, however.

The larger laboratory was empty, with the windows still curtained. Joseph wasn't likely at Number 28 then; opening the lab was one of his first duties.

It presented the perfect opportunity to see what she could find, if anything, in Narramore and Quinn's work that might be worth stealing. She tugged the curtains aside, illuminating the maze of shelves and workbenches.

She approached the corner where Entomology was set up. The wooden workbenches were clear save for the trio of vivariums. Saffron had seen insects skittering around inside them but hadn't paid much attention before. With the curtains open, the wriggling creatures had fled to the cover provided by the foliage growing inside the tanks, but a few stragglers were still crawling around. Earwigs, a crop pest, were the main focus of Entomology. Saffron spotted a few creeping along a bare branch in the middle of one of the vivariums.

Apart from the glass tanks, however, there was little to see. The drawers were locked save for the top one, which contained only pens, pencils, and inexpensive measuring tools. Glancing at the clock on the far wall, Saffron tried to gauge just how long she had if she wanted to attempt picking the drawer locks—

A chorus of voices exploded somewhere down the hall.

Saffron scuttled away toward her own workbench, as the tumult of voices increased in the hall.

Sutcliffe's bellow echoed into the lab. "Absurd! The boy isn't clever enough to even start to—"

"*Dr. Sutcliffe*, please," came Mary's plaintive voice, quickly overtaken by Quinn's brisk voice saying, "I saw it myself! They were leading the boy away from the house in handcuffs. How else do you explain it?" There was a trace of smugness in her tone.

Someone threw one of the laboratory doors open. The three scientists marched inside.

"He might have broken in to steal something," Sutcliffe replied, his color high. "Calderbrook said yesterday someone had broken in. Place was a mess. No doubt he went back to find whatever he missed the first time 'round."

Mary walked behind him, her hands twisting in their white gloves. She'd pulled her mask down around her chin, so her worry was plain.

Quinn, on the other hand, seemed delighted to be sharing gossip. "I tell you, Joseph was the one to do Wells in. He was caught in the man's house. I'd wager he was *hiding* evidence." She sniffed, crossing her arms. "I always thought something was off about him. He's far too quiet. He came back from the battlefields with not *only* an eye missing, if you ask me."

Anger spiked through Saffron with a force that made her breathless. "What a perfectly wretched thing to say."

Quinn, Sutcliffe, and Mary turned to her at once, surprise on their faces. They hadn't noticed her presence.

"Wretched it might be, but true," Quinn said stiffly.

"There could be a dozen reasons why Joseph was in Mr. Wells's house," Mary said, seeming to pluck up the courage to disagree with Quinn now that Saffron had.

"Like what?" barked Sutcliffe. When Mary gave him a hurt look, he added gruffly, "If you're putting forth a hypothesis, you better have some evidence to back it up."

"He might have been looking for Mr. Wells's keys," Mary said. "Dr. Calderbrook might have asked him to retrieve them."

Missing keys, or missing papers, Saffron thought with excitement. "Has Joseph actually been arrested?"

Quinn sniffed again. "I don't know. All I know is that this morning, I saw them leading him away from Poets Court in handcuffs. The obvious conclusion is evident."

"But not proven," Mary said. She was just as stiff as Quinn, her face a little pale. "How dreadful. What are we to do?"

"Hire a new fellow to run errands," Quinn muttered. "One who isn't touched in the head."

Saffron fought to keep her voice cool. "I would appreciate you not ridiculing those who sacrificed in service to our country."

Quinn flushed an unpleasant brick red and began sputtering.

Saffron continued to glare at her. She'd never spoken out about such mutterings before, but she found she couldn't let them go unchallenged any longer.

Dr. Calderbrook hurried into the room. His teeth worried his flushed lips beneath his mustache. "I know we are all in quite an uproar over poor Joseph, but a representative from the ministry just arrived and he wishes to speak to everyone."

Behind him, Nick Hale entered the lab.

CHAPTER 29

"Good morning," Nick said, scanning the room before coming to rest on each scientist for a moment. He wore a somber navy suit with a matching tie beneath his fine wool overcoat, which apparently no one had taken. "You might recall that I am Nicholas Hale from the Agricultural Ministry. A member of your staff was arrested this morning by local police after he attempted to break into the home of Jeffery Wells. I am here to discuss this and other recent . . . developments, here at the lab."

He was utterly serious and had the faintest hint of menace that put Saffron and the others on edge. Another carefully crafted persona he'd slipped on.

His pause was equally calculated to raise the tension further. Mary was pale, while Sutcliffe's color was slowly rising as if he were a kettle preparing to boil. Quinn looked more alarmed than Saffron would have expected. Only Narramore, who'd walked in behind Nick, seemed unaffected.

"You are a new face," Nick said, and Saffron realized he was speaking to her.

"I am, sir," she said. "I was hired last week as the new assistant in Horticulture."

Nick flicked a look at Dr. Calderbrook, who confirmed this with a nod. "Saffron Everleigh," Dr. Calderbrook said, "down from London."

"I'll start with you, then, Miss Everleigh. Dr. Calderbrook, if I may have use of your office?"

Soon, Saffron was sitting before Nick in Calderbrook's pink office. Nick waited until the door was closed and the sounds of Calderbrook's footsteps faded before he broke into a grin.

"Well, well," he said, leaning back in Calderbrook's chair. "We've had quite the development. I assume you've already heard that Joseph Rowe broke into Wells's home this morning?"

"I don't think Joseph killed Wells," Saffron said. "I have no evidence to the contrary, just . . . just a feeling."

"Unlike you scientific types, I don't need definite proof to believe you. I don't think he killed Wells either. They had no quarrel, according to what I've heard."

The facts and theories about the staff Saffron had collected poured out of her. "Quinn doesn't much like Joseph, though. She just essentially accused him of stealing her notes and materials as well as doing in Wells. And Mary takes issue with Burnwell, the botanist, which means that Joseph had an issue with him too."

"Why is that?"

"Because he's sweet on Mary and finds Burnwell vile," Saffron said.

"I see," Nick said, an eyebrow raised. He reached into his pocket. "Very interesting, then, what was found on Joseph Rowe's person when he was arrested."

He passed her a folded sheaf of papers. Saffron saw Mary's neat script. She flipped through a few of the papers, finding them to be records of the care of a particular specimen, referred to in the top right corner of the paper as Specimen No. 28923.

The papers were daily notes from the twenty-ninth of October until November twelfth. The last in the sequence noted that the specimen had failed, meaning it had died.

She stared down at the papers for a long moment. "These were in Jeffery Wells's house."

"That is my guess," Nick said.

She glanced up at him. "Joseph didn't say?"

"He refuses to speak about it. Admitted to breaking in, said he wasn't there for any reason to do with Wells's death, but won't stay what his actual reason was."

"This is the reason," Saffron said, lifting the papers from her lap. "These papers. He was retrieving them for Mary. I've heard Sutcliffe's reaction to missing papers. She'd want to avoid him learning she'd lost reports."

Nick hummed, a finger tapping his chin. "So Joseph broke in for the girl he's sweet on, or because he wants to sell the papers to interested parties?"

"These wouldn't do much to help someone," Saffron replied. "The specimen they describe ended up dead."

"Perhaps that information is vital to someone."

"It could be . . ." Saffron shook her head, thinking. "Sutcliffe isn't working on beneficial fungi. He's working on killing harmful ones."

"So you're saying that he was successful."

"Yes, but if that had been the goal of this experiment"—she shook the papers slightly—"then there likely would have been a note about positive results, that they'd gotten their desired outcome."

"This report isn't complete; it's missing a page or two."

"Have you searched Wells's house?" she asked Nick. "Apart from when we visited, I mean. The others mentioned the house was a wreck. It was messy when we went there, but certainly nothing out of the ordinary for an ill bachelor."

One of Nick's brows shot up. "Do the others know that Joseph Rowe was caught with papers?"

So, he was avoiding the question. What did that signify? "I don't think so."

"Good. I can make it seem unrelated. Don't want to spook them with a suggestion that the papers might be linked to the death." Nick sighed, running a hand over his jaw. "Did you find out about the *Mucor indicus*?"

"I haven't yet," Saffron said, adding dryly, "We've had rather an eventful morning here. I take that to mean that you confirmed that our identification was correct?"

"A severe infection would cause the sort of necrosis we saw in his wound. The coroner did seem puzzled by the severity of his, ah"—he lifted his brows—"gastrointestinal symptoms, however. A cutaneous infection doesn't generally cause that level of disruption, apparently."

That was a delicate way of saying that Wells ought not to have been relieved of all but his intestines from an infected cut. "Will they continue looking for an explanation?" she asked.

"They will. Ask about the fungus today, and if you find out the mycologists are working with it, get me word. I'll be here all day." During the pause that followed, his gaze turned unreadable. "How are things?"

Saffron blinked. "Things are fine."

"Going back and forth between here and London isn't too much?"

She hadn't thought much about it. "I don't care for it, but it's not a burden."

"Must be hard, not working alongside your beau."

Ignoring his mischievous grin, she replied, "I do enjoy sharing the North Wing with Alexander, but the place is a hotbed for gossip. As soon as word gets 'round that we're seeing each other . . ." She sighed, just realizing it herself. The chin-wagging would be endless.

"Good to know," Nick said. He propped an elbow on the desk and gave her a perfunctory smile. "Well, off you go. We can catch the train back to town together if you like."

Saffron gave him an indifferent reply, unsure if she wanted to invite more time with Nick, and returned to the lab.

CHAPTER 30

Saffron hadn't intended on screaming when the hand landed on her shoulder, but the walk to the train station that evening had been dark and lonely—her own fault, for avoiding Nick—and with what she'd learned about the goings-on at the lab, fear had curdled in her stomach. She was prepared for the worst up until she'd reached Harpenden's brightly lit high street, when she relaxed just enough to be scared out of her wits when a hand fell on her shoulder.

Her alarmed screech broke off the moment she wheeled around and saw Elizabeth flattening her hat over her ears.

Glaring, Elizabeth ground out, "Oh, for heaven's sake, Saffron!"

"You snuck up on me!" Saffron shot back, face flaming as she realized half the street was staring at her. She hurriedly took Elizabeth's arm and continued toward the station. "What are you doing here?"

"Well, hello to you too!" Elizabeth huffed.

Saffron narrowed her eyes at her friend. She was flushed, and her lipstick was nearly gone. "What have you been doing?"

"Been down the pub." Elizabeth winked. "Where I've had several very interesting conversations I'll tell you all about on the train. Let's get a move on, we have places to be!"

Elizabeth was keen to tell Saffron about all the things she'd discovered in the Dancing Sparrow. She was clearly quite proud of herself for taking the initiative to go to the pub from which Jeffery Wells had collected so many receipts, and frankly, Saffron was impressed,

206 ～⟩ Kate Khavari

not only that she'd recalled that negligible detail from Saffron's description of Jeffery Wells's house, but that she'd managed to learn so much.

Jeffery Wells, according to Elizabeth's report, was often to be found drinking ale in the evenings at the public house. Most nights, he'd chat with the locals. But the barkeep, whom Elizabeth described as "magnificently authentic" to the "rustic setting" of the Dancing Sparrow, remembered that on several occasions, Wells would scoff at the local beer and order hard liquor, but only when his friend from London came to town. They'd share a few drinks and talk, and those talks were not always friendly.

"And you'll never guess who Wells was getting so cozy with," Elizabeth whispered, eyes widened dramatically. "Do you remember those few months I was stepping out with Sammy Lambert last year?"

Saffron could scarce forget; Sammy had been one of Elizabeth's less worthy suitors. She'd been rather relieved when Elizabeth had broken off with him. "Don't say Wells was meeting up with Sammy!"

"No, it wasn't him. Sammy took me to a cabaret a few times, the one down on Fentiman Road. The dancing was just average, but the place was always packed, and I could never understand why until one evening Sammy got bored and decided we ought to go gambling instead. I told him I didn't want to pay to be dragged all over London so he could have a good time—you know he never took the bill for anything—and he said the gaming was to be found there at the cabaret. And then I asked him—"

Saffron withheld a sigh. She knew Elizabeth would get to the point eventually.

"—if they took bets on how many beads would fall off the dancers' bodices with all the shimmying they were doing!" She snorted. "Then he took me to the back room of the cabaret. It was a proper gaming hall in miniature, all shoved into some room off the main floor. I was quite disappointed we didn't need a password or something like they do at those little drinking holes in America."

Now impatient, Saffron asked, "And you recognized the description of the man Wells was drinking with as someone you saw at the gambling room?"

"Yes, darling!" Elizabeth beamed. "The barkeep described him quite inadequately, but I've heard of him. He's a middle-aged man who walks with a limp. He frequents the gaming room. Everyone just calls him Alfie."

"Alfie," Saffron repeated, wracking her brain for if she'd heard that name recently.

"We've got to go to Le Curieux Cabaret and speak to Alfie. Having unfriendly talks with a dead man is definitely suspicious!"

It took ten minutes of Elizabeth coaxing and cajoling her until Saffron had to agree there was some merit in the idea. It wasn't incredible that a second-rate cabaret might have a secret casino hidden in the back. Such things were reported in the papers—which Elizabeth was sure to point out to her, as she'd usually at least heard of the places, if not actually visited—she just didn't see how it could possibly relate to the lab.

Elizabeth was convinced, however, and ready with a plan. Considering she'd already taken it upon herself to search out clues relating to Petrov's and Wells's deaths twice now, Saffron was sure Elizabeth would end up asking questions around the gaming room regardless of whether Saffron agreed to accompany her.

The actual plan, Saffron was even less confident about.

Alexander had mentioned he would not be available to see her that evening—he planned to go to Kingston to check in on his brother—thus she'd stayed at the laboratory late. Elizabeth didn't think that was a problem in the least. She refused to telephone her brother's hotel, saying breezily, "We don't need him to sit down at the card table."

They did need an escort, however, and Elizabeth's suggestion of who ought to accompany them surprised Saffron, even more so when he agreed to go with them to Le Curieux Cabaret.

Yet there Lee was, waltzing into their flat at a quarter to ten that evening, decked out in his evening kit and looking as fresh as a daisy.

"Everleigh," he said, dropping a kiss on her cheek. "Elizabeth, a pleasure." He kissed her hand.

Despite her frequent protestations that she despised Lee, Elizabeth grinned. She and Saffron were already dressed in their third-best gowns on Elizabeth's orders, and Elizabeth was sipping a sherry. She handed Lee his own glass. "Ready for a bit of fun?"

"I would have agreed had you stopped at cabaret, my dear," he said, lifting the sherry in a toast. "But add in a secret casino and nefarious characters, and you would have to pry me loose from the pair of you."

Saffron glanced warily between her two friends as they drained their glasses. She had the suspicion that, of the three of them, she would be the most reasonable, and that was absolutely unnerving.

CHAPTER 31

Le Curieux Cabaret was no Criterion Club, which Saffron had joined Elizabeth in visiting a number of times, but the owners had done their best to make the space elegant. It was housed in a large building that Saffron guessed had once been a bank, or something like it, as it had tall ceilings decked with columns and entablature whose flaking paint had been painted over, giving it an oddly crackled texture. Deep red fabric hung from high points on the walls, gathered and lit to create dynamic shadows that rippled slightly each time someone passed them by. It was an interesting solution to the problem of either damaged walls to hide or a lack of pleasing artwork. The round tables covered in white cloths were crowded, and the air smelled of smoke, sweat, and too-sharp scent.

The wood dance platform, built overtop the stone floor, was empty of dancers, save for one.

A girl danced in the center, a spotlight trained on her as she leaped and hopped. It wasn't the dancing that arrested Saffron's interest—though it was rather avant-garde—it was her outfit. Saffron had known she was in for an interesting experience, coming to a cabaret where things were rumored to get particularly lurid, but this was something else altogether. The dancer was dressed in what was essentially a pair of tap pants and a brassiere top—both made of white fur. Matching fur ears attached to a fluffy bandeau wrapped around her head and a delicate tail, no doubt lined with wire to keep it at a jaunty angle, was attached to her behind. It bobbed with each of her skittering leaps.

"Absolutely incredible," Lee murmured as the girl did a jump that forced her legs parallel to the floor.

A moment later, a tall, lithe man emerged from a little structure on the platform Saffron hadn't noticed. He rose to his full height, stretching languorously, which allowed his skintight white suit painted with brown and black spots to hug his impressive figure. The man finished his stretch, then froze as he apparently caught sight of the feline dancer. They stared at each other, the tension between them emphasized by a few short blasts from a trumpet. Then the music broke, and the man—clearly a dog, now that Saffron saw he wore floppy ears—scampered over to the woman. The crowd tittered as he caught her, then swept her up and over his head. The cat dancer lunged backward. The man swung her up and over his head again, then, with startling efficiency, tossed her into a series of acrobatic maneuvers that made Saffron's head spin.

She'd seen some strange things in Elizabeth's company, but this had to top them. She glanced at Elizabeth, but she was murmuring into the ear of a handsome, tuxedoed waiter.

Meanwhile, the female dancer had wrapped her legs around the male's neck as he spun, leaving the woman suspended in midair. A glance at Lee told her that he was ready to burst from either laughter or amazement.

Elizabeth leaned over to whisper in her ear. "We're to wait until the end of this number, then that fellow will show us in." She nodded to the waiter she'd spoken to, now lurking in the corner, avidly watching the dancers.

At the conclusion of the number, to the blaring of trumpets and crashing of drums as the canine dancer swung the feline dancer into his arms one final time and then retreated with her into the little doghouse structure at the edge of the dance floor, Elizabeth got up. She looped her arm through Saffron's, and Lee trailed them as they followed the waiter.

He wove between pillars and past tables until they reached a stretch of the room that was more populated by potted palms than people. The waiter stopped before an open door that led to a dark hall.

"Second door on the left. Knock twice," he instructed in a thick Cockney accent that didn't match his suave appearance. He slipped away.

Elizabeth squeezed Saffron's arm. "Let's see if we can find Alfie."

Saffron might just keel over, Elizabeth thought the moment they entered the smoky back room of Le Curieux Cabaret. And Lee might just kiss her for bringing him here.

It was just as she remembered. Green baize poker tables stacked with chips, roulette wheels spinning away, and dice flying across hazard tables—there was no doubt what this place was, though they likely had clever ways to hide the obvious gambling paraphernalia should the police ever come knocking. Elizabeth guessed that the cheap wood paneling lining the walls hid a number of places to stash the stuff. Though alcohol was still plenty legal in England, unlike across the ocean, gambling raids were a common thing. A number of her friends had spent uncomfortable nights in jail cells because of them, and Elizabeth had no intention of joining their ranks. If there was a sniff of trouble, she'd kick their way out if she had to.

But it wasn't the prospect of a police raid that had Elizabeth eyeing Saffron—it was the girls working the floor of the room. They were clad mostly in beads, and those beads did not hide much. It was surprisingly well done, making the girls look exotic rather than tawdry, Elizabeth thought. But Saffron, for all her modernity, could be frightfully naïve at times despite Elizabeth's best efforts to educate her.

She tugged Saffron away from the curious looks of the men at the nearest table, next to which Saffron had come to an abrupt halt, and linked their arms together as they wandered over to watch a roulette wheel spin to a clicking stop.

"Lee and I will stay here and make some delicate inquiries about our pal Alfie," she whispered to Saffron.

Her friend's worried eyes flashed to hers. "And I'll do what, exactly?"

"You're going to have a look in their back office."

"What back office?"

"These sorts of places always have a place where precise records are kept of who owes what and when their time to repay their debts expires. You ought to check to see if Jeffery Wells or Petrov—or anyone else involved—owed these people money. That's a powerful motive for murder."

Saffron swallowed hard, audible over the renewed clattering of the roulette wheel. "Where is the back room?"

Elizabeth glanced around, but saw nothing readily apparent in the dim corners of the room other than the handful of bruisers who didn't bother making themselves look like anything but the hired muscle they were. They stood at intervals about the room, plainly keeping watch over the patrons.

"Let's take a walk and find out," she murmured to Saffron. She pressed a kiss to Lee's cheek to give herself the chance to mutter, "Play the part, and I'll find you shortly."

Elizabeth chose a meandering path, the two of them idly moving from table to table to get a feel for the place and keep an eye out for Alfie. She'd never met the man herself, but she'd heard he was the sort of fellow who drew one's attention. If he was in the room, she was sure to spot him sooner rather than later.

The air was heavy with smoke and the sort of sickening anticipation that those who needed to win often emitted. She didn't care for it. When she was in the mood for debauchery, she found a place with the sort of easy atmosphere that encouraged bad behavior. This place made her feel like she needed a long, hot bath, and she'd barely been inside for five minutes.

In addition to the waitresses in their glittering strings of beads, a number of women sat at the tables or stood behind their male partners. Elizabeth recognized a woman from a literary salon she'd attended a few months ago and approached her to chat.

"Darling," Elizabeth drawled, bending to kiss the short woman's cheek. She couldn't recall her name, but the radical things she'd said during the meeting were unforgettable. With high cheekbones and a nose like a mountain, her features were equally memorable.

"My dear," the woman crooned back in a thick Slavic accent, pressing her cheek to Elizabeth's. She likely didn't recall her name either. "How are you?"

"Very well," Elizabeth said. "Haven't seen Alfie about, have you?"

The woman frowned slightly at Elizabeth's casual question. "No, I have not seen him. Most unlike him. He usually keeps a close eye on his tables."

Elizabeth's stomach swooped unpleasantly. Alfie's tables, were they? She kept her voice light. "Hasn't made an appearance yet, then? I suppose I can while away some time somehow." With a wave of her white-gloved fingers, she wafted away, drawing Saffron along in her wake.

She kept this up, wandering here and there, placing a bet on occasion at roulette, until she and Saffron had stopped drawing so much attention from the patrons and guards. The bruisers' eyes were sharp, and their poorly fitted dinner jackets bulged in unlikely places, suggesting concealed weapons. That was a change from her previous visit. Elizabeth wondered if it was the gaming tables that had gotten more dangerous or something else. Regardless, their presence wouldn't help with getting answers or slipping around unnoticed.

On one turn about the room, Elizabeth saw what she'd been looking for. Hidden along the wall panels was the outline of a door. Naturally, it was situated exactly three steps away from two of the guards. She nudged Saffron and darted her eyes toward the door. Saffron followed her gaze, then inhaled sharply when she spotted it. Elizabeth drew them in the opposite direction.

Across the room, Lee had engaged the patrons around the roulette table with what looked to be a rousing tale. He was an obnoxious creature, with more good looks, money, and intelligence than anyone was worthy of, but Elizabeth was glad he was at least putting it to good use for once.

A few of the thugs who lined the walls wandered over to the guards close to the hidden door. She overheard one mutter something about needing to check a newcomer at the poker table, and the other grunted, "Go on, then—but 'urry it up."

One of the thugs disappeared through the hidden door. That was confirmation enough that the room contained information rather than a toilet or something. The door was far enough away from the tables that it would be obvious if someone tried to get in. Elizabeth needed a distraction.

A solution came to her, and the moment the man came back through the hidden door, she deposited Saffron at the nearest table and sauntered over to the group of thugs. On the pretense of straightening her glove, she muttered out of the corner of her mouth, "The fellow with the mole at the hazard table is cheating."

One of the guards jerked his head around to her. "What—?"

"Don't look at me, you idiot!" she hissed. "If anyone sees me ratting him out, I'm through. But there's a lot of clams on the line, and I'd rather Alfie owe me a favor."

The guard hesitated.

"If anyone asks, I know nothing, all right?" Elizabeth said harshly and made for Saffron.

She counted to five in her head, waiting for the guard to move. At five, she glanced over her shoulder to see the thug was signaling for the others to converge on the hazard table. Elation swept through her, and she pushed Saffron toward the hidden door.

Chapter 32

Saffron's heart stuttered as the door shut behind her. On the other side of the door, there was some sort of uproar, no doubt Elizabeth's doing, but that unnerved her less than the fact that the room was *tiny*. She could barely take three steps across within, it was so small and crowded with furniture. Her breath stuck in her chest.

From Elizabeth's conjectures about records, she'd expected a filing cabinet or something, but she saw only a desk with a tiny lamp, a heavy chair, and a rug that was rolled at the edges of the room, too large for it. It was all good quality, better suited to a real office than this hole in the wall.

She rounded the desk with difficulty, her thighs squeezing between the desk and the wall, and sat in the chair. It was dreadfully uncomfortable for how plush it looked.

The desk drawers were unlocked, to her surprise, but held only pens, ink, spare poker chips. She ran her fingers over the insides of the desk drawers in hopes of a secret compartment. That was just the sort of thing one would expect to find behind a secret door in a secret gaming room.

She leaned forward, digging her hand all the way back into a drawer, and let out a yelp as pain bit her in *quite* an intimate place. She jerked out of the chair, only to see that a sharp corner had been raised within the leather that ought to be well padded.

For a long moment, she stared at it. Then she let out a disbelieving laugh and went to her knees. She curled an arm under the chair

216 ✑   Kate Khavari

and brushed the underside of the seat, only to encounter a familiar feeling: the binding of a book.

With some careful maneuvering, she shifted the book until it was extracted from the crisscross of iron just beneath where the cushion ought to be. A grin spread across her face as she lifted the book to the desk.

It was a ledger, simply bound in black leather and absolutely enormous. Half the pages had the wrinkled look of having been written on. She flipped open the first page.

Secret codes should be added to her list of disappointments for the evening; this was a plain accounting of the patrons and their debts to the club. Alfie's name was nowhere to be found, but when Saffron flipped to the year 1923 and scanned down the list of alphabetical names, Jeffery Wells was there. And he owed a considerable sum.

Saffron frowned down at the number. A large amount, about a thousand pounds. Enough to sink a fellow, and far more than someone would kill over. But did it have anything to do with the lab? Was there a connection between Alfie and Wells, apart from a gambling debt? Perhaps Alfie had been sent to Harpenden to insist Wells repay his debt.

That was a tidy solution, but it wouldn't explain why Wells had died the way he did nor how it might connect to Petrov's death.

Petrov! She flipped the page, scanning the list for the Ps. Her whole body jolted, however, when her eyes lit on another name.

The book had to be wrong—but how could it be?

Why would whoever did the accounting for this illicit casino write in an entry about Colin Eugene Smith, age twenty-eight, living on Berwick Street in Soho, if it was not *Elizabeth's* Colin Eugene Smith, age twenty-eight, living on Berwick Street in Soho?

Her stomach roiled with the knowledge that the man her best friend had been seeing was in deep, dark debt.

It was not . . . unbelievable that Colin was a gambler, nor that he could have found his way to a place like this. The number on the paper, however, boggled the mind when one considered Colin's expensive clothing and his purported hobbies. She just wished she didn't have to now tell Elizabeth.

Gritting her teeth, she finished her search. The P section of 1923 was missing any Petrovs, as was the rest of the book, going back to its beginning in 1920. She replaced the book and was just straightening up when a renewed disturbance beyond the little office stopped her heart in her chest. What had happened now?

CHAPTER 33

The first sign something was wrong was that the cabaret's music, which could be heard over the chatter of the gamblers, stopped abruptly. The aftermath of the supposed cheater's loud expulsion from the room had taken a good deal of time to settle, so few patrons noticed the sudden lack of music. Elizabeth watched as they shrugged it off and went back to their gaming.

Lee noticed, and sent her a questioning look across the poker table over which they both stood. He'd sidled over to her during the hubbub and they'd exchanged a few terse whispers before moving apart again, the better to keep an eye on the room and the hidden door. The moment either of them saw any indication that Saffron was ready to emerge, or that one of the guards planned to enter the room, they'd create another distraction.

The music falling silent was not a cause for alarm—that is, until a subtle rattle began to make ripples in the drinks on the poker table.

The other patrons noticed that. The room slowly quieted.

Then one of the tuxedoed waiters from the cabaret burst through the casino's entrance. Face glistening with sweat, he spoke only one word, and it was sufficient to throw the room into chaos. "Raid!"

Noise and movement surrounded Elizabeth, buffeting her before she'd fully processed the waiter's announcement. Then her hand was in Lee's and he was dragging her in the opposite direction of the crowd. The frantic patrons were making for the doors—doors that had not been there moments before, the half-sized ones the bruisers had opened by tearing the paneling from the walls.

Once she realized Lee was pushing in the direction of the secret office's door, she did her best to shove her way forward. They were there in moments, only to be thwarted by the door being locked.

Elizabeth yanked on the embedded handle, then stared blankly at this unexpected obstacle. Who'd locked the bloody thing, and how were they meant to get Saffron out without drawing the attention of the guards who hadn't yet escaped? The room was already draining of patrons scrambling for their chance to flee through the tiny doors. They'd miss their own chance to get out before the police busted in if they didn't get cracking.

"Break it down," Elizabeth ordered.

Lee looked agog at her. "Break down the door? Are you mad? Those thugs will break me in half!"

"How else are we meant to get her out?" hissed Elizabeth.

Harassed as he was, Lee managed to give her a disparaging look. "You could try knocking."

He did so, pitching his voice low to call, "Everleigh, open up. We've got to breeze."

To Elizabeth's immense relief, the door opened. Saffron took in the scene behind them with parted lips. "What on earth—"

"Oi!"

Their heads whipped around to see a guard a dozen feet away with beady eyes locked on them.

That was the last thing they needed now! Elizabeth grabbed Saffron's arm and hauled her toward the nearest exit, eyeing the guard attempting to muscle his way toward them past the tide of patrons.

But it was then that the first bobby materialized and the shrill of his whistle threw the room into greater chaos. Cursing and pushing became shouting and shoving as black-clad bobbies flooded the room like so many ants pouring from their hill.

Fear blazed like a hot anvil in the center of Elizabeth's chest, but it soon transformed into angry determination. Damn it all, she was *not* going to be arrested!

Still gripping Saffron's arm, she pushed as forcefully as she dared through the remaining people gathered at the nearest makeshift exit.

A gap opened up as two patrons argued who'd go first, and she dove for it—only to be stopped abruptly by a hard jerk on her arm and the blast of a whistle directly in her ear.

Elizabeth wheeled around, screeching inelegantly at the pain ringing in her ear and fully prepared to sock the fellow touching her right on the nose, even if he was a policeman.

A familiar pair of hazel eyes glared down at her from beneath the custodian's helmet.

Elizabeth gasped in recognition and outrage, only to snap her mouth shut. How the devil was Nick here and in uniform? But she was too aware of the precariousness of their position to argue with a friendly face in the midst of such chaos.

She stopped struggling against Nick's grip on her arm and allowed him to escort her from the gaming room, Saffron in tow.

They were led through the pandemonium filling every corner of the gaming room and the cabaret. Patrons bodily fighting off bobbies, and bobbies raising nightsticks between blasting on their wretched whistles, made Elizabeth feel she'd stepped into a particularly violent film. Her hand nearly slipped from Saffron's a dozen times as Nick threaded them past the worst of it.

Outside, police vehicles were swarmed with bobbies loading disgruntled patrons inside. Nick did not lead them to one of the motorcars, however, but moved confidently to the edge of the action. Elizabeth managed a look behind her and saw with great relief that Saffron and Lee were following.

When at last Nick let go of her arm at the mouth of an alley, leaving it prickling uncomfortably along with the ache of future bruises, he doffed his custodian helmet and slipped from his bobby jacket with two quick movements, shoving them into a rubbish bin. Nick swept his eyes briefly over Elizabeth and the others. "Come on." He struck out with his ground-eating strides into the alley.

The street on the other side was quiet, but the noise from the raid echoed there. Nick made for a nondescript motorcar sitting at the curb.

"Dr. Lee," Nick said curtly, "I trust you'll be able to make your way home from here."

"Will do," Lee said. "Thanks very much for the help."

Now Elizabeth got a look at him, he seemed a tad shaken. No doubt he feared, as he had before, that his reputation as a medical professional had come dangerously close to being demolished tonight. His attempt at a charming smile didn't quite succeed. "Ladies, good night."

He took off down the street, hands in pockets and pace slow enough not to gain attention.

Elizabeth returned her attention to Nick, only to see him glaring at her. She wrinkled her nose. "If you expect me to fall on bended knee in thanks—"

"Get into the car. We'll discuss this back at your flat."

"Oh, goody," she muttered, "a lecture."

The drive back to Chelsea was suffocating.

Elizabeth was fuming, Nick was silent, and Saffron's head was aching from the stress of the evening, coming off a very long day at the lab. How had it only been a few hours since Elizabeth had made her jump out of her skin outside the Harpenden train station?

The silence pressed her all the way until the three of them were safely ensconced in the parlor of their flat. Elizabeth, clearly not in the mood for the lecture brewing, took her time removing her gloves before settling on the couch across from where Saffron stood near the radiator. She felt frozen to the bone and wrung out but was too keyed up to sit.

Nick rounded on them. "What were you thinking?"

"I was thinking I was going to have a night out with my mates," Elizabeth drawled. Her posture was tight, however, as was her expression. "What were you doing there? How did you know we were there, for that matter?"

"Alfie Tennison is dangerous," Nick said.

That gave even Elizabeth pause long enough for Saffron to get in a question. "Do you know that Wells owed Alfie—he owns the gaming room, I'm guessing—a good deal of money?"

Nick's nostrils flared. "Yes. And I do not want to know how you came to know that."

"I want to know why you didn't bother to tell us that Jeffery Wells owed some dangerous bookie!" Elizabeth cried. "Don't you think that's key information in investigating his *murder*?"

Nick bore down on her, leaning over the couch with arms crossed. "*You* are not investigating anything. Did it ever occur to you that it would be the work of a few hours, if that, to discover who you are, where you live, and that you are employed by the government? What would Alfie have made of learning you work for a minister and you were poking around in his things? You took information from a dangerous man, one whose allegiances are available for purchase, and the current highest bidder opposes the sitting government."

Surprise rioted through Saffron—what was Nick implying?

Elizabeth let out a frustrated scoff. "How the devil was I supposed to know that?"

"You are supposed to have nothing to do with this!"

"Then why are you spying on me? Why are you following me around? How else would you know we'd be at the cabaret, let alone in the gaming room? And where did you get the bloody bobby getup?"

"I was not spying on you," Nick said sharply. "There are a great many more important things on my mind than the shoddy places you spend your time, Eliza."

Elizabeth went bright red, but with a great effort, she forced a patient tone. "I am trying to help, Nicholas. If it weren't for me—"

"I don't need your help."

"So you're willing to accept—*invite*—Saffron's assistance, but not mine? Am I not educated enough for you?"

"In this case, no," Nick said bluntly. "You're meant to be at home. In bed. Preferably alone, though at this point that's probably too much to ask."

Saffron stared at him. He wasn't speaking through any identifiable mask; he merely seemed tired and irritated. But she couldn't believe that Nick would be so tactlessly disrespectful to his own sister.

"Nick," she said in a softly scolding tone, stepping forward in a half-hearted attempt to encourage him to stop towering over Elizabeth.

"No," Elizabeth snapped, pushing to her feet. It forced Nick to step back, and she stood so they were nearly nose to nose. "How right you are, Nick. It *is* too much to ask for me to behave like a good little girl. Are you sure you've been out of touch with our parents? You sound exactly like them. I'd wager you'd like me to put on a virginal white gown and command me to stand perfectly still while men three times my age sniff around me. Maybe you could hold my lips back so they can inspect my teeth like I'm a damned horse for sale!"

Withholding a wince at the increased volume of Elizabeth's growing rant, Saffron did her part and glared at Nick. He showed no reaction whatsoever.

"If I wanted my family to judge and scold me like I'm a child, I'd go back to Bedford. I'm too old for this by far." She let out another frustrated groan, her shoulders bunching. "How stupid I was to believe you'd be any different from them. That you might believe in *me*, might agree that I should live my life how *I* see fit. How idiotic I was to think you might have been more like Wesley."

Silence fell as Elizabeth's voice broke on her brother's name. Saffron went to her side, took her hand and squeezed it.

Elizabeth let out a shuddering breath. "You may exit my life now and stay gone from it this time. Better I have no brothers than one who'd use me, only to censure me for trying to help."

Nick's jaw worked, but his voice was cool when it came out. "I see. I will do just that if that is what you truly want. But tell me, should I extricate myself entirely, or would you prefer to keep your job with Lord Tremaine?"

Elizabeth went stiff. "What is that supposed to mean?"

Nick shrugged. "Consider it a parting gift."

He left the room, and a moment later, the front door shut quietly behind him.

CHAPTER 34

Saffron entered the kitchen warily the next morning, unsure what sort of mood Elizabeth would be in. A moment after Nick left, she'd let out a rage-filled shriek before stomping off to her bedroom and refusing to emerge, even after Saffron attempted to get her to talk by offering wine through the bedroom door. Elizabeth had opened the door just long enough to snatch the bottle before closing it again.

"Good morning," Saffron ventured, sitting in her customary seat at the kitchen table.

"Good morning," Elizabeth said. She slid a hot plate of eggs and roasted tomatoes onto the table before Saffron.

Unsure of what else to say, Saffron offered, "Jeffery Wells owed Alfie Tennison close to a thousand pounds. It was in a ledger in the back office."

Elizabeth took the topic in stride. "Based on Nick's not-so-subtle comments last night, Alfie seems be involved in shady politics." She sat down, poured herself a cup of coffee, and inhaled its steam rather forcefully. "But not the sort he suggested, necessarily. In the gaming room, I saw a woman from one of my more radical literary salons. She likes to get on her soapbox and is in favor of the 'burn-it-all-down' approach rather than the 'change-over-time' strategy, or the 'complain-but-do-nothing' attitude that so many of my dear friends languish with." She took a sip of coffee, and her eyes took on a speculative gleam. "I got to thinking—what better way to destroy a government than to use their own discoveries against them? The radicals could get hold of some science experiment from the Path Lab, use it to a deadly end, reveal the government was the one to create it, then incite the people to overthrow the government."

Saffron reached for the coffeepot. "If we're going to speak about government coups, I need coffee first."

Elizabeth allowed Saffron silence to consume her breakfast and contemplate her idea. "A radical political group," she mused as she set her fork and knife on the empty plate. "I would like to think that it's all too far-fetched, but the actions of such a group were what started the war. Millions of people died because a handful of angry people did something about their anger."

"Precisely," Elizabeth said with a firm nod. "I'll be able to find out more soon enough. That particular literary salon dissolved some months ago, but I'll get a message to Jarl—you know, the Dane who makes the atrocious wine. He always knows who is meeting and where. I'll see what the rumors are and see if anything rings a bell."

Saffron knew better than to argue. Investigating radical political groups seemed like a far more dangerous prospect than infiltrating a plant pathology laboratory, but after last night, there was absolutely no way Saffron would try to put her off. She cleared her throat and began, "Nick was so very wrong, Eliza."

"He was," Elizabeth said, pouring herself more coffee. "But he was right about one thing. I believe he did get me my position."

"But of course he didn't!" Saffron declared. "No one deserves that job more than you."

"Nick might have *gotten* me the job," she said, "by putting a word into the right person's ear, but *I* kept it. I am a damned good receptionist. Lord Tremaine is lucky to have me, and if he felt otherwise, he would not have kept me on longer than most of his private secretaries."

Despite her proud words, a shadow of doubt passed over Elizabeth's features. Saffron reached for her hand. "You're right, Eliza. You *are* the best receptionist."

Elizabeth sighed, squeezing her hand back. "Thank you, darling."

It seemed the time had come to tell her what else she'd learned in Alfie Tennison's books. "Colin has debts with Alfie as well. Serious ones."

Elizabeth took in this news with pursed lips. After a moment, she seemed to come to some sort of conclusion. She sighed again. "He seemed so wretchedly dull! He goes on and on about his family and their connections. He told that ridiculous story about his mother spending hundreds of pounds buying up every tonic she could get her hands on. That's the last time I step out with a dull man in hopes of a more settled relationship, mark my words."

"Do you suppose his family is in trouble? Or they cut him off?"

"Either is possible. He might also just be a poor gambler. Figures." She let out an abrupt groan, planting her forehead on the kitchen table. "Damn that Nick! He knew!" She glared at Saffron from between sandy waves of hair. "All those pithy comments about horse racing and Lady Fortune. He knew about Colin's gambling and never said a thing to me! The wretch."

Saffron had to agree. Shifting the conversation away from Nick before Elizabeth could get too far into her temper again, she asked, "You're going to toss Colin over, aren't you?"

Elizabeth scoffed. "I most certainly am! The way he speaks, you'd think he owns half of London rather than owing it. It's entirely dishonest. The only pity is that I'll have to see him 'round the office. He'll still ask me to pull dozens of files for him, and I won't even be rewarded for it." Her cheeks went a bit pink. "And for all his faults, Colin does know how to please a girl."

Saffron cleared her throat. "Well, then. I suppose I ought to be off. Even if I feel I'd rather sleep for weeks, I've got to go to the lab."

The telephone rang.

Elizabeth sighed. "Well, you get a wiggle on and get dressed." She left to answer the telephone, and Saffron rose to wash the dishes before dressing.

But a moment later, Elizabeth was calling from down the hall, "Do you want to take a call from the U?"

At this time in the morning, just after half past eight, it might be Alexander. She hurriedly dried her hands and made for the hall. The operator connected the call, and Saffron said, "Yes?"

"Mademoiselle Everleigh," said a soft, accented voice. "I beg pardon for interrupting your morning, but *le chef* wishes to see you immediately."

Saffron swallowed hard. "Thank you for letting me know, Monsieur Ferrand. I will be on campus shortly."

He rang off without mentioning why Dr. Aster wanted to see her, but Saffron feared she already knew.

CHAPTER 35

Mr. Ferrand's encouraging smile before shutting the door to Aster's office behind her did little to lift Saffron's spirits.

When Dr. Aster lifted his sphinxlike gaze from the papers on his desk, he fixed her with an icy frown. "Sit."

Saffron did, feeling the lack of greeting to be the warning that it was. For all his coldness, Aster was fastidious in his manners. "Good morning, sir," she ventured.

"I received word of a most disturbing change in your career trajectory, Miss Everleigh," he said briskly. "Dr. Jonathon Calderbrook mentioned last evening while we dined, as we do once a month with others who are interested in rigorous research into our field, that he recently took on a new assistant at his laboratory. The man had the gall to boast of his new acquisition. Especially because he knows that you are currently in my employ."

Mouth dry, she said, "I can explain."

Aster's frown deepened, reducing his eyes to slits within his heavily wrinkled face. "There is no need. You took advantage of my acceptance of your request to spend a few weeks researching outside of the university and leveraged my exceedingly generous advancement to full researcher into another position. What I fail to understand is the desire to move down to an assistant, especially at a small government research station in Hertfordshire. In *horticulture*."

His disdain was plain, but Saffron saw beneath it a surprising amount of emotion. The perceived betrayal had brought the barest hint of pink to his papery cheeks. "Dr. Aster, I apologize for any awkwardness the situation has caused you. I . . . I am apprenticing at the lab, but not because I wish to leave the university and work there." She blew out a breath. "At the Paris conference, I ran into Dr. Ingham."

"Ah." The whole of Aster's opinion of the former professor was expressed in that single derisive syllable.

"And he mentioned that my father had been approached by Dr. Calderbrook at Kew. To join the same lab that Dr. Calderbrook now runs in Harpenden."

"And?"

Silence fell between them. He no doubt felt it was as weak an explanation as she knew it was. Curse Nick for making her wait for his ministry's support until after the Path Lab's matters were settled! She doubted Aster would appreciate her need to understand her father. Aster had told her that her father's research was not up for discussion when he promoted her in the spring. She doubted that had changed. She would be sacked and likely hoping to keep her position at the Path Lab after all.

An all-too-familiar feeling of helplessness settled over her shoulders. Eyes on the spotless desk rather than on Aster, she said, "I just wanted to know. I wanted to know what my father had been working on. After what Berking said to me—"

"Berking was, and no doubt continues to be, an imbecile. I thought you, of all people, had perceived that."

Startled at the amusement in his tone, Saffron looked up. Aster's face told her nothing. "I assure you, I am well aware, sir."

Aster scoffed lightly. "Have you spoken to Dr. Calderbrook regarding your father's work?"

"No," she admitted. "The lab has experienced two sudden losses of scientists, so we've been scrambling to make up for it. I haven't had the opportunity."

The truth was she had had time. Dr. Calderbrook attended their afternoon tea breaks, and she'd spoken with him on a few occasions. He'd even mentioned her father during one, but she hadn't tried to ask him why he'd wanted him to join the lab. She wanted her father to be simply a brilliant scientist. As much as she wanted to know the truth, she worried what it would be. She longed to put the matter to rest, but she was a coward in the end.

"As it happens," Aster said, steepling his fingers, "I received a visit from a member of the Agricultural Ministry just this morning. He intimated that your presence in the laboratory related to an issue with which he required your assistance. I believe his name was Hale."

Saffron nodded dumbly. Why hadn't Aster mentioned this first? He clearly enjoyed watching her squirm.

"A relation to your flatmate or a coincidence?" The barest hint of musing in his voice disappeared as he shook his head. "I understand the . . . assignment is considered confidential. I am forced to comply with their wishes, lest the future of collaborations with that institution be put at risk. Next time you wish to venture into government dealings, Miss Everleigh, I require to be made aware of it. Had I not been informed of your cooperation, you would be walking out of the premises with only your temporary position at Dr. Calderbrook's laboratory to support you." His voice went colder. "And the next time you attempt to deny interest in work carried out while under contract from the government, I will be sure to remind you that you risked your career here at the university in order to assist that same government. I daresay I need not mention the hypocrisy of your decisions."

Saffron left the office a few minutes later, head reeling. Aster had given her leave to finish at the lab, but it was a hollow victory. She did feel like a hypocrite. She'd been so eager to solve the mystery that she'd convinced Nick to let her help, despite the fact she'd knowingly damaged her career by refusing to add her name to the government-funded study she'd worked so hard to complete.

But associating her name with the government and information about dangerous plants was different than volunteering to work in an agricultural laboratory in order to solve a murder.

Saffron stopped walking, barely aware that she'd made her way halfway down the hall and now stood in the center of it, interrupting the sparse traffic of the upper level of the North Wing.

Wells had died from a fungal infection. Alexander had mentioned that *Mucor indicus* lived in soil, and she'd accepted that the infection was a coincidence. But what if it wasn't? What if Wells had died from contracting the infection from a specimen the mycologists had strengthened, just as she'd feared her father would have been doing?

A sick feeling overtook her. Such work would have been easy for her to miss. She'd never seen documentation of the specimens Sutcliffe and Mary worked on; she'd asked about *Mucor indicus* and accepted it when they said they didn't work with it. They could have very easily lied, and Saffron would never be any the wiser. She needed to get into the mycology lab and examine all the notes *and* the specimens to find out the truth herself.

Her plans were immediately arrested the moment she walked down the stairs to the second floor of the North Wing.

"Have you just been standing here, lying in wait for me?" Saffron asked Nick.

He shrugged cheerfully.

She shot him an unamused glare. "Step into my office, if you will. I'd like a word."

The air in her office was nearly as cold as it was outside. She'd moved her plants into Alexander's office in anticipation of her absence, and she missed their presence in the window.

"Why did you not tell me that you planned to tell Aster what I'd been doing at the Path Lab?" she asked, not bothering to offer him a seat or take one herself. She wanted an explanation, then she needed to get to Harpenden. She was already going to be considerably late. "You said you weren't going to tell him until matters were concluded."

"Matters are concluded where you are concerned," Nick said smoothly. He quickly slipped his gloves off and offered his hand to her. "The Agricultural Ministry thanks you for your assistance."

Saffron ignored the hand. "The case isn't solved. We don't know how Alfie Tennison fits in with Wells, nor do we know for certain how Wells or Petrov died."

"It was the fungus you and Alexander identified," he replied. "That was the bit I needed help with, and you delivered. Again, thank you."

"We don't know—"

"We know all we need to."

Saffron studied him; there were shadows under his eyes that his pleasant expression could not hide. "Is this because of Elizabeth?"

"I doubt you'll believe me any more than she would if I told you that her involvement in all of this is the furthest thing from what I want." He sighed, his broad shoulders falling a bit.

"I believe you that you wish to keep Elizabeth from danger, but I also agree with her that it's hypocritical for you to engage my cooperation."

His brows shot up. "You're a trained scientist—"

"Whom you took to discover a dead body!" Saffron frowned as she realized how truly unnecessary that had been. "You could have just shown me the autopsy report, or even waited for the coroner or another expert to work on the sample of the *Mucor*. Why did you take me with you and bring me the sample? I'm not a mycologist."

Nick's slight frown didn't waver. "Yet you figured it out—with Alexander's help, I admit—within hours."

"You knew Wells was dead," Saffron countered, "yet you took me to his house. There wasn't anything plant-related there, and you knew that. Why did you take me to see his body?"

Nick gave her a look she couldn't understand. "Why did you agree to go?"

Exasperated, she hissed, "Because you implied I was needed to help plug a hole in national security!"

"You were, and you did. You've provided me the information I needed, and now your part has come to a close." Nick's indecipherable look turned speculative. "Unless you believe you can do more."

Her immediate impulse was to say yes, yes, she did think there was more she could do. She wanted to find the rest of the puzzle pieces and lay them down so she could see how they all fit together. But for some reason, it felt like Nick wasn't asking her to help solve the rest of this mystery.

"What do you mean?" she asked slowly.

"I mean something beyond being a mole in a lab."

"I don't . . . I don't know what you mean," she repeated.

Nick's lips hitched into a crooked smile, suddenly charming. "You're smarter than that, Saffron. Think it through. Do you really think I just happened to desire to reconnect with my sister right now? That it's coincidence?"

Indignation on Elizabeth's behalf welled within her. "You used Elizabeth to get to me? But why?" Her mind raced ahead. She was far from the only botanist in the city and definitely not the only one Nick could have used as a mole in the lab. She was young and female, which might have made her seem an easy target, but Nick had shown no lascivious interest in her whatsoever.

Her voice wavered as she said, "You used me."

"I *employed* you, Saffron. There is a difference. Compensation is the main one. It would be generous and stable. Not to mention what it would do for your career. Publications would just be the start."

"I don't want publications. I turned down the chance to be published because I didn't want my name attached to the government."

"I know," Nick said, taking a small step toward her. His brow furrowed. "I understand. Your father died from chlorine gas. And Wesley . . ."

Pain stabbed in her chest at their mention.

Nick's eyes did not leave hers. "I lost my brother and dozens of men who were like brothers to me. I understand." His hand rested on her shoulder, heavy and warm. "That's why I chose to take this work on. To prevent things like this from happening again."

"Your work—"

"Is not so different from yours. We could both be working to prevent disasters, Saffron."

Visions of the fields of Ypres and Flanders clouded her mind. Muddy wastelands where, years after war tore it to pieces, things were barely coming back to life. "Scientists didn't prevent the greatest disaster of our time, did they? They made it worse. More traumatizing. More deadly."

Nick merely looked at her, the impatience in his gaze making her aggravation burn hotter.

"Thank you for the offer, but no," she said firmly. "I took this on because you led me to believe it was essential I help discover what

happened to Petrov and Wells and ensure the security of the laboratory. I realize now you had a bigger scheme in mind, and I want no
part of it."

"I never took you for the type to turn your back on those in
need."

"I don't," Saffron replied. She went to the door and opened it.
"You, and the government, don't need my help to destroy things.
Once I tell Elizabeth the real reason why you came to town and
rekindled your relationship, you'll finish destroying anything you've
repaired with her."

He followed on silent feet. Once he was inches away, she wished
she saw regret in his eyes but saw only intense focus. "You would hurt
her so badly?"

A pang of sadness rang through her chest. It would hurt
Elizabeth. But it was better that she know. "I would protect her. She
should know the kind of man you turned out to be."

CHAPTER 36

Nick left, leaving Saffron reeling once again. She looked around her office, desperate for a comfort or distraction, but there was only a cold chair by a cold window and stacks of books that had already accumulated dust.

She closed the door gently behind her, locked it, and walked down the hall. At the door of Alexander's office, she knocked softly and went inside at his word.

"Saffron." He smiled at her from his desk.

"Aster called me in to ask me about the Path Lab." She crossed the office, and without invitation, simply sat in his lap.

His chair squeaked in protest as Alexander's arms came around her. She closed her eyes, willing the stiffness in his embrace to melt away so she could take comfort from his presence and warmth. After a moment, he loosened up, and his cheek came to rest on her collarbone.

She poured out the whole ridiculous story of the previous evening, ending with recounting the conversation that had just transpired between her and Nick. By the time she'd finished, she'd gotten to her feet and was pacing the small room. The more she explained, the deeper the depths of her own stupidity appeared.

"I cannot believe I thought I'd convinced him that I should work in the lab. It was clearly a ploy to get me to want to do it. I've tangled myself up with two other investigations, and he knew I'd leap at the chance to do it again." She sank onto the chair opposite Alexander, feeling idiotic. "I'm so wretchedly transparent, aren't I?"

He gave her a sympathetic smile. "You'd not be the first to be taken in by Nick Hale. It is his job, after all."

Surprisingly, that made her feel better. She propped an elbow on the arm of her chair and let her chin rest in her palm. "Will you tell me what happened between the two of you in Greece? Why do you dislike him so?"

He pondered it for a moment before saying, "I will tell you part of it. The part that wouldn't get me accused of treason."

She waited impatiently for him to collect his thoughts, idly aware that she ought to be heading to Harpenden but unwilling to leave all the same.

"I was recruited by a friend of a friend who knew I'm fluent in Greek. I'd been home for a few weeks after my release from the convalescent hospital, and I wasn't doing well." He paused, shaking his head. "It was a hard time. When the opportunity came up, my father all but pushed me out the door."

Surprised, she asked, "He was quick to send you out again after you were hurt?"

"He was eager for me to do something other than stare out of the window," Alexander said dryly. "My mother didn't speak to him for weeks after I left, apparently. She wanted me to stay home. She still would prefer I be at home." He wore a fond smile, which faded as he continued. "I joined the party and went to Greece. I'd been there to visit family a few times before, but the war had changed so many things. I did what I was asked to do, and I'm afraid I can't give you many more details than that." He shot her a rueful but humorous look.

She stifled a groan of frustration. She wanted to know more, but she understood why he shouldn't tell her. "And Nick?"

"He was working there too. As fellow Englishmen, we socialized. There was a hotel where many of us stayed, and I saw Nick most evenings. I didn't know what he was doing there, but he wore a uniform and I . . . I was generally not sober enough to care who anyone was or their business." Saffron bit her lip at the self-disgust she heard in his voice. "At that point, I'd quietly drink myself into a stupor in a corner each night, and so I saw the comings and goings of the others. I noticed Nick paid a good deal of attention to one of the English businessmen living in Salonika who hung around with the English officers."

Alexander cleared his throat, an uneasiness coming over him. "One evening as I dragged myself up to my room, I saw Nick inviting the businessman into his room. They looked . . . intimate."

Saffron blinked. Nick, intimate with a man?

Alexander pressed on. "That, alone, was not anything that surprised me. I'd seen a good many men act differently at war than they might at home, and I've seen enough of the natural world now to know that it isn't the unnatural inclination most believe it to be. I hope we can agree on that." Saffron nodded. "The businessman was found dead three days later. Not in Nick's room," he added hurriedly. "But in his own house. It was a gruesome sight, according to those who'd stopped by for a look. I heard it looked like an execution." At her shocked inhalation, he shook his head. "The representatives in charge of our party made a point of involving themselves, as the fellow had been English. The investigation into his death concluded it was a business rival, but no one was ever arrested."

"But you suspected Nick?"

"No," Alexander said. "Not at first, anyway. I watched him work his way through a number of men and women during our stay at the hotel. Some were rumored to be involved in political dealings, others in business deals directly related to the war effort. Some were just people, from what I could tell, and no one else ended up dead. But several were arrested for crimes like treason, a few were ruined financially or socially, and at least one turned out to be a spy for Germany. I've no proof Nick had any part of those consequences, but I find it suspicious."

She couldn't help but gape at him. "And you didn't say anything when you realized Elizabeth was his sister? How could you never even hint—"

"You made it seem like they were estranged when you showed me the photograph in your parlor. Elizabeth doesn't speak about her family. I never thought it would come up."

She sighed. "I suppose you're right. I just can't believe it. And I can't believe I fell for it. I'm no better than all those people he seduced into revealing their secrets."

Alexander gave her that sympathetic look again. "People in Nick's line of work don't look at people and see individuals with lives and families. People are either tools or obstacles. They either can be manipulated to suit their purposes, or they are removed. And you won't know which you are until it's too late."

A heavy silence fell between them. She didn't know what that meant for her. If Nick believed her to be an obstacle rather than an asset, what would he do? Would her rejecting an offer of employment impact her career in the long run? The one thing she kept coming back to was why he'd offered her a job in such a roundabout way to begin with. Why go through the trouble of enticing her with solving the mystery at the Path Lab?

The question ate at her. "I just don't understand why Nick wanted me, specifically. He could have had his pick of botanists. He could have taken someone from a science park, or walked into any university in town, or even gone to Kew and requisitioned someone from there. Why me?"

"Why not you?" Alexander asked, his head tilted slightly to the side as if he was considering the question himself. "You're trained by a university known for its botany program. You've worked in greenhouses and labs. You're intelligent and tenacious, and willing to do things differently. And, as you mentioned, you've caught murderers before." His eyes warmed, and his lips formed a little smile. "You'd be at the top of my list. You *were* at the top of my list."

And with that, Saffron felt something had changed between them, something more than the shift from uneasy friendship to rekindled romance. Though she wouldn't have thought it possible even minutes before, she found herself feeling grateful to Nick.

It was close to noon when Saffron finally managed to telephone the Path Lab and tell them that she was not able to come in that day. Her surprise could have knocked her off the stool in the cramped telephone room when Joseph's gruff voice was the one to answer the telephone.

"Joseph!" she exclaimed. "You're back in the lab. The police concluded you were innocent of everything, I suppose."

"Aye," he mumbled. "What did you need, miss?"

"I'm unable to come to the lab today. I'm afraid I'm under the weather. Please apologize on my behalf for calling so late."

"Right."

In the background, she heard Joseph relaying that Saffron was unwell. The other side crackled, then Dr. Calderbrook's anxious voice spoke into her ear. "Is it serious, Miss Everleigh? Only with the recent issues, I'm afraid news of yet another staff member ill might be cause for alarm."

"Oh, er—" She wanted *not* to raise an alarm. Screwing up her face, she said, "Female troubles, I'm afraid, sir."

Dr. Calderbrook made a choked sound. "I see, I see. Never you mind, then. I do hope you, er, recover quickly."

Still wincing, Saffron rang off. Well, that was one problem solved. Now to face a greater one.

Lord Tremaine's rooms were on the third floor of a grand old building in Westminster. Saffron had been there twice since Elizabeth began working there five years ago, and she remembered the way up the palatial stone steps that wound around the middle of the building. Thick carpets muffled her steps, adding to the overall hush of the building.

But, Saffron reflected as a familiar voice drew her down a hall, things never stayed quiet for long when Elizabeth Hale was around.

". . . not at all what I meant," Elizabeth's strident tones said. "There is no need for accusations."

"It is not an accusation if the man all but said it to the entire party," Colin Smith replied.

Saffron approached the open door from which the voices emanated and peered inside. Elizabeth stood in the middle of a long room full of filing cabinets. She and Colin wore matching frowns. Colin stood with his arms crossed over his chest, a blotchy flush reddening his face and neck.

"Nick has nothing to do with our relationship," Elizabeth ground out, her own color high.

"Yet you had no complaints until he came into town," Colin countered.

"It is a woman's prerogative to change her mind."

"Changeable. Yes, that is a good word for you," he said, his tone turning sneering. "I'd no idea you were so inconstant, for all your stubbornness."

"There's no need for insults," Elizabeth replied. "We don't suit, and that's that."

"More like you believe you can find a better prospect in this office," he shot back. "I've been warned a dozen times about your flirtations with everyone who walks in the door. Hoping to catch a minister or lord, are you? I doubt they'd deign to lift your family—"

Colin caught sight of Saffron and froze. His color went deeper, and he straightened up. "I must return to my duties," he said stiffly. He walked past Saffron with an indifferent nod.

Saffron ventured into the filing room. "Took it well, did he?"

"Obviously," muttered Elizabeth. She didn't seem affected by Colin's accusations, though Saffron knew she was seething inside. She eyed Saffron. "What brings you here?"

It was exceptionally poor timing, considering the scene she'd walked in on, but it couldn't be helped. "We need to talk about Nick."

Elizabeth's expression hardened. "What did he do now?"

When Saffron was finished with her report of the conversation, and Alexander's observations, Elizabeth looked ready to go to battle.

"We don't need a chat; we need a bloody war council." She took a few angry paces in one direction, then switched to another. "I am finished with Nick. He's a manipulative, lying, unfeeling bastard, and I want to be rid of him as soon as possible."

"He said I'm done with the case," Saffron said. "I hope that means he's off."

Elizabeth scoffed. "You think he'll let go of this notion of convincing you to work for him—with him?—so easily? I very much doubt that." She scowled at the nearest cabinet, on top of which sat a stack of files. "Colin didn't even take the wretched files. He likely did it on purpose, so I'd have to play delivery girl for him." She snatched the files off the cabinet and rounded on Saffron. "We need to figure out what's happening in that lab. That's the only way Nick will get a new assignment. Otherwise, he has an excuse to hang around and approach you again."

Saffron had to agree. "How do you suggest we do that?"

"I'm going to see Jarl and find a meeting where I can ask some subtle questions about Alfie Tennison's possible radical connections. If Wells owed him money, Alfie could have forced him to do something crooked at the laboratory. And you . . ." She swung around, still pacing. "You'll have to go back to Harpenden."

"I haven't had luck finding out what's going on there. It's too hard to look around where I'm not meant to without someone noticing."

"Then go when no one is around and look at everything you can get your hands on," Elizabeth said grimly. "We'll break in. Poke around. Tonight."

"You just said you need to see Jarl."

"Drat." Elizabeth propped her hands on her hips. "Take Lee. He seemed to enjoy our outing to Le Curieux Cabaret."

"I'll take Alexander," Saffron said as the idea came to her. "He's the one who identified the fungus, after all. He knows laboratories better than any of us." She pursed her lips, recalling how Lee's hand had lingered on the small of her back, how his eyes had dipped to her lips during their adventure at the cabaret. "You should take Lee with you instead. You're right, he did enjoy the outing, but I think it was for the wrong reasons. I don't want him to get ideas."

"I'd wondered if you'd noticed that." Elizabeth's lips pursed. "It's Alexander, isn't it?"

"Well, yes," Saffron said, surprised by her suddenly serious tone. "He and I are together now."

Elizabeth's expression softened. "No, darling. It's *been* Alexander, hasn't it?"

The truth of what Elizabeth suggested sank through her, sending her heart fluttering. She nodded, temporarily robbed of words.

With a comforting hand on her shoulder, Elizabeth gave her a bracing smile. "For all his flaws, Lee is a decent fellow. I doubt he'll hold it against you." She smiled rather viciously. "But if he does throw a fit, feel free to toss him right into the bin along with Colin. Poor fellow will need some company."

CHAPTER 37

Breaking and entering was best done in the warmer months, Saffron decided. Summer would be ideal, for lurking outdoors would be pleasant rather than cold. She'd never plan criminal activities for the winter again.

She and Alexander had arrived at sunset in Harpenden. He'd agreed immediately to her scheme, asking only once if she felt it was a good idea, and had kept quiet after she admitted she was wary but determined to get Nick out of their lives.

She'd known there was a cluster of new homes being built further down Milton Road, providing a convenient, if uncomfortable, place from which to watch the activity at Number 28. The windows of the lower level, where the laboratories were, had been dark for hours already. It was nearly ten in the evening. Another hour, and Saffron was sure the few lingering lights above stairs would be extinguished.

A gust of wind swept through the half-finished house, and Saffron burrowed further into her coat. The cold had set in as twilight came upon them. She'd not thought to wear trousers, and her freezing legs were complaining about it. She'd already wrapped her scarf around her ankles.

Alexander's voice drifted through the dark. "You can see the house fine from here."

"But then I can't see the road. Believe me, I would much rather be taking advantage of your body heat."

His chuckle faded quickly, and they went back to sitting in silence.

They'd eaten sandwiches from the Dancing Sparrow soon after they'd settled in the defunct house, but they'd neglected to bring anything to drink. Her mouth was sticky and dry, and not just from the corned beef. Her realization about the extent of her feelings for Alexander had kept her tongue-tied, unsure what, if anything, she ought to say to him about it.

"I had to do this during the war," he murmured. He was all but invisible, just a black shape against a dark wall, but she perceived him turning to her.

"I often took night watch," he said. "I preferred it to the daylight duties on offer between bouts of shelling. Better to watch and wait than clean dishes or shore up the breastworks."

Saffron had no idea what to say to that. She didn't often hear about the mundanities of war, and she'd least expected them from Alexander. After poking at his secrets for the past few weeks, she didn't imagine he'd tell her much willingly.

"I thought it would be exciting," he continued, "being the one to raise the alarm if I caught sight of a light or heard gunfire."

"Did you?" She'd never thought of him as the sort of person to seek out excitement in the form of outright danger. He'd been scolding her off such pursuits for nearly the length of their acquaintance.

"I did," he said, almost wistfully, but it disappeared from his voice as he continued. "That was how I came to be injured. Command planned to take a place called Sugarloaf. It was a small rise that the German bulge occupied. We were to attack from the west. A division of Australians were to come at them from the east. I volunteered to do some scouting. I had no business going, but I was sick of standing around waiting. It was a warm, quiet day, the sort that once you got far enough away from camp, you might have forgotten we were at war." He shifted in the darkness. "We lingered too long and were caught by surprise when the shelling started before the attack. I don't remember much after the shelling began, but I remember seeing movement in the grass, and my companions yelling to take cover. I can only guess what happened, but I think someone panicked and threw a grenade. The blast caught us, but I was damned lucky. The debris set my uniform on fire, but the ground was wet, so only my right side burned. The remaining member of my party dragged me back to camp. I missed the attack, which proved to be my salvation. I was unconscious, on my way to the field hospital while my peers ran to their deaths."

Without making the conscious decision to do so, Saffron rose and went to where Alexander sat. She sank down next to him so she faced him, his face touched by faint silver light.

He had not fallen into his recollections, she realized. His depthless eyes were sharp on her.

"The leadership had vastly underestimated the Germans' preparations. They—" He broke off with a sigh. Her hand moved to cover his. The leather of their gloves kept their skin from touching, but she felt the connection nonetheless. "Suffice it to say, it was a disaster. Nearly an entire battalion of Australians were killed. My own division came out badly as well."

In the heavy, silent darkness, Saffron was struck with understanding of his reluctance to speak about his days as a soldier. They'd been short and harrowing, but his injury marked a mistake, a mistake that allowed him to keep his own life while thousands of his fellows perished. She could not fathom the guilt he must have felt, the unwarranted shame of it.

Her throat went tight, and she found the potent mixture of fear, relief, and sympathy was overwhelming.

"I am glad, then," she managed to say, voice too high. "For the shelling, and the grenade. That you were hurt before you could be sent out." This was perhaps not the right thing to say, given the way he was staring at her. She hastened to add, "I know that your injury has given you no end of trouble but I . . ." She faltered and blinked rapidly at the emotion threatening to spill from her eyes. "I would have never known you otherwise."

"I admit I am grateful for it too," he said softly. "I wish I could go back in time and tell myself that one day I would be glad for what happened to me."

A tear slipped from her eye, leaving a stinging trail on her cheek in the cold night air. She forced a lighter tone. "I doubt your past self would trust it. I doubt he believed in time travel any more than the present Alexander does."

His fingers tightened on hers briefly before letting them go. "You're right. I would have thought the concussion was playing tricks on my mind."

She didn't reply to that, choosing instead to focus on the press of his leg against hers and the resulting warmth. She knew she ought to return to her window to watch if anyone was coming or going from Number 28, but she felt an increasing pressure to share some of her own grief.

"I went to the battlefields," she blurted after a moment of indecision. "When I was at the conference. After it, rather. I went to Lijssenthoek, to see where Wesley was buried. And Ypres."

Alexander was silent, but his hand found hers again. She took it, gratefully. "It was Elizabeth's idea to go. She booked train tickets to Belgium and planned to find us a guide who could show us to the cemeteries, to see Wesley's grave and my father's." Her words had withered to a whisper. "But she had to return before we could go. I felt I'd be a coward not to go simply because I was alone. But I wish I hadn't gone. I wish . . ." Emotion stole the remainder of her voice.

"Past Saffron made a brave choice to go."

"Past Saffron did as she always does," she said with a wavering sigh. "She rushed into something without considering what the reality would be. Example A, going to the war-torn countryside and expecting a peaceful place to say goodbye."

Lijssenthoek Cemetery had been anything but peaceful. She'd seen photographs of the place in the newspapers years ago, sullen rows of mismatched crosses over uneven dirt. Work had been done since then to beautify it. Most of the crosses had been transitioned to uniform white stone markers. Shrubs and trees had been planted, a stone arch built, and the place was silent but for the barest breeze rustling what leaves had been left on the young tree branches.

But it had brought Saffron no peace. She'd been unable to take a full breath the entire time, unable to stop tears from falling in a torrent. She sobbed violently the entire brief visit, pausing only to whisper a prayer when she at last found Wesley's marker.

She knew now that the unending tears had been as much for herself as for Wesley and the dozens of men buried there. She had not lost her life, but she lost a future with the boy she loved. She lost a piece of innocence the moment she realized that the war would not be the quick, righteous fight the politicians had anticipated, and it would crawl on and on, dragging down thousands of innocent people with it. Visiting Wesley's grave had only emphasized feelings she thought she'd reconciled long ago.

After that, she dreaded going on to Ypres. She had not known exactly where her father had been buried, and Elizabeth had suggested they visit the few British cemeteries to search for him. But the prospect of doing so had frozen her. She'd made it off the train, barely, but the idea of even leaving the train station had been too much.

She stayed inside, sitting wide-eyed and motionless on a bench until some kind soul with an enormous mustache and gentle eyes asked her if she needed assistance. He helped her find the train back to Paris and board it.

That was when a fresh wave of tears came—when she realized she'd taken from herself the opportunity to find her father, to say goodbye, even if it was a miserable goodbye.

She said all of this to Alexander, who listened while his thumb ran over the top of her hand in steady, slow strokes.

"And now I'll never be able to say goodbye," she whispered. "And I want to. I want to put to rest all the . . ." She hesitated to admit it. "The doubts I have about him."

"Berking?"

"Yes," she murmured, grateful he remembered her confession of Berking's suggestions. "And I found out that Dr. Calderbrook, the director here, invited my father to work at Kew Gardens in his lab. I don't know why my father wouldn't have told me about it. Kew was . . . It was a special place for us. It was the greatest treat to go there. I don't know why he would not have even mentioned it to me, that he'd been offered the chance to work there."

"I've never been to Kew," Alexander said. "I imagine it must thrill you."

At the warm humor in his voice, her lips lifted into a tremulous smile, even as recollections of running through lush tropicals in a massive glasshouse set off more pangs in her chest. "I was like a child in a toy shop."

"You haven't been there recently?"

"I haven't been since before the war."

He was quiet for a moment. "Was the laboratory at Kew different from this one?"

"My understanding is that it simply moved here. The fields of study have expanded, but it's still a plant pathology lab at its core."

He hummed thoughtfully. "And you worry that your father was working to make his subjects more dangerous, rather than resistant to disease and pests."

"That was Berking's implication." She sighed. "It seems such a stupid thing to worry about. Breeding a plant to increase its toxicity does not mean my father planned to do anything nefarious with it. I know that. But after all that I've seen with what the plants already in existence can do, and knowing that the government has an interest in those plants . . . I cannot help but wonder."

"He could have been experimenting with the natural defenses of the plant. Many of those toxins are simply biological defenses. Maybe he was testing to see what level of toxicity was needed to prevent insects from eating them. Or studying how to use those toxins for medicinal purposes."

"I suppose." She'd thought of that, but it was comforting to hear Alexander suggest it as a possibility.

He went still next to her, a subtle change she might not have noticed had she not been pressed against him.

"The last of the lights have been extinguished," he murmured. "Time to go."

CHAPTER 38

Saffron and Alexander made their way along the line of trees blackening the east side of the lot under construction. The next plot was nothing more than a patchy field with a handful of trees they darted between until they reached the edge of Number 28's property. Saffron's breath came out in tight little bursts of white from her mouth, more from anxiety than exertion.

She led them forward until they were crouched in the darkness of the shrubbery of the dead garden that bordered the patio of the lab. Saffron couldn't see anything within; the curtains were drawn.

Alexander's low whisper sent shivers down her spine. "This is familiar." It was familiar, she realized with a smile. They'd crept around gardens together before.

She darted across the garden and winced when her shoes crunched on the gravel path surrounding the patio. She slowed to hop gingerly across the path, which brought her to the French doors. She attempted to press the handle and push the door, but it was locked. She hadn't hoped it might be somehow open—she was aware of the additional locks on the interior of the doors—but it would have been foolish not to check. She went window to window next, but they too were locked.

The windows on the rest of the house were too high or too small for them to enter through, so they made for the kitchen door, protected from the eyes of passersby by the unoccupied mews that housed only a cart and crates of supplies for the laboratory and greenhouses.

The kitchen door was locked, naturally. But Saffron had come prepared for that. Slipping a hand into her pocket, she pulled out a pair of hairpins and went to work.

Alexander kept himself pressed to her side, facing outward to the path leading to the greenhouse and the mews. Their breathing and the subtle scrape of metal on metal were the only sounds; the night didn't breathe even a whisper of wind.

She pushed and pulled, turned and twisted the slender metal picks. She removed her gloves after realizing how much harder it was to pick locks with them on. One pin broke, and she retrieved another from her pocket. Her fingers grew stiff in the cold as she struggled. All her senses told her that she and Alexander would be caught at any moment, and her heart raced as if it might head off a chase.

Alexander's elbow nudged her. He breathed, "Someone is coming."

Saffron inhaled sharply. Hand on her arm, he guided her away from the door and into the nearest pool of shadows, a few dozen feet from the door. They eased back into it, their dark clothing hopefully doing its job to hide them.

The sound of approaching footsteps grew louder. Someone wasn't bothering to avoid the gravel as they had. A figure of a man rounded the corner a moment later. His head was covered by a cap and angled down, but Saffron recognized his uneven gait.

It was Joseph Rowe. He walked to the kitchen door, planted a key inside the lock, and swung the door open. He wasn't making any effort to be quiet. He shut the door, and a flickering light caught within the kitchen window a moment later.

Suspicion and surprise flared. Joseph had already proven he had no problem breaking into Wells's house, but he'd just been caught doing so—by the police, no less. Why would he do so again? Perhaps this was a last-ditch effort to get whatever he'd been looking for. But if so—why was he being so obvious about it?

To Alexander, she whispered, "That's Joseph Rowe. I'm going to look in the window for a moment."

She slipped away. Her toe caught a rock, sending it pinging away, and she froze. No sound came from the kitchen.

The window revealed a stub of a candle flickering next to Joseph, who stood, knife in hand. Sudden, primal fear gripped her, until she saw what he was doing. He was working the blade into a loaf of bread.

Saffron blinked. He was *eating*. Had he broken into the Path Lab to eat?

Saffron shrank from the glass as Joseph looked up and over at the window. Knife in hand, he walked purposefully forward. Her mind screamed at her to flee, but she found herself unable to do so. Her fingers clung to the brick of the windowsill as she crouched down. He paused, silhouetted by the meager flame of the candle at his back. He set the knife down on the counter, then filled a mug with water and gulped it down before returning to his loaf of bread.

She was to Joseph's left, where his missing eye prevented him from seeing her. She eased back until he was no longer in view and crept back to Alexander.

"He ate bread and drank water," she reported.

"Does he live in the house like the director?" he asked.

"I've never heard of it, but I suppose he might. Joseph said Dr. Calderbrook gave him a job, brought him out here to continue on when the lab moved. It seems he's fond of him."

They waited in silence until the candle in the kitchen went out.

Saffron rested her forehead on Alexander's shoulder, sighing. "How long should we wait to try to get in?"

"Not long enough for him to recall he hasn't locked the kitchen door," Alexander said. "He'll likely be getting washed up for bed, making noise. Best get into the lab before he settles down."

They waited two more minutes, Saffron bouncing on the balls of her feet, before entering the house. The kitchen smelled like smoke and fresh bread, a scent that faded as soon as they stepped into the hall. The rest of the house smelled like soil.

They crept down the long hall. She used her own keys on the double doors leading into the main lab.

It was black as pitch inside. She had to resist the sensation of being swallowed whole as she led them to her workstation by feel;

Alexander's hand light on her shoulder. She managed a full breath only when she'd found the gas lamp on the counter and lit it.

It flickered to life, and Alexander whispered, "What first?"

"Missing records," she said. "I've looked over Horticulture. I'll check Botany, and you can check Entomology."

"I ought to check Mycology first. If we have to get out of here quickly, that's more important."

Saffron nodded hesitantly. She hadn't a key for that room. She took another lamp from the counter to light it. "I'll come do the door."

"No need," he replied, slipping a hand into her pocket. For some reason, it made her heart leap when he held up a pair of hairpins. "I practiced."

Her mouth fell open. "When?"

"Not much to do on a long voyage from Brazil."

Baffled and charmed, she stammered, "And you let me struggle with the kitchen door?"

"I had to let you try it." He brushed a kiss on her forehead, took her lamp, and was gone.

She shook her head slowly. Alexander was forever surprising her. At least this time, it was a good thing.

Mycology fell into a strange no-man's-land between botany and zoology, in Alexander's estimation. Fungi were not plants, not animals, and were far too large to be included in his own personal realm of study, bacteria, but they shared a great many similarities. For one, the labs that studied them looked more or less the same.

The microscopes, glass plates, petri dishes, dozens of bottles and jars of liquids, and everything else made Alexander feel right at home. Every surface was covered in equipment and rows of dishes of growths in various stages of development. He wished for daylight, for he was sure there would be a rainbow of color contained within those plates.

But records were his priority, not the growths.

The filing cabinet wedged into the corner next to an incubator was his first destination. He set the oil lamp on the top and found that the lock had not been engaged. Saffron had mentioned a date in October. He pulled open the cabinet drawers until he found the correct time period and set to searching.

He'd read up more on mycology since Nick had come to town, talking of fungi. Still, unfamiliar terms filled his vision as he flicked back page after page. He kept his eyes on the dates instead, pausing whenever days were skipped. Some notes had numbered pages, which was useful, but others did not. Some reports were written in four or five different hands, others were typed.

He paused, hand ready to push the first drawer closed. Joseph Rowe had been found in Jeffery Wells's house with actual lab reports, not copies. If Alexander were stealing information from a laboratory, he would copy the reports, not take them. Someone would notice—*had* noticed—that they were missing. Yet Wells had taken the papers themselves.

Then he remembered Saffron's story from the previous evening. Alfie Tennison might have been the one receiving the reports, for use . . . in something. He could have worried Wells would copy them wrong, leave something out or get a measurement incorrect. He'd want the most accurate information possible.

Three files contained information from the two weeks or so in October. He saw a series of reports on a strain of *Alternaria alternata* and its effect on pyrethrum, the flower the laboratory was studying. That genus of fungi was familiar; he'd seen it in the other files. Those files were complete, from what he could tell.

He dug further back, keeping his ears open to any sounds in the hall beyond. Saffron would have numerous places to hide should someone come around, but this room was tiny. There was no furniture to hide behind, and the closet was merely a series of shelves in an alcove. He'd be spotted the moment anyone crossed the threshold.

He took each file out one by one, scanning the papers for anything interesting. Saffron had explained how the lab worked with other research stations and farms around the country; reports and samples were sent in over the course of weeks and months. They were analyzed, and occasionally products developed by the lab were sent out for field testing. These papers did not detail those exchanges but the actual work of the laboratory. The daily logs were written in neat, feminine script, occasionally interrupted by a brash, broad hand that Alexander guessed was the chief of mycology rather than his assistant. He found no references to the papers Joseph had.

Frowning, he opened the cabinet above it to search earlier in the year. August and September were jam-packed. A busy time for the laboratory given their areas of study. Only measurements of materials and dry descriptions of the growth of fungi, boring even to him.

One line of the daily log caught his eye, however. A dissection, done by N. Narramore, showed a sample from "Farm E" was discovered to have been infected by a fungus, Specimen No. 28923, and had been turned over to E. Sutcliffe for identification. Saffron had mentioned that specimen.

But as Alexander paged back through the reports of the following weeks, he found no further information regarding Specimen No. 28923. In fact, the records were missing entire days' worth of notes: from the twenty-ninth of October to November twelfth, the exact dates of the papers found in Joseph Rowe's possession.

He wanted to see the original reports and find out exactly what those insects had been infected with, and why Jeffery Wells and then Joseph Rowe had stolen the reports of it.

CHAPTER 39

Although Saffron had already done a fair bit of creeping around the main area of the laboratory, it was something quite different to do so in utter, silent darkness. Light and shadow flitted over the rows of glass and metal equipment as she moved toward the rear of the lab to Entomology.

A soft ripping noise made her jump. She jumped, flinching away from the noise, and found she was being pulled back. Flailing, she staggered away, only to find it was her skirt, caught on a brass valve sticking out from a workstation. The wretched thing had ripped her skirt and nearly given her a heart attack to boot. Glaring at the valve, she turned away and hurried toward Entomology.

She hadn't gone a handful of steps before she swallowed a terrified gasp. Something loomed out of the darkness.

Hand pressed to her thundering heart, Saffron forced herself to slow her frantic breath. The largest vivarium dominated the first workstation. Within lay a massive piece of driftwood, which, in the bleaching light of her single lamp, looked like an alien skull. Worse, it was crawling with insects.

Saffron brought her lamp to the glass and cringed when the dark, shining bodies of dozens of earwigs scuttled away from the light and into the crevices of the driftwood and rolled newspaper littering the bottom of the vivarium. Earwigs did not go into the ears of humans to nibble on the insides of one's head as they'd once been believed to do, but that did not mean Saffron wanted to spend time with the creatures.

Quinn had explained that Entomology had recently shifted its focus to testing the pesticides the Path Lab was developing from the oil of the pyrethrum daisies on a handful of insects, earwigs among them. This was their second round of earwigs, she had said. Some of the previous year's brood had been used to test the pesticides over the summer, and they'd kept the other half to breed. Half of the brood set to hatch in 1924 had been set aside in a small vivarium to test the pesticides on the egg and larval stages, and the rest was in a third vivarium, apparently empty, to grow into maturity and continue the cycle.

Saffron uneasily watched an earwig frantically scuttle across the glass, its little pincers waving. These insects hadn't been used as test subjects yet, just to breed more earwigs.

She was suddenly quite glad she studied plants and not things that could crawl away from her. Resolving to ignore the creeping earwigs, she started her search.

After ten minutes, all she'd found were supplies and a collection of dead bugs. There were none of the fascinating shapes and colors one might find in an entomological display at a museum, just beetles and flying insects that Saffron had seen a hundred times over in the country.

She'd hoped that the drawers might have revealed something relevant rather than just headless pins and forceps and a number of preservation chemicals, the names of which were familiar to her from the list she'd given the Datta siblings, but she was disappointed.

On to Botany, then, Saffron thought with a deep, bracing breath.

The workstations were clear. Within the drawers were familiar tools and materials. Nothing stood out to her. The last drawer contained a stack of weathered and stained field notebooks dating back to 1911, all marked with the chief of Botany's name: A. Crawford. She flipped through the pages, willing something useful to make itself known, but found only a series of charming sketches of leaves and flowers. The rolling cursive showed the notebooks contained mostly field notes from various farms in Hampshire.

She closed the drawers and relocked them, then sank onto a stool to think. She heard only silence from the rest of the house. Alexander was apparently still searching Mycology. If he found nothing useful in there, she wasn't sure what she would do. Would she have to give up this venture and trust that Nick really could figure out what was happening here at the Path Lab?

Doubt nipping at her heels, she carefully made her way into the hall.

She'd never seen anyone go in or out of the records room, but she knew which key would open the door. The tiny room smelled like paper and that indefinable soil scent and had no more space for two people to stand within at once. Blowing out a breath, she stepped inside and shut the door. She couldn't risk anyone coming to the hall and seeing the door open, but she immediately felt the difference, as if the closed door had reduced her lung capacity.

The lamp flickered as she set it down on the floor. Shelves lined the walls to the ceiling, each stuffed with row upon row of paper sheaves wrapped in string. She pulled the first one from the nearest shelf and saw the date was April 1921. Working backward, she found the records from the latter half of 1923.

Each farm and research station had its own file for each month. Unfortunately, there were twenty-two research stations that shared information with the Path Lab, and still another handful of private farms that sent in reports and samples.

She scratched nearly illegible notes in her notebook on the floor as she pulled down file after file, noting anything promising, only to dash them off as she found the concluding notes for each tidbit of information. A rash of mosaic virus that took out a massive portion of tomatoes, the loss of acres of young potatoes to blight, a curious fungus that was identified and eliminated, with thanks to Dr. Sutcliffe for his recommendations.

By the time Saffron reached September, her knees were aching from kneeling on the hard, cold floor. The dates from the reports Nick had shown her echoed in her mind as she meticulously worked through each set of reports in search of a mention of Specimen No. 28923.

The specimen number didn't show up as she reached the relevant dates, but, as she untied the papers from the week of September twenty-fourth through twenty-eighth, she realized that the specimen number *was* the date. Her fingers shook with poorly suppressed excitement as she sorted through the papers. But there was no report from Friday, September twenty-eighth in the stack.

She groaned with frustration. Wells must have taken it. Blast, but she wanted to see what it said! Would they have made copies of any of the reports? She would possibly have to get into Dr. Calderbrook's office . . .

She hastily tied the twine around the papers and shoved them back onto the shelf. The force of her frustration caused a cascade of sheaves to fall to the floor.

"No, no, no, no!" she whisper-shouted.

Half of the sheaves had slipped apart, leaving a heap of papers on the floor. Borrowing a few of Elizabeth's favorite curses, she hurriedly began shuffling papers together again.

The door opened. Saffron jerked back, gasping. The lamp cast eerie shadows on his face as Alexander took in the mess on the floor. "What happened?"

Saffron's explanation died in her throat at the sound of a floorboard squeaking. "The stairs," she whispered. "Someone is coming down!"

Alexander stepped inside the records room and closed the door. "Lamps."

They blew them out at the same time. In the darkness, Saffron could make out the sound of fabric swishing. She sensed Alexander kneeling down a moment later, then heard his shoes crinkle over the papers littering the floor.

"Sit down," he breathed, and she shifted so her bottom was on the floor rather than her knees. He did the same, and they ended up pressed together from hip to ankle.

Soft footsteps padded across the floor in the distance. Saffron could trace their path in her mind: coming down the stairs, then around the corner past the library and lavatory. Down the hall, toward them.

She blew out a shaking breath. Alexander's hand found hers. She clung to it, wrapping both her cold hands around his warm one. The rise of his chest slowed and deepened. She tried to focus on the rhythm, will some of his calm into herself. But the darkness of the room bore down on her. She knew the room was tiny, knew they barely fit inside. It was suffocating.

Her chest tightened. Her heart thudded wildly. She squeezed Alexander's hand tighter, but even with him as her anchor, the storm of her panic only grew stronger.

When Saffron had told him that she didn't care for small, enclosed spaces, Alexander thought she merely had a distaste for them. He realized now that she had far more than mere dislike. She was on her way to over-breathing.

He didn't dare move to comfort her. The footsteps were in the hall beyond the door, shuffling along unevenly. Should they stop outside the door, they'd likely be able to hear Saffron's heaving breaths.

So he turned toward her, used his other hand to tilt her chin up, and kissed her.

It wasn't a scientifically sound way to cope with triggered anxiety, but it was effective.

He'd always had luck snapping himself out of attacks by disrupting patterns dragging him deeper into panic. Focusing on a mundane object could snap him out of visions of war, or a sharp, unusual smell might help clear his head of the remembered stench of blood or smoke. Saffron's frantic breathing needed to be interrupted. Kissing her was a quiet, effective way to do that.

It was hard to tell her reaction from the half second of frozen stillness. His hand moved to cradle the back of her head, and his fingers slid along the back of her neck.

Her grip on his other hand eased. He smiled against her lips in relief. With tentative pressure, she kissed him back. It was brief and firm, as if she was saying, "*Thank you.*" Their foreheads rested against one another. He slowly stroked the soft nape of her neck.

The sound of muffled footsteps was receding.

They sat like that for a long time, well after the house had gone silent again, his hand on her neck, sharing her breath.

At long last, Saffron whispered, "Do you think we can get up?"

He nodded. By feel, he reached for his coat. He'd removed it and rolled it against the bottom of the door in the hope that it would block the smell of the extinguished lamps from wafting into the hall. The coat was no doubt covered in dust now. He grimaced at the thought.

Beneath his feet, papers crinkled. He reached into his pocket for the matches he'd begged off the barkeep when they bought their pub sandwiches and lit one.

Saffron was kneeling on the floor, retrieving her lamp. Just as their eyes met, the match went out. He lit another, and she was lifting the lamp to him. He took it, the light dropping out for a moment as the wick of the lamp caught.

"Wait!" Saffron hissed, nearly making him drop the lamp. "The light! Bring it back!"

He turned the handle to make the lamp brighter. Saffron was scrambling to her feet, a paper in hand and eyes huge.

She shoved the paper at him. "Alexander, *look!*"

He winced at the clear imprint of his shoe's tread on it. Anyone looking at this paper, or any of the others still under his feet, would know something had happened with the reports. "We'll have to hope no one wants to look these over any time soon."

"Not the footprint." She jabbed the paper. "*This.*"

"*Erratic behavior*" was his first indication of what Saffron meant, followed by "*prolific destruction.*"

He set the lamp on the nearest shelf and read over the entire paper, Saffron peering over his shoulder. It was a report, but a second or third page, as the page had no introductory information and the first line was a continuation of a sentence. It seemed to refer to an insect or group of insects, a sample of which a certain farm, referred to as "Farm E," had sent into the laboratory.

"What does this mean?" he asked.

"I have no idea," Saffron admitted. "But I've never seen any reports referring to prolific destruction! That has to be meaningful."

He had to agree. "Where do they keep the samples from the farms? Maybe they still have it."

Color had returned to Saffron's face, along with the enthusiasm he found so damned irresistible. "Help me sort these, then I'll show you."

CHAPTER 40

Though her body was fairly vibrating with the need to search the stored samples, Saffron forced herself to look over each report before she and Alexander carefully organized them back into their original sheaves and returned them to the shelves. None of the other papers Saffron had spilled provided meaningful information about the specimens in question.

Alexander peered out of the cracked door, and seeing no one lurking in the hall, opened it wide for her.

Getting back into the hall was a relief she'd been waiting for. Even after Alexander's timely kiss, she'd felt like she was being buried alive. Had anyone else seen her in such a state—even Elizabeth, who knew well Saffron's fear of enclosed spaces—she'd have been mortified. But Alexander understood. She felt no judgment for nearly getting them caught from her panic.

She was grateful to see the sample room was larger. It was narrow but long, with rows of little glass bottles and vials with matching green labels. Each stated, "Harpenden Phytopathological Service," in bold black letters, followed by a series of typed words and lined spaces that were filled out with handwritten identifiers for fields, plots, and dates. Most were filled with soil, but there was a section for insects too.

Saffron wrinkled her nose at the heaps of dead insects inside the finger-sized glass jars at the back.

"We need samples from September," she murmured.

"October," Alexander said with a frown.

She shook her head. "September was when they received the samples. The fungal specimen is 28923, that's the date of receipt."

After five minutes of carefully shifting the specimen jars to see the ones at the back of the shelves, Saffron huffed out a frustrated breath. "It's not here."

"We shouldn't be surprised. Most of the information regarding the specimen was taken. Where else would they have written down information about it?"

"Entomology's daily logs didn't have anything," Saffron said. "Though now I know better what to look for, I ought to check again."

"What about personal notes? I didn't find any in Mycology. Perhaps Entomology keeps them at their workstations."

"We can check," Saffron said. "I didn't spend a lot of time looking at anything that looked like field notes."

It was nearing one in the morning. Saffron could feel her body was tired, but her mind was whirring at double speed. She felt if she could just find one more piece of information, things would come together.

Alexander observed the vivariums with interest as they approached Entomology.

"Those are earwigs," she told him.

"Test subjects for the pesticides?"

"Yes." She unlocked the first cabinet again, rolling out the drawer for Alexander's inspection. She held her lamp low for him to sort through the materials within. "Earwigs aren't the worst pest, but they are annoying. My grandfather complained of them on occasion, though I believe they don't generally affect his crops."

Alexander arched a brow at her. "He grows crops?"

"His tenants do." She frowned at the insects. "I wonder why they chose to study earwigs. They are omnivores, according to the records I looked through. Some of their observations suggested they prefer meat or even sweet foods to plants."

"Perhaps they mean to protect the meat industry against invasion by earwig too."

Saffron shot him a look. "Ha, ha."

"If they're omnivores, they likely eat other insects. They could be trying to breed a new generation of carnivorous earwigs so they'll target troublesome pests rather than be pests themselves."

"That is a terrifying thought."

Alexander worked his way through the contents of the drawers and handed Saffron anything that looked promising.

A low creak sounded down the hall.

They froze. Saffron's hand moved to close the drawer, but Alexander stopped her. He picked up the lamp on the counter and moved to the right, to the far side of the room. They knelt behind the last workstation and doused their lights.

Saffron held her breath. She heard no further footsteps, but she sensed another presence enter the laboratory as if the air had notice-ably shifted.

There was a click, and an electric torch glared right into their faces, causing Saffron to wince away into Alexander's shoulder.

"Who are you, and what do you want?" asked a voice attempting to be stern. It was terribly familiar.

Saffron sighed and turned toward the light. "Hello, Sergeant Simpson."

It was clear Sergeant Simpson was not pleased to see them, to say the least. He'd dropped the torch, causing it to crash to the ground and crack the bulb, plunging them back into darkness. When it became clear none of the household had awakened at the noise, Alexander lit one of the lamps.

Simpson glared at them. "What are you doing here?"

"We're investigating, of course!" Saffron said in hushed tones. "What are you doing here?"

"Me? *I'm* investigating!" he shot back.

"But you're in Harpenden," Alexander said. "That's well outside your jurisdiction."

Simpson's youthful face went pink. "I might be . . . I might have come up here on my own."

"But why?" Saffron asked. Now she looked at him, he wasn't wearing a uniform. His fair hair was under a cap, his clothing plain and dark.

"Inspector Green told me we were off the case," Simpson replied. "But it didn't feel right. As much as the inspector believes in hard evidence, he always told me I had to follow my instinct too. We came up here a time or two, and it always gave me a feeling. When Jeffery Wells was found dead, my instincts were shouting at me. But a few days ago, we were told our part in the investigation was done. The inspector didn't like it, but he has other cases to work and moved on."

"And you didn't move on?" Saffron asked.

Simpson shook his head. "Didn't feel right, miss."

"You're investigating Wells's death on your own?" Alexander asked. "That is a risky thing to do. You don't worry that Inspector Green will reprimand you?"

Simpson straightened up so his height nearly matched Alexander's. "If I discover a cover-up, Mr. Ashton, I think I'll be up for a promotion."

"And if you don't, and someone finds out you're poking around what is now a government investigation, you'll be sacked."

Simpson's mouth fell open. "A government investigation?"

Saffron nodded, feeling sorry for him. She had no doubt that Inspector Green had been told that someone, if not Nick, was taking it over. "The ministry has people working on it."

"And you're working with them?" Simpson asked. His surprise gave way to enthusiasm. "You've been working here at the lab. I'd thought you just were hired on, but you're here to investigate? I have information for you, then. I've been watching this place. And sorting through the rubbish bins for clues."

It was Saffron's turn to gape. "You've been going through the rubbish bins?"

He went scarlet once again. "It's nasty work but turns up evidence."

"Like what?"

"Come to the place I've been staying, and I'll show you."

Sergeant Simpson's place turned out to be a second-cousin's house, where he'd been sleeping on the couch in the parlor.

"Got to be quiet," he muttered as he unlatched the door. "They've got three young ones and it'll be my head if we wake them."

He'd taken not two steps into the entry before he kicked something. Saffron held her breath as Simpson scrambled to right whatever he'd knocked over, but the little row house remained quiet.

In the parlor, a shabby but cozy space littered with toys for small children, they settled on a pair of armchairs and the couch. Alexander winced as he tugged a wooden toy boat from under him. He set it on the floor and asked, "What did you find in the rubbish bins, Sergeant?"

Simpson reached for a knapsack tucked next to the couch. It was full of crumpled papers that had been smoothed out. "Found these two weeks ago, just after Petrov died but before Wells. I'd been up to interview the staff and thought I'd see what someone might be trying to hide. Not many fires in that place, and even with the burners in the lab, no one could burn papers without someone noticing. Only place to do it is above stairs or in the kitchen, and that kitchen maid, for all she's quiet as a mouse, you can't get nothing by her. She's run me off the few times she's caught me lurking."

Saffron took the papers, split the pile in two, and gave half to Alexander. She scanned receipts for chemical purchases and records of mail received from the other research stations, nodding to herself. She was impressed; Simpson had found things that could have been relevant to Petrov's death.

"Saffron," Alexander said.

At the choked way he said her name, she looked up. He was staring at a bit of paper, his jaw clenched. Putting a hand on his arm, she asked, "What is it?"

All the color had washed from his face. "If this means what I think it means, it is not good. It is actually very, *very* bad."

CHAPTER 41

G iven the lateness of the hour, Simpson had reluctantly offered them the use of the parlor for the remainder of the evening. Saffron was forced to take the couch, while the two men did their best to make themselves comfortable in the armchairs.

Saffron didn't sleep. She knew Alexander didn't either, from the dark glitter of his eyes beneath lowered eyelids. He waited until Simpson's snores became regular before he rose and went to the couch to sit next to her.

Whispering, he said, "I might be misunderstanding the note."

"I wish you were," she whispered back. "But I think it's obvious what it means."

His throat bobbed as he swallowed, and that nervous action made her stomach turn. Alexander worrying made her own anxiety spike. She retrieved the crumpled note from her bag, where she'd tucked it away for further examination. The light was so low it was hard to make out the words, but she'd read it over so many times already that she hardly needed to see them. She could practically hear Quinn speaking.

The insect in question suffered a distended thorax covered in dark green growth. Microscopic observation confirmed fungus, tubular protrusion discovered to be ready to burst through exoskeleton. Neville gave it to Sutcliffe despite warning.

The paper had one ripped side, which clearly came from Quinn's personal notebook. The reference to Narramore by his Christian name was evidence enough for Saffron, further emphasized by the messy handwriting and uneven lines. After seeing Quinn's writing in the daily logs, Saffron guessed she'd been in a rush to write these observations now, possibly angry that Narramore had given the sample to Sutcliffe. *"Despite warning"* bothered Saffron. Warning of what? Simply that Sutcliffe was disagreeable, or something more?

She shuddered, both at the implications about Sutcliffe and the horrible visual that Quinn's description had provided. Worse was what Alexander had said.

"I've heard of this," he'd told her as she read the note over the first time. "The local Brazilian guides told stories about a fungus that took over insects' bodies. There was a species that took over ants' bodies, changed their behavior. They'd find the ants attached to the bottom of leaves; their bodies covered in tiny spores."

"But that was in Brazil," Saffron had said. "A tropical fungus."

He hadn't replied, just as he did not speak now as she stared down at Quinn's words on a separate paper, similarly crumpled then smoothed.

Absolutely outrageous that no one but me sees the potential. Initial results showed stupendous potential for predatory pest control. There is work to be done to correct the problem of the earwigs eating everything in sight, but a few years of development—

The note stopped there, leaving Saffron deeply uneasy. Quinn's scrawls, in addition to the words from the report they'd found in the mixed-up pages from the record room, painted a picture Saffron didn't care to imagine. *"Eating everything in sight"* and *"prolific destruction"* added up to something potentially catastrophic.

Eventually, Alexander tugged the papers from her hands and set them on the floor. He inched over to the side of the couch, bringing Saffron with him, and wrapped an arm around her so she leaned her head on his chest.

Despite the increased comfort of having him near, she was too worried about what exactly it meant that the Path Lab had apparently been sent a new fungus that infected insects and made them cause prolific destruction with their insatiable appetites—only to have a staff member steal those secrets and then be killed. She wrapped an arm around Alexander's waist to settle closer but did not bother attempting to sleep.

After they were fed breakfast by a remarkably unfazed woman Simpson introduced as his second-cousin Nelly, Simpson walked them to the train station and saw them off with promises of adding their discoveries in the lab to his report. Alexander held his tongue about demanding Simpson leave out their breaking into the lab. He'd deal with that issue another time.

His first goal was to get Saffron safely to her flat so he could get on to the most important business of the day: finding Nick.

Saffron was dead on her feet. Her words were slurred with exhaustion, earning him some scathing looks from the people on the train who no doubt thought he'd kept his girl out all night drinking. He had kept his girl out all night, but it had been the furthest thing from a fun night on the town that he could imagine.

The train back to London was packed with folks commuting to work in the city, but he snagged a seat for Saffron while he stood. Her head sagged onto his hip, and he kept her upright but asleep the whole way back. She was adorably groggy when he woke her and clung to his arm as he walked them to the bus stop. Even with her half-asleep, after her reaction to being trapped in the records room last night, he wasn't going to attempt to take her on the Underground.

His heart gave a pang to recall how she'd struggled to breathe, and he tightened his grip on her arm.

She looked up at him with a squinting smile. "I won't fall over, don't worry."

He forced a smile back. He couldn't put a finger on what he was feeling, but it wasn't worry. Not over her falling asleep walking, anyway.

Alexander retrieved her keys from her handbag, slipping the papers from Simpson out as he did so, and unlocked Saffron's door. He helped her inside, told her to go to bed, and was surprised when she gave him a very thorough kiss in reply.

Something about how she clung to him, the door hanging open behind them, made him wary rather than inflamed. He eased away from her, placing a final chaste kiss on her lips. "Go to sleep, Saffron."

"I'll have horrible dreams," she said, burrowing her face into his neck.

He wasn't sure if she meant that as the invitation it sounded like. "Telephone me at the university when you wake up, please."

"You're going to the U?"

"Someone has to keep your plants alive."

She sighed, her breath tickling his throat. "Very well. Be responsible. I'll telephone you and we'll make a plan for what to do with Simpson's information. I'm not sure what it all means yet, but I'll think on it."

He hummed noncommittally, kissed the top of her head, and left the flat before he could change his mind.

From the beginning, he'd known Nick would bring nothing but danger to Saffron and Elizabeth, but now he cursed Nick anew. He might not be manipulating politicians and businessmen anymore, but he'd forced himself, and Saffron, into something just as dangerous. He had no doubt Nick would keep plaguing her about joining up with the very scientists who had inadvertently stumbled into what could very well be an incredibly destructive biological threat.

Nick's hotel was close, so Alexander went there on foot. He was rapping on the door in minutes, not stopping until Nick answered. He wore shirtsleeves with no collar, tie, or shoes, but he did wear a neutral frown of confusion. "Alexander?" He must have recognized Alexander's cold determination for the warning it was, for his expression snapped into the same cool competence that meant Alexander should be careful. "What's wrong?"

Alexander stepped inside and shut the door. "Saffron and I found something. I will give it to you if you will personally guarantee that you and anyone else working with you will leave her alone."

"You will give me all of the information regardless," Nick snapped. He seemed to regret it immediately. He propped his hands on his hips. "You know I can't promise anything. I'm here on a job. And I'll do my job."

"Saffron isn't part of the job."

Nick's reply came too slow. Alexander unclenched his jaw and ground out, "Saffron *isn't* a part of the job, Nick."

Nick sighed. "Let's cope with whatever crisis brought you here first. What happened?"

Alexander had just finished explaining the events of the previous evening when the door to Nick's room exploded. They both fell back, showered with splinters of wood from the door. Alexander's ears rang even though he saw, as two massive men shouldered their way into the room, that there had been no explosion, only a pair of heavily booted feet that kicked the door in.

They hauled him to his feet.

"This ain't the right one," grunted one of the men.

"I believe you're looking for me," Nick said, coming around the bed with a pistol aimed steadily at them.

Alexander stopped struggling against their grip.

The one to Alexander's left nodded, a slow grin spreading across scarred features. "Aye, you're the one, all right. Drop that little barker, or your friend gets a knife to the belly."

"What do you want?" Nick asked, not lowering his weapon.

From just behind the two bruisers, someone pronounced, "You."

Alexander couldn't see the speaker, but he could see Nick, his face twisted with rage for a split second before going completely smooth. Voice cool, he said, "I knew I should have gotten rid of you when I had the chance."

CHAPTER 42

A pounding knock at the door awakened Saffron an indeterminate time later. She'd fallen into bed fully clothed, and scrambled out of bed now, squinting at the bright light coming in through her window telling her it was still morning.

She stumbled into the hall, imagining Alexander had returned, and stopped short when she saw Elizabeth, in a similar state of dishabille, emerging from her own bedroom. They stared at each other for a moment before renewed knocking jerked them out of their confusion.

"You get it," croaked Elizabeth, turning for the kitchen. "I need sustenance."

Saffron peered through the grate and started when she found Colin Smith's face not two inches away. She leaped back with a little shout.

"Miss Everleigh!" Colin cried, pounding on the door again. "I must speak to Elizabeth! Please!"

"I don't believe she wishes to see you, Colin," Saffron called to him, loud enough that Elizabeth could hear from the kitchen.

She poked her head out with a scowl. "Tell him to shove off."

"I don't wish to speak to her for my own sake," Colin said, muffled through the door. "They telephoned Lord Tremaine's office to contact her. It's her brother."

Elizabeth stomped past Saffron to jerk the door open. "What's wrong with my brother?"

"He's been hurt," Colin said. "Come along, I'll take you to the hospital. Quickly!"

Elizabeth stared at him for a long moment before turning on her heel and dashing into her bedroom. Saffron stared after her, sadly not at all surprised that Elizabeth would snap into action on Nick's behalf.

Just behind her, Colin said, "I think you ought to come too, Miss Everleigh." She turned to him in surprise. His expression was grave. "Nick is . . . he is in a bad way. Elizabeth will need your support."

Heart in her throat, Saffron hurried to tidy herself. Not two minutes later, she and Elizabeth were pulling on their coats and following Colin down the stairs and into a waiting cab.

The door slammed shut, and Colin, on the far side of the vehicle next to Elizabeth, sighed.

"Where is Nick?" Elizabeth asked. "What happened to him?"

Saffron peered around her to look at Colin when he didn't answer. His eyes were closed, his head resting on the uncomfortable back of the seat.

"Colin!" snapped Elizabeth.

"Oh, do shut up," he groaned. "I was awoken terribly early this morning and five minutes of quiet would be ideal."

Elizabeth inhaled sharply. "What?"

Behind his spectacles, Colin opened one eye. "Shall I speak slower? Even you can understand simple words. Shut. Up."

Elizabeth went totally still. Perhaps she was as completely baffled as Saffron, who was just realizing that they were not alone in the cab. The driver was driving, of course, but the other seat in the front was occupied, and the man had turned around in his seat to watch them.

Saffron swallowed. She recognized him from the gaming room. She nudged her friend. "Elizabeth."

"Don't interrupt me, Saff, I'm deciding how I want to kill this imbecile next to me."

She jabbed her with her elbow. "*Eliza*."

Elizabeth swung around to glare at Saffron, who pointed to the man watching them with a crooked grin. Elizabeth blanched, then scowled. "Damn you, Colin Smith."

"Is my brother actually hurt," Elizabeth said, turning back to Colin, "or was that merely a ruse?"

"Oh, no, he is definitely injured. Unfortunately, he is nowhere near a hospital."

Her hands itched to hit him or close around his throat. "Where is he?"

"You ask so many questions, Elizabeth," he drawled. "It makes you seem so simple. Better to hold your tongue until I want to make use of it."

Red-hot anger flooded her, fueled by humiliation. This cad had *used* her, and in more ways than one. The suspicion had taken root while she'd dug out yet another set of files Colin had demanded the previous day, and now she'd seen his true colors, it blazed to full life.

"What does Alfie Tennison want with records about immigrants?" she demanded.

Colin's eyes shot open, and he stared at her for a long moment before a cruel smile curled his lips. "What, brother dearest didn't tell you? You'd think he'd crow it from the rooftops, all he'd discovered about me and my friends. He made such charming little comments about my preferred entertainments."

"Like visiting the gaming room hidden in Le Curieux Cabaret's back room," Elizabeth cut him off. "You owe Alfie Tennison an exorbitant sum. That's why you're doing his bidding."

Chagrin leaked through Colin's sneer. "So Nick did tell you, then? That's why you threw me over, I suppose. Not rich enough to bail your family out of their troubles."

"I have no need for or interest in anything you might have offered me."

"Oh, we both know that isn't true." His displeasure melted into a leer.

Elizabeth regarded him coolly. "I was passing time with you, Colin, nothing more."

Colin placed a hand over his heart. "Oh, how that stings."

"Of course, you decide to have a personality now," Elizabeth grumbled, more to Saffron than Colin. Saffron gave her a worried look, angling her head toward the window. They were passing Willesden Junction. They were going out of the city, and Elizabeth was quite sure she knew where they were going.

She wished she could brazen this out, put Saff's mind to rest, but they had no way out of this motorcar, save risking getting smashed up trying to jump from it as it sped further and further out of London.

Very well. Colin was at least talking. They could get some answers, even if he wouldn't tell them what had happened to Nick. If anything had happened to him.

Frustration burned through her again, this time at herself. She was furious with Nick, and had told him she'd never speak to him again, yet the moment Colin had said he'd been hurt, everything had fled from her mind.

To make matters worse, Colin—*Colin*—was one of the villains in this drama. He'd not only tricked her into believing he was a respectable man but had apparently known her so well as to know the perfect way to trap her.

"What exactly are you doing, taking Saffron and me?" Elizabeth asked him. "You know we haven't any money, and neither does my family. You'll get nothing out of either of our families."

"Don't think so little of yourself, my dear. Besides, *you* are not the hostage."

"Who is?" Saffron asked.

Colin smiled banally. "You'll find out, soon enough. No use getting upset over it now." He closed his eyes again.

Elizabeth turned her questions to the fellow in the front. "You, there. What is your part in all this? Certainly, they didn't invite you along to brighten the place up."

He was a great brute of a man, with enough dark hair to make it hard to distinguish him from a gorilla. He frowned, bringing his heavy brow low. "No need to be insultin'."

"Quite right, my apologies," Elizabeth said briskly. "How did you end up carting this idiot around?"

The man flicked a glance to Colin, who snorted. "I do me job, miss. This is business. Don't take it personal."

"Seems awfully personal to me. Where are you taking us?" She could see through the window where they were well on their way to going, but she wanted it confirmed.

"Boss sent us on a little errand," the man said.

"Would that be to the laboratory in Harpenden?" Elizabeth asked.

He squinted at her, then at Colin. "Maybe."

Blast and damnation, Elizabeth thought. He'd looked to Colin. That meant Colin was the one in charge, and that made this all the more complicated.

"Why are you taking us to the laboratory?" Saffron asked. "There are people there now. You can't break in to steal anything."

"Don't need to break in," grumbled the man driving. He was as bulky as the other in the front, but his bright red hair distinguished him. His eyes found Saffron in the mirror. "You can just waltz in there."

"I see," Saffron mumbled.

Elizabeth exchanged a look with her, and though they said not a word, they were in agreement. This was not good. From the panic on Saffron's face, Elizabeth took it that she'd discovered something worth stealing from the lab. If only they'd been able to speak before Colin turned up!

"Jeffery Wells was paying off his debt to Alfie with information, wasn't he?" Saffron asked suddenly. "The police found papers from the lab in Wells's house. But he started holding out on Alfie. Was that why he was killed?"

The two men in the front exchanged a look, all but confirming Saffron's guess. Beside her, Colin spoke without opening his eyes. "In a word, yes. Wells was an idiot. I didn't know him myself, but anyone crossing Alfie is digging their own grave. Unfortunately, the man Alfie works for is even worse. He was tired of Wells attempting to pull the strings."

"Ol' Alfie ain't going to be pleased you said he ain't the one in charge," grumbled the gorilla-like man.

Colin dismissed him with a superior sniff. "We all know I'm too valuable for him to do much about it." The man scoffed. "As I was saying, the other fellow involved in this is the sort to give even a man like Alfie pause. He called him a ruthless radical, and that's saying something, considering the people he usually consorts with. I hope that information inclines you to cooperate. We all know radicals can get a bit edgy when things don't go their way."

CHAPTER 43

They stopped on the outskirts of Harpenden. The driver pulled over and remained in the car, but the dark-haired thug pulled Saffron and then Elizabeth out and made them stand on the side of the road next to the cab.

The midmorning sun, though high and bright in the clear sky, did little to warm Saffron. Next to her, Elizabeth was bouncing on the balls of her feet and puffing out angry white clouds.

"Why are we here?" she asked, waving a hand to indicate the empty field next to the road.

"Waitin' for someone," said the dark-haired man.

"And why can't we wait inside?" she demanded, pointing to where Colin sat in the cab.

He shrugged and lit a cigarette.

"Ridiculous," Elizabeth muttered.

Saffron inched a bit further away from the man and whispered, "Should we run?"

"They have guns, I have no doubt," Elizabeth replied. "What did you find at the lab last night?"

"Someone discovered a fungus that reminded Alexander of one he heard about in Brazil, one that can alter the behavior of insects. The bit of the report we saw said it had devastating potential."

Elizabeth's mouth dropped open. "I cannot even begin to understand that. Do they have it in the laboratory?"

"I think Wells stole the samples and the reports on it. He must have given them to Alfie to pass to the radical. We found only bits and pieces of evidence left over at the lab. And Sergeant Simpson was there, he had more information." Saffron quickly explained about Simpson's efforts to solve the mystery on his own.

"So he's in town, and he knows what is going on!" Elizabeth looked relieved.

"But how can we communicate with him? We're stuck with these . . . people," Saffron whispered back, nodding toward the cab and the bruiser leaning against it, trails of smoke obscuring his face.

"One of us will have to get away. Considering you know where Simpson has been staying and I do not, it'll have to be you."

"But they need me to get into the lab."

"That is a problem." Elizabeth blew out another steaming breath on a sigh. "Now would be an excellent time for Nick to show up out of the blue."

As if in answer, a sleek red motorcar slowed on the road and came to a stop behind theirs.

Saffron gave Elizabeth a look. "If that worked, I'll have to take back everything I said about that phony psychic in the 5th arrondissement."

"Darling, if it's Nick in that motorcar, I'll take up as a performing psychic myself."

The occupants were hidden behind the glare of the windshield. One emerged, the other remained inside. The one who came out was not Nick.

"Guess no one will be calling me Madame Elizabeta," Elizabeth grumbled. "That is Alfie Tennison."

Colin stepped out of the cab, smiling grimly at Saffron and Elizabeth. "Ladies, come meet your new employer."

Alfie Tennison approached the cab. He walked with a slight limp, as Elizabeth had reported he would, and wore a brown pinstripe suit with a bright yellow and green striped tie beneath a rather luxurious fur-collared overcoat. His face was ruddy and worn, and its age didn't match the too-even muddy brown color of his hair. He held out his hands as he approached them.

"Miz Hale and Miz Everleigh," he said with an exaggerated bow. His accent matched his broad smile. "A pleasure. Coulda knocked me over with a feather when one of my boys told me one of you had managed to sneak into my office the other night. I should skin the pair of you, but I love a woman with gall, I do."

"Perhaps your fondness for bold women will extend to the favor of letting us go," Elizabeth said with a charming smile.

He smirked. "Not even if you were willing to put that pretty mouth of yours to good use. Heard you could, but, ah, no time for that."

Elizabeth rolled her eyes. "More's the pity."

Saffron elbowed her. She didn't trust Alfie's cheerful demeanor for a moment.

Alfie chuckled. "Indeed. Now, my friend has some information he's in need of. Not pleased at all by the delay." He jabbed a finger at Saffron. "You're the one been in that laboratory. You're the one to go in to get what I want."

He paused, looking almost expectant. "Usually, this is the part when folks get their backs up and say stupid things like, 'And if I don't?'"

Elizabeth and Saffron exchanged a look. Saffron cleared her throat. "We like to avoid saying stupid things."

"It's clear you have my brother," Elizabeth said. "I assume you're going to use that to make us do as you like."

"If I was making you do as I like, luv, we'd be in that motorcar going somewhere a bit cozier than a laboratory. No, you and your friend will be getting me what I'm due. My first scientist failed to get me all the pieces and parts for my associate. Once you've collected for me, I'll let you collect your friends."

"What friends?" Saffron asked at the same time Elizabeth said, "You said you have Nick."

"Didn't say nothin' about who I had," Alfie said with a twinkle in his eye. "But I will say I've got two strappin' young men in my care who are none too pleased with my hospitality."

A sudden suspicion dropped into Saffron's stomach like a brick.

"I might be offended," Alfie continued, "but I've seen the place they're being kept, and I'd surely be unhappy with such accommodations myself." He sighed melodramatically and patted his paunch. "And the state they're in, I hope you ladies can be quick about it. Anything could happen if you dawdle."

"Who do you have?" Saffron asked.

Alfie turned the full weight of his gaze on her, and in his gray eyes, she saw no hint of the charm of his smile. "Pretty sure you already know, luv."

Alexander. Alexander was trapped along with Nick, and one or both of them were hurt. Her knees went weak.

Elizabeth's arm came around her shoulder. "So we go into the lab, find . . . something, and then we all go free? I somehow doubt that's how things are going to go."

Alfie's brows rose. "I am offended you'd suggest I'm not a man of my word."

"I am offended that you think we're that stupid!" Elizabeth retorted. "I want assurance that we'll go free."

With a patronizing smile, Alfie said, "Like what?"

"I have a friend in Harpenden. Doesn't know anything about this, or the lab," Saffron burst out as an idea struck her. "You tell her we'll be at her house for lunch."

Alfie blinked. "Why the devil would I do that?"

"Because if someone is expecting us, they'll know if we go missing," Saffron said.

"I could just make a telephone call," Alfie said easily. "Say the fellows in my care are to no longer be among the livin'. How's that for an assurance?"

Saffron swallowed hard and stepped out of Elizabeth's protective embrace. Keeping her voice low, she said, "You've got a man in Lord Tremaine's office. You've got people infiltrating at least one government research station. And you've got any number of men who look very capable of wielding the weapons they carry. But it's been two weeks since you killed Jeffery Wells." The placid smile Alfie wore flickered. Saffron pressed on. "Two weeks during which you could have sent someone to break into the lab for the rest of the information, but you haven't. Because you don't know what it is you need."

Elizabeth stepped up next to her. "Your collaborator is getting impatient. I hear he is a frightening man. Someone who'd be angry if the information goes unretrieved."

Alfie's lip curled. "You're all talk, ladies. I'm getting that information, or bodies are going to start turning up downriver. You do what I want, or you'll be the first to make a splash."

After Nick had revealed more about Alfie Tennison's identity, Saffron had wondered why Alfie would meet with Wells himself in the Dancing Sparrow. He was at the top of his hierarchy. It didn't make sense for him to be a go-between, but now that she saw how badly Alfie wanted the information from the lab, badly enough to take hostages and drop the niceties after only a few minutes, it made more sense. He was desperate for the information from the Path Lab. Desperate for payment, or desperate to stay in his radical collaborator's good graces? Either way, this situation was growing more dangerous by the minute.

"We're at a stalemate, Mr. Tennison," Saffron said, hoping her estimation of Alfie was correct, and that her voice revealed none of her fear. "You need us. We want to walk away from this alive and well, and our friends returned safely. Unless you're willing to compromise, you'll have to find another way into the Path Lab."

⸙

"You're going to dislocate something if you keep that up."

Alexander ignored Nick, as he had for the past two hours. He also ignored the sting of his wrists as he continued to tug at where they were bound behind his back. The scratchy rope had rubbed his skin raw. But unlike Nick, he wasn't content to sit and do nothing.

He'd fought against Alfie Tennison's men when they took them from Nick's hotel, and attempted to get away when they shoved them into the motorcar waiting in the mews behind the building. Blood crusted his upper lip and his ribs ached for his trouble, while Nick had come out of it with not a scratch. He leaned on the wall across the room from Alexander, his hands bound and attached to the radiator. Alexander was tied to the iron grate embedded in the fireplace's grimy tiled hearth and had no comfortable way to sit, as Alfie's men had seen fit to tie his ankles together too.

They'd been tied up and left alone in the small, cold room. They could hear murmurings and movements beyond, as well as the smell of something frying, weighing down the musty air. With dust clinging to every surface and the single window covered with a tacked-up sheet, it was clear this place was a temporary hideout. It was in London, somewhere along the Thames. He'd lost track of the streets as he struggled to push his way out of the motorcar.

Alexander had counted three men in total when he and Nick were hauled inside. If he and Nick could get free, he was confident they could escape, either by going through them or sneaking past. If Alfie had come after Nick, it was likely he'd sent someone after Saffron and Elizabeth as well. Staying here and waiting to see if they'd drag the girls into the little house wasn't an option.

He gave an almighty tug, trying yet again to muscle apart his wrists, and a sharp, deep pain shot through his right shoulder, accompanied by an ominous pop. Alexander could barely make out Nick's sigh over the harsh, uneven sounds of his breathing.

"And now you'll be halfway to useless. But you learned to be left-handed, didn't you? You can still throw a punch or pull a trigger, I wager," Nick said.

Alexander was too caught up in the pain to be annoyed that Nick knew he'd taught himself to use his left hand after his injury.

After a minute of breathing through his teeth to get the pain under control, he ground out, "Do you have a plan for when I might need to do those things?"

Nick's reply was as opaque as his expression. "Just be ready."

But as the pain in his shoulder worsened and the minutes passed to hours, Alexander began to suspect that Nick didn't have a plan, at least one he would enact from this room. They'd have to wait for something to happen, and Alexander was impatient for whatever that was just as much as he dreaded it.

CHAPTER 44

It was hard to maintain a steely composure when one was shivering like a frightened greyhound, but Saffron was determined not to give way to fear or the cold. She stared into Alfie Tennison's eyes until he harrumphed and waved a hand to the cab.

"Smith," he barked, and Colin came forward.

"Mr. Tennison," Colin said with a strange mixture of deference and smugness.

"You're to take the girls to their friend's house. Have a little chat with the friend to give them peace of mind—no funny business— then take them to the lab. Make sure they do what I want them to do."

Saffron was tempted to lie and say that Colin wouldn't be allowed inside the laboratory, but that would mean Elizabeth wouldn't be allowed in either, and she had no desire to force Elizabeth to stay behind with Alfie and his bruisers. "And what precisely do you mean for us to find?"

"Anything related to this," Alfie said. He dug into his breast pocket and pulled out a paper. He handed it to Saffron.

It was a page of notes written in Quinn's hand from the middle of October, something that looked torn from a notebook. She'd listed a dozen species names in her neat script, but each had been crossed out. She knew precisely what it was and what Quinn had been trying to do by listing them out.

But she lied to Alfie. "This is just a list of species. I don't recognize them as anything they're using in the lab."

"Regardless," he said with a nasty smile, "that's what you're looking for. I want the information related to what's on that list and anything about Specimen No. 28923."

"And if we can't find anything?" Elizabeth asked.

"Then me and my men get to take bets on which of your friends will wash up at Deadman's Dock first."

"And don't bother attempting to fabricate information," Colin said. "Mr. Wells tried that, and you know how well that ended for him."

Saffron squeezed her freezing fingers together. That meant they had a scientist who could sort real pieces of information from false ones. It was infuriating to think that she was just supposed to give them information that could be potentially disastrous in the hands of someone capable. Worse, she didn't think there was a way to give them any information at all. She and Alexander searched the entire lab last night and found only the sparsest information. Even the papers she'd gotten from Simpson hadn't added much to their understanding, merely said what the fungus infecting the earwigs from Farm E did.

She exhaled slowly, glancing at Elizabeth. Her chin was raised, her eyes hard, but when their eyes met, Saffron saw Elizabeth had no more solutions than she did. "Very well," Saffron said. "We'll speak to our friend, go to the lab, and—"

Elizabeth cut her off. "And the moment we see my brother and our friend walking away from you, unharmed, you'll get whatever we find. Not before."

Alfie's genial smile was back in place. "We've got a deal." He laughed when Elizabeth stuck her hand out for a shake. "Don't let me down, ladies. Else we'll all likely be taking a dunk in the Thames."

"I've got to get into Dr. Calderbrook's office," Saffron said. "If there is any information about the specimen or a report that I missed, it has to be there."

Elizabeth shifted so she was facing Saffron in the back seat of the cab. With their party down to themselves, Colin, and the dark-haired driver, they had more space to move. "I'm to be the distraction, then?"

Saffron nodded. "Just keep everyone in one place for as long as you can. Maybe you could pretend to be a relative of Petrov or Wells, or another ministry agent, demanding answers."

"Answers for what?"

"How Wells died, for one," Saffron asked. "Colin admitted that Alfie's associate killed Wells, but Nick said he died of a fungal infection, the *Mucor indicus*. I doubt he plotted for him to die of mycosis."

From the seat next to the driver, Colin sighed with apparent exasperation. Elizabeth glared at him over her shoulder before muttering, "He's been looking at the files of immigrants for weeks. I bet he's trying to find someone willing to shrug off their recently professed loyalty to king and country." She raised her voice to ask Colin, "Found anyone willing to sell Alfie secrets, Colin? Maybe you go 'round Alfie and simply approach them yourself, then find someone to sell them to."

Colin jerked around, glaring at Elizabeth. "Shut your mouth, or I will shut it for you."

"Ooh, you are so very frightening," she cooed at him. "The intimidating private secretary. I am *quaking*—"

In a flash, Colin lashed out and snatched a handful of Elizabeth's hair. He jerked her forward, and she let out a cry. Saffron tried to get at Colin, to hit him or something, anything to get him to let go of Elizabeth, but the driver reached around to press a beefy arm over her chest and prevented her moving an inch.

"You'd better be quaking," Colin hissed, his face radiantly red. "This will seem like a gentle caress compared to what Alfie and his partner will do to you if you fail."

He let go and Elizabeth curled away from him into the corner of the seat. From beneath her ruined curls, she glared daggers at him. "You better hope I don't live long enough to ensure you get what you're due, Colin Smith."

Wisely, Colin didn't reply.

CHAPTER 45

*W*easel. *Traitor. Selfish bastard. Treacherous, scheming cad. Moron.*
    That last bit of her litany was directed at Elizabeth herself, of course. Colin Smith may have been the worst sort of bastard, but she was the one who'd never thought twice about sharing herself with him. If only one really could shoot fire from one's eyes, she was sure she would have set the back of Colin's head on fire. He and Saffron had returned from their errand to Sergeant Simpson's cousin moments ago, and though Saffron had given her an encouraging look when she slid back into the cab, Elizabeth's mood was low and still sinking.

Anger was the only thing from keeping her falling apart.

So she clung to her anger, reciting in her head all the ways Colin had been horrible—he'd worked her to death at the office, he was drowning in debt and had decided to provoke people into selling secrets to resolve it, and he'd made her listen to his dreadfully boring commentary on the statistics informing current immigration policies. And his face glowed like a bloody neon sign anytime he was the least disturbed.

"We're here," Saffron murmured as the cab came to a stop. They got out, and the cab puttered off down the street.

Elizabeth glared at Colin. "How are we to get inside, then?"

"Through the front door, of course." He gave her an evil, sly smile. "As Miss Everleigh said, you're to be the distraction. I will accompany Miss Everleigh in her search for the files." He opened his overcoat, pulling aside his suit jacket to show her the pistol tucked into the front of his waistband. "And you'll behave, Eliza."

"I hope that misfires right there," she hissed at him.

He ignored her and opened the hip-high gate for them with mocking courtesy. Elizabeth followed Saffron up the path to the house. She looked about for something that could be of use to them—a convenient hole to shove Colin into would have been marvelous—but saw only the building and its garden, the next house too far to see more than the roof. Saffron's Path Lab was housed in a tall, stately manor that, while not falling apart, had fallen into a genteel state of shabbiness, with the red brick striated with frostbitten ivy and the garden in its sad winter slumber.

Saffron opened the door, and they trooped inside. Colin stood uncomfortably close.

"Eliza," Saffron murmured, "you're to be with the ministry. Nick has the whole place well and truly afraid they'll be shut down, so all you need to do to get them to cooperate is make them think they're in trouble. Get them all into the mycology lab, if you can. It has only one door for you to guard."

Elizabeth wanted to warn Saffron against whatever she planned to do to Colin, for that bleakness in her eyes said her dearest friend wasn't planning to give away any dangerous secrets without a fight. She feared what the result would be. Colin was armed and desperate, not to mention that if they didn't comply, Nick and Alexander would be in even more danger. But Saffron knew that, and she'd never endanger her brother or the man she loved. Hopefully.

Elizabeth exhaled shakily, willing herself to recapture some of that furious confidence she'd cultivated in the motorcar. Time to put the poet on the stage and see what yarns she could spin.

Saffron and Colin went upstairs, Saffron speaking to him in a low voice lost to the creaking steps. Elizabeth stood motionless in the foyer, thinking.

She required a prop.

There was a small library to her left. She marched inside, plucked a notebook and pen from the nearest table, and opened it. She scrawled some nonsense she hoped would be convincing on the page. With a deep breath to lift her chest and chin, she began down the corridor Saffron had indicated.

There were voices coming from the end of the hallway, where two doors stood open to reveal a massive room full of scientific stuff. It was a veritable maze of glass, brass, and soil. Good Lord, but they had a lot of soil.

"Who are you?" asked an acerbic female voice.

Elizabeth turned to the left where a woman even taller than she stood. She was graying at the temples and had a pair of spectacles on her nose. "Ah," Elizabeth said in her best posh tones, "you must be Dr. Quinn."

"Miss Quinn, actually," said the man sauntering up behind her.

Elizabeth scrutinized him. He was also tall, but where Miss Quinn was a robust woman with the look of an obnoxiously healthy schoolmarm, this fellow was lanky and sallow of skin. Even from more than an arm's length away, she could smell cigarette smoke on him. Elizabeth couldn't place him in any of Saffron's descriptions of the scientists at the lab.

"Victor Burnwell," he said with a smile that had Elizabeth putting him in the "Smarmy" column in her mind. "How do you do?"

Then the name registered in her mind. Burnwell! Saffron had been at school with a fellow with that name and had been inclined to despise him. Saffron had mentioned he worked here, she now recalled. "Aren't you and your colleague meant to be at the other research station?" Elizabeth asked. She pretended to look at the notebook she held in the crook of her arm.

Quinn's and Burnwell's expressions turned to confusion. Elizabeth cleared her throat, looking at them expectantly. "Well?"

"I beg your pardon," Quinn said imperiously. "But I'm afraid I have no idea who you are."

"I see my own colleague failed to mention my arrival. Allow me to apologize on behalf of Mr. Hale, he can be the most unreliable of devils. Frankly, I don't know why the ministry hired him." She sighed with brisk annoyance. "I'm here to finish his inquiries, and I require all of you to gather so I may do so. Where are the others?"

Burnwell shrugged. "Since Crawford and I were absent the last month, I suppose we're free to carry out our work."

"You suppose wrongly," Elizabeth snapped. They couldn't very well be wandering about when Saffron was doing whatever it was she was doing. With Colin. And his *gun*. She needed something ironclad to keep them in place. Inspiration was close at hand. "You shared a workspace and collaborated with Dr. Petrov and Mr. Wells, and are therefore suspect in their deaths, as are the rest of the staff of this research station."

Burnwell gaped at her. Quinn gasped.

"I see you understand the seriousness of this matter," Elizabeth said, nodding. "Now, please assemble your colleagues. The mycology lab will do very nicely."

"Dr. Calderbrook," Saffron said, peering in the open door. The director sat at his desk and startled at her interruption.

"Miss Everleigh," he said. "What can I do for you?"

Saffron cleared her throat. "Sir, there's someone from the Agricultural Ministry here. She's following up on Mr. Hale's investigation and she's . . . I'm very concerned she thinks something is afoot. She's gathering everyone to question them now."

Dr. Calderbrook blinked rapidly behind his round spectacles. "Good Lord. I see. Well." He stood, knocking his chair back with a screech. He looked thoroughly bewildered. "I see. I've been summoned too, have I? This woman from the ministry—what is her name?"

"Miss . . . Hamilton," Saffron said.

He didn't notice her hesitation. "We'll just answer her questions. It's all just a horrible mistake. A strange, horrible coincidence."

Saffron gave him a reassuring smile. "Of course, sir."

Calderbrook hurried from the room, too distracted to notice Colin lurking in a corner of the landing, or that Saffron didn't follow him down the stairs.

"Well?" Colin drawled, approaching the doorway.

Saffron withheld a sigh and went to Dr. Calderbrook's desk. She had no idea if this search would turn up anything, let alone something she could conceivably turn over to Alfie and his collaborator.

It was possible, she reasoned as she started scanning the labels on the files in Calderbrook's desk drawer, that nothing would come of turning over the information about the entomopathogenic fungus. She imagined it would take years to study, being an unidentified species possibly belonging to an equally unknown genus, as proven by Quinn's attempts to name it that Alfie had shown her. Any attempts to engineer it into something the government could use would likely take years as well. If one ignored the thirst for deadlier weapons and the rate at which the development of those new weapons had occurred during the war, one could convince oneself that this potential weapon would never see the light of day. But Saffron could not ignore it. It was an icy fear, growing under her skin.

Colin had closed the door and stood in front of it, gun in hand. Its barrel followed her as she moved from Calderbrook's desk to the next filing cabinet.

Papers went through her hands like sand through a sieve, their contents making similarly temporary impressions on her mind, until she'd reached the end of the first cabinet having found nothing. Colin tapped the pistol's grip impatiently.

The only time she paused in her search was when she saw her own surname. This was her chance to see what Calderbrook wanted with her father.

Colin's watery blue eyes did not leave her as she opened the file and searched the papers. Her own employment contracts were first, followed by a few of her father's published articles relating to phytopathology.

"What did you find?"

Saffron jerked the file shut at Colin's sharp words. "Nothing," she said quickly. Regretfully, she shoved the file back into the drawer. There were more papers within, but she didn't dare risk Colin growing impatient.

Dread and relief created a curious lightheaded feeling when she finished the last drawer of the final filing cabinet. "There's nothing here," she said.

"You missed something," Colin said, straightening up. Sweat dotted his brow. Was he as nervous as Saffron was that they'd been in the office for twenty minutes already? Surely, someone would return here soon, Dr. Calderbrook or Joseph. And Saffron couldn't allow them to be dragged into this. "Or, you found it and hid it."

"I wouldn't do that," Saffron said. "Two other lives are at stake, not to mention Elizabeth's and my own. You left her alone in this laboratory, knowing that she wouldn't do anything to jeopardize their safety or mine. I wouldn't either."

"The evidence says to the contrary," he said, stepping forward and raising his gun slightly. "Yours are not the only lives Alfie will take if he's disappointed. Give me the information. Now."

Alarmed, Saffron stepped back, her hands automatically coming up in a placating gesture. "Colin. There is nothing here. Wells probably destroyed whatever of the research is missing."

"Wells was a fool, but he was a greedy one. He didn't destroy it. He hid it somewhere. It wasn't at his house; Alfie's boys searched it. And it's not among the papers here in the lab." He raised his gun higher, his eyes going slightly manic. "Where is it, then? Where could he have hidden it?"

Saffron's mind raced, working double-time to think of how to calm Colin and find the answers he was desperate for. She'd hoped by now her gamble with Nelly would have paid off, but it seemed she would have to rely on her wits alone to get out of this. Until said wits decided to produce a brilliant scheme, she needed to stall.

"The greenhouse," she said. "Wells would have hidden whatever you're looking for in the greenhouse."

CHAPTER 46

There were six scientists gathered in the mycology lab, marked by their white coats, and one young man with a patch over his eye and an annoyed expression on his scarred face. Elizabeth knew that was Joseph Rowe. He stood next to a younger woman she guessed was Mary Fitzsimmons, by her youth and brown hair.

"I really must insist," Mary said breathlessly, "that everyone don their protective equipment while in this laboratory."

Everyone ignored her. Quinn and Sutcliffe—identifiable by his shouting about invaders of his domain—were already arguing. Burnwell and the other botanist, an older man, sat against one of the walls on metal stools. The older botanist watched the scene with far less amusement than Burnwell. His rounded cheeks were flushed and his bespeckled eyes bounced between Quinn and Sutcliffe as they shouted. That left the silent man towering over the scene with a slight frown, who must have been the other one who studied bugs.

Dr. Calderbrook, wiry and nearly shaking with apprehension, had come jogging down the stairs moments ago. He'd been eager to help shuffle everyone into the tiny room. Elizabeth appreciated he had no inclination to gainsay her right to shove them all into the mycology lab.

A final person entered the room, a slip of a girl with dark hair covered by a cap and a mousy manner to her that Elizabeth imagined was ideal in a maid. She edged into the room, eyes darting all around.

When she caught Elizabeth's eye, she shied away, as if she thought Elizabeth might bite.

Considering how the day was going, she might do just that.

"Thank you for assembling so quickly," Elizabeth said. The shouting scientists quieted down.

Dr. Calderbrook, rocking on his heels, said, "I understand you have questions for us, but Mr. Hale already spent a good deal of time interviewing each staff member, even Betsy." He nodded to the quivering maid.

"My colleague is woefully inadequate at his job," Elizabeth said with real satisfaction. "I was sent here to finish what he couldn't. Now." She cleared her throat and took her time looking from face to face. They were apprehensive, save for Burnwell, who watched her with shudder-inducing interest. She might as well ask the questions she really wanted the answers to while she had them there. "First, I would like to know what happened to Specimen No. 28923."

The reactions were disappointing. Confusion tightened the faces of some of the staff. All but Mary, Sutcliffe, and Quinn. The other bug scientist just looked bored.

"Well?" Elizabeth prodded. She glanced at Quinn. "You took notes about the specimen. Said it had potential."

Quinn's mouth fell open. "How could you possibly—where did you—?"

With a grim smile, Elizabeth said, "I have my ways. What happened to it? My colleague was unable to find any trace of it here at the lab."

"Now, see here!" began Sutcliffe.

"I do see, that is the problem, Dr. Sutcliffe!" she called over his brewing tirade. "I see that specimens and reports have gone missing. I see that your colleagues have died mysteriously."

"Specimens and reports are misplaced all the time," Quinn said, darting a glance at the large, dreamy fellow next to her. "And our colleagues became ill."

Incredulity crept into Elizabeth's voice. "At the exact same time? Just when dangerous specimens have gone missing?"

The others were getting restless. Burnwell was muttering to the old fellow at his side. Joseph Rowe, who'd been silent at Mary's side, was looking antsy. And Dr. Calderbrook looked as if he might faint. She'd have a mutiny on her hands before long, and these people had to know something. She couldn't count on Saffron being able to find any information about Specimen No. 28923, because if she didn't, Nick was going to die. Alexander was going to die. And she and Saffron would no doubt be just behind them.

Elizabeth's eyes caught on the counter nearest her, where something black was festering in a sealed glass dish. An idea sparked, fueled by fear and the rage caused by helplessness.

She stepped back to the lab's door, grabbed the handle, and slammed it shut behind her. Then she picked up the glass dish covered in blackness for them to see. "I'm afraid I'm not going anywhere until I get the information I need, and neither are any of you. You're going to tell me, or we'll all get to carry out a little experiment. Anyone have a hypothesis for what will happen if I smash this?"

Number 28 was quiet as Saffron and Colin descended the stairs. She led him through the kitchen at the back of the house, fragrant with tea that had been left on the counter to steep. Every step, every breath, reminded her that she had a gun pointed at her back. Her neck wouldn't stop prickling.

Cold air met them as they stepped outside, then warmth as they entered the greenhouse. It was empty, but birds hopped on the glass roof, tittering and warbling at one another.

"Damned hot," Colin muttered.

"They keep it warm, since the daisies prefer warmer temperatures," Saffron said absently, looking intently around the greenhouse. Everything was perfectly in order. The daisies were as bright and fresh as they might have been on a summer morning.

What could she do? She'd wagered on stalling, but it looked like she'd be scrambling for something to hand over to Colin and Alfie after all.

She went to the shelves full of equipment and chose a shovel. She could just start digging in the dirt. At the very least, she could buy some time by giving Alfie something. A pot of dirt she could say contaminated the fungus from Farm E, or a plant she could claim was infected by it, or—

"What are you doing with that?" Colin snapped.

Turning, she saw Colin had the gun aimed at her again, clearly unnerved by the weighty shovel in her hands. She swallowed hard. In a careful, soothing voice, she said, "I believe Wells buried the materials. I'll have to dig for them."

"Fine," Colin spat. He was losing his composure, likely fearful that this was taking too long. Alfie had given them only an hour, and it was nearly up.

Saffron wandered down the rows, wondering where she should start. Colin wouldn't believe the fungus was simply living in the dirt, would he?

Her eyes swept over the plots, pausing on plot 13. The daisies there were still stunted, their white heads barely visible over the other plots' growth. They'd evened out some since she'd first observed their pell-mell arrangement, almost as if they'd adjusted to stretching their necks up high at the odd angle.

Her feet stopped on the brick, frozen by the understanding ricocheting through her mind.

But it couldn't actually be as simple as that, could it?

With equal parts anticipation and dread, she strode to plot 13 and drove the shovel into the dirt. Black earth and snapped daisies were tossed aside as she struggled deeper into the soil. Disregarding her shoes, she stepped into the plot and stomped on the ridge of the shovel blade's base to drive it deeper.

The beds were deep, and by the time she'd dug nearly to the bottom, she was panting and sweating and flecked with damp dirt. Colin was across the plot from her, watching with a mixture of malice and anticipatory greed.

She set the shovel down and started running her hands through the dirt, discarding mauled daisies and roots. Her fingers reached something hard and angular.

Heart thundering in her chest, she dredged it up out of the dirt.

It was a large box, two feet long and three feet wide. A briefcase.

The leather was stained with mud, for the bottom of the raised bed was wet. It hadn't been there long; the lock had only a speck of rust beginning in the center at the keyhole.

"Give that to me," Colin said, reaching his free hand out.

Saffron hesitated. This was doubtless what Alfie and his conspirator were after. A case hidden in the flower beds Wells had tended? There was nothing else it could be. It also explained why the daisies' growth pattern was strange; Wells had dug them up to hide this, then replaced them over top.

"Give it to me, now," Colin barked.

Saffron stood on the spongy earth, clutching it to her chest. "You'll telephone and tell them I've done what Alfie asked. You'll tell them to let Alexander and Nick go, and when I see they're safe, then you can have the case."

"You'll hand it over now." Colin's face twisted into a cruel grimace of a smile. "You don't want me take it from you."

CHAPTER 47

No one moved.

All the eyes in the lab were on Elizabeth, or, more specifically, the dish in her hand.

"Sutcliffe?" The older man at the other end of the room spoke with a wheeze. "Is that something we need to worry about?"

Sutcliffe's established flush bordered on violet. "Yes," he spat. "Look here, you daft woman, put that down, before you—"

"I will not," Elizabeth said, raising the glass dish higher. "You heard me. I want answers."

"Petrov and Wells were ill," Burnwell said angrily. He'd gotten to his feet. "Sudden bouts of sickness."

"Then why is your laboratory being investigated?" Elizabeth asked. "Why am I here, threatening you all with mold?"

"That isn't mold." Mary spoke timidly, fingers twisting together. "It's a fungus, one that will—"

"Sorry, darling, but I don't give a damn." She needed to maintain control of the room and keep them distracted. Plus, she would love to be able to tell Nick at the end of all this that *she* had solved the murders after all. "I want to know what happened to Wells and Petrov, and I want to know what happened to the missing specimen."

"Nothing happened to them," Quinn said. "We've already told you—"

"It wasn't an accident," Elizabeth snapped. "Good Lord, I thought you lot were meant to be intelligent! Two of your colleagues die within weeks of each other and you all just shrug it off as bad luck?"

The room stilled again, the faces of the scientists showing they were thinking it over, and many of them were drawing the natural conclusion. Several looked alarmed.

"This entire situation is mad," said the older botanist, removing his spectacles to rub tiredly at his eyes.

The scientists all started to speak at once, their arguments and accusations layering on top of one another. Their voices bubbled up like milk left over the heat, and Elizabeth was likely to be the target when it finally boiled over. She cleared her throat, preparing to make another threat to get them all quiet again, but a small voice cut through the din.

"It was me."

The entire room turned as one to the person who spoke so miserably, their expressions as stunned as Elizabeth's own.

Recovering herself, Elizabeth demanded, "What do you mean, it was you?"

Misery in every line of her face, Mary said, "It was me. But I never meant to kill anyone, I swear!"

Saffron inched backward over the uneven dirt of the raised bed. "The people Alfie will sell this information to will do terrible things with it."

"And Alfie will do terrible things to your beloved Alexander if you don't give it to me," he hissed.

There was a flicker of movement beyond the condensation-blurred walls. Saffron resisted following it. It could be any number of people, including Colin's conspirators, coming to tell them that time was up. She couldn't afford to hope otherwise.

She reached down to the shovel, struggling to balance, clutching the case's handle in her hand as she knelt on the uneven ground. "The information contained within this case could destroy entire countries, Colin. Don't you care?"

Her fingers closed around the shovel's handle, and she rose, her eyes never leaving Colin's.

His eyes narrowed on the shovel. "Don't you dare."

With wide-eyed innocence, she said, "I have to put it back. The dirt too. Otherwise, someone will notice and start asking questions."

"People are already asking questions!" he cried. "That's the whole bloody reason for Nick Hale being here, isn't it? He caught wind of our scheme and came to put an end to it." A sneer stretched his face. "But he's been caught. Like a fat fly in a spider's web."

She looked to the wall of foggy glass, then to the door. If she made a run for it—

The bricks before the door caught her eye. They were uneven, just like the soil of plot 13. Joseph hadn't finished reinstalling them properly after tending to the broken pipe beneath. The one with the faulty fixture.

"I think I know where more information is hidden," she said with false enthusiasm. "This can't be it. Wells wouldn't have put it all together in one place. And this spot, over here"—she walked swiftly down the brick path parallel to Colin's—"these bricks have been disturbed!"

Taking care to keep the case and the shovel at her side, she got on her knees and began pulling bricks from the ground. Sweat trickled down her temples. Her fingernails tore as she dug the bricks away, until at last the grate was exposed. She lifted it and let out a soft exclamation as she peered down into the large gap filled with pipes.

"What is it?" Colin asked. He'd followed her and stood a few feet away.

"There's another case down there," she said, standing. "You'll have to get it, it's too far away for me."

He was already striding to the hole in the ground. "Move off over there."

Saffron bit her lip. That was not what she wanted. She had to stay where she was for this to work. "Er, but—"

"Over there," barked Colin. He kicked the shovel away from Saffron.

She backed up, picking up the case. Without the shovel, she'd have no way to make the pipe burst, providing her with the distraction she needed to run.

The gun was in Colin's left hand, the one he was bracing on the ground as he knelt and peered into the hole. Could she reach it?

A light knocking sound came from outside. Someone was there, knocking on the kitchen door of Number 28. Colin's colleagues wouldn't knock on the door.

"Help!" Saffron yelled, lunging toward the greenhouse door. "I need help, quickly!"

Colin let out a howl of rage. She turned to see him jerk up, his face contorting with anger. "Shut up, damn you!"

Footsteps thudded on the ground outside. Colin rose to his knees, his gun raised. Cold from the open greenhouse door met her sweaty back. Saffron was pitched forward as something hard hit her shoulder. Her head cracked against the door frame. Her knees hit the hard bricks. A gunshot rang out, followed by a hiss and a scream.

Dizzily, Saffron clambered to her feet. The humid air was strangely acrid. Sergeant Simpson was sprawled next to her, his gun a foot away. Colin was screaming and writhing, his body on the ground next to a column of steam from which came an ear-splitting whistle.

Scrambling up, Simpson gaped at Colin before seeming to recall Saffron. He rushed to her side, reaching for her when she took an uncertain step forward. "Miss Everleigh, are you all right? My cousin gave me your message, but it took ages to place all the telephone calls."

"I'm fine," Saffron said, reaching a hand to her head, where a sizable lump was already growing. "We've got to do something about Colin." He was still howling on the ground, his hands against his face, which Saffron could see was violently red.

Simpson ran his hand through his short blond hair, his cheeks nearly as red as Colin's. "By God, they're never going to let me live this down. I didn't mean to fire. The gun was in my hand, and when I tripped—"

Simpson had tripped over her, accidentally discharged his weapon at the pipe, and possibly given her a concussion and Colin Smith severe burns. But she couldn't argue with the results.

"I think you're right, Sergeant," Saffron said, spotting the case laying on the ground where she'd fallen. She stooped to pick it up, head throbbing, and pressed it into Sergeant Simpson's arms. "I don't think you're going to live this down. But I think it'll be for a much better reason than you expect."

CHAPTER 48

Sutcliffe rounded on Mary and asked with such vicious vehemence that even Elizabeth winced, "What the devil are you talking about?"

She didn't flinch at him shouting in her face, but her eyes filled with tears. "I . . . I did it. I made them ill. I contaminated their workstations." She bit her lip, and a tear rolled down her cheek. "I was so tired of Wells and—and Burnwell—"

"What?" Burnwell stepped forward, face darkening. "What did you do to me?"

Mary glared at him through watery eyes. "You and Wells flouted our health and safety protocols constantly! You all do!" She waved a white-gloved hand helplessly. "We work with dangerous substances and specimens, and none of you bother to protect yourselves—or others. You could breathe in spores of dangerous fungi, or have them cling to your person, and just walk out with them, spreading them all around!"

Burnwell took a few angry steps forward. "So you infected us with something? To teach us a bloody lesson?"

"No," Mary said, retreating until she was steps away from Elizabeth. "No, I didn't! It was the pyrethrins. I dabbed the oil on the counters and on your tools."

Elizabeth interrupted her. "What are pyrethrins?"

Mary gave her a confused look. "The chemicals we're studying, from the pyrethrum daisies. I thought if Burnwell and Wells were dizzy, maybe had headaches, they might realize how dangerous it was to go without their protective equipment." She looked from person to person with growing distress. "I didn't mean to seriously harm anyone! I knew nobody here had a serious allergy to it! But I don't understand how it killed Dr. Petrov or Mr. Wells!"

"Petrov was already ill," growled Sutcliffe. "He was ill before he left Russia, for Christ's sake. His kidneys were failing and nobody knew why. Introducing more chemicals into his body would have worsened his condition and weakened him further."

The room went silent as Mary realized what she'd done. Her face drained of color. "My God. My God, I'm sorry. I didn't realize—"

"Shut up!" Sutcliffe turned to Elizabeth. "Now you see it was an accident. She meant nothing by it other than a foolish attempt to make people wear their damned masks and gloves. Put the bloody dish down!"

That certainly explained some things, like how Petrov had actually died. A glow of satisfaction suffused her. She had solved it after all.

This was a fascinating turn of events, indeed. One of the scientists had poisoned Petrov. She might as well keep prodding them to see what other confessions might come oozing out.

"What about Wells?" she demanded of the room. "Wells was not ill like Petrov, was he?"

Quinn jabbed a finger toward Mary. "We've all been ill thanks to that idiot!"

Mary let out a noise of protest, and Sutcliffe barked, "You all know the pyrethrins last only a few days before their potency fades. Even if she meant to teach Wells and Burnwell a lesson, the oil hasn't been out in the lab for weeks."

"That's true," the tall man said softly. "Wells died of something far more serious."

"Unless the bitch gave him a double dose," Burnwell snarled at Mary.

"I didn't!" she protested. "I haven't done anything since Burnwell went away.'

"Wells had a wound on his hand. A large cut to his palm," Elizabeth said. "It was blackened and absolutely vile to behold, I'm told. It was a fungal infection, *Mucor* something-or-other."

The old botanist in the back of the room spoke in a wheezing voice. "If it was blackened, it could have been necrosis. That's a serious infection, then."

Burnwell crossed his arms, glaring at Mary. "Gave Wells something you grew here, did you?"

"I would never infect him with something like that!" At Burnwell's incredulous snort, she turned wide, pleading eyes on Elizabeth. "You said it was *Mucor*? That's a common genus in the materials we work with, decaying food and soil. Wells never wore gloves, not when he worked in the laboratory or the greenhouse. He likely contracted it from the soil."

"*Mucor indicus*," Sutcliffe said gruffly. "The Everleigh girl asked about it. What does she have to do with this? She spying for the ministry?"

"No" was all the reply that Elizabeth gave, for although Mary was going on about what sounded very scientific and likely informative, the sole window in the room, just opposite where Elizabeth stood, was suddenly full of a very welcome sight: Saffron, filthy as anything, waving frantically at her. She was mouthing equally welcome words at her through the glass.

Sweet relief flooded Elizabeth, and she nearly dropped the glass dish in her hands. The population of the room had gone quiet, more than one craning their necks toward the window, clearly wondering what she was staring at.

"I beg your pardon," Elizabeth said perfunctorily. "A poor time for wool-gathering."

"You have the answers to your damned questions," Sutcliffe bit out. "Put the petri dish down!"

"If Wells had stolen from the lab and infected himself in the process," Elizabeth said, ignoring Sutcliffe's demand, "he likely worried he'd contracted something from the specimens he stole, and worried he'd have to explain how he came into contact with it, I suppose."

But then why did Colin and Alfie say the mysterious collaborator killed Wells, if he'd died from the fungal infection? Regardless, it seemed it was time for her to go. Elizabeth set down the dish.

The entire room exhaled.

"What about Mary?" asked Joseph gruffly.

"And what you do you mean, Wells stole from the laboratory?" asked Burnwell.

"Dr. Calderbrook!" Quinn cried, pointing at Mary. "Dismiss this lunatic at once."

Elizabeth stole a glance at Dr. Calderbrook, who'd gone terribly pale and collapsed onto the stool next to the old botanist.

"No," the tall man said. "We need the police."

"Oh, the police will be here any minute," Elizabeth said cheerfully. Saffron's signal through the window had told her as much. She winked at Mary. "Good luck."

It was somewhat surreal to walk into the flat that evening. It seemed like years since they'd last been at home, not hours, and Saffron felt like she barely recognized the place. But that might have been the head injury.

She was not concussed, according to the doctor who had examined her while she and Elizabeth gave their statements in the aftermath of the events at the Path Lab. Nick had shared enough of Saffron's involvement with his superiors that they were taken to a private room at the local police station to report to someone from Nick's "office" rather than the constable. She'd left out certain parts of the truth, just as she was sure Nick had left out certain parts of his dealings with her. She felt it was fair play, in the end.

Saffron breathed a great sigh of relief when she finally got into her bathroom to disrobe. She tugged out all the bits and pieces she'd accumulated through her adventure, dumped them into a basin on the tiled floor, and emptied a bottle of peroxide over the whole mess.

There was a trail of dirt on the bathroom floor by the time she settled into a steaming-hot bath. While Elizabeth had made a beeline for the wine bottle, the bath was the first thing Saffron wanted—the second, actually, but she didn't know when she would get to see Alexander.

Saffron and Elizabeth had been promised that Alexander and Nick would be rescued in short order. Without Colin to report back what had happened to Alfie, two of his thugs had shown up at Number 28. The police had promptly arrested and interrogated them, and between their reluctant confessions and what the London police and Nick's "office" already knew of Alfie Tennison, Saffron had to think that Alfie and his hostages would be found soon. She forced herself to believe it. Colin was under arrest in a hospital bed, and therefore Alfie couldn't know what had occurred. Alexander and Nick would be safe.

A knock on the front door had Saffron scrambling out of the bath. Her head and body throbbed, but she didn't care. She wrapped herself in her dressing gown and peered down the hall.

Elizabeth, wine bottle in hand, stood at the front door. She was speaking to a man in a police uniform. Elizabeth stepped aside, and the man, followed by another in uniform, came inside. Saffron quickly retreated. Elizabeth knocked on the bathroom door and said through the door, "Saff, the police have sent some fellows to wait with us until the rest of this is settled. Said not to mind them, they're just here to ensure Alfie doesn't catch wind and make good on his promises about the river."

From the loose way she spoke, Saffron guessed Elizabeth had already made good headway on the wine, and perhaps the cooking spirits too. She sighed, turning to the mirror to dry off properly. Her head was tender from Simpson banging the greenhouse door into her. Poor Simpson. For all his heroics, he seemed to have been rather forgotten in the shuffle after the police arrived at Number 28. She hoped he'd manage to get some recognition. After all, if not for his telephone calls to Inspector Green and the local police and arriving when he had, the story would have had a very different ending.

She dabbed some ointment on her bruise and thought about Elizabeth. She was likely to be the only one who came out of this physically unharmed. But mentally . . .

Elizabeth projected worldly confidence like a blazing summer sun, but she also had a tender heart capable of great love and craved it in return. Saffron wasn't sure what it would do to her to have had her boyfriend betray and use her so. She would have to keep a close eye on Elizabeth.

She put on comfortable, cozy clothing. She went through the ritual of combing and braiding her long hair but found it gave her little comfort. From the smells and sounds from the kitchen, she knew Elizabeth was cooking something. Saffron had no appetite herself, and she doubted Elizabeth did either. She was relying on her own comforting routines. Saffron wondered if she ought to leave her alone to brood. Still deciding, she stepped into the parlor to greet the police officer.

He turned from the window as she entered the room.

"Hello," Saffron said. "Have you had any news regarding Mr. Ashton or Mr. Hale?"

"I expect you'll see them soon, Miss Everleigh," he replied.

She exhaled. "That's good news."

His thin lips lifted in a half-smile. "It certainly is."

Curious, she asked, "Your accent is so hard to place. Are you English?"

"Certainly," he replied. "As English as a girl born and raised in Bedford."

He said it like it was a common turn of phrase, but it definitely was not. "I—yes, I suppose I am quite English." She wet her lips, unable to place the unease winding through her. "What did you say your name was?"

"I didn't," the officer said. "But, please, call me Bill."

She was definitely uncomfortable now. Something in the nonchalance of his voice, the steadiness of his gaze. She forced a light laugh. "That's rather too informal for someone I've just met."

He canted his head to the side. That half-smile played at his lips again. "What makes you think that you and I haven't met before?"

CHAPTER 49

Saffron stared at the man she was now certain was not a police officer. "We haven't met before, I'm sure of it."

"No, you're not." Bill took a step forward, and Saffron took an automatic step back. With exaggerated purpose, he lowered himself into an armchair. He gestured for her to sit too.

She hesitated, tempted to run to the kitchen to Elizabeth, or even to the telephone. She wet her dry lips. "Where have we met, then?"

"I'm hurt you don't remember me. We've known each other for years, in one way or another."

She didn't know how to respond to that. He had plain features, dark brown hair swept back from his forehead, and soft eyes that would require closer inspection to determine the color. She couldn't determine his age either. He was certainly older than Alexander, who was in his early thirties, but not yet middle-aged. His nose was on the larger side, but it wasn't memorable. Nothing about his face was. She swallowed hard. "Well, if we're such good friends, perhaps you should let me go."

Bill's brow puckered. "You are at liberty to leave any time you like. You are not a prisoner here."

She caught his unspoken meaning. "I suppose you wouldn't leave if I asked politely."

"I will, after you give me what I want."

"I don't have it."

Bill's lips pressed together in a stern line, but his eyes danced. "Saffron, it's unnecessary to lie to me. Give me what you took from Jeffery Wells's case, and you'll never have to see me again."

Again, she caught the nuance. "But you'll be seeing me regardless?"

Bill let out a soft chuckle. "You always were clever. Even as a little girl, I recall you getting into all sorts of mischief with that active mind of yours."

She found her lungs did not want to fill with air. He acted as if he'd known her as a child. But he couldn't—

"You think I must be lying." Bill leaned forward in his chair. With his elbows on his knees and his face forward, he gave the impression of earnestness. "I assure you; I've watched your progress just as surely as you watched your strychnos seeds sprout. Except you haven't been watching them. You've allowed Alexander to tend them for you. A good idea, too, as you're not too popular at the university, especially at the moment. Dr. Aster may have forgiven you for your absence to help Nick, but the rest of your colleagues see it as a continuation of the preferential treatment they think you've been receiving since you were a student. Luckily, Alexander doesn't see you in so negative a light. Despite your differences of opinion, I believe he's in love with you."

A choked sound came from Saffron's throat.

"I shouldn't distress you by telling you before he does," Bill said. "But it illustrates the point you must understand if our conversation is to progress: I know everything, Saffron. I know who you care for. I know who they care for. I know about the flowers and vines you draw in your notebooks. I know the shop where Elizabeth prefers to buy her wine. I know what Alexander's shaving soap is scented with. I can't say for sure whether or not you like it, but I'd wager you do."

Throat constricted by the flood of fear at his gently spoken words, she managed to ask, "What do you want?"

"You know what I want. I want what you took from Wells's case."

"I didn't take—"

Warning laced his quiet voice. "Did I not make my point clear? I know everything, including that you took materials from the case before you turned it over to Nick's friends and the police. I want it."

Saffron believed him. If he'd been spying on her and the others—but *why* would he?—then he likely would know. He might be the scientist Colin had warned would examine the materials to ensure she hadn't swapped out anything. She didn't see the point in lying, then. "I can't give it to you."

Bill was silent for a beat. "Why not?"

"I destroyed it," she whispered.

"Show me," Bill ordered. He rose, straightening to an unimpressive height, though straight-backed as an arrow.

He squashed her hopes of enlisting Elizabeth's help by murmuring, "I have a colleague keeping Elizabeth company. Let's not interrupt them."

Shivers broke out over her body, pebbling her skin. Elizabeth was in just as much danger—more, probably. Bill must know how much Saffron loved her friend, and he would be furious when he realized Saffron wasn't lying about destroying the stolen materials.

In the bathroom, still damp and muddy, Saffron pointed him to the basin on the floor.

Bill walked slowly over, kneeling beside it. His nose wrinkled as he took in the trio of vials, their contents soaked.

"Hydrogen peroxide," he muttered. He picked up a piece of paper, the ink long since muddled by the acid. "Clever."

He stood, and as he did so, he rolled his shoulders. The action of a man attempting to collect his temper.

Saffron swallowed hard. She knew she'd done the right thing, stealing and destroying the information, but what would the consequences be?

Bill walked slowly, deliberately, to the door where Saffron stood. He stopped just before her. This close, she still couldn't see the color of his irises. His lashes were straight, shading them somewhat as he studied her.

"You owe me, Saffron Everleigh," he murmured. "You owe me something big to make up for this loss."

"I—I won't steal secrets for you," Saffron stammered. "I won't. If Alfie had gotten his hands on that specimen, it could have killed hundreds of thousands of people."

"Alfie?" Bill smirked. "He was going to give it to me. *I* would have killed hundreds of thousands of people with it."

Fear gripped her at his cool manner. Bill was Alfie's collaborator, the one Colin and all his men feared. The prospect of being responsible for the deaths of so many people didn't bother him in the least. "Who are you? Why are you doing any of this?"

"Bill Wyatt. Please, continue to call me Bill."

He held his hand out for her, which she could not have been paid a thousand pounds to take. "I've made you uncomfortable. I apologize. In my eagerness to finally speak with you in this open way, I'm afraid I've forgotten my manners."

She was torn between demanding answers from him and wanting desperately for him to leave. But she didn't know how to do either without threatening herself or Elizabeth.

"I am a member of an organization that . . ." he hummed thoughtfully, "disseminates information. I gather it, and interested parties offer me trades to receive it."

"People pay money for the secrets you steal from the government."

He shrugged. "I cannot deny that some information does come from within governments. It is often those same governments that pay me for similar information, strangely enough."

She wasn't going to be tangled up in his subtleties. He stole and sold secrets, dangerous ones. And now he thought she owed him something. Too boldly, she said, "And you kill those who refuse to do your bidding."

"Like any good gardener, I remove the weeds." Bill's lips stretched into a smile that shone in his eyes. "But I always leave behind sprouts with the potential to grow."

Ignoring that strange smile, she asked, "How did you manage to kill Wells so quickly with *Mucor indicus*?"

"A strange coincidence, that," Bill replied. "It might have killed him if left to fester long enough. But I had access to something a little quicker. Nearly impossible to identify in the human body after just a few hours."

A poison, no doubt. Saffron wet her dry lips. "Another secret you stole?" Bill only smiled. "Did you kill Petrov too?"

His sense of levity disappeared. "I did not kill Demian. I liked him, in fact. I think it a great pity he never found a solution to his *Aristolochia* problem."

Saffron blinked, bewildered by the gentle bitterness in his tone. But she had no opportunity to ponder it.

Bill canted his head again toward the front door. A pale scar, thick and ugly, was notched just below his ear. "Ah." He turned to the kitchen door. "Time to go," he barked in a commanding tone.

The kitchen door opened, and the other man in a policeman's uniform came out. He was tall but slender and wore a faint mustache. His hair was covered by a custodian's helmet.

Bill took his own helmet from the table just inside the front door, donned it, and gave her a little bow. "I'll be seeing you, Saffron. Good evening."

They exited the flat. Indecision froze her in place. Did she telephone the police? Nick's flat? Should she run after them, to try to see where they went?

She was still standing in the hall when the door flew open, and two men appeared in the frame.

Saffron stood in the hall, her face stark white. Guilt lashed Alexander. He'd all but kicked in the door, likely terrifying her. He was no better than the thugs who'd abducted him and Nick.

He'd been told what Saffron and Elizabeth had gone through: being tricked out of the flat by Colin Smith, forced to search the Path Lab again, and the strange conclusion with Sergeant Simpson. He ought to have been gentler about this.

But none of his feelings were gentle now. He stormed inside, not caring about Nick, standing just behind him, and took Saffron in his arms.

He buried his face into her neck and held her for a long time. His heart, which hadn't stopped racing since he'd heard Colin had forced them into Alfie Tennison's clutches, finally eased to its usual steady rhythm, and he came back to full awareness. They stood in the hall, and Saffron was stroking his back. She was saying the same thing over and over again, "I'm fine, Alexander. I'm fine."

He couldn't bring himself to be embarrassed. He'd thought he might die today. Saffron might have died, and he wouldn't have been able to do a thing about it.

He'd known it for ages, maybe from the moment he stepped onto the ship to Brazil and felt he was making a terrible mistake leaving her behind. It was too soon and too late, but there was nothing else to say. Staring into her eyes, such a precious shade of blue, he said, "I love you."

A strange emotion flickered in their depths before they filled with tears. Her breath caught on a sob. "I love you, Alexander. I'm so—"

He cut her off with a searing kiss. He ignored the burning ache of his shoulder and ribs, the twinges of his bruised nose, the stinging of the bandages chafing at his raw wrists. Nothing mattered but this.

Neither attempted to break apart for a long time. Eventually, Saffron pulled back enough to rest her forehead against his. He didn't loosen his grip on her waist. He wasn't going to be able to let her go for a long time. Maybe never.

"Alexander," she whispered.

His whole body tensed up at the trepidation he saw in her eyes.

With a shuddering breath, she said, "I have to tell you about Bill."

CHAPTER 50

The building that housed Nick's so-called office was in Westminster, an ugly sand-colored brick with minimal white stone flourishes around the windows and doors. When Nick had strolled in, cheerful as ever, and invited Saffron along to "wrap up a few loose ends," she and Alexander had exchanged wary glances. It was nearly a week after she'd thought it was all over, save for whatever strangeness Bill's promises ensured.

"That sounded rather ominous, didn't it?" Nick chuckled, shaking his head. "I mean only that I'll be speaking to a few of the scientists from the Path Lab and wanted you to sit in on the interviews to answer any questions I might have about the scientific aspects."

Saffron hummed disbelievingly. Elizabeth had tearfully embraced Nick before shoving him hard and telling him she never wanted to speak to him again, then warned him if he ever went so long without visiting, she'd sic Alfie Tennison's bruisers on him. Nick seemed to have accepted the drunken warning for the forgiveness it was. Saffron, however, was not sure she'd ever forgive Nick for inviting her into the Path Lab mess. She wasn't sure she'd forgive herself for endangering Elizabeth and Alexander with her choice to pursue the mystery.

Saffron had acquiesced to Nick's invitation, only because she wanted to assure herself that nobody—not even mysterious, terrifying Bill Wyatt—could get their hands on information about Specimen 28923.

Now she, Nick, and Alexander, who'd refused to be left behind, walked into the building. It was just as ugly within, with white tile that had seen better days and water-stained ceilings.

"Charming place," Saffron muttered to Nick.

He winked at her, though his attempt at charm seemed to slide right off his face. By the time they'd crossed the foyer and checked in with the receptionist, Affable Brother Nick had disappeared behind a hardened mask. He'd made the same rapid switch when she told him about Bill. He'd listened raptly, particularly to her description of his appearance. He and Alexander had both been shocked that they'd passed him and his man on the stairs, but neither had made any sort of impression on them.

But in the end, Nick had only told her that he would look into Bill and his supposed network of secret-stealers. It occurred to Saffron long after he'd departed that evening that he might have already known about Bill's involvement.

Nick led them through a maze of halls until they reached a door on which he knocked. Two men were within, and the younger of the two rose and gave Nick a polite nod before exiting.

Nick held the door open for Saffron but blocked Alexander's way. "Stay outside, Alexander," he said casually.

Saffron nodded at Alexander, and he stepped away from the door reluctantly. Nick closed it.

The other man, who sat in a chair opposite an empty desk, craned around in his seat to glare at her. "What are you doing here?"

"Hello, Dr. Sutcliffe," Saffron said, venturing further into the room. It was a plain office holding only the desk, a few chairs, and a pair of lamps whose muddy yellow light mixed oddly with the blue morning haze from the windows lining the far wall.

"Brought you in for interrogating too, did they?" Sutcliffe glared at Nick as he went to sit behind the desk.

Nick settled in his chair, calm but alert. "I'm glad to see you're alive and well, Dr. Sutcliffe. From what I gather about those involved in this matter, you could have been in considerable danger."

Sutcliffe snorted, clearly disbelieving.

"After the statements given by various involved parties in the event last week, and thanks to the cooperation of multiple institutions, the contents of Alfie Tennison's private residence and his various places of business were thoroughly searched. We found a good deal of stolen information from a number of research facilities around London, including yours."

"Wells deserved what he got, that traitor."

"Indeed," Nick said dryly. "However, the information recovered belonging to Number 28 was incomplete. The case recovered from the greenhouse had some materials, but the majority of what you and the others reported missing was not recovered."

Saffron resisted shifting guiltily. She'd taken those materials knowing that Nick and his colleagues would be looking for them. She stood by her decision, but she felt bad that Sutcliffe had been hauled to London to answer for her actions.

Nick dipped a hand into a pocket to retrieve a few folded papers. He read, "The original specimen of the infected insect from Farm E—that's the one just outside Eynsford, if you recall—is missing, as well as the soil and plant samples the insect arrived with."

Saffron's hands twitched involuntarily. There hadn't been a plant sample among what she'd taken from the case. That meant it was still out there, somewhere, possibly in Bill's hands. What if he'd stolen it from Alfie before his properties were searched?

"I destroyed it," Sutcliffe barked. "Obviously!"

"You destroyed it?" Nick repeated, and Saffron was pleased to see he was truly nonplussed.

"Damn right, I did," Sutcliffe said, shifting in his seat. "I killed the growth Mary had been tending, then I took the samples—or what that rat Wells hadn't taken—soaked them in nitric acid, and burnt the whole mess until there was only ashes left."

Nick had regained his calm quickly. Voice flat, he said, "You are admitting to destroying invaluable government property."

Sutcliffe jabbed a finger at Nick. "I would do it again, a hundred times over. You like eating, Hale? You like having a stable life in a country not plagued by insects puffing out spores left and right, then eating everything in sight? Something like that fungus wouldn't stay locked away in a laboratory for long. If it wasn't stolen, it would be used, as you damn well know."

"You should be arrested," Nick said blandly.

"Go ahead! Arrest me! Call me traitor." He leaned forward, and Saffron imagined that he thought he was lowering his voice. It came out just as loud and brash. "But you and I both know that I made the right choice. If you think for a moment it would stay in whatever godforsaken field you people dropped it in, you're daft. This is *nature*. Nature always finds a way. It adapts! It worms its way into everything! How do you think a fungus like that got here in the first place? You know how few entomopathogenic fungi are in this area naturally? They travel on anything and everything. It probably came in on an innocent-looking ship bringing coffee or bananas from some tropical place! Damned if I can tell how it didn't manage to spread over the whole country, with how quickly it progressed."

"How do you know how quickly it progressed?" Nick asked sharply.

Sutcliffe opened his mouth, then mashed it shut. After a moment, he ground out, "Because I studied it, didn't I? How do you think I knew to destroy Mary's samples? I grew it, infected some of Narramore's earwigs, and the damned things went mad! Burnt those to a crisp too. I had to destroy the entire vivarium, and Quinn lost her mind over it! They ate everything I gave them. Probably would have found a way to eat their way out of their enclosure. Something about that damned fungus made their appetite insatiable. If the danger of infecting other insects and upsetting the ecosystem wasn't bad enough, it was the possibility of the infected insects eating anything in their path. They wouldn't stop at crops, I'd wager," he finished darkly.

"It wasn't your right to make that decision."

Sutcliffe lurched to his feet. "The entire ecosystem that your greedy stomach relies on would collapse if it got out!" His face had gone an alarming shade of puce. He sat back down heavily, chest heaving.

"He's right," Saffron murmured.

Nick gave her a quelling look, but she was quite done taking instructions from him. "Dr. Sutcliffe is right," Saffron repeated.

"Of course I am," he grunted. "Humanity isn't mature enough to not use something like that."

Nick didn't reply, but she saw calculation in his eyes. A wave of exhaustion washed over her. She was so tired of this. So tired of the contrivance and manipulation. She wanted someone to do something good and right without it costing something.

But as she departed the ministry building soon after, arm in arm with Alexander, she wasn't sure that was how things would ever be with Nick Hale. Luckily, she didn't plan to see him, or any of his colleagues, ever again.

EPILOGUE

Three Months Later

The night was dry but cold, making the warm air of the flat all the more welcoming when Saffron and Alexander stumbled inside. In truth, Saffron stumbled, giggling, and Alexander followed with a fondly exasperated expression. As soon as the door closed, that fell away into a heated look she'd come to anticipate.

His mouth had just captured hers when a throat cleared.

Alexander stepped back, and Saffron turned to Elizabeth, blushing. Apparently, her encouragement for Elizabeth to leave the house and go out that evening had not been effective. She stood at the end of the hall, dressing gown tied at her waist and a mostly empty glass of wine in her hand. At least she wasn't drinking straight from the bottle as she'd been doing almost every evening for months.

"Sorry, Eliza," Saffron said, stifling another giggle. She'd definitely had one too many cocktails, but keeping up with Alexander on the dance floor was thirsty work.

"Don't mind me," Elizabeth drawled. "Only you received a telephone call that sounded rather urgent."

"Who from?" Saffron asked.

"That lawyer fellow, Mr. F.," Elizabeth said.

"Feyzi?" Saffron asked, frowning. She'd not heard from Mr. Feyzi since she and Alexander visited him in November.

"Said to telephone his office, no matter the hour."

The last of her tipsy glow left her. "That cannot be good." She reached for the telephone.

Alexander frowned. "Would you like privacy?"

She paused, hand on the receiver. She had no idea what bad news Mr. Feyzi might tell her—for that was the only kind of news one received at nearly midnight. "Yes, thank you," she said softly before speaking to the operator.

Alexander disappeared around the corner, ostensibly going to the parlor. She was glad he hadn't decided to leave. Things had been going very well between the two of them lately, and she wasn't quite finished with him this evening.

"Miss Everleigh," Mr. Feyzi's voice said.

"Yes, good evening."

"I apologize for requiring you to telephone so late," he began, "but I received news from Ellington that I am obliged to pass on to you as quickly as possible."

Saffron's stomach dropped. "What is it?"

"Lord Easting has suffered a heart attack."

"Is he—" She couldn't bring herself to ask if he was alive.

"He is alive and conscious," Mr. Feyzi said, anticipating her. "I know scarce more than that. Mrs. Everleigh requested I pass on the message that the family has installed the telephone in the manor and awaits your telephone call."

Surprise and delight momentarily chased away the worry for her grandfather. If Ellington had a telephone, that meant she could speak to her mother whenever she wanted. They'd been relegated to letters for a very long time, since her mother never left the house anymore.

"I will 'phone there now. Thank you, Mr. Feyzi." She rang off before he'd finished saying goodbye.

She tucked an errant strand behind her ear while she awaited the connection to Ellington. Bobbing her hair only last week had been another ploy to bring Elizabeth out of her bitter melancholy, but boasting victory over Saffron's long tresses lasted only a day or two before she'd sunk back into her bad mood.

"Hello?" came a cool voice on the telephone.

"Kirby!" Saffron could hardly believe the crusty old butler was speaking on a telephone. "This is Saffron."

"Miss Saffron," the somber voice said. "Allow me to summon your mother."

There was a brief crackle, then her mother came on the line. "Saffron, my darling, are you there?"

A sharp ache in her chest had tears flooding her eyes. "Yes," she choked out. "I am. Oh, Mama, I'm so happy to hear your voice."

"My dear girl," her mother gasped. "I cannot tell you—but I must tell you about your grandfather."

Her mother explained that her grandparents had visited a nearby friend's estate, where her grandfather experienced pain in his arm he told no one about until after he'd fallen off his horse during a hardy morning ride. Saffron gasped, but her mother reassured her that apart from a few bruises, the fall had done him little harm. "The heart attack was far more serious." She spoke so quietly that it was hard to hear her. "Lady Easting sent for a specialist from town and has hired him to look after Lord Easting for a few weeks. They returned to Ellington just today, and Dr. Wyatt arrived this evening."

It must have been her mother's low voice that made Saffron question what she thought she heard. "What—what is the doctor called?"

"Dr. Wyatt. He's a cardiologist, in fact. It was terribly good luck that he was available to come to Bedford so quickly."

It seemed it was too good of luck. But it *couldn't* be. "What does this Dr. Wyatt look like?"

"What does he—what does it matter, darling? Now, I've looked at the train timetables—"

With too much urgency to be gentle, Saffron repeated, "What does he look like, Mama?"

The line went quiet for a long moment, then her mother said, "He's a middle-aged man, with dark hair and spectacles. He wears a short beard, and he stoops slightly."

Saffron released a relieved breath. "I'm sorry to shout, Mama, I'm just worried for Grandpapa."

"I understand, my dear," her mother said quietly. "Oh, and a scar."

"A scar?"

"Yes, Dr. Wyatt has a rather significant scar. It's just below his ear."

Her vision swam. *Bill.*

She gripped the small table on which the telephone rested and curled her fingers tighter around the mouthpiece. "Mama, listen. This is very important." How could she possibly explain Bill? If she revealed what she knew about him, she'd have to explain about the Path Lab and her investigations and everything she'd been keeping from her mother for the past year. Her mother was fragile. She didn't want to upset her on top of her worry for Lord Easting.

"I'm coming up there," she said firmly. "I know that Grandmama might not wish to see me, but I am coming to Ellington as soon as possible. If you could please smooth the way—"

"That is what I'm trying to tell you," her mother said. "Lord Easting has asked for you. He's asked for you and John. Even your grandmother can't deny him that. John and Suzanne and their little boy will be arriving in a few days. Do you think you could join us at Ellington now?"

"Yes," Saffron said, a drop of hope mixing with her worry. If John was coming, everything would be all right. For all that her grandfather argued with John about living so far away and plagued him with complaints about inheriting the title someday, John's presence would soothe her both grandparents. Not to mention she would have another ally against Bill.

Her mother spoke about the train times and transportation to the estate for a few minutes before Saffron said she had to ring off. Her mind buzzing like an angry wasp, she slumped against the wall.

Bill Wyatt was in her family's home masquerading as a physician. That put him into direct contact with each of her family members, not to mention he would be at his leisure to give her grandfather anything under the guise of medication.

But why now? She'd heard nothing from Bill since that evening. She didn't suddenly have access to any dangerous secrets he could pluck from her.

"Everything all right?" Alexander asked, making her jump. He was peering out of the parlor. Next to him, Elizabeth stood with a shoulder leaned on the kitchen door jamb, a fresh glass of wine in her hand.

With effort, Saffron pasted on a smile she didn't think either of them would believe. "It seems I've been invited to Bedford. How would the two of you feel about a little trip?"

★ ★ ★

Author's Note

Science-themed espionage is a topic that I adore, but I find it tends to center on the Big Bads: nuclear warheads and their codes, viruses and poisons that will kill within moments of exposure, unhinged AI programs threatening to end humanity. In short, the sort of things James Bond would be charged with preventing landing in the wrong hands. These possibilities are terrifying, but there are other problems that are actively but quietly being dissected in labs full of people who, to all appearances, just put on their white coats and fiddle around with things that would put the average person to sleep.

Espionage was certainly happening in World War One and the interwar years, and while there is a dearth of real facts readily available for public consumption, there is a shocking amount of information at the click of a button about England's government laboratories. Harpenden Phytopathological Service, for example, was real. The laboratory at Number 28 existed, as did its predecessor, Jodrell Lab at Kew Gardens. I have to tell you I was immensely disappointed to learn that the lab was no longer at Kew in 1923; I wanted desperately to send Saffron there to snoop. Maybe in a future story?

The lab's work as described in this book is a reflection of the records I found. Among other horticultural interests, the Path Lab worked on developing resilient crops, more effective pesticides, and defenses against fungi. The research into the pyrethrin oil and its efficacy against pests was a real focus of the laboratory, and the Path Lab scientists carried out the research in association with nearby Rotham-sted. Earwigs were also mentioned a number of times.

Another facet of truth found in the depiction of the Harpenden Path Lab and Rothamsted is the presence of women among the staff. There were a number of women at these institutions and dozens of others. It was strange to come across their names and realize that many of my assumptions about women in science in the 1920s were apparently wrong. Like many, my knowledge of female scientists was limited to the few I was taught about in school, and it's only been through researching Saffron's adventures that my eyes have been opened to the ways women have been participating in science for centuries. They were often hidden behind genderless initials—when they were recognized at all—but they were there, generating and perpetuating knowledge.

If you're a fan of a certain popular zombie TV series, you might have recognized some aspects of the mysterious fungus the Harpenden scientists discovered. The basis of both the zombies' origins and the mysterious fungus are the same: the real-life entomopathogenic fun-gus genus, *Cordyceps*. Many *Cordyceps* species infect insects and use them as a host, eventually consuming them as they burst forth to infect more insects. When I began writing this book, I had no idea that this would be the Big Bad that the scientists had discovered, but after learn-ing more about fungi and how intertwined they are in every facet of the world, I grew to respect fungi's potential to completely turn the world upside down. As Dr. Sutcliffe says, nature will find a way.

I find all the science behind Saffron's solves fascinating. But like Saffron, I found that politics were an inescapable aspect of life in 1923. Alexander and Adrian's background became more complicated the more I understood what had occurred in Greece in the twentieth century. Relearning what high school had taught me about the Rus-sian Revolution became necessary. I found both topics a trial simply because there are so many subjective layers to sort through, but it was enlightening to see just how many strings were still strung across the Continent and the Channel and how tugging on one or two could cause mayhem. I can't wait to explore how one man tugging at those strings will cause chaos in Saffron's life, too.

ACKNOWLEDGMENTS

Thank you to my loving, long-suffering husband, Erfawn. You make it all possible, and never doubt that I appreciate all the hours you spent listening to me rattle on about fungi and poisons while I worked on this book. Thank you to my son for inspiring me to learn all I can about poisonous plants: I pass on that knowledge to you hoping that the weird and wild of the world will inspire you to keep exploring (and so I worry less when you wander). Thank you to my newly arrived daughter: I loved working on this book as you rolled around in my belly, and I cannot tell you how much I appreciate your arrival's impeccable timing.

My parents, Tracy and David, are also owed a great big thank you for each of my books. I love how you ground me in fiction and reality, not to mention the extra-loving care you gave me finishing this book while very pregnant and anxious. Thank you for always being there, even across an ocean.

Thank you to Melissa, my editor, for being willing to listen and work with me on this slightly out of the box idea. You helped me keep Saffron on track while encouraging my imagination! And of course, thank you to the team at Crooked Lane for their patience, professionalism, and hard work.

I have so many friends and family who continue to amaze me with their loving support for me and my books. Please know that every face in the crowd, every message and comment, every book purchased, and every reshare on social media and among your friends make all the difference to me.

My readers are incredible and I'm always so humbled to be a part of your reading experience. Thank you for reading, reviewing, requesting, and recommending. Knowing I get to share Saffron's adventures with you makes sitting down at my computer every day a joy.